S0-AAN-254

SCARY GRAPHICS

STONE ARCH BOOKS
a capstone imprint

Scary Graphics is published by Stone Arch Books,
an imprint of Capstone.
1710 Roe Crest Drive
North Mankato, Minnesota 56003
www.capstonepub.com

Library of Congress Cataloging-in-Publication Data is available on the Library of Congress website.

ISBN: 978-1-4965-9796-0 (library binding)
ISBN: 978-1-4965-9800-4 (ebook PDF)

Summary: When the phone that Emma dropped into the ocean starts behaving oddly, she'll discover that she brought back more than just photos from her beach vacation. A spirit has followed her home, and it's tired of swimming alone . . .

Editor: Abby Huff
Designer: Brann Garvey
Production Specialist: Katy LaVigne

Printed and bound in the USA.
PA117

BEACH NIGHTMARE

BY **STEVE FOXE**

ILLUSTRATED BY **ALAN BROWN**

WORD OF WARNING:

BE CAREFUL WHAT YOU BRING BACK FROM THE BEACH.

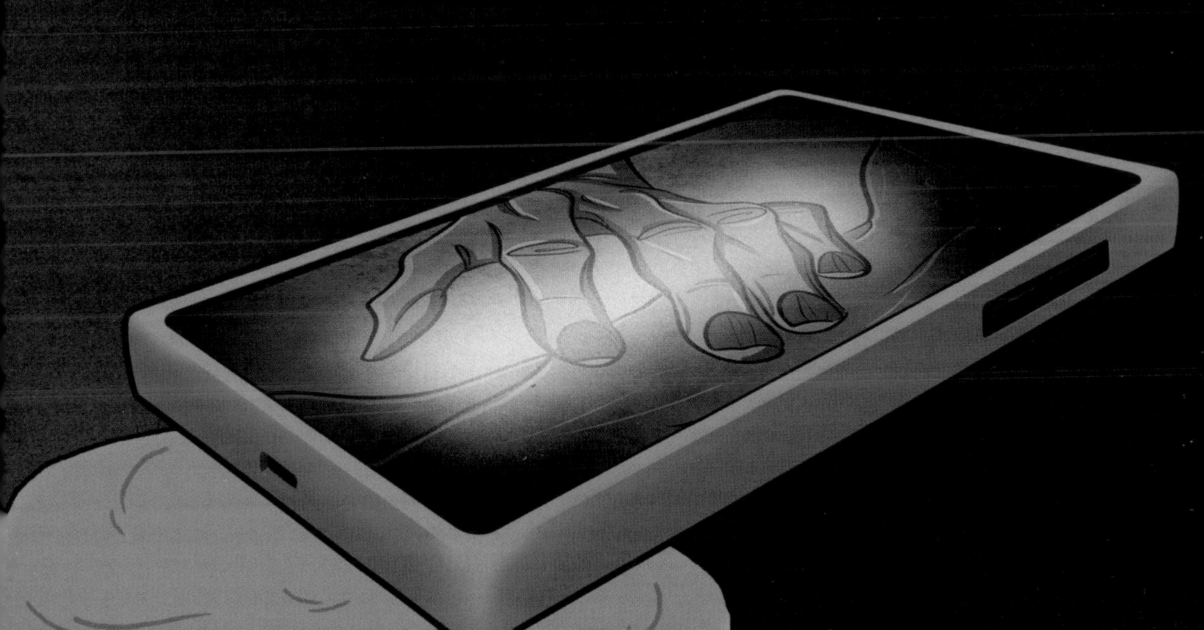

On a dark and stormy coast, Emma Park was trying make the most of the final day of her beach vacation.
WARNING
DANGER:
Flash!
WARNING
DANGER: STAY OFF ROCKS
Almost...
SKRRT!
Whew! That was close.

Everyone is gonna *freak* when they see I came out all this way.

SPLASHHH!
WHOA!
EMMA

No! My phone!
CLACK!
SPLOoSH!

Ugh, and it was brand new too.

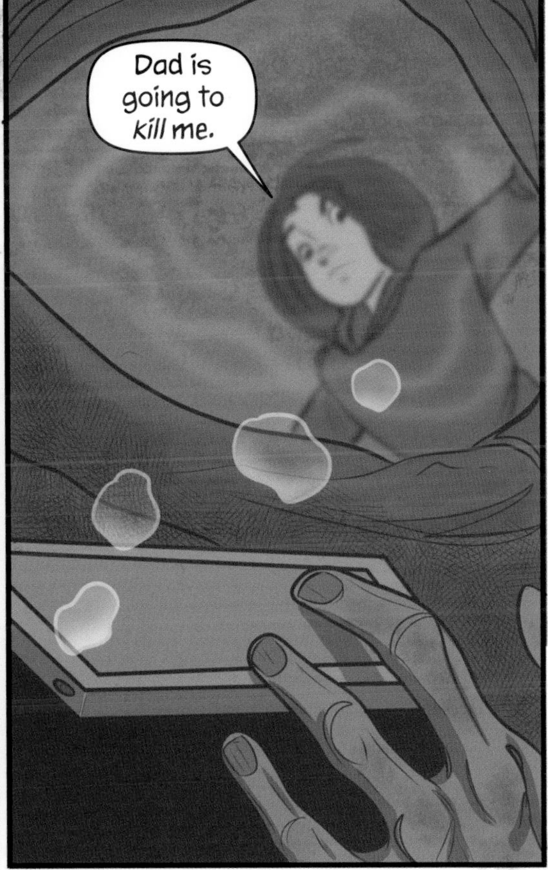
Dad is going to *kill* me.

A little while later...
You *lost* it?
Emma, I just bought you that phone. What were you doing out there?
I didn't want to waste the whole week napping on the beach. I wanted adventure!

Sigh
C'mon, Ms. Reckless Adventurer. It's a gloomy day anyway. Let's go back to the hotel.
Can we order a movie?
Sure, but it's coming out of your new-phone fund.

Ah, Mr. Park? Someone left something for your daughter.
For me?

My phone!

But I *just* lost it. How—

Wow, that was a nice twist of fate. Who returned it?
I'm afraid I don't know.

I found it sitting at the front desk. It's a good thing Emma's name is on the back.
EMMA

Lucky us! Thanks again!
Yeah. Thanks...

Back in the hotel room...
Hmm...
At least the pictures turned out.

Ahh!

Is that ...
sand?
Shhhhhfff

Emma, is
something
wrong?

I thought
I saw...

Nothing,
Dad. It was
nothing.

The next day...

Ugh, I can't believe vacation is over already. I've gotta call Tati and Sheena to catch up.

We should leave your phone in rice tonight. That'll soak up any water in it.
Dad, I've had no signal for a whole week. I need my phone *now*.

Okay, but don't blame me if it starts acting up.

Later...
Emma! Time for bed!
TIK
TIK
TIK
9:56
p.m.

3:31
a.m.

BRING!
BRING!
UNKNOWN CALLER
BRING!
BRING!

Hullo? So late. Whoizzit?

COME BACK TO THE BEACH, EMMA...
EMMA
What?! Who—

KRRRISSSSHHHH
It's just static. Almost like ... waves?

Guess Dad was right about the rice thing...

Emma! You don't want to be late for your first day back.

Soon...
Can you put my pillowcase in the wash? My phone leaked water on it overnight.
If that phone doesn't work because you couldn't wait a few *hours* to text your friends, I'm *doubling* your chores.

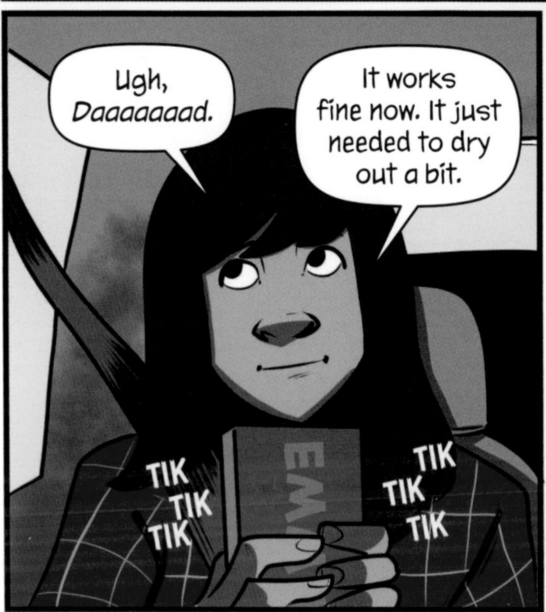
Ugh, *Daaaaaaad.*
It works fine now. It just needed to dry out a bit.
TIK TIK TIK
TIK TIK TIK

Let's hope so. Turn it off before you get to class. You don't want it randomly going off again like it did last night.
Have a great day!

Last night? But I thought that was just a dream...

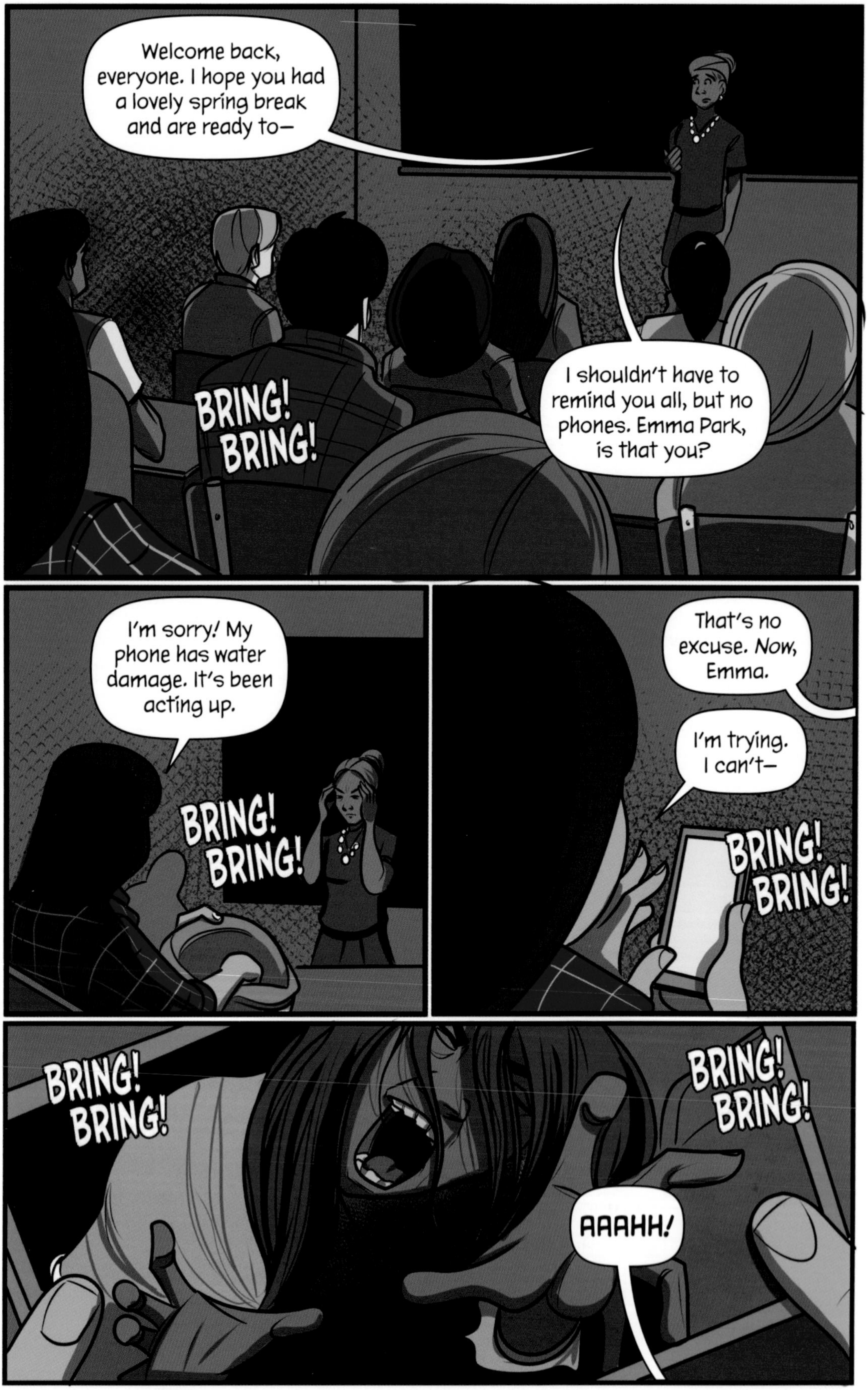

Welcome back, everyone. I hope you had a lovely spring break and are ready to—

BRING! BRING!

I shouldn't have to remind you all, but no phones. Emma Park, is that you?

I'm sorry! My phone has water damage. It's been acting up.

BRING! BRING!

That's no excuse. *Now,* Emma.

I'm trying. I can't—

BRING! BRING!

Again?! Who was that?
BRING! BRING!
If you can't turn your phone off here, you can turn it off in *detention.*

BRING! BRING!
Sorry, I'll take care of it!

BRING! BRING!
Why won't you—*ugh*—turn off! And what is so *heavy* in this bag?

BRING! BRING!
Agh!

BRING! BRING!
More sand. How ... how is this possible?
EMMA

Excuse me, do you need help?
No, I—
Where did the sand go?
Sand? What sand?
And the ringing stopped.
Are you sure you're okay?
Yep, all good! Thanks! Just headed to the library.

Okay. Something seriously weird is going on with my phone.
Something *ghostly*...
Tap
Tap
Tap
McCammon Beach death
Click
...and it's time to figure out why.
LOCAL GIRL LOST IN MCCAMMON BEACH RIP CURRENT
Whoa.

"Nancy Lindqvist, 13-year-old daughter of the local Lindqvist shipping family, disappeared during a storm on McCammon Beach this weekend."
"Due to rough waters and the dangerous rocky coast, the family was sadly..."
drip
drip
drip
"...unable to recover her body."
What a horrible way to go. And her skeleton has just been stuck in the ocean for almost a hundred years...

No wonder her spirit is so restless.

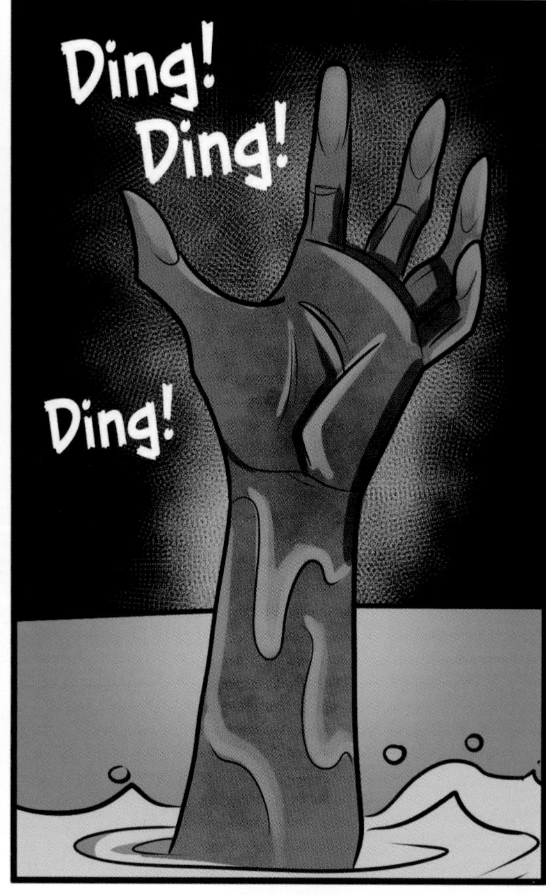
Ding!
Ding!
Ding!

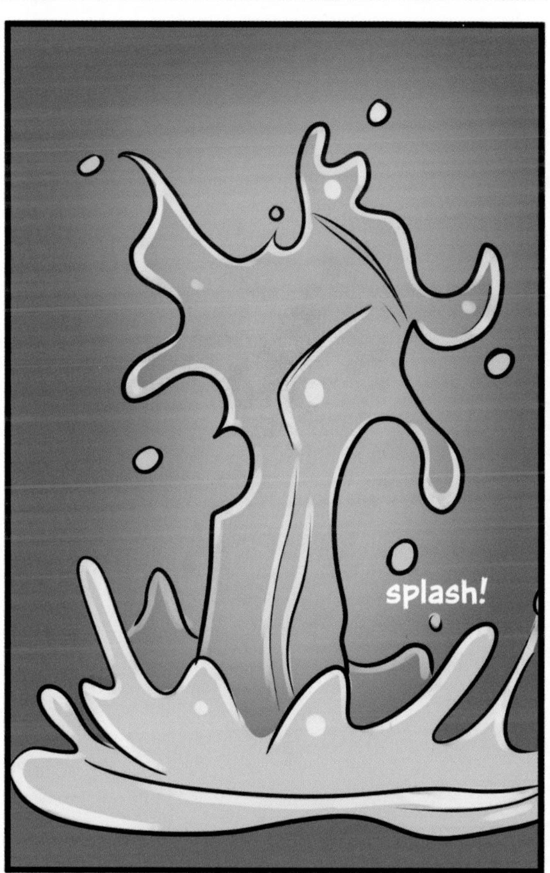
splash!

Sorry, Nancy. I'm off to next period.
I don't like being haunted—and I don't think you like haunting me.
But if you are creeping around my phone, I'll find a way to put you to rest.

After school...

Whoa, someone is in a hurry.

Sorry, I really want to get started on my ... homework.

Well, can't argue with that.

Hey, did your phone give you any problems?

...Nope. All good.

But maybe we can do your rice thing? Just to cover all the bases?

Later...
Okay, Nancy Lindqvist, how do we get you to your eternal slumber?
It says here that "ghosts often haunt the living when their bodies aren't properly buried."
And according to the creepy photos on my phone, she's stuck in the rocks near the beach.
I can't exactly go back there, but maybe we can call—
Emma!
It's past your bedtime. Hit the hay, kiddo.
10:14

COME SWIM WITH ME, EMMA...

Ahh!

This can't be happening!

It's not real. It's not–
I'VE BEEN SWIMMING ALONE FOR SO, SO LONG.

I'm trying to help you! Leave me alone!

STOP HAUNTING ME!

Emma! What's going on?

Dad?

"Authorities believe that Lindqvist's body was washed out into the ocean..."
And you think Nancy is the girl you saw in your room?

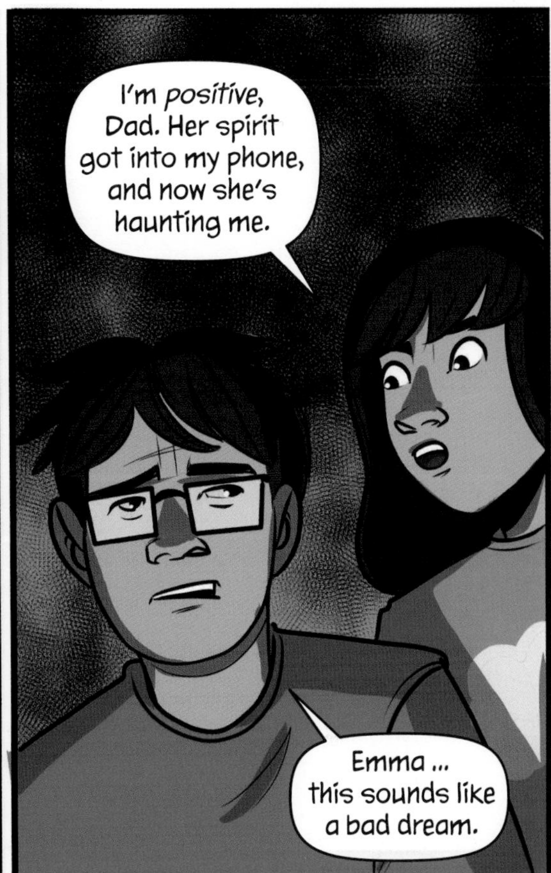
I'm *positive*, Dad. Her spirit got into my phone, and now she's haunting me.
Emma ... this sounds like a bad dream.

You saw my room! How else would it get *that* wet?
All right, all right. I'll call the McCammon Beach police station in the morning.

Nancy has been stuck in the water for so long. The police have to get her out of those rocks. It's the only way to make this stop.
I'm *sure* of it.

I hope so. Until then, get some rest.
You're going to be a mess at school tomorrow.
There's no way I can fall asleep after—wait.
Em? Where are you going?
I have to do *one* more thing. Just to be safe.

Em?
Thwack!
Thwack!
Thwack!
Thwack!
Now I can get some rest.
Fair.

The next morning...
Yawwwwn.

After nine...? Dad, you let me oversleep.

Dad?

Dad? This isn't funny. Not after last night.

Dad! You are officially starting to freak me out.

Maybe he's out back talking with the cops...

Pfft!

Tastes like ...
salt water?!

BRING!
BRING!

But ...
I smashed
the phone. I
smashed it...
BRING!
BRING!

What...
Oh no.
BRING!
BRING!

BRING!
BRING!

BRING!
BRING!

WHOOSH!
THE WATER IS LOVELY, EMMA! COME SWIM WITH ME!

FWOOSH!

LOOK CLOSER

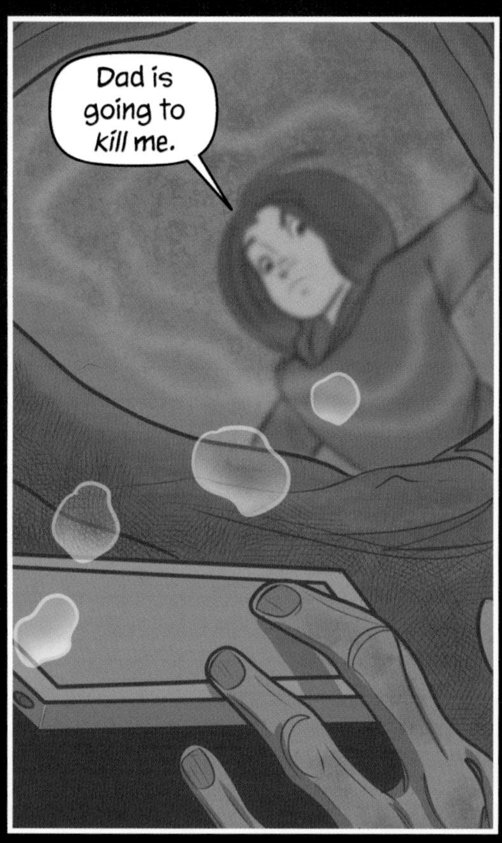

1. Whose hand is reaching for Emma's phone? How do you know? Why is this an important moment for the rest of the story?

2. Even before Nancy's spirit appears in Emma's room, a number of ghostly things happen. Look through the story and find three examples.

3. The background of this panel doesn't show any details. It's only a burst of color. Why do you think the illustrator made this choice? How does it connect to what's happening in the story? (Check pages 10–11 if you need a hint.)

COME SWIM WITH ME, EMMA...

Ahh!

4. Why is the spirit's word balloon different than others? What does it tell you about the character? Brainstorm other ways the balloon could look.

5. In your own words, describe what's happened to Emma at the end. Were you surprised by this? Why or why not?

THE AUTHOR

Steve Foxe is the author of more than 40 children's books and comics properties including Pokémon, Transformers, Adventure Time, Steven Universe, DC Super Friends, and Grumpy Cat. He lives in Queens, New York, and enjoys visiting the beach . . . but only with plenty of sunscreen and zero ghosts.

THE ILLUSTRATOR

Alan Brown is a freelance artist from the United Kingdom. He's worked on a variety of projects including Ben 10 Omniverse graphic novels for Viz Media, as well as children's book illustrations for the likes of Harper Collins and Watts. He has a keen interest in the comic book world, where he's at home creating bold graphic pieces. Alan works from an attic studio, along with his trusty sidekick, Ollie the miniature schnauzer, and his two sons, Wilf and Teddy.

GLOSSARY

bury (BER-ee)—to put a dead body in a grave

coast (KOHST)—the land next to an ocean or sea

eternal (ih-TUR-nuhl)—lasting forever

fate (FAYT)—events in life that are out of a person's control or are thought to be decided by a greater power

haunt (HAWNT)—for a ghost to keep coming back to a living person or to a place, often in a way that causes strange things to happen

properly (PROP-er-lee)—done in a way that is right

reckless (REK-lis)—not caring or thinking about the bad things that may happen as a result of your actions

recover (ri-KUHV-er)—to get back

restless (REST-lis)—unable to rest or be calm; when a ghost is restless, it causes troubles for the living because a problem in its previous life needs to be worked out

rip current (RIP KUR-uhnt)—water that flows strongly and quickly away from shore that can be dangerous to swimmers

slumber (SLUHM-ber)—sleep

spirit (SPIHR-it)—another word for ghost; some believe the spirit is an invisible part of a person that leaves the body after death

SCARY GRAPHICS

NOT SCARED YET? DARE TO READ THEM ALL...

ONLY FROM CAPSTONE

W9-ABC-901

THE MUSIC FORUM

Volume III

THE MUSIC FORUM

Volume III

Edited by WILLIAM J. MITCHELL *and* FELIX SALZER

HEDI SIEGEL, EDITORIAL ASSISTANT

Columbia University Press 1973 New York and London

Library of Congress Catalog Card Number: 67–16204
ISBN: 0–231–03522–5

William J. Mitchell (1906-1971)

William Mitchell's untimely death is a grievous loss not only to the readers of *The Music Forum* but also to the international community of musical scholarship. My personal sorrow over the disruption of a long and close friendship is deepened by my sense of the loss of an irreplaceable musical colleague. I know that many others will also miss the invaluable advice of a scholar whose unfailing judgment—based on a profound knowledge of the art of music and its history—was always available to his musical friends and colleagues. His sense of obligation to musical scholarship, to music education, and to musical standards in general manifested itself in ceaseless activity on behalf of all those individuals and groups with whom he was associated. In contrast to a strong present-day trend, he was no mere specialist. To be sure, he had intimate and detailed knowledge of many special fields, among them thorough bass, Renaissance theory, and the development of nineteenth-century chromaticism. However, one could turn to him for much valuable insight into compositional, theoretical, and historical problems of virtually any period of Western music. It was this breadth of knowledge that made him so much more than the meticulous scholar which he most certainly was.

His memory will be a continuous inspiration to me personally as well as to all of his other friends and colleagues at *The Music Forum.*

FELIX SALZER

Preface

THIS ISSUE of *The Music Forum* still carries the name of William J. Mitchell as co-editor since most of the editorial work was completed before his death. It would have been a great source of gratification to him—as it is to us—to have learned that Lewis Lockwood received the Alfred Einstein Award of the American Musicological Society for his article "The Autograph of the First Movement of Beethoven's Sonata for Violoncello and Pianoforte, Opus 69," published in Volume II.

Starting with the next issue (Volume IV), Carl Schachter will be Associate Editor, I shall continue as Editor and Hedi Siegel as Editorial Assistant.

F. S.

Contents

Thames Hickman again provided the expert autography

Contributors

Walter Hilse is Assistant Professor of Music at Columbia University

Alfred Mann is Professor of Music at Rutgers University

William J. Mitchell was Professor of Music at the State University of New York at Binghamton

Arbie Orenstein is Assistant Professor of Music at Queens College of the City University of New York

Felix Salzer is Professor of Music at Queens College of the City University of New York

Carl Schachter teaches at the Mannes College of Music and is Visiting Associate Professor of Music at Queens College of the City University of New York for the academic year 1972–73

THE MUSIC FORUM

Volume III

The Treatises of Christoph Bernhard

translated by
WALTER HILSE

TRANSLATOR'S PREFACE

CHRISTOPH BERNHARD, according to all available sources, was born in Danzig in 1627.[1] He received his earliest musical education in his native city under Paul Siefert, organist at St. Mary's Church, and (probably) Christoph Werner, the future cantor at St. Catharine's Church, and then seems to have joined the electoral chapel at Dresden as a singer as early as 1645. At the Dresden court he quickly won the highest esteem of his master, Heinrich Schütz, so that already in 1649 the vocal training of the choirboys of the chapel was entrusted to him, and in 1655 we find him promoted to the rank of Vice-Kapellmeister. Between 1664 and 1674 he sojourned in Hamburg, serving as cantor of the Church of St. James, and as co-director, with Matthias Weckmann, of that city's famed Collegium Musicum. Thereafter Bernhard returned to Dresden to serve as tutor for the elector's grandson and, once more, as Vice-Kapellmeister. He finally became full-fledged Kapellmeister of the chapel in 1681, a position that he retained until his death in 1692.

1 All information concerning Bernhard's life has, unfortunately, come to us second- or thirdhand. Probably the most authoritative sources of information available today are Bruno Grusnick's article, "Christoph Bernhard," in *Die Musik in Geschichte und Gegenwart*, Vol. I (Kassel, Bärenreiter, 1951), hereafter cited as *MGG*, and Joseph Maria Müller-Blattau's preface to his *Die Kompositionslehre Heinrich Schützens in der Fassung seines Schülers Christoph Bernhard* (Leipzig, Breitkopf and Härtel, 1926; reprinted by Bärenreiter in 1963). Most of what they say, however, is traceable to the nineteenth-century historian Moritz Fürstenau, especially his *Zur Geschichte der Musik und des Theaters am Hofe der Kurfürsten von Sachsen* (Dresden, Rudolf Kuntze, 1861), or to accounts (hardly always reliable) found in eighteenth-century writings such as Johann Mattheson's *Grundlage einer Ehrenpforte* (Hamburg, 1740) and Johann Gottfried Walther's *Musikalisches Lexikon* (Leipzig, 1732).

Bernhard left us three major treatises: *Von der Singe-Kunst oder Manier* (On the Art of Singing; or, Manier), *Tractatus compositionis augmentatus* (Extended Treatise on Composition), and *Ausführlicher Bericht vom Gebrauche der Con- und Dissonantien* (Thorough Account on the Use of Consonances and Dissonances). These are available in a modern edition prepared by Joseph Maria Müller–Blattau. Each of the treatises offers valuable insights to the present-day student of music theory.

Twice during his earlier Dresden period (the first time seemingly between 1651 and 1656, the second time in 1657), Bernhard was sent by Schütz to Italy to recruit singers for the chapel. He thus was able to gain firsthand knowledge of the latest developments in Italian music and also to meet some of the leading musical figures of that nation, most notably Carissimi. Already in Danzig, however, the young Bernhard must have been thoroughly exposed to the "newer style" of composition emanating from the South, which was being spread enthusiastically to all corners of Europe by Italian musicians employed abroad, and by Germans returning from study in Italy. It was an Italian, the highly regarded Marco Scacchi, who held the position of Kapellmeister at the nearby, very prestigious Warsaw court, and Danzig had two distinguished Italophiles of its own —the elder Kaspar Förster, Kapellmeister at St. Mary's,[2] and Werner.

This "newer style" was still, fundamentally, Monteverdi's *seconda prattica*, subject only to the inevitable modifications and extensions of a younger generation that included such brilliant musicians as Carissimi and Schütz. Even so, the battle for its acceptance—fought and won in its home country long ago, most spectacularly in the form of the Monteverdi–Artusi controversy—was still being waged most bitterly in the Northland four decades later.

Chief opponent of the newer ways was Siefert, who engaged in constant polemics over the matter with the elder Förster, his associate at St. Mary's. Scacchi eventually entered the fray on the side of Förster, and a celebrated exchange of tracts and pamphlets between him and Siefert ensued, including: 1) Scacchi's *Cribrum musicum ad triticum Syfertinum* (Venice, 1643), which sought to prove not only that Siefert did not understand the *seconda*

[2] See *Tractatus* note 56 for biographical details on Scacchi and Förster.

prattica but, even more, that he was not even master of the *prima prattica* (numerous excerpts from Siefert's compositions are quoted to support this claim); 2) Siefert's *Anticribratio musica ad avenam Scacchianam* (Danzig, 1645), basically a spirited answer to the preceding; and 3) Scacchi's *Judicium cribri musici* (Warsaw, ca. 1649), which printed letters by many of the most eminent musicians of the day—including Schütz himself—who supported his position.

Among the various documents which address themselves to this dispute, a letter written by Scacchi to Werner around 1648 is of particular interest to us,[3] for, besides the expected remonstrations against Siefert, it offers a division of (vocal) music into three styles: the *stylus ecclesiasticus* is the old *prima prattica* and covers the more traditional species of church music; the *stylus cubicularis* includes the less radical innovations of the *seconda prattica* and is suited especially to the various genres of vocal chamber music—a cappella madrigals, monodies, and concerted works; and the *stylus theatralis* or *scenicus* contains, in addition to everything found in the *stylus cubicularis*, the more daring elements of the *seconda prattica* and is meant, above all, for stage productions.

These three styles seem so closely aligned, in both characteristics and domains, with those proposed by Bernhard in his *Tractatus compositionis augmentatus*, that our curiosity is immediately aroused with regard to the relationship between the two theorists. Was Bernhard's primary influence actually Scacchi, rather than his beloved mentor, Schütz? We must be doubly careful here, for in an age whose stylistic diversity is dwarfed only by that in our own day, nearly every thoughtful musician evolved his own categories of musical style.[4] Thus two men might have arrived at similar schemes quite independently of one another; also, the same designation (e.g., "*stylus ecclesiasticus*") might stand for somewhat different things in different classifications.

A second question is raised by a reference in Schütz's preface to his *Geistliche Chormusik* (1648). Schütz spoke there of a musician, "highly experienced in both theory and practice," "whom I know well," who would

3 Printed in Erich Katz's dissertation, *Die musikalischen Stilbegriffe des 17. Jahrhunderts* (Charlottenburg, W. Flagel, 1926), pp. 83–89.

4 *Ibid.*

"soon bring a treatise of particular benefit to us Germans to the light of day." What musician, and what treatise, was he referring to?

Joseph Maria Müller-Blattau has given his own answer to both these questions unequivocally, in the title of his modern edition of Bernhard's three treatises: *Die Kompositionslehre Heinrich Schützens in der Fassung seines Schülers Christoph Bernhard.* He thus not only regards the *Tractatus* as the fulfillment of Schütz's prophecy, but furthermore has postulated that this work, and to a lesser degree the other two treatises, constitute faithful presentations of Schütz's musical views. Müller-Blattau's hypothesis has recently been sharply contested: by Bruno Grusnick in his article, "Christoph Bernhard," by Claude V. Palisca in his article, "Marco Scacchi," and by Peter Benary in his review of the 1963 reprint of Müller-Blattau's edition.[5]

In these newer writings it is pointed out, among other things, that Bernhard's references to certain contemporaries in chapter 43 of the *Tractatus* all but guarantee that he could not have written that treatise as early as 1649 (Müller-Blattau's supposition), but most likely issued it in the late 1650s.[6] (A late limit for the appearance of the *Tractatus* seems to be 1664, the year Bernhard moved to Hamburg, as he is identified on the title pages of the manuscript copies as the Vice-Kapellmeister at Dresden.) These same scholars also cite a Schütz letter, dated 1648 and seemingly addressed to Christian Schirmer of Danzig,[7] which conveys the fervent hope that a "counterpoint treatise" promised by Scacchi would soon be completed—a treatise which, says Schütz, would be of great service "especially to our German nation"! I might add, as a further argument against Bernhard as the fulfiller of the prophecy in Schütz's preface, the improbability that any twenty-one-year-old, no matter how talented, would be referred to as "highly experienced."

Nevertheless, the case for Scacchi is not quite airtight. His only known

5 Claude V. Palisca, in *MGG* (1963); Peter Benary in *Die Musikforschung*, XV (1965), 452.

6 In particular, we should mention his references to Vincenzo Albrici, born in 1631, and to Marco Giuseppe Peranda, whom Bernhard himself fetched to Dresden from Italy in the early 1650s. See *Tractatus* note 56 for more details on Albrici and Peranda.

7 This letter is printed in the original Latin in Erich H. Müller, *Heinrich Schütz: gesammelte Briefe und Schriften* (Regensburg, G. Bosse, 1931), p. 190; it appears in a German translation in Hans Joachim Moser, *Heinrich Schütz: sein Leben und Werk* (Kassel, Bärenreiter, 1936), p. 161.

theoretical work dating from 1648 or later is the *Breve discorso sopra la musica moderna*, published in Warsaw in 1649. The date of the work is promising, but it is in Italian, and thus would not be "of particular use to us Germans," as Müller-Blattau emphasized, I think rightly.

As to the matter of the chief influences on Bernhard, it may be said that if Bernhard's three styles do resemble Scacchi's to a striking degree, his manner of presenting them seems to echo most clearly the viewpoint outlined by Schütz in his 1648 preface: namely, that the more recent innovations in musical style were all, essentially, extensions or elaborations of *stylus gravis*—that the latter is the foundation, as it were, for the former. Again and again in all his treatises, Bernhard demonstrates how passages replete with ornamentation can be stripped of the latter, leaving skeletons fully in accord with the older practice. The adjective "natural" (*natürlich*) is consistently applied to these "unornamented versions," as to *stylus gravis* in general, suggesting that it is this style which Nature, with its immutable acoustical laws, has, so to speak, "given" to the composer (or performer), and that anything added thereto constitutes, almost by definition, an "artifice."

The right of the newer styles to coexist with the older, which was Scacchi's principal concern as Siefert's adversary, is taken for granted by Bernhard. His energy is rather spent in trying to fit these seemingly opposed modes of thought into one common framework—in showing that they are, in fact, not opposed at all. Insofar as he succeeds, his treatises, and the *Tractatus* in particular, may be said to represent the final resolution of the Monteverdi–Artusi controversy.

Schütz certainly made this view his guiding principle as a teacher, introducing the *stylus gravis* to his students first, as the point of departure for anything more adventurous and modern. According to Mattheson, the young Bernhard, newly arrived in Dresden, "composed diligently in the Palestrina style,"[8] and we possess Masses in that style from both his hand and that of another outstanding Schütz disciple, Johann Theile.[9] True,

[8] Mattheson, p. 18.

[9] These two Masses are found in *Das Chorwerk*, No. 16, Rudolf Gerber, ed. (Berlin, 1932), the Theile work on pp. 4–22, the Bernhard work on pp. 23–30. Like many Lutheran settings of the Mass, these consist of *Kyrie* and *Gloria* only. The Bernhard Mass is based on the chorale, *Christ unser Herr zum Jordan kam*.

this method of instruction does not seem to have been Schütz's uniquely: Buxtehude, although not connected with the Dresden circle as far as we know, issued precisely the same type of Mass.[10] But if the "bilingual" composer—the composer fully conversant in both the old and the new styles—was a common phenomenon in the seventeenth century, Schütz nonetheless had the training of a particularly bright assemblage of such composers to his credit. And Bernhard must be ranked among the best of them.

Five of Bernhard's compositions in the concerted church style are printed in *Denkmäler deutscher Tonkunst*; two others have been published separately by Bruno Grusnick.[11] These works suggest a highly competent, if not often inspired mind, with instances now and then of truly arresting writing—the first few pages of *Ich sahe an alles Thun*, for example.[12] In the realm of stage music we unfortunately know of no compositions which are his for certain, although at least one attempt has been made to attribute such a work to him.[13] Walther says that "some sonatas of his appeared in print,"[14] but we have no trace of these published works.

It appears to be as a composer in the *stylus gravis* that Schütz thought especially highly of Bernhard, as is suggested by his entrusting him, shortly before Schütz's death in 1672, with the task of writing a five-part funeral motet on the text, "Cantabiles mihi erant justificationes tuae in loco peregrinationis meae," in the Palestrina style. Bernhard, in Hamburg at the time, soon sent the piece to Schütz; and the latter, deeply touched by its quality, wrote back that he "could not have bettered one note."[15]

In view of much of the above, I feel that Schütz may indeed deserve reinstatement as the single greatest influence on Bernhard. Nevertheless, it

10 Gottlieb Harms and Hilmer Trede, eds., *Dietrich Buxtehudes Werke* (Hamburg, Ugrino Abteilung Verlag, 1931), IV, 12–19. Like the Bernhard and Theile compositions, this is a "short Mass"—i.e., a setting of *Kyrie* and *Gloria* only.

11 Max Seiffert, ed., *Denkmäler deutscher Tonkunst* (Leipzig, Breitkopf and Härtel, 1901), VI, 111–72, hereafter cited as *DDT*; Bruno Grusnick, ed., *Fürchtet euch nicht* and *Jauchzet dem Herren alle Welt* (Kassel, Bärenreiter, 1933, 1934).

12 *DDT*, VI, 128–31.

13 See Gerhard Bittrich's dissertation, *Ein deutsches Opernballett des siebzehnten Jahrhunderts; ein Beitrag zur Frühgeschichte der deutschen Oper* (Leipzig, Frommhold and Wendler, 1931).

14 Walther, p. 89.

15 This funeral motet, unfortunately, has not been found.

remains patently extravagant to label the latter's writings as renditions, pure and simple, of the former's musical thought. Bernhard, quite clearly, is also indebted to other men for many of his ideas. In particular, much of the *Tractatus* can be traced back to Gioseffe Zarlino's *Istitutioni harmoniche*, a work that left a deep imprint on other prominent treatises of the future—for example, Thomas Morley's *A Plain and Easy Introduction to Practical Music* (London, 1597),[16] and the so-called *Kompositionsregeln* pieced together by Sweelinck's disciples. In the Notes section, I frequently draw attention to whole paragraphs in Bernhard which essentially restate Zarlino, especially in the chapters of the *Tractatus* dealing with "fugues" and double counterpoint. (Interestingly, Morley often echoes exactly the same passages.) Yet the full extent of Bernhard's debt to the great Italian theorist is only realized, I think, when it is pointed out that innumerable shorter, seemingly off-the-cuff remarks, such as that about "*contrasonus*" in chapter 1 of the *Tractatus*, also derive from him. Whether or not Bernhard actually had access to the Zarlino work is immaterial (although he probably did). As shown in the *Kompositionsregeln* of the Sweelinck school, the Dutch master embraced and faithfully passed on much of Zarlino's thought. We can expect Paul Siefert, a devoted disciple of Sweelinck, to have relayed many of these same ideas to Bernhard as his first teacher—and, in view of Siefert's notoriously reactionary bent, to have stressed precisely such topics as "fugues" and double counterpoint.

On the other hand, some of the descriptions and illustrations of "figures," found in both the *Tractatus* and the *Bericht*, strongly suggest a source more nearly of Bernhard's own generation than Schütz, not so much in the daring of some of these species of dissonance treatment—no one could outstrip the early monodists in sheer daring—as in the degree to which they have already been sorted out and rationalized. Moreover, we must recall that Schütz, by the late 1640s, had reverted to a much more conservative style than he had cultivated two or three decades earlier. The *Geistliche Chormusik*, which strives to recapture the esthetic of a cappella vocal music, typifies this trend on his part. It is particularly in this connection that Bernhard's reported

[16] Gioseffe Zarlino, *Istitutioni harmoniche* (Venice, Francesco de i Franceschi Senese, 1558, 1562, and 1573; facsimile edition, Ridgewood, N.J., Gregg Press, 1966); Thomas Morley, *A Plain and Easy Introduction to Practical Music*, R. Alec Harman, ed. (New York, Norton, 1963).

encounter with Carissimi seems to invite further investigation, as well as other meetings with eminent musicians he may have had during his stays in Italy. This, too, may have been the area where Scacchi influenced him most tellingly.

Our discussion thus far has revolved almost exclusively around the *Tractatus*—which is fully understandable, in view of its sheer bulk over against the other two treatises, its great variety of subject matter, and its central position in the debate concerning the role of Schütz and others in the formation of Bernhard's musical thought. Yet the much shorter treatise, *On the Art of Singing; or*, *Manier*, also merits serious consideration. It demonstrates most vividly the almost total domination of German musical life by Italian style and taste. Vocal music, needless to say, followed Southern fashions unreservedly; but instrumental music also (with the sole, highly significant exception of organ music) assumed a predominantly Italianate cast—if only because, as Bernhard recalls again and again, instrumentalists could and constantly did adapt features of prevailing vocal style to their own media.

The *Art of Singing* is, without question, the earliest of the Bernhard treatises, almost surely written in 1649 or shortly thereafter, while he had the responsibility of instructing the Dresden choirboys. A passage in the *Tractatus* seems to refer to it, strongly supporting the theory that it is the earlier work.[17] The postulation of a direct connection with his teaching duties is, furthermore, encouraged by the delightful bits of humor which are injected into it along the way. (One wishes that similar passages would enliven the other two works!) Appearing as it does around 1650, Bernhard's singing treatise occupies a position at the head of a long series of voice manuals which were to appear in Germany during the later stages of the seventeenth century, all seeking to acquaint their readers with contemporary Italian performance practice. It may be true that several earlier works on the same subject had been produced by German writers—Johann Andreas Herbst's *Musica Practica sive Instructio pro Symphoniacis* (1642) certainly deserves mention. But these all had at least one of the following drawbacks: either they did not enjoy wide circulation, and so made little

[17] *Tractatus*, ch. 2, para. 3; see also *Tractatus* note 5.

impact (Herbst's work was very shortly out of print, not to reappear until its second edition in 1658); or they were in a foreign language, and so were accessible only to a limited audience; or they did not present the material nearly as thoroughly as Bernhard did. Here, as in the other treatises, our author may often be infuriatingly inaccurate and unsystematic in matters of detail, with a literary style the sheer clumsiness of which verges on the comical; but, in the larger view, he succeeds admirably in giving an intensive, well-ordered exposition of the domain under consideration—with musical sensitivity evident to a very high degree.

The third treatise, *Ausführlicher Bericht vom Gebrauche der Con- und Dissonantien* (hereinafter referred to as the *Bericht*), has much less to offer than the other two. Written during Bernhard's Hamburg period, it is substantially a rehashing of much of the material found in the first forty-two chapters of the *Tractatus*, with abridgments of statements in the *Tractatus* far outnumbering elaborations or clarifications. As it does not add anything really new, but is interesting mainly for its subtle variants of things said in the *Tractatus*, I have chosen not to print it separately as an entity, but rather to present its various segments side by side with passages in the *Tractatus* that cover the same subject matter.

This has necessitated a considerable jumbling of the contents of the *Bericht*, with chapters—and often different paragraphs within chapters—appearing in a completely new order. Hopefully the reader will find this admitted inconvenience outweighed by the intriguing divergences that this format reveals, at least some of which may reflect important changes in attitude and/or technique which took place in the (probably) ten or more years elapsing between the appearance of one treatise and the other. For those who wish to read the *Bericht* in its intended order, I have provided a table, listing the chapters and paragraphs of the *Bericht* opposite the sections of the *Tractatus* where they may be found. The table, on page 30, precedes the two treatises.

Prior to Müller-Blattau's 1926 edition, none of the Bernhard treatises had appeared in print. Yet, despite the lack of publication in their own era, these works were to exercise considerable influence in Germany for at least a century, circulating widely through various manuscript copies. Among those who apparently had intimate knowledge of them were such distinguished figures as Johann Kuhnau, Gottfried Heinrich Stöltzel, Heinrich Nikolaus Gerber, Johann Philipp Kirnberger, Johann Gottfried Walther, and Johann Mattheson. The last-mentioned quoted numerous examples from the *Tractatus* in his *Der vollkommene Capellmeister* (Hamburg, 1739), sometimes identifying his source, often not.

Müller-Blattau, in his Foreword, gives detailed information concerning known manuscript sources, and lists, in particular, four different copies of the treatise on singing, two of the *Tractatus*, and six of the *Bericht*.[18] Not all of these, he points out, give their respective works intact, and many variants occur between different copies of the same work. I, in general, have followed Müller-Blattau in his choice of variants. In the few instances where I disagree with him, a note or footnote appears to that effect. Brief comments of this nature, and simple cross-references to other sections of the treatise or treatises concerned, appear in footnotes, keyed by a symbol. More substantive material, including historical backgrounds, musicological information, and extended editorial comment, appears in separate Notes sections, one following the *Art of Singing* treatise and one following the *Tractatus/Bericht* treatise.

Müller-Blattau also mentions a fourth treatise purportedly by Bernhard, entitled *Resolutiones tonorum Dissonantium in Consonantes*. This is a very brief work, seven chapters in all, and consists, according to Müller-Blattau, almost wholly of examples of ways to resolve various dissonances—a subject which certainly is amply covered in the *Tractatus* and in the *Bericht*. Hence I feel no great loss as a result of his not having included it in his publication.

The "Anhang" concerning double counterpoint, which appears as chapters 64 to 70 of the *Tractatus* in the printed edition, indeed seems to have been an appendix—or, we should rather say, a separate treatise. It is found in only two manuscript sources, tagged onto the end of the *Tractatus* proper in one, and onto the end of the *Bericht* in the other. I follow Müller-Blattau in giving it at the end of the *Tractatus*.

My translation of the Bernhard works is based throughout upon the

[18] Müller-Blattau, pp. 8–10.

printed edition—both the text as given therein and the critical commentary which precedes it. It preserves the chapter and paragraph numbering found there, to facilitate reference. I have followed Müller-Blattau in assigning Arabic numbers to the chapters of the *Tractatus*, Roman numerals to those of the *Bericht*. Musical examples are reproduced faithfully, except that all of them have been rendered in the treble and bass clefs,[19] and black breves and semibreves have been replaced by white equivalents. Any questionable features of these examples, as found in the printed edition, will be discussed in notes and footnotes. Certain obvious errors of printing or copying will be corrected without mention.

Müller-Blattau's brackets, consistently employed by him not only for editorial interpolations, but also for readings not found in all the sources, have been mostly retained. Whenever there is no explanation for bracketed material, the reader may assume that it appears that way in the printed edition. Additional bracketed material introduced by me will, on the other hand, always be accounted for in a note or footnote. Italics are kept wherever they seem significant.

A word should be said here about the term *Manier*, which occurs repeatedly in the treatise on singing. According to Müller-Blattau, this word is found on the title page of only one of the manuscript sources for that work. There the title reads "Kurze Reguln von der Manier oder Künstlicher Art zu singen. . . ." The titles in two other manuscripts contain the Italian *Maniera*: "Von der Singe-Kunst oder Maniera," and "Manductio brevior ad Maniera." The remaining source reads, simply, "Von der Singe-Kunst." I choose to retain the German form, *Manier*, as this even today can refer to musical ornaments or grace notes, whereas neither the English *Manner* nor the Italian *Maniera* has any such musical connotation. Moreover, the latter term can be used in music to refer to something quite different.

A suitable English equivalent for *Manier* was sought in British treatises of the time, but not found. Thus Christopher Simpson, in the *Division Violist* (1659), speaks of the "Gracing of Notes," which seems to cover everything except diminutions, referred to under the separate heading of

[19] Except for two, where special reasons call for the retention of the old C-clefs (Examples 311 and 329).

"minuritio." Thomas Mace simply speaks of "Graces" (*Musick's Monument*, 1676) a term with similar shortcomings. John Playford, in *An Introduction to the Skill of Musick* (published in 1703), uses phrases such as the "Italian manner of Singing" and the "noble manner of Singing," which may be all-inclusive but too cumbersome. F. T. Arnold has translated "manierlicher" as "more elaborately," which suggests "elaboration" as a possible equivalent for "Manier."[20] But do *piano* and *forte* really constitute elaborations, as we understand that word? "Artifice," used to mean the antithesis of the "natural" (see above), seems a fully satisfactory translation of *Manier* when the latter refers to a specific category of refinements, but does not seem quite right when the same term is used in its most comprehensive sense, including all the various types of refinements.

[20] F. T. Arnold, *The Art of Accompaniment from a Thorough-Bass* (London, Holland Press, 1961), p. 230.

ON THE ART OF SINGING; OR, MANIER

1. To earn the title of Singer, it is not enough to execute skillfully all that appears [in the music].[1] Besides a good voice, a certain artistic style, commonly referred to as *Manier*, is required, and therefore must be learned. Only when the elaborations* of this style are observed and applied is one entitled to the name of Singer.

2. This *Manier* is twofold, one part preserving the notes,† the other changing these.

3. Moreover, the part preserving the notes is again divided in two, one part considering only the notes themselves,‡ the other also taking the text into account. These last two kinds of *Manier* are referred to by peculiar names, and partly because of their inherent features the first is called *cantar sodo*, the second *cantar d'affetto*. The altered kind, however, is called *cantar passagiato*.

4. They are also named after the regions wherein they are especially popular, the first being referred to as *cantar alla romana*, the second as *alla napolitana*, and the last as *alla lombarda*. These kinds shall now be described in order.

5. *Cantar sodo* [*alla romana*],§ the kind dwelling only upon the notes themselves, is called "plain"[2] or "even" singing, not because it is easy to learn, nor yet because it is undesirable to sing in this way (for it is the hardest way of all, the most taxing, and the foundation for the other kinds), but rather because notes are not altered therein through passage-work,|| each

* "Kunststücke."

† "bei den Noten bleibend," i.e., keeping to the notes written in the score.

‡ "nur auf die Noten sehend," i.e., looking upon the notes as purely musical entities, without regard to any text.

§ The bracketed material is mine.

|| "*passagiren.*"

note being separately accorded its own graces. One who does not employ either of the other kinds, possessing neither a throat fit for passage-work nor an understanding of the text, must still be acknowledged a fine singer.

6. The refinements used in *cantar sodo* are the following: a) *fermo*; b) *forte*; c) *piano*; d) *trillo*; e) *accento*; f) *anticipatione della syllaba*; g) *anticipatione della nota*; h) *cercar della nota*; i) *ardire*.

7. *Fermo*, or the maintenance of a steady voice, is required on all notes, except where a *trillo* or *ardire* is applied. It is regarded as a refinement mainly because the *tremulo* is a defect (except on the organ, where all the voices can tremulate simultaneously,* and where it sounds well because of the alteration).[3] Elderly singers feature the *tremulo*, but not as an artifice. Rather it creeps in by itself, as they no longer are able to hold their voices steady. If anyone would demand further evidence of the undesirability of the *tremulo*, let him listen to such an old man employing it while singing alone. Then he will be able to judge why the *tremulo* is not used by the most polished singers, except in *ardire* (about which more will be said below). Basses, however, are permitted to use it elsewhere, but with the stipulation that it be applied infrequently and on short notes only.

8. *Piano* and *forte*, just as the other refinements, will henceforth be referred to by special symbols, the former by *p*, the latter by *f*. We treat them together, as they indeed must alternate with one another in singing.

9. *Piano* and *forte* are either used together on a single note, or successively on different notes. The former occurs on whole and half notes,† the latter on notes of shorter value.

10. On whole and half notes it is customary to employ a *piano* at the beginning, a *forte* in the middle, and a *piano* once more at the end, as: [Example 1].‡ Care must be taken not to shift too abruptly from the *piano*

EXAMPLE I

* "zugleich *tremuliren* können."

† "in gantzen und halben *tacten*."

‡ All example numbers are mine.

to the *forte* [or vice versa], but rather to let the voice wax and wane gradually. Otherwise, what ought to be a charming refinement will instead sound absolutely abominable.

11. On short notes, some are sung *piano* and others *forte*, in alternation. But more often than not, one begins with a *piano* and, in any case, ends with one.[4] [Example 2]

EXAMPLE 2

12. The *trillo* is the hardest device of all but also the most ingratiating, and no one can be regarded as a good singer who does not know how to employ it. Although it is impossible to describe verbally in a manner such that one can thereby learn it, and although it is better learned by listening, yet we can indicate approximately how it should be done. Note, however, that at times voices arise from the chest, but at other times they are formed only in the throat, or "in the head" (as the *musici* would say). Hence it follows that not everyone can strike the *trillo* in the chest, where the best ones otherwise originate, but certain people (and contraltos in general) are obliged to produce them in the throat. Above all, however, one should take great care not to change the quality of the voice in striking the *trillo*, lest a bleating sound result. Hence it is also to be observed that one who does not execute it well should keep it short, so that his audience may not become aware of the shortcoming; on the other hand, an expert may extend it for as long as he can, appearing the more gracious and wonderful in so doing. Furthermore, one should not strike a *trillo* too fast, but rather let the voice simply beat, as it were;* and too slow a *trillo* is also not to be recommended. It is best to find a good medium speed—although, if I myself had to choose one over the other, I would rather hear one that is somewhat too fast than one that is altogether too slow.

13. The *trillo* is first of all made wherever a *t* is to be found over the notes

* "die Stimme gleichsam nur schweben lassen."

(this being a sign whereby a *trillo* is indicated). One may apply it in other places as well, but only upon careful reflection. Good use of the *trillo* is better learned through practice and the example of others than through any specific written precepts which would describe its use and thereby deny the singer his freedom. His good taste will be able to pick out the notes on which a *trillo* can be made. One should nevertheless remark that it must not be overused. It is like a spice which, when employed moderately, adds to the attractiveness of a dish, but if used in excess can indeed spoil it. But our primary concern here is merely to explain all the refinements of *Manier*. Their use can better be learned through practice.

14. It is very agreeable to hear *forte* and *piano* on long trills, and this happens in two ways: a) when the *trillo* is begun *piano* and the voice is allowed to increase its intensity gradually; b) when the *trillos* are doubled (*quando si fa trilli doppi*), as in the example.[5] [Example 3; one manuscript has a variant (Example 3a) beginning with the fifth quarter note.]*

EXAMPLE 3

15. *Accento* is a little refinement,† formed at the conclusion of a note by means of an aftersound which, as it were, only hangs on.‡ He errs, therefore, who would employ a bold, strongly forced shout§ in place of a gentle *accento*; for while he intends to impart elegance to his singing, in reality he horrifies his audience with the abusive shout.

16. The *accento* is used on descending notes,[6] on repeated notes,[7] and on closing notes. [Example 4]

* The bracketed material is mine.
† "ein so genanntes Kunststücklein."
‡ "mit einem gleichsam nur anhenckenden Nachklange."
§ "einen starck herausgestossenen Jauchzer."

EXAMPLE 4

a
a
a
[a]
t
a
Do - mi - ne ex - au - di o - ra - ti - o - nem me - am

17. Two successive notes cannot both be graced with an *accento*. If the first has one, then the second must remain without an *accent*.[8] A third note can again have one.

18. Also, an *accent* is only permitted on syllables which in speaking are long. Short syllables must remain without an *accent*, with the exception of the last syllables of words, which may be accented in song even if repressed in speech. All this may be observed in Example 4.

19. *Anticipatione della syllaba* is denoted by *S*, and is (as the name implies) a device wherein a syllable assigned to a given note is delivered in part on a fraction of the preceding note, as: [Example 5].

EXAMPLE 5

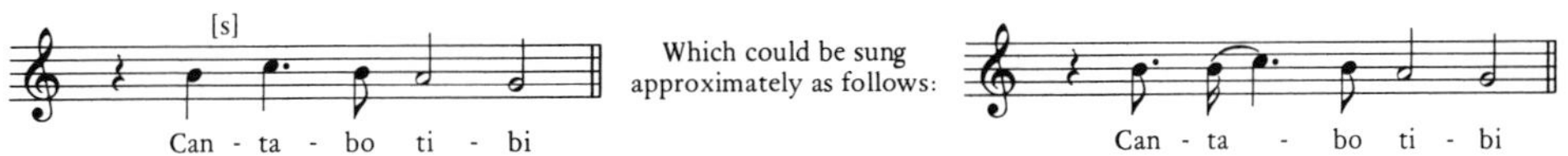
[s]
Can - ta - bo ti - bi
Which could be sung approximately as follows:
Can - ta - bo ti - bi

20. *Anticipatione della syllaba* is used: a) commonly when a note lies a step higher than the preceding note; b) rarely when the notes rise or fall a third; c) still more rarely when the notes fall a fourth, fifth, or sixth; d) most rarely of all, when they rise a fourth, fifth, or sixth. Now when the second note lies a step higher than the first, the syllable belonging to the second note is applied to the end of the first, as is to be seen in the above example. When the notes rise or fall a third, a fraction of the antecedent note is given over to the note between them, while the syllable of the consequent note is applied to that fraction, as: [Example 6]. When the notes fall a fourth, etc.,

EXAMPLE 6

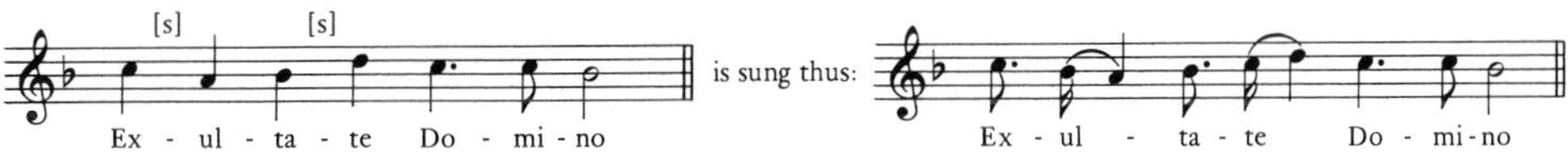
[s]
[s]
Ex - ul - ta - te Do - mi - no
is sung thus:
Ex - ul - ta - te Do - mi-no

the first note is divided as follows: [Example 7]. The last case, wherein the notes rise a fourth, etc., is seldom encountered, but occurs in this manner [Example 8].

EXAMPLE 7

EXAMPLE 8

Lau - da - bo Do - mi - num Lau - da - bo Do - mi - num

21. *Anticipatione della nota*,* denoted by *N*, is, as the name suggests, a refinement wherein a fraction of a note is given over to the note following it. It is employed when the notes rise or fall a second.

22. When the notes rise a second, the first note is divided, and the last part thereof drawn to the pitch of the next note;† one does the same when the notes fall a second. [Example 9]

EXAMPLE 9

23. *Cercar della nota*‡ means a searching out of notes, and is marked by *c*.

24. It is used either at the beginning or during the course of a phrase. At the beginning of a phrase, one sings the note immediately beneath the initial note very briefly and softly, then glides from this quite imperceptibly to the initial note: [Example 10]. During the course of a phrase, it can be

EXAMPLE 10

* See *anticipatio notae*, in ch. 23 of the *Tractatus*; see also ch. XV, para. 4 of the *Bericht*, given opposite ch. 24 of the *Tractatus*.

† "in den *Tonum* der nachfolgenden [Note] gezogen." The bracketed word is mine. See also para. 33 and its footnote.

‡ Cf. *quaesitio notae*, in ch. 33 of the *Tractatus*; also, *subsumtio*, in ch. 24 of the *Tractatus* and ch. XV of the *Bericht*.

used equally well between two notes of the same pitch* or between notes a leap apart.[9] When the notes are of the same pitch, one goes from the first to the second by way of the note immediately above or below: [Example 11].

EXAMPLE 11

If one would apply *cercar della nota* to two notes differing by a step, then *anticipatione della nota* must first be employed, and thereafter the preceding rule followed, as:† [Example 12]. When the notes rise or fall a third, one

EXAMPLE 12

employs *cercar della nota* in the following manner: [Example 13]. If, how-

EXAMPLE 13

ever, the notes rise or fall a fourth, fifth, etc., then *cercar della nota* occurs either a step lower or a step higher. We only give examples of descending leaps, as *cercar della nota* is indeed rarely employed on ascending intervals of this type: [Example 14].

EXAMPLE 14

* "bey den nebeneinander stehenden . . . Noten."

† The example is given exactly as found in Müller-Blattau. (The "*sic!*" is his.) Probably the questionable quarter beat should consist of an eighth, a dotted sixteenth, and a thirty-second, though an interpretation in triplets also seems possible.

25. *Ardire*, denoted by ♯, is a *tremulo* performed on the last note of a close.[10] It is indeed used by few, and then only by basses, whom it also suits best, since these are in general permitted to make wider application of the *tremulo* than others. It is well to remember, however, that one should never use it on the last note of a piece, which is called the *Final Note*.

So much briefly for that *Manier* which is called *romana*, of which all musicians—instrumentalists as well as singers—should partake.

Now we turn to the one called *napolitana*.

26. *Cantar alla napolitana*, or *d'affetto*, is a style meant for singers only, as they alone are confronted with a text. Even so, instrumentalists can to some extent apply its principles, insofar as they know how to produce and control joyous or melancholy sounds* upon their instruments.

27. It consists, however, in the singer's diligent observation of the text, and in his regulating his vocal production in accordance with it.†

28. This happens in two different senses, as he takes heed, first, of the words alone‡ and, second, of their meaning.

29. The first consists in the proper pronunciation of the words which he must set forth in song. Burrs, lisps, and other forms of bad diction must be eschewed, and a graceful, blameless manner of speech cultivated. In his mother tongue, he should certainly adopt the most elegant way of speaking, so that a German will not speak Swabian, Pomeranian, [etc.], but rather Misnian or as close to the accepted manner as possible,[11] and an Italian not Bolognese, Venetian, or Lombard, but rather Florentine or Roman. If, however, he is to sing in a language other than his mother tongue, then he must read that language at least as fluently and correctly as those people to whom it is native. Latin he is free to pronounce as is customary in the district where he is singing, since it is pronounced differently in different countries. If, however, someone should choose to pronounce Latin in the Italian way, as indeed most singers are wont to do, I would judge this not only admissible but also right and prudent, for weighty reasons (which cannot be spelled out here). Germans should strive, above all, to make a clear and noticeable distinction between *b* and *p*, *d* and *t*, *f* and *v*; as also to

* "frölicher oder kläglicher *Harmonie*."

† "nach Anleitung [desselbigen] die Stimme *moderirt*."

‡ "blosen Worte," i.e., the words regarded as sounds pure and simple, completely apart from what they mean.

render *st*, not in their usual manner—as in the word *steten*—but rather as in the word *besten*. *Sp* and *sc* should be handled similarly. A singer must especially not confound vowels with one another, but give them their natural sounds. *A* must not sound like *o*, or *o* like *a*, or *e* like *i*, etc.

30. Still more necessary than the preceding is an adequate understanding of the text. Accordingly it is to be deplored that only a few singers concern themselves with a proper and solid grounding in Latin and Italian—two languages which, besides their mother tongue, all singers ought to understand passably, if not indeed speak well. The anger of learned listeners is therefore all too frequently aroused by singers who apply passage-work to a word like *confirmatio*, or place an ascending run on one like *abyssus*, bringing their ignorance to the light of day.

31. The words, once understood, suggest what affects, occurring therein, should be elicited.* The noblest affects which can be represented in music are Joy, Sorrow, Anger, Contentment, and the like.

32. In Joy, Anger, and similarly strong affects, the voice must be strong, valiant, and hearty. Notes must not be decorated in special ways;† rather, they should more frequently be sung as written, for any further application of *Manier*, and of *piano*, *cercar della nota*, *anticipatione della syllaba*, and *anticipatione della nota* in particular, would sound somewhat more melancholy than these affects require.

33. On the other hand, for sorrowful, gentle, and like words it is better to employ a milder, softer voice, to slur and slide between the notes,‡ to employ frequently the refinements of *Manier* mentioned directly above, and to use *forte*, *ardire*, and *trillo* somewhat more sparingly than for stronger affects. For this type of affect one should also choose a slower tempo, for the other a quicker one. A good singer will derive further rules through his own judgment and from the example of other singers.

34. The question may here be raised, whether a singer's face and bearing should reflect the affects found in the text. Thus let it be known that a singer should sing modestly, without special facial expressions; for nothing is more upsetting than certain singers who are better heard than seen, who

* "Aus den verstandenen Worten sind die *affecten* abzunehmen, so darinnen fürkommen."

† "nicht sonderlich geschleift . . . werden." See para. 33 and its footnote.

‡ "die Noten ziehe und schleife." See para. 22 and its footnote for use of "gezogen," and para. 32 and its footnote for use of "geschleift."

arouse the expectations of a listener with a good voice and style of singing, but who ruin everything with ugly faces and gestures. Until they learn better facial expressions and manners, such singers should only be heard in the choir,[12] behind the grating, but not openly, within sight of everyone.

In ordinary music-making,[13] especially in the performance of motets and the like, it is in my opinion not proper to use even simple theatrical gestures.* Rather, he who would follow my advice will withhold even these until he undertakes a role in a play with song, wherein they will stand him in better stead—indeed be absolutely essential, as he then must present not only a trained voice, but a sympathetic, theatrical personage as well. So much then briefly for the second type of singing.

The third type, *cantar passagiato*, follows.

35. The *Manier* called *cantar passagiato* [or *alla lombarda*] is a type of singing wherein one does not adhere to the designated notes, but rather changes them either through *diminution* or through *colorature*.

36. In *diminution*,† one divides the written notes into shorter notes which correctly preserve the measure.‡ Thus a note which has the value of a half note may rightly be divided into four eighth notes, eight sixteenth notes, or sixteen thirty-second notes.§ Instead of staying on the given note, one ventures forth from it gracefully, as in this illustration:|| [Example 15].

EXAMPLE 15

Examples of similar *diminutions*# may be found in abundance everywhere.

37. The following rules govern such *diminutions*:

They should be used sparingly, lest the singing, through constantly recurring runs of this type and the concomitant neglect of other devices,¶

* "auch nur *comoediantische* Geberden [gebrauche]."

† See *variation*, in ch. 25 of the *Tractatus* and ch. XVI of the *Bericht*. See also *transitus*, in ch. 17 of the *Tractatus*, ch. 12 of the *Bericht*, and note 26 on p. 183.

‡ "in richtiger Beobachtung der *Battuta*."

§ "Halben Tact" again is rendered by "half note." The other note values mentioned in the text are respectively, "*Fusen*," "*Semifusen*," and "*Subsemifusen*." See para. 9 and its footnote on p. 14.

|| I give the example exactly as it appears in Müller-Blattau.

Here, and in the sequel, the text reads "*Diminutionen*" rather than "*Diminutio*."

¶ "durch stetige solche Läufe und wegen weniger auf solchen Fall fürkommender Veränderung[en]."

become difficult and tiring for the singer, and unpleasant for the audience. For it is quite ridiculous that one should let nothing be heard but steady passage-work. Rather this *Manier* also should be used in the same way as pepper and salt.

Second, such diminutions should not venture up too high nor down too low, nor too far over or under the scale, and certainly not out of the natural setting or key; for through this the composition will easily be ruined, and soon here, soon there, a horse-fifth, cow-octave, or miserable unison will creep in; one voice (soprano, alto, or tenor) will trespass upon the territory of another, or the second upon that of the first; and so the judiciously planned harmonic scheme will, whether intentionally or not, be brought to naught.[14] Third, all types of uncomfortable leaps and difficult intervals must be avoided, since such not only fail to produce a good effect, but also are irksome for the throat, and hence much easier and far more comfortable for an instrumentalist than for a singer.

38. *Colorature* are runs which are not so exactly bound to the measure, but which often extend two, three, or more measures further. It must be remarked, however, that such runs should be made only at chief closes,[15] not too often, and not always in one and the same manner. Now and then one may find further precepts to follow in well-written solos by conscientious composers who understand the voice. Otherwise there is no great difference between *colorature* and *diminutions*, and what is to be observed about one also holds for the other.

39. In *colorature* it is better and more musical for a singer or instrumentalist not to stray from the notes at cadences, but rather to return modestly to these notes once again. It would, accordingly, be bad to adorn cadences with this sort of *coloratura* or *diminution*: [Example 16]. For fifths, fourths, octaves, and unisons would be produced against the other

EXAMPLE 16

voices. Instead of the foregoing, it is better to use the following sort of variation:* [Example 17].

EXAMPLE 17

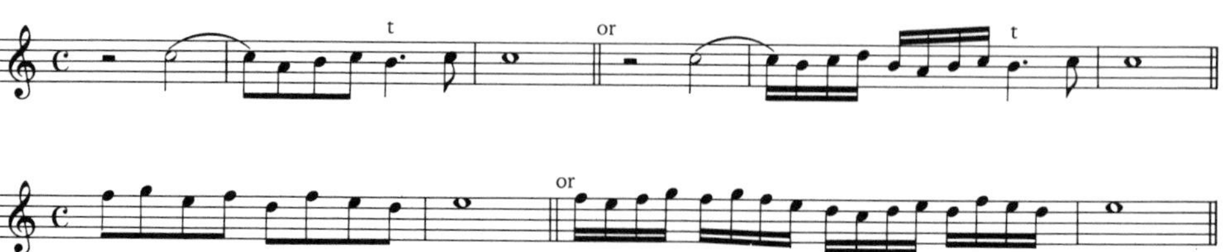

40. When music is made to the accompaniment of an organist or lutenist alone, the above rule is not observed as strictly as when a harmony of several voices is involved. But one should beware of applying passage-work or *diminution* without careful consideration. In the bass, no rapid passages or *colorature* should be employed at all, except for that which is indicated by the composer; otherwise the groundwork of the piece will be disrupted and the voices left without a foundation, and nothing but a disagreeable dissonance will be heard. The verse of the Mantuan should be heeded: *Bassus alit voces, confortat, fondet* et *auget.*[16] Other voices, however, should introduce *diminutions* in such a way as not to beget musical defects.† These can notably be avoided if the *diminutions* are ended on the same degree as that on which they were begun. Finally, one must know those pitfalls which a good singer and sophisticated musician, familiar with the qualitative and quantitative properties of sound, can avoid:‡ A singer should not raise his voice in connection with the affect of humility or love; nor let it fall several tones when anger is to be shown. In the recitative style, one should take care that the voice is raised in moments of anger, and to the contrary dropped in moments of grief. Pain makes it pause; impatience hastens it. Happiness enlivens it. Desire emboldens it. Love renders it alert. Bashfulness holds it back. Hope strengthens it. Despair diminishes it. Fear keeps it down. Danger is fled with screams. If, however, a person faces up to danger, then his voice must reflect his daring and

* "folgender Gestalt zu *variiren.*" See *variation* in ch. 25 of the *Tractatus* and ch. XVI of the *Bericht.*

† "*Vitia Musicalia.*"

‡ "Ferner ist zum Beschluss annoch zu wissen von Nöthen, dass ein guter Sänger oder *Subtiler Musicus,* der mit *Qualitate* und *Quantitate Toni* weiss umb zugehen."

bravery. To sum up, a singer should not sing through his nose. He must not stammer, lest he be incomprehensible. He must not push with his tongue or lisp, else one will hardly understand half of what he says. He also should not close his teeth together, nor open his mouth too wide, nor stretch his tongue out over his lips, nor thrust his lips upward, nor distort his mouth, nor disfigure his cheeks and nose like the long-tailed monkey, nor crumple his eyebrows together, nor wrinkle his forehead, nor roll his head or the eyes therein round and round, nor wink with the same, nor tremble with his lips, etc.

NOTES FOR THE *Art of Singing*

1. The bracketed material is mine. In this paragraph, the distinction is made between *ein Singer*—apparently anyone who engages in singing—and *ein Sänger*—one who has truly mastered the art of singing. As this distinction in terms is not easily rendered in English, I have chosen to equate *Sänger* with the English *Singer*, and to change the sentence structure in the one place where the German *Singer* occurs: ". . . diejenige Kunststücke sind, welche ein Singer beobachtend und anbringend eines Sängers Nahmen verdienet."

2. "schlechte." An untranslatable pun on this word is involved here. Just below, Bernhard uses the word in its more familiar sense of "bad" ("schlechter Dinge," rendered in the translation as "undesirable," the sentence structure having been slightly altered). See *Tractatus*, ch. 70, para. 1, and its footnote.

3. "wegen der Veränderung wohl lautet." By "Veränderung" Bernhard may be referring to the uniform change in tone color which the tremulant stop seems to produce. In that case it would appear to be precisely this uniformity which renders the *tremulo* acceptable on the organ.

4. The example seems hardly ideal, as each of the melodic fragments (after the initial note) begins *f*. Müller-Blattau (henceforth referred to as M-B.) points out that one manuscript source has only the indication *p* over the initial note, rather than the *pf* found in all the others.

5. In Example 3 and subsequent ones, M-B. seems to have substituted the modern *tr* for the indication which Bernhard himself had prescribed for the trillo, namely *t*. I prefer to employ Bernhard's *t*, especially since *tr* refers in our own day to an entirely different ornament. I give the *p*'s, *f*'s and ♯s as they appear in M-B. Obviously the sharp hould hold sway through the final cadence.

6. It is very possible, though hardly certain, that the *accento* here mentioned is identical with the *accentus*, or *superjectio*, discussed in ch. 22 of the *Tractatus* and in ch. XIV of the *Bericht*. From para. 15 of the present treatise it is clear that a short, ornamental "note," probably of somewhat higher pitch, is involved in the execution of the *accento*. Thus it seems strikingly analogous to the *accentus*, carefully illustrated in the other works. However, the fact that this "note" is not written out here in Example 4, might suggest that it is not precisely a step above the main note, as is the case with the *accentus*. Also, according to the other two treatises, *accentus* only occurs on falling notes; *accento*, however, can also occur on notes of the same pitch and on final notes. Further

comparison of the accounts of the two devices will reveal still other (possibly) significant differences. See note 8, however.

7. "nebeneinander in einem *Clave* stehenden . . . Noten." The word *clavis*, as used by Bernhard both here and in the other treatises, usually seems to refer to an individual degree of the scale (and will generally be translated as "degree" or "pitch") rather than to a whole scale, clef, or key. See note 14, however.

8. Here, and in the sequel, the word *accent*, rather than *accento*, is found. Interestingly, *accent* is also used interchangeably with *accentus* in the *Tractatus* and *Bericht*. See note 6.

9. "bey den . . . springenden Noten." Example 12, however, shows that *cercar della nota* may be applied to notes a step apart as well as to notes a leap apart, even if the application is somewhat more indirect.

10. "bey der letzten Note einer *Clausul*." I translate *Clausul* in the most usual way for the period, namely as *close*, but must remark that the word was also sometimes used to refer to any melodic fragment whatsoever.

11. "Meissnisch oder der Red-Arth zum nächsten rede." Meissen, for many hundreds of years, was a far-ranging, influential margraviate, located on both sides of the middle Elbe. It encompassed the city of Leipzig—considered by many to have been the most distinguished intellectual and cultural center in all of Germany—and also, perhaps significantly, Dresden.

12. "im Chor." It seems that *Chor* is employed here not only in its most common sense, i.e., an organization of singers, but also in the sense of the part of the church (also sometimes called "choir" in English) where they would sing. In former times, a sort of screen or "grating" (*Gitter*) often separated this part of a church from the nave.

13. "in *Musiciren*." Seemingly, musical performances not involving any kind of acting or character portrayal are meant here.

14. "Zum Andern, dass solche nicht gar zu hoch noch zu tief, oder zu weit über oder unter die *Scala* oder gar aus dem natürlichen Satz oder *Ton* gehen, wodurch gar leichtlich die *Composition* verdorben [wird], und bald hier, bald dar eine Ross-*Quint*, Küh-*Octav* oder verdriesslicher *Unisonus* sich einschleichet und entweder der Erste *Discant*, *Alt* oder *Tenor* in des Andern, oder der Andere in des ersten seinen Clavem einlaufet, und also die wohlgesetzte *Harmonie nolens volens* vernichtiget wird." By *Scala* Bernhard seems to suggest a concept somewhat akin to that of ambitus, and by *Satz* and *Ton* the diatonic setting of the octave (devoid of any chromatic alterations) holding sway in the section of the piece under consideration. (Compare the use of *natürlich* and *Satz* in ch. 12 of the *Tractatus* and ch. III of the *Bericht*. Also, see my preface regarding Bernhard's use of "natural" in general.) For *Ross-Quint*, *Küh-Octav*, and *verdriesslicher Unisonus*, several explanations seem possible, among which it is

difficult to choose since Bernhard does not elaborate on the matter. These may be chromatically altered intervals, derived simply through the ill-advised introduction of pitches foreign to the diatonic setting. They may be commatic deviations from perfect intervals, which recklessly added chromatic tones produce against an unequally tempered accompanying instrument (or another voice). Bad intonation may also result from straining on the part of the singer, when, ignoring Bernhard's advice, he ventures unnaturally high or low. Zarlino already had observed that remaining in a very high or low register over a substantial period of time will cause a singer to strain and produce "dissonant sound": Gioseffe Zarlino, *Istitutioni harmoniche* (Venice, Francesco de i Franceschi Senese, 1573; facsimile edition: Ridgewood, N.J., Gregg Press, 1966), p. 241. Finally, the phrases *Ross-Quint*, etc., may each possibly refer not to a single interval, but rather to two parallel intervals. (See para. 39.)

I have chosen to interpret *Clavem* not the way I do elsewhere—that is, as referring to a particular degree of the scale (see note 7)—but rather as referring to the *range* of each of the voices in question. The reader will note the close relationship between range and clef in all vocal music before the nineteenth century. Pedro Cerone had used the word *clave* throughout his *El Melopeo y Maestro* (Naples, 1613) simply to mean *clef* —a meaning which it has retained in modern Spanish. (See especially pp. 873–932.) On p. 912 of that work, he advised that voice parts should not overstep the boundaries of their respective five-line staves, forcing the introduction of ledger lines ("reglas falsas ò añadidas"); thereby he quite clearly linked clefs with voice ranges. I have taken the phrase, "*Discant*, *Alt* oder *Tenor*" as an appositive to "*Erste*," as suggested by the capitalization of the latter. This is consistent with my interpretation of *Clavem*, for Bernhard is then probably speaking of two voices with different ranges (and, hence, different clefs) interfering with one another, rather than of two voices with the same range.

15. "Haubt-*Finalen*." *Colorature*, as defined here, thus seem very much akin to what we call *cadenzas*. Bernhard's use of the word in ch. 25 of the *Tractatus* is quite different, however: the word refers there, as "*diminution*" does here, to divisions which preserve the measure.

16. I am indebted to Denis Stevens of Columbia University for information concerning the source of this quote and the identity of the "Mantuan." The poet in question is Teofilo Folengo (1496–1544), called the "Mantuan" because he was born near that city—though more precisely at a village called Cipada. The quote is from canto 20 of his *Baldus*, a lengthy mock-epic poem which frequently mentions music. In the spot where this line appears, Baldus and his three friends are singing in harmony as they ride along together, and Folengo describes the role which each voice plays in the harmony:

Plus ascoltantum Sopranus captat orecchias.
Sed Tenor est, vocum rector, vel Guida canentum.
Altus Apollineum carmen depingit et ornat.
Bassus alit voces, ingrassat, firmat et auget.

Zarlino quotes these same four lines (referring to Folengo not by name, but just as "the playful Mantuan poet") on p. 282 of his *Istitutioni harmoniche*, in a section discussing composition in more than two parts; he substitutes "fundat" for "firmat." We next encounter the line concerning the bass by itself, in Michael Praetorius, *Syntagma Musicum* (Wolfenbüttel, 1619), p. 94, in the following form: "Bassus alit voces, ingrassat (confortat), fundat et auget."

Praetorius refers to this as the "Vers des Mantuani." Thus it seems very likely that Bernhard owes this quote to Praetorius, who in turn must have come across it in Zarlino. A characterization of the "bass," very similar to this quote, is still found in Jean-Philippe Rameau, *Traité de l'harmonie* (Paris, 1722), p. 49. Rameau in fact calls it a quote of Zarlino, though the correspondence of words hardly seems precise: "la Basse a la proprieté de soûtenir, d'établir et de fortifier les autres parties." However, the French theorist is correcting, or updating, Zarlino's ideas, as he does elsewhere; thus the term "bass" is to be understood here as a "basse fondamentale," in Rameau's own, very special sense.

GUIDE TO INTENDED ORDER OF THE *Bericht*

Bericht		Tractatus
chapter paragraphs		chapter paragraphs
I:1–10	appears opposite	4:1–6
II:1–2		4:10
3–6		8:9
III:1–25		12:1–21
IV:1		6:4
2–5		6:7–8
6–9		9:4–5
V:1–4		8:4–5
5–8		6:6
VI:1–4		11:4–5
5–8		6:9
VII:1–4		8:7–8
5–7		9:6
VIII:1–4		11:7–8
5–7		9:9
IX:1–4		13:1–3
X:1–2		14:5
3–7		16:3–4
XI:1–11		19:1–15
XII:1–4		17:1–3
5–6		18:1–2
XIII:1–6		21:1–7
XIV:1–3		22:1–3
XV:1–7		24:1–2
XVI:1–9		25:1–12
XVII:1–4		26:1
XVIII:1–3		37:1–4
XIX:1–2		38:1–4
XX:1		41:1–3
2		41:6
XXI:1		40:1–2
XXII:1		39:1–3

THE TRACTATUS

Q.D.B.V.*

Chapter 1

Of Counterpoint in General

1. Composition is a science† which erects a harmonious contrapuntal structure‡ out of well-disposed consonances and dissonances.

2. Thus the object of composition is Harmony, or the euphony of several distinct voices. The *musici* call this *counterpoint*, since in olden times, before the invention of the notes in use today, only points§ were used, and so two or more voices, indicated through such points, were referred to as *contrapunctus*. In the opinion of some, *contrasonus* would be a better term.

3. The building blocks of counterpoint are consonances and dissonances. Of the latter, however, only those are employed which stem from the division of the octave into its tones and semitones; not the others, which are so unnatural, and hence inimical to harmony.

4. Beauty|| consists in the artistic alternation and intermingling of consonances and dissonances, hence in the observation of the General and Special Rules of Counterpoint.[1] From differing applications of these rules and from their natural influence, it results that one composition is good, but another better, that the audience may be more or less pleased, and that a composer is made famous.

Chapter 2

Of the General Rules of Counterpoint

1. The first rule, from which all others follow, is that every voice in a contrapuntal structure should permit itself to be sung to good effect.[2]

* *Quod Deus bene vertat.*

† "*Wissenschaft.*"

‡ "einen *harmoni*schen *Contrapunct.*"

§ "*Puncte.*"

|| "Die *Forma.*" This Latin word also can mean "form" in general.

Hence it is better to compose in fewer voices, all of which are melodious,[3] than in a greater number of voices, many of which will sound disagreeable by themselves.

2. To this end it is particularly important that text and notes should be in accord with one another, for otherwise it can happen that notes which in themselves make a good melody may sound bad because of the setting of the text, and vice versa.

3. A contrapuntal structure of singable lines* should adhere to a regular meter.[4] This matter is given more extensive treatment in the *Art of Singing*.[5]

4. No voice should be set too high or too low, lest it appear too difficult, or indeed unnatural, for the singer or instrumentalist.

5. No voice should stay on one note,† especially one that is rather high or low, for too long; for nothing renders a melody as attractive as the skillful alternation of upward and downward motion by the voice. Nevertheless, *falsi bordoni* are not to be rejected on this ground.[6]

6. In ascending and descending, one should beware of unnatural step progressions or leaps,‡ such as the leap of a seventh, the step progression or leap of a false fifth or fourth—especially when these are augmented§—and also the augmented second. [Example 18] Even so, certain of these progressions and leaps are permitted in contemporary composition, par-

EXAMPLE 18

* "aus *Notis cantabilibus.*"

† "auff einer *Chorde . . . obteniren.*"

‡ "unnatürlichen Gängen und Sprüngen."

§ "*Superfluae.*" Diminished intervals are often called "*deficientes.*"

ticularly in the recitative style. Their use is left to the discretion of the composer.

7. Every voice, and hence the whole contrapuntal structure, should conform to one of the twelve modes, which will be discussed below.*

8. One should not repeat the same kind of melodic figure† too often. Even so, fugues and imitations have their merits.[7]

9. Contrary motion‡ should be present in a three-part piece, where it is always appropriate, except when consecutive sixths have thirds in their midst.§ In a four-part piece, it must always be found, without exception.

10. In a four-part piece, all consonances should be sounded wherever possible;[8] but this is particularly true in a five-part piece.

11. Counterpoint should begin and end with perfect consonances. However, when the voices do not begin together, the voice which follows should commence at a perfect interval with respect to the first note of the voice that began. In this situation, the fourth is counted as one of the perfect intervals, particularly in plagal modes.

12. Voices should not have false relations with one another, such as a tritone, a diminished fifth,[9] an augmented octave, etc.: [Example 19]. Yet

EXAMPLE 19

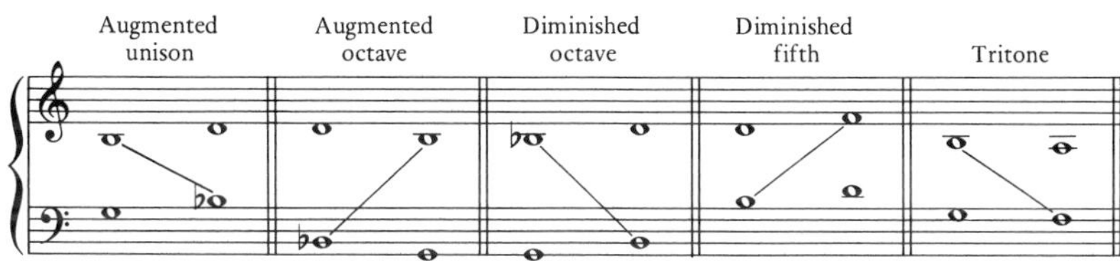

this rule cannot be rigorously enforced in selections with more than two voices.

13. Voices should not stand too far—i.e., more than a twelfth—apart. Thus men of former ages are not found to have composed for soprano and

* The modes are discussed in chs. 44 to 56.

† "einerley *Modulation.*"

‡ Müller-Blattau (henceforth referred to as M-B.) gives "*Modus Contrarius,*" but clearly "*Motus Contrarius*" is meant. The latter appears several times below, e.g., in ch. 8, para. 6 and in ch. 11, para. 9.

§ "wo die *Consecutio* der *Sexten* durch *Tertias* gemittelt wird." That is to say, where we have successive $\frac{6}{3}$ chords.

bass alone.* Nevertheless, composers today are doing this, in dialogues,[10] etc., so that this rule also is not too binding.

14. Similarly for this next rule: namely, that very high or low consonances† are forbidden in two-part pieces.

15. In contemporary composition it is none the worse when two-part pieces are written in such a way that they may also be sung without any support (such as thorough-bass).‡ This is not, however, absolutely necessary. In three-part works, I hold it to be a defect if the lowest voice is not the support of the other two. *Omne trinum perfectum.*

16. High voices should seldom go underneath the low, or low voices above the high.

17. If, in a four-part piece, three voices rise or fall together, then it is sufficient that the fourth voice stand still, if it does not proceed in contrary motion.

Chapter 3

Different Types of Counterpoint

1. The main division of counterpoint is into *contrapunctus aequalis* and *inaequalis*, which some call *simplex* and *diminutus* or *floridus*, respectively.

2. In *contrapunctus aequalis*, all the notes of two or more voices have the same time values over against one another.§ It is not, however, necessary that every voice consist of only one type of note. Rather, one can indeed use various note values in each voice, but those above and below should at all times be similar to one another.

3. Such counterpoint consists entirely of consonances, without the interpolation of any dissonances.

4. In *contrapunctus inaequalis*, *diminutus*, *floridus*, or however one might choose to call it, one voice is fashioned out of slower notes, the other out of faster ones.

5. This type consists of dissonances as well as consonances, which are artfully intermingled with one another, consequently producing a harmony more pleasing to the ear than that which *contrapunctus aequalis* produces.

6. Counterpoint could, moreover, be divided still further, into *motets*,

* "*Canto e Basso solo.*"

† "gar zu sehr *acutae* oder *graves Consonantiae.*" That is to say, consonant notes in extreme registers.

‡ "dass sie auch ohne einig ander *Fundament* (als *General Bass*) können gesungen werden."

§ "gleicher *Mensur* sind."

concerti, *madrigals*, *canzonette*, *arias*, *sonatas*, etc.; only, these are not so much species of counterpoint as genres of composition.

7. Similarly, it is not ill to divide counterpoint into *gravis* and *luxurians*, which others call *stylus antiquus* and *modernus*.

8. *Contrapunctus gravis* is the type consisting of notes which do not move too quickly, and few kinds of dissonance treatment. It does not consider text as much as it does harmony; and since it was the only type known to men of former ages, it is called *stylus antiquus*—as also *a cappella* and *ecclesiasticus*, since it is better suited for that place* than for others, and since the Pope permits this type alone in his churches and chapel.

9. *Contrapunctus luxurians* is the type consisting in part of rather quick notes and strange leaps—so that it is well suited for stirring the affects†—and of more kinds of dissonance treatment (or more *figurae melopoeticae*, which others call *licentiae*)[11] than the foregoing. Its melodies agree with the text as much as possible, unlike those of the preceding type.

10. This can again be subdivided into *communis* and *comicus*, the first being used everywhere, the second most of all in theatrical productions, although something recitative-like is also often employed in church or table music. No style succeeds as well in moving the heart as *theatralis*.‡

Chapter 4

Of the Consonances

1. *Contrapunctus aequalis* easily holds first place [among the species of counterpoint],§ dominating all others because of its consonances (which are the soul of harmony).

2. Consonances are the proportions of those intervals‖ which are capable of making harmony with one another. Hence the unison

THE BERICHT

Chapter I

Description of the Consonances

1. Consonances are of two kinds: first, those which are always consonances, such as the third, the fifth, the sixth, and

* The church.
† "die *Affecten* zu bewegen."
‡ "*theatralis*" = "*comicus*."
§ The bracketed material is mine.
‖ "*proportiones* derer *Intervallorum*."

and the fourth are not really to be regarded as consonances in every instance.

3. Consonances are of two kinds: perfect and imperfect.

4. The perfect consonances are those which consist in the proportions *dupla* and *sesquialtera*,* i.e., the octave and fifth, as also the twelfth, fifteenth, and all other sounds arising from the octave by itself, or with octave and fifth combined.†

5. The unison, passing for a consonance according to the usage of all composers, also belongs to the perfect intervals.

the octave; second, that one which is sometimes consonant, sometimes dissonant, namely the fourth. The latter is a dissonance in all two-part pieces, as also whenever it is taken against the lowest part in pieces having a greater number of voices. Otherwise, however, among the middle voices themselves, or between these and the uppermost, it is a consonance.

2. Those which always remain consonances are again of two kinds: perfect and imperfect. The perfect ones are those which keep their magnitude unchanged, namely, the fifth and octave.

N.B. The unison is actually no consonance; yet it is equated with the octave.‡

3. A fifth occurs when one voice stands three tones and a semitone above the other, as:§ [Example 20].

EXAMPLE 20

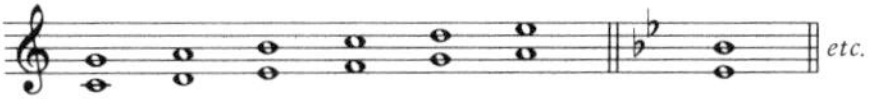

4. An octave occurs when one voice stands five tones and two semitones above the other, as: [Example 21].

* *Dupla* = 2:1; *sesquialtera* = 3:2.

† "aus der *Octava* an ihr selbst, oder mit *Octava* und *Quinta* verdoppelt herrührend."

‡ "wird aber der *Octav* verglichen."

§ In M-B., the key signature for the last fifth is given a third too low for the clef.

6. The imperfect consonances are those which derive from the remaining proportions comprehended in the *senario*,[12] namely *sesquitertia*, *sesquiquarta*, and *sesquiquinta*,* either taken in themselves† or combined with the octave. The fourth, the major third, the minor third, the eleventh, the major tenth, and the minor tenth belong here.

* 4:3, 5:4 and 6:5, respectively.
† "*sowohl bloss.*"

EXAMPLE 21

5. The imperfect consonances are those which do not keep their magnitude unchanged, but sometimes are smaller, sometimes larger, such as the third and sixth.

6. The third is of two kinds: major or minor.

7. Major, when one voice stands two whole tones above the other, as: [Example 22].

EXAMPLE 22

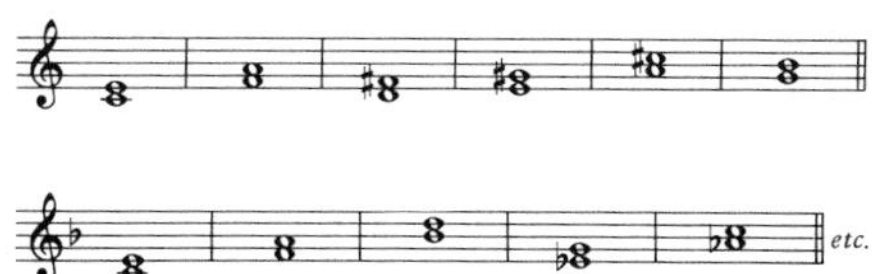

8. Minor, when one voice stands a tone and a semitone above the other, as: [Example 23].

EXAMPLE 23

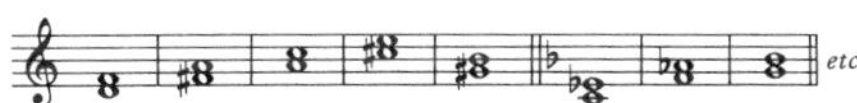

9. The sixth is also major or minor. Major, when one note stands four tones and a semitone above the other, as: [Example 24].

EXAMPLE 24

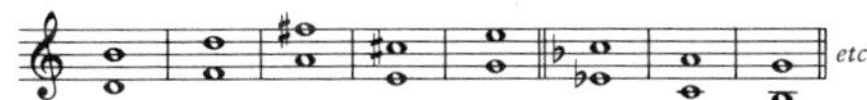

10. The sixth is minor when one voice stands three tones and two semi-

tones above the other, as: [Example 25].

EXAMPLE 25

7. The fourth cannot always be considered a consonance, and especially not in a two-part composition or against the lowest voice, since it does not divide the octave harmonically but only arithmetically,[13] and for other reasons which the *musici* have. Even so, it is the mother of other consonances, such as the major sixth, the major thirteenth, the minor sixth, and the minor thirteenth, as is demonstrated through the division of the monochord. 3 : 5 is the major sixth, the number being specified which divides the two harmonically—3 : 4 : 5.[14] 5 : 8 is the minor sixth, the number being specified which divides the two harmonically—5 : 6 : 8.[15]

8. *Affectio consonantiarum* means a succession of consonances. The following general rules pertain thereto.

9. Perfect consonances begin and end a composition.

Chapter II

Of the Use of Perfect Consonances among Themselves

10. Two perfect consonances of the same kind cannot follow one another directly, except in standing still, or occasionally in contrary motion. [Example 26]

1. Two perfect consonances of the same kind cannot rise or fall together, as: [Example 27].

EXAMPLE 26

Bad

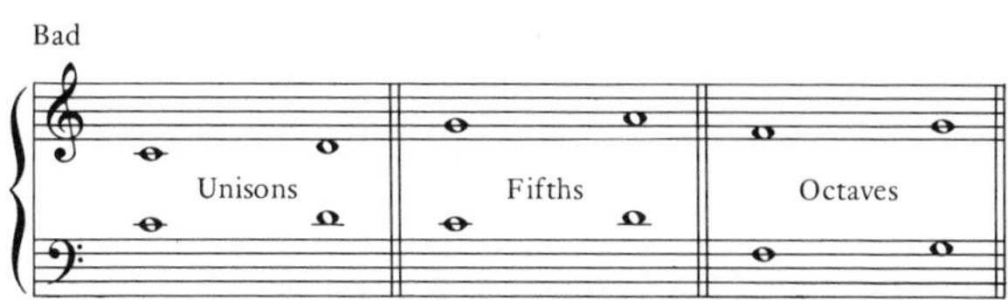

Good

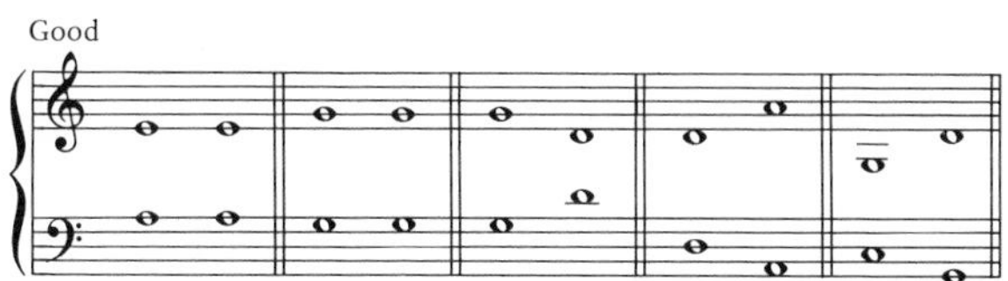

EXAMPLE 27

2. But leaping in opposite directions, or standing still, they indeed follow each other well, as: [Example 28]. In this way, fifth can follow fifth, and octave can follow octave.

EXAMPLE 28

11. Imperfect consonances follow perfect ones well, and perfect ones the imperfect, except when a bad leap is produced, as will be shown below.

12. Two imperfect consonances follow each other well, except for çertain cases, which will be discussed in the Special Rules for successions of intervals.

13. Imperfect intervals are employed at the beginning and end of a four-part piece, since the perfect ones do not suffice there—and since, also in a three-part piece, the third is placed more frequently amid the fifth than the fifth [is placed] amid the octave.* In the middle of a composition, many imperfect consonances should occur, since a work would be rendered unattractive by a succession of nothing but perfect ones.

14. Leaps arising from disagreeable successions of consonances are indeed prohibited; yet it is not always possible to avoid them in many-

* "weil die *Tertia* die *Quinta* oft mehr vermittelt als die *Quinta* eine *Octavam.*" (*sic*)

voiced compositions. However, they should not occur in the outermost or principal parts, but rather must be concealed here and there among the middle and less important parts.

15. Although perfect consonances are ordinarily the best ones, yet there are cases where they must not be used. When the lowest and hence fundamental part has a b♮ or b♭,* then the third and sixth are more suitable than the fifth and octave. Degrees† in the lowest voice which are raised by sharps are dealt with similarly. If, however, a cadence is formed out of such notes, or on such a note, then the situation is different, seeing that the same cannot be consummated without perfect consonances, especially in many-voiced pieces. Likewise in transposed systems.‡

16. In the following I really speak only of simple consonances, i.e., those which are not compounded with the octave. Yet successions of composite consonances are altogether similar, so that no special rules are required. The tenth, twelfth, etc., share the nature of their simple counterparts, the third, fifth, etc. Thus, one will also find that I have occasionally written composite intervals where I mention only simple ones.

Chapter 5

Of the Unison and Its Successions

1. A unison occurs when one voice dwells upon the same pitch as does another,§ with not the slightest interval in between.

2. Its nature is that it should be used infrequently, since it does not make harmony as well as the other intervals do. Rather, it is the coming together of two or more voices at the same pitch,|| and hence is not appropriate for composition, which is eagerly bent on making two or more distinct voices sound well together.# Even so, endings on a unison are not infrequent.

3. From the unison, one goes to the minor third.[16] [Example 29]

* "das ♮ *durum* oder ♭ *molle* hat."

† "*Chordis.*"

‡ "*item* in *Systematibus transpositis.*" That is, analogous statements can be made (with changes only in the pitch-classes involved) if a piece has flats or sharps in its signature.

§ "wenn eine Stimme mit der andern in eben einem *Sono* . . . sich befindet."

|| "einen *concentum* zweyer oder mehrerer gleichlautender Stimmen."

"2 oder mehr ungleiche Stimmen zu *accordiren* bemühet ist."

EXAMPLE 29

1. 2. 3. 4. 5. not too good 6. likewise 7. likewise 8. bad 9. bad

4. From the unison, one goes to the major third. [Example 30]

EXAMPLE 30

1. good 2. 3. 4. 5. 6. not good 7. likewise 8. likewise

5. From the unison, one goes to the fifth. [Example 31]

EXAMPLE 31

1. not too good 2. good 3. good 4. good 5. good 6. not good 7. not good

6. From the unison, one goes to the minor sixth. [Example 32]

EXAMPLE 32

1. good 2. not too good 3. not too good 4. good 5. not too good

7. From the unison, one goes to the major sixth. [Example 33]

EXAMPLE 33

1. good 2. not too good 3. not too good 4. not too good 5. bad 6. good

8. From the unison, one goes to the octave. [Example 34]

EXAMPLE 34

1. bad 2. good 3. good 4. not too good

9. From the unison, as from other consonances, one also goes to the fourth. But this happens either against the lowest voice, and so is a kind of syncopation, or between the upper and middle voices, where it does not produce so noticeable a clash. That is why I consider the fourth neither here, in connection with the unison, nor further on, in connection with other consonances. Rather I will save it until we discuss syncopation.

Chapter 6

Of the Minor Third, and the Consonances which Follow It

1. The minor third, or *semiditonus*, is an interval containing a tone and a semitone. It is ordinarily situated between re and fa, or mi and sol; also, where a flat occurs in the upper voice, or a sharp in the lower.

2. Its nature is that it is used infrequently at the beginning, and never at the end. Also, it should rarely be employed before or within proper cadences.* In general we may note that differentiation between its use and the use of the major third is left more to the composer and his judgment than to any rules which could possibly give precise formulations. The minor tenth is treated similarly.

3. From the minor third, one goes to the unison. [Example 35]

EXAMPLE 35

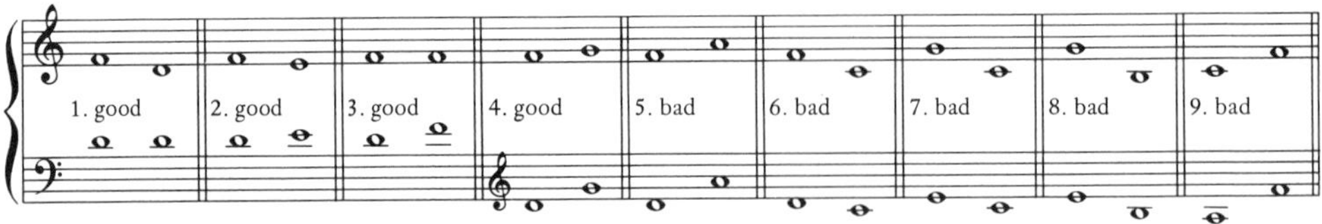

* "massen sie auch sonst selten für, oder in rechten *Cadentzen* soll gebraucht werden." See also ch. 12.

4. From the minor third to the major third. [Example 36]

EXAMPLE 36

1. good
2. good
3. good
4. good
5. good

6. good
7. good
8.
9. good
10. not too good

5. From the minor third, one goes to the minor third.* [Example 38]

EXAMPLE 38

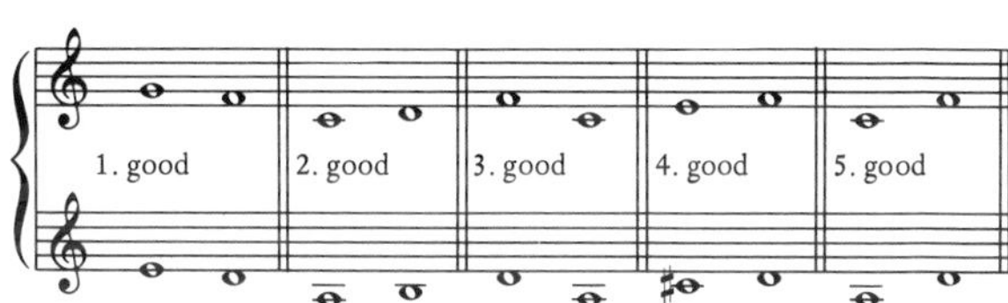

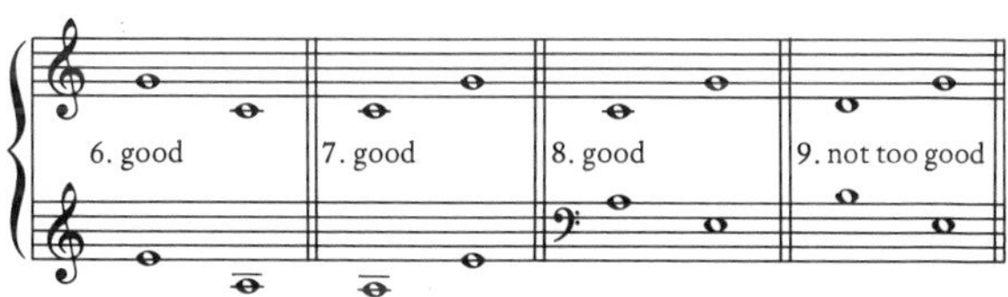

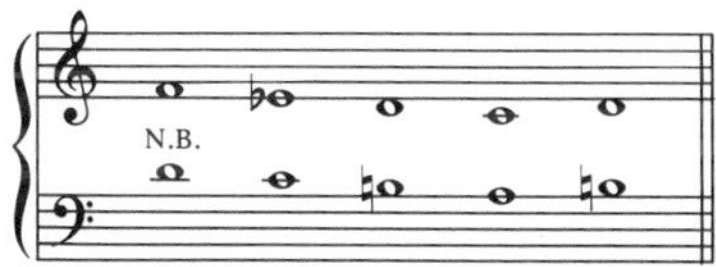

Chapter IV

How the Imperfect Consonances Follow One Another

1. Two or more sixths or thirds follow each other well, as: [Example 37].

EXAMPLE 37

* In M-B., the N.B. was given at the conclusion of the example for paragraph 4; but it seems much rather to belong here.

6. From the minor third, one goes to the fifth. [Example 39]

EXAMPLE 39

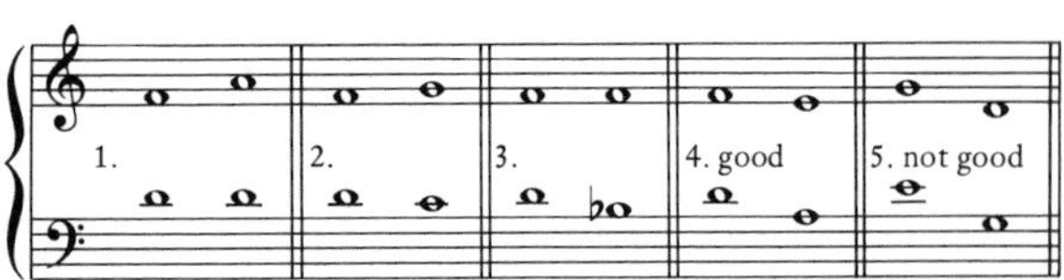

Chapter V

5. A third proceeds correctly to a fifth when one voice stands still, as:* [Example 40].

EXAMPLE 40

6. However, it is forbidden when both fall, as: [Example 41].

EXAMPLE 41

7. It is always forbidden when both rise.

8. When, however, they go in contrary motion, it is indeed correct, as: [Example 42]. The other kinds have no value.

EXAMPLE 42

Chapter IV

7. From the minor third, one goes to the minor sixth.† [Example 43]

2. A sixth follows a third well when one voice stands still and the other leaps a fourth, as:‡ [Example 44].

* Since major and minor thirds are treated together in these paragraphs, see also *Tractatus*, ch. 7, para. 6.

† I give no. 11 as it appears in M-B. Nos. 4 and 6 are indeed identical in M-B. In his *Revisionsbericht*, M-B. indicates that he has given variant comments for examples such as this. Bracketed comments within the examples are given here as they appear in his edition, and almost surely constitute variants of just this kind.

‡ Since major and minor thirds are treated together in these paragraphs, see also *Tractatus*, ch. 7, paras. 7 and 8.

EXAMPLE 43

1. 2. 3. 4. 5.

6. good 7. [not good] 8. [not good] 9. good

10. not too good [good] 11. not too good [good] 12. good

8. From the minor third, one goes to the major sixth.* [Example 47]

EXAMPLE 47

1. 2. 3. 4. 5.

6. 7. not too good 8. good 9. good

9. From the minor third, one goes to the octave.† [Example 49]

EXAMPLE 44

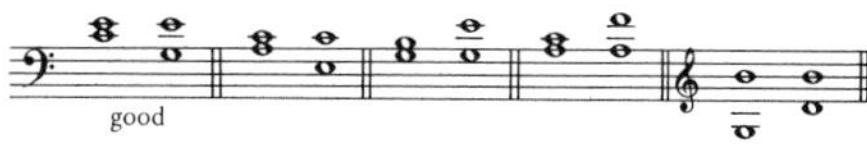

3. When both fall, the following is to be avoided: [Example 45].

EXAMPLE 45

4. When both rise, avoid only this: [Example 46].

EXAMPLE 46

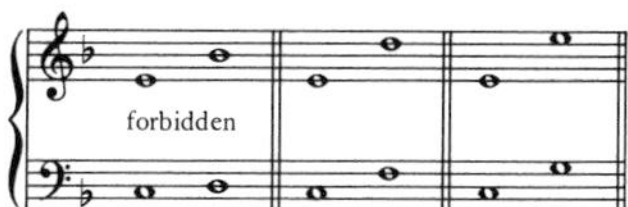

5. A sixth follows a third well when they proceed in contrary motion, as: [Example 48].

EXAMPLE 48

Chapter VI

5. A third proceeds correctly to an octave when one voice stands still.‡ [Example 50]

* I give no. 3 as it appears in M-B.

† I give no. 12 as it appears in M-B. In view of no. 7, it is not certain that B♮ was meant to read B♭.

‡ Since major and minor thirds are treated together in these paragraphs, see also *Tractatus*, ch. 7, para. 9.

EXAMPLE 49

1. 2. 3. 4. 5.

6. not too good 7. not too good 8. good

9. good 10. good 11. not good [good] 12. good

EXAMPLE 50

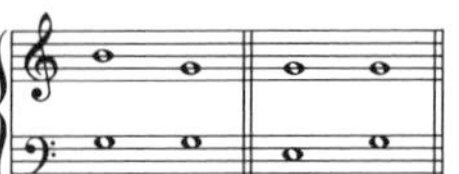

6. Likewise, when both rise, as: [Example 51].

EXAMPLE 51

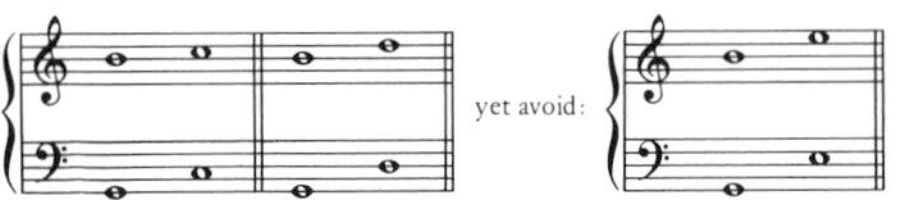

7. Likewise, when they move in contrary motion. [Example 52] All

EXAMPLE 52

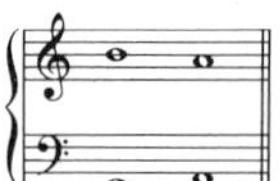

other examples of this type are forbidden.

8. It is forbidden to go from a third to an octave when both voices descend.

Chapter 7

Of the Major Third, and How Consonances Are Employed after It

1. The major third, or *ditonus*, is an interval comprised of two whole tones. It is ordinarily situated between ut and mi, or fa and la; also, where a sharp occurs in the upper voice, or a flat in the lower.

2. Its nature is that it begins not infrequently, and always is present at the end, and also in and before natural, full-voiced cadences.* Beyond this, its use is left to the discretion of the composer. Let the same be said of the major tenth.

3. From the major third, one goes to the unison. [Example 53]

EXAMPLE 53

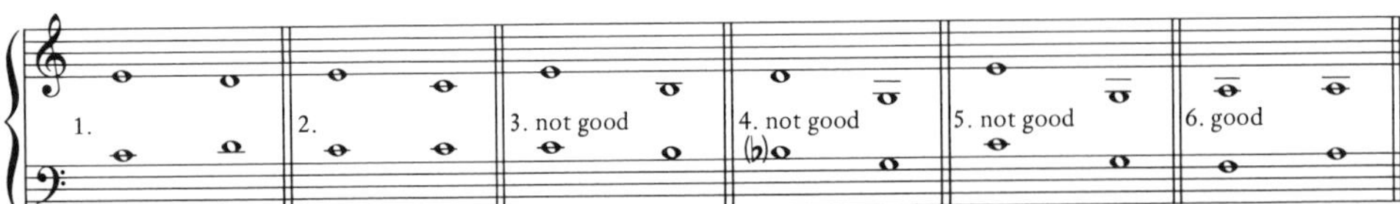

* "natürlichen vollstimmigen *Cadentzen*." See also ch. 12.

EXAMPLE 53 (*continued*)

7. good | 8. good | 9. not good | 10. not good

4. From the major third, one goes to the minor third.* [Example 54]

EXAMPLE 54

1. | 2. | 3. | 4. | 5. | 6. | 7. not too good | 8. not too good | 9. not too good

5. From the major third, one goes to the major third. [Example 55]

EXAMPLE 55

1. | 2. | 3. not too good | 4. not good | 5. good | 6. good | 7. good | 8. good

9. good | 10. good | 11. good | N.B.

6. After the major third, the fifth follows. [Example 56]

EXAMPLE 56

1. | 2. | 3. | 4. | 5. not too good | 6. not good | 7. not too good

8. not good | 9. good | 10. good | 11. good | 12. not good

* The paragraphs from the *Bericht* which correspond to the paragraphs of this chapter are given opposite portions of ch. 6, since the *Bericht* treats major and minor thirds together.

7. After the major third, the minor sixth follows in contrary motion.* [Example 57]

EXAMPLE 57

1. not too good 2. good 3. good 4.

Yet the following examples are good.† [Example 58]

EXAMPLE 58

1. 2. 3. 4.

8. After the major third, the major sixth follows. [Example 59]

EXAMPLE 59

1. 2. 3. 4. 5. 6. 7. not too good 8. not too good

9. From the major third, one goes to the octave. [Example 60]

EXAMPLE 60

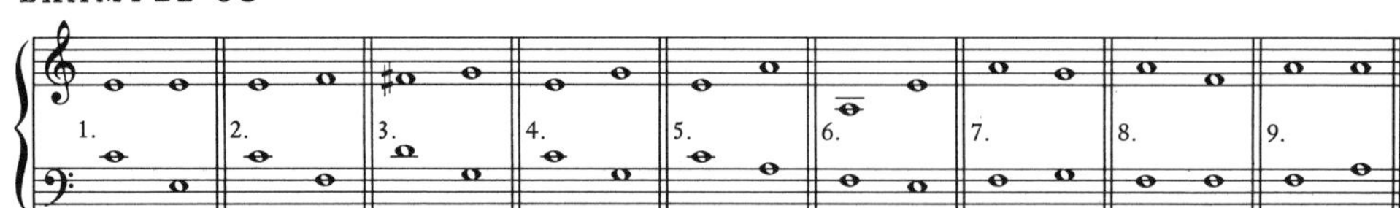

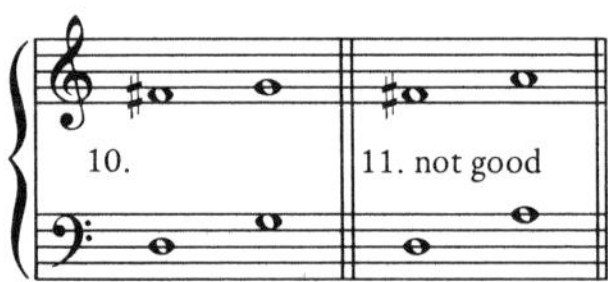

* I give no. 1 as it appears in M-B.

† An alto clef appears in parentheses in the lower voice of no. 4, after the tenor clef had held sway there for nos. 1-3. I give the reading with the alto clef, since the vertical intervals are then correct; however, the augmented fourth in the lower voice casts doubt on the favorable judgment accorded this progression.

Chapter 8

Of the Fifth, and How the Other Consonances Follow It

1. The fifth, or *diapente*, is an interval consisting of three tones and a semitone, and is ordinarily situated between ut and sol, re and la, mi and mi, or fa and fa. When it is deficient by nature, one aids it through a flat, sharp, or natural sign.

2. Its nature is that it begins and ends at all times, and in the middle also is used more frequently than the sixth, which can never stand with it, except in rare instances*. [Example 61]

EXAMPLE 61

3. From the fifth, one goes to the unison. [Example 62]

EXAMPLE 62

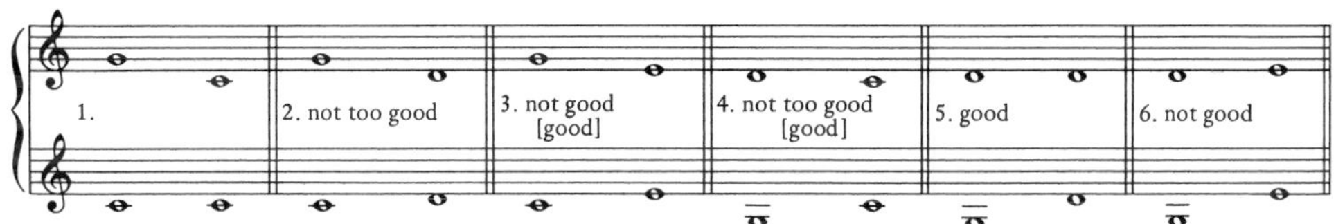

4. From the fifth, one goes to the minor third. [Example 63]

Chapter V

Of the Use of the Fifth and Third after One Another

1. A fifth goes nicely before a third when one voice stands still. [Example 64]

* Of two variant readings, M-B. prefers "im folgenden seltenen Exempel" to "in seltenen Exempeln." I, however, deem the latter more plausible.

EXAMPLE 63

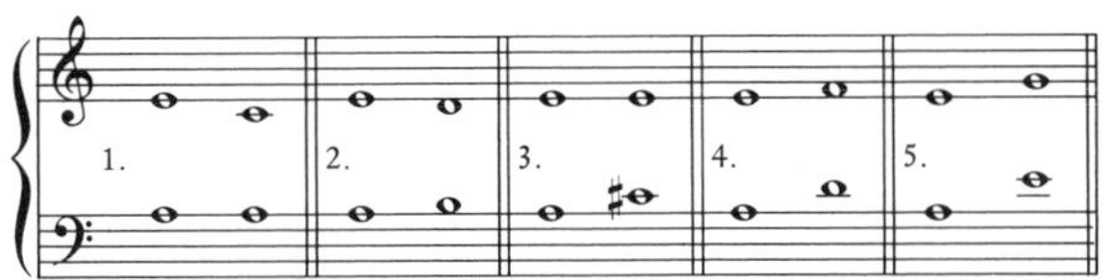

6. not good | 7. not too good | 8. | 9.

10. | 11. | 12. | 13. | 14. rare

5. From the fifth, one goes to the major third. [Example 66]

EXAMPLE 66

1. | 2. | 3. | 4. | 5.

6. not good | 7. not good | 8. not good | 9. not good

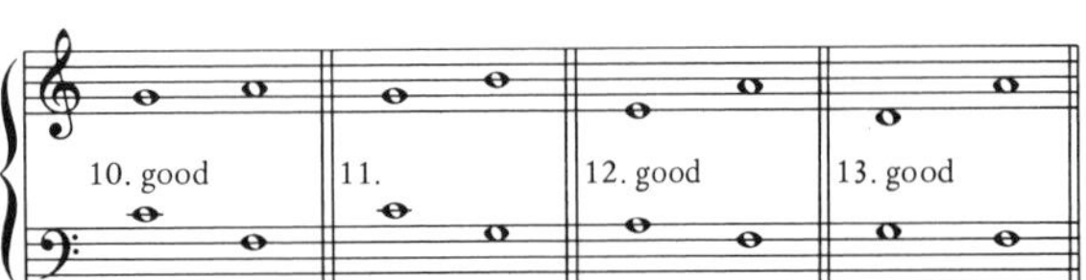

14. not good | 15. good | 16. not good | 17. not good

EXAMPLE 64

2. Likewise when both rise, as: [Example 65].

EXAMPLE 65

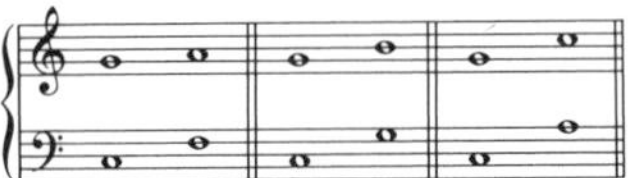

3. If they both fall, then the upper voice must fall a fifth and the lower voice a third. The other kinds are prohibited. [Example 67]

EXAMPLE 67

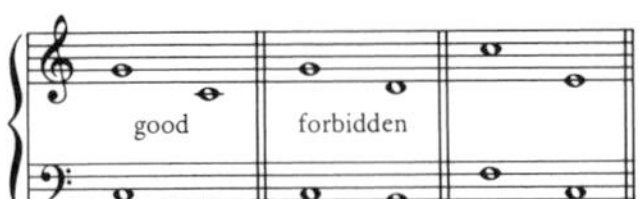

4. In contrary motion, they indeed go well, as: [Example 68].

EXAMPLE 68

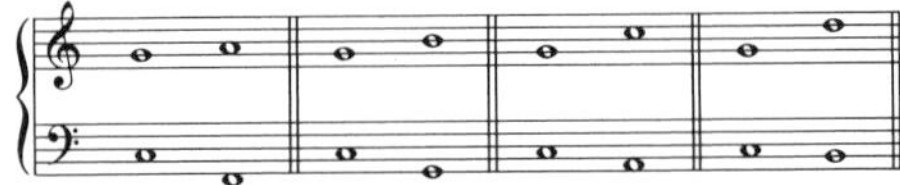

6. One only goes from the fifth to the fifth in standing still, or in contrary motion. See above, chapter 4, paragraph 10.

7. From the fifth to the minor sixth. [Example 69]

EXAMPLE 69

6. [rare] 7. rare 8. not good 9. not good 10. not good

8. From the fifth to the major sixth. [Example 72]

EXAMPLE 72

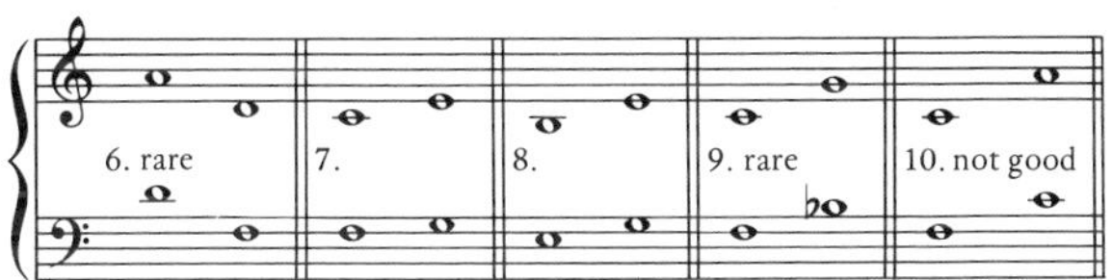

Chapter VII

Of the Use of the Fifth and Sixth after One Another

1. A fifth lets a sixth follow it when one voice stands still. [Example 70]

EXAMPLE 70

2. When, however, they both descend, it is prohibited, as: [Example 71].

EXAMPLE 71

3. When they both ascend, it is sometimes good, sometimes forbidden, as: [Example 73].

EXAMPLE 73

4. In contrary motion, however, they indeed proceed well. [Example 74]

EXAMPLE 74

9. From the fifth to the octave. [Example 75]

EXAMPLE 75

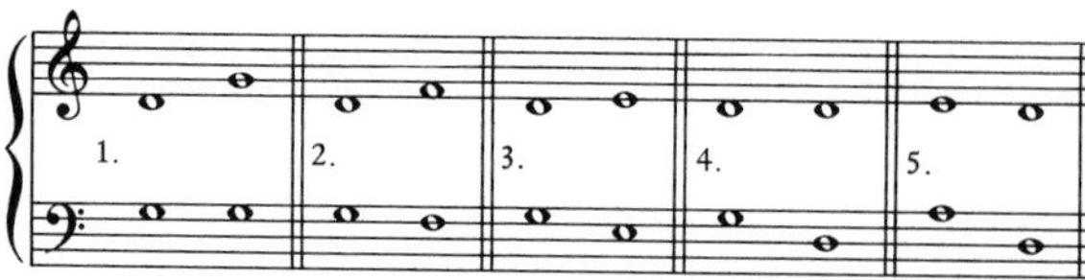

6. not good
7. good
8. not good

9. not good
10. good
11. good

Chapter II

3. But now it is to be said in what way an octave can follow a fifth. This occurs when one voice moves stepwise, the other by leap, as: [Example 76].

EXAMPLE 76

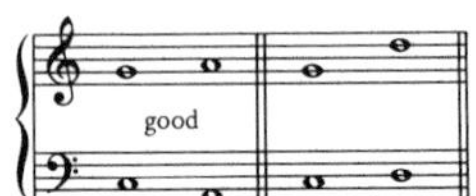

4. Likewise, when one stands still and the other leaps, as:* [Example 77].

EXAMPLE 77

5. It is, however, forbidden to go from a fifth to an octave when both voices have leaps, as: [Example 78].

EXAMPLE 78

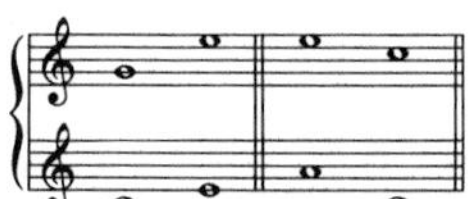

6. An exception is made if contrary motion occurs. Thus, these go well:* [Example 79].

EXAMPLE 79

* In M-B., the intervals of the second succession are given in reverse order.

Chapter 9

Of the Minor Sixth and the Consonances which Follow It

1. The minor sixth, or *hexachordum minus*, is an interval consisting of three tones and two semitones, or of a perfect fifth and one semitone. In *systema durum*,[17] it is ordinarily situated between e below and c above, or between a below and f above; in *systema molle*,[18] between d below and b♭ above, or between a below and f above. When it is too large, one aids it through a flat, sharp, or natural sign.

2. Its nature is that it never starts or finishes. Even so, it could more readily appear at the beginning than at the end. In the middle, it is not used as often as the fifth; and it requires a third in its midst.[19] The composer must employ the same discretion with regard to the use of minor and major sixths as is demanded of him concerning minor and major thirds. See chapter 6, paragraph 2 and chapter 7, paragraph 2.*

3. It is never very good to go from the minor sixth to the unison. [Example 80]

EXAMPLE 80

4. From the minor sixth to the minor third. [Example 81]

EXAMPLE 81

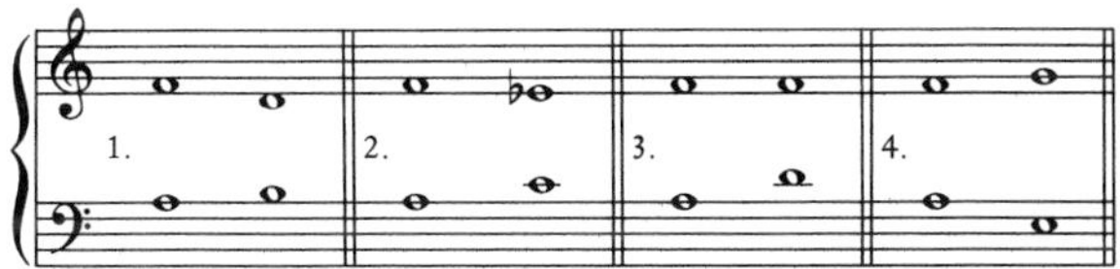

Chapter IV

6. A third follows a sixth well when one voice stands still, as:† [Example 82].

EXAMPLE 82

* See also ch. 12.

† The last two successions of Example 82 read as follows in M-B.:

As they stand here, they are identical with the last two successions of the example found in the previous paragraph of the *Bericht* (given opposite ch. 6, paras. 7 and 8 of the *Tractatus*). I replace them with successions of the kind that Bernhard surely meant. Since major and minor sixths are treated together in these paragraphs, see also *Tractatus*, ch. 10, paras. 4 and 5.

EXAMPLE 81 (*continued*)

5. rare 6. rare 7. 8.

5. From the minor sixth to the major third. [Example 84]

EXAMPLE 84

1. 2. 3. 4. rare

5. not good 6. better

6. From the minor sixth to the fifth. [Example 87]

EXAMPLE 87

1. 2. 3. rare 4. not good

5. good 6. good 7. not good 8.

7. Likewise, when both fall. Yet avoid the following: [Example 83].

EXAMPLE 83

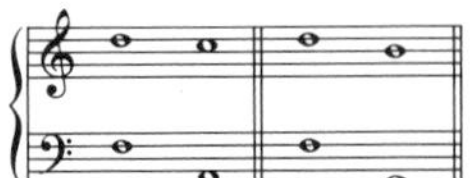

8. Likewise, when they proceed in contrary motion, as:* [Example 85].

EXAMPLE 85

9. It is forbidden, however, to go from a sixth to a third when both voices rise. [Example 86]

EXAMPLE 86

is still good

Chapter VII

5. A fifth follows a sixth equally well when one voice stands still, as:† [Example 88].

EXAMPLE 88

* I give the third progression exactly as it appears in M–B.

† Since major and minor sixths are treated together in these paragraphs, see also *Tractatus*, ch. 10, para. 6.

7. From the minor sixth to the minor sixth.* [Example 91]

EXAMPLE 91

1.
2. not good
3. rare
4. rare
5. good
6. not good
7.
8. rare
9. not good
[is good]

* See *Bericht*, ch. IV, para. 1, given on p. 43.

6. When they proceed in contrary motion, it is partly good, partly bad: [Example 89].

EXAMPLE 89

7. However, they may not either rise or fall together. [Example 90]

EXAMPLE 90

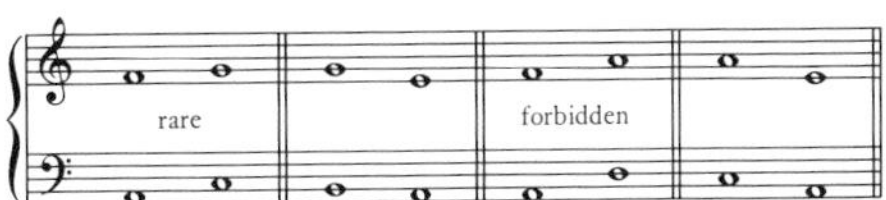

8. From the minor sixth to the major sixth.* [Example 92]

EXAMPLE 92

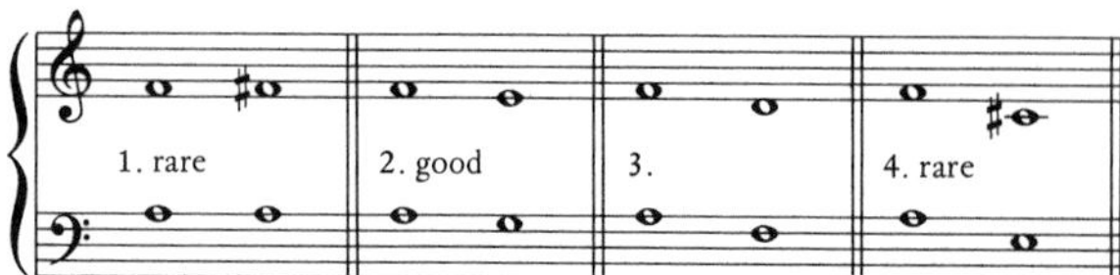

9. From the minor sixth to the octave. [Example 93]

EXAMPLE 93

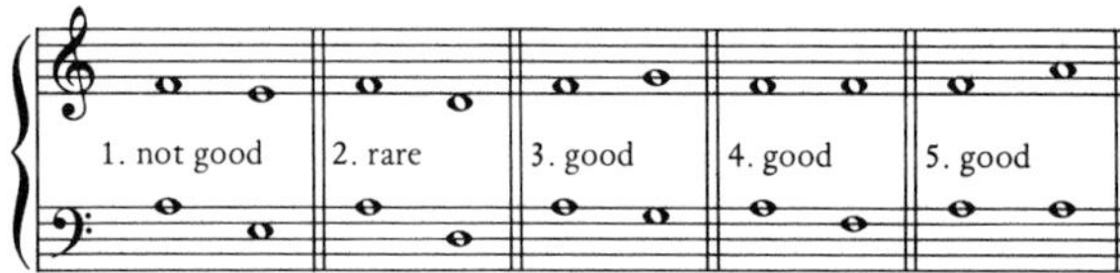

Chapter VIII

5. After a sixth, an octave indeed follows correctly when one voice stands still.† [Example 94]

EXAMPLE 94

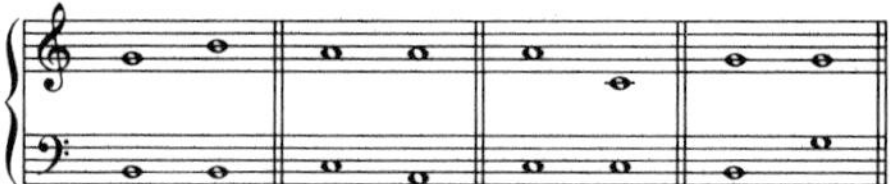

6. Likewise, sometimes when they proceed in contrary motion: [Example 95].

EXAMPLE 95

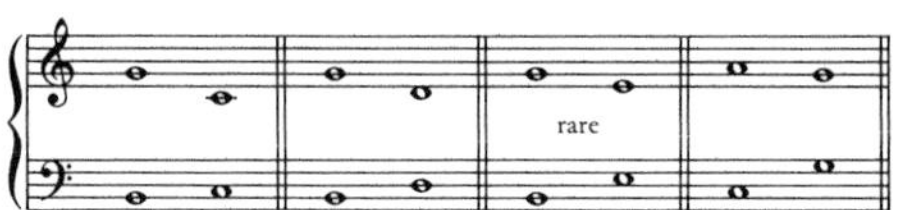

* See *Bericht,* ch. IV, para. 1, given on p. 43.

† Since major and minor sixths are treated together in these paragraphs, see also *Tractatus,* ch. 10, para. 9.

7. But it is prohibited when they rise or fall together, as: [Example 96].

EXAMPLE 96

Chapter 10

Of the Major Sixth and the Consonances which Follow It

1. The major sixth, or *hexachordum majus*, is an interval consisting of four tones and a semitone, or of a perfect fifth and a whole tone. It is ordinarily situated between ut and la, in *systema durum* between d below and b♮ above, and in *systema molle* between g below and e above. In other places it is formed by affixing a flat, sharp, or natural sign.

2. The nature of this consonance is like that of the preceding one, never beginning or ending, and occurring in the middle less frequently than the fifth. Just as the preceding one, it requires a third in its midst, above the lower voice. The discretion of the composer pertaining to the minor sixth is required in its use as well.*

3. It is never good to go from the major sixth to the unison. [Example 97]

EXAMPLE 97

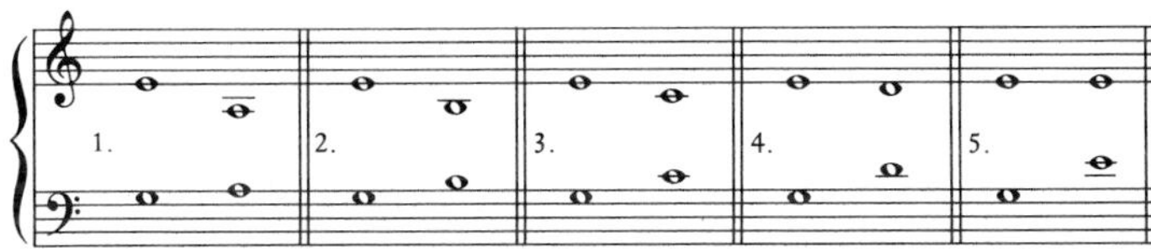

* See ch. 9, para. 2; also ch. 12.

4. From the major sixth [one goes] to the minor third.* [Example 98]

EXAMPLE 98

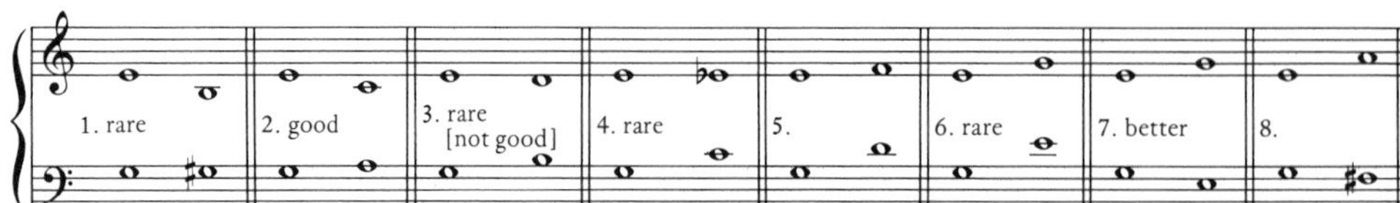

5. From the major sixth [one goes] to the major third. [Example 99]

EXAMPLE 99

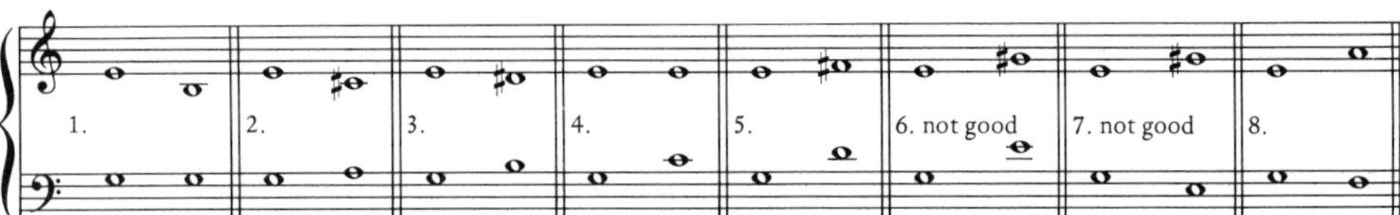

6. From the major sixth [one goes] to the fifth. [Example 100]

EXAMPLE 100

1. 2. 3. 4. rare 5. not good 6. [not good] 7. [rare] 8. [not good]

7. From the major sixth [one goes] to the minor sixth. [Example 101]

EXAMPLE 101

1. rare 2. 3. 4. rare 5. [rare] 6. good 7.

8. From the major sixth [one goes] to the major sixth. [Example 102]

EXAMPLE 102

1. 2. not good 3. not good [good?] 4. 5.

* The paragraphs from the *Bericht* which correspond to the paragraphs of this chapter are given opposite portions of ch. 9, since the *Bericht* treats major and minor sixths together.

9. From the major sixth one goes to the octave. [Example 103]

EXAMPLE 103

1. 2. 3. 4. rare 5. rare 6. not good

Chapter II

Of the Octave and the Consonances which Follow It

1. The octave is an interval composed of five tones and two semitones.

2. Its nature is that it is particularly good to use in the beginning, middle, and end. Even so, it should seldom be applied in *cantus durus** upon the b♮, or in *mollis* upon the e, or upon degrees raised by sharps, and then only in pieces with very many voices, in a middle part, in degrees already stated,[20] or to form a cadence therewith.

3. From the octave, one goes to the unison in many-voiced pieces, chiefly in doubled basses. [Example 104]

EXAMPLE 104

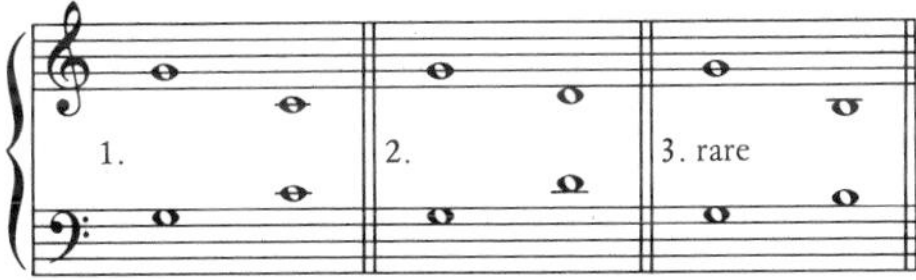

4. From the octave to the minor third. [Example 105]

EXAMPLE 105

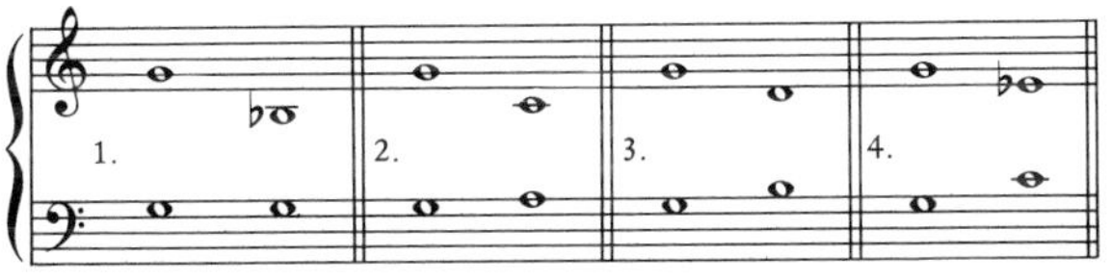

Chapter VI

Of the Use of the Octave and Third after One Another

1. An octave goes before a third well when one voice stands still: [Example 106].

EXAMPLE 106

* *Cantus durus* = *systema durum*; *cantus mollis* = *systema molle*.

EXAMPLE 105 (*continued*)

5. From the octave to the major third. [Example 108]

EXAMPLE 108

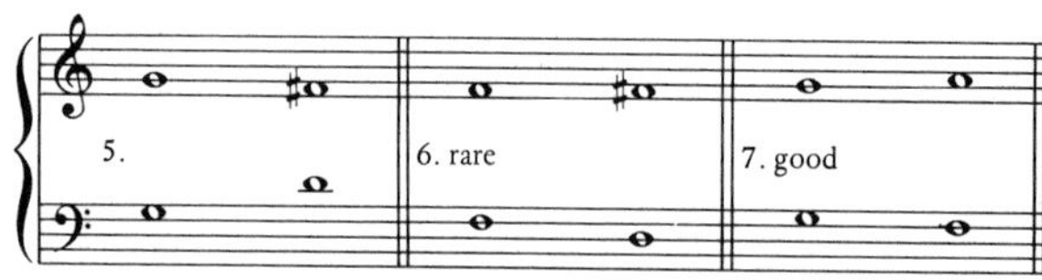

6. From the octave to the fifth. [Example 110]

2. Likewise, when both descend. [Example 107]

EXAMPLE 107

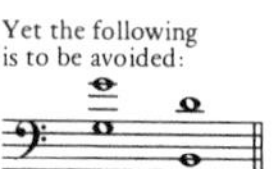

3. Likewise, when they move in contrary motion. [Example 109]

EXAMPLE 109

4. On the other hand, it is always forbidden to go from the octave to the third when both ascend.

EXAMPLE 110

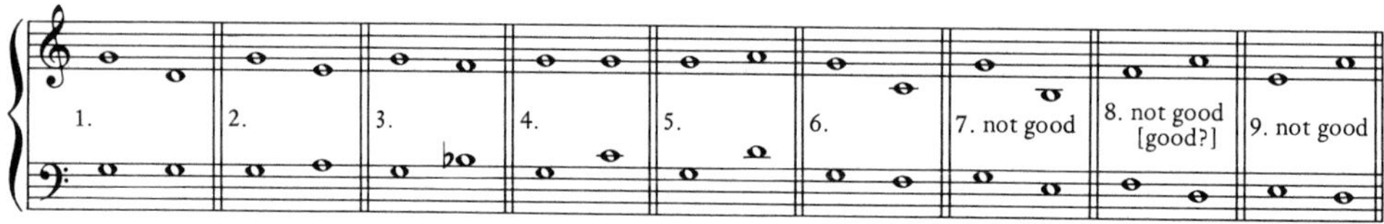

7. From the octave to the minor sixth. [Example 111]

EXAMPLE 111

8. From the octave to the major sixth. [Example 114]

EXAMPLE 114

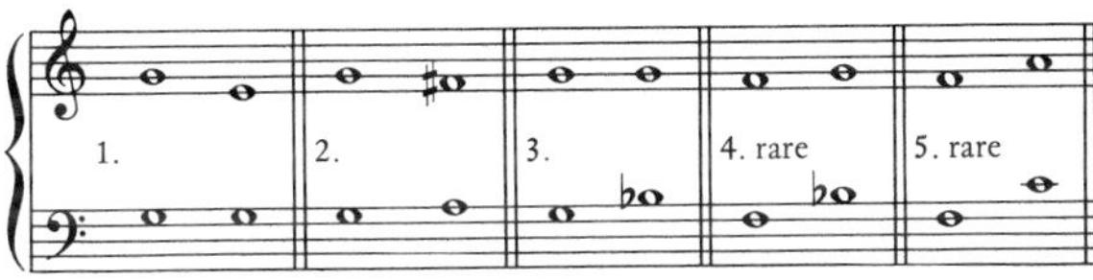

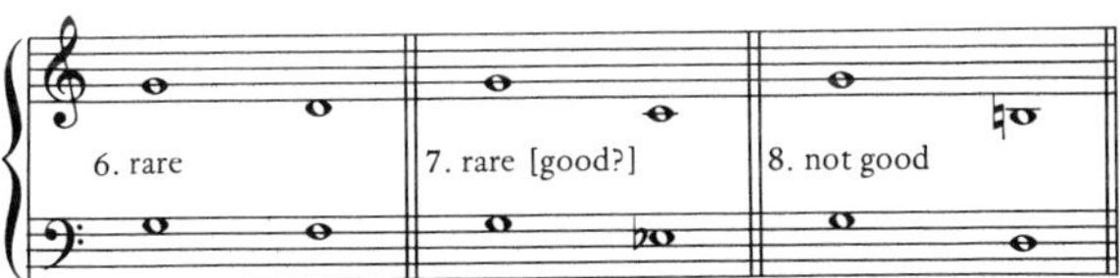

9. From the octave one goes to the octave only when both voices stand still, or when they are conceived in contrary motion. [Example 117]

Chapter VIII

Of the Use of the Octave and Sixth after One Another

1. A sixth follows an octave correctly when one voice stands still.* [Example 112]

EXAMPLE 112

2. Likewise, when both fall, as: [Example 113].

EXAMPLE 113

3. Likewise, when both rise: [Example 115].

EXAMPLE 115

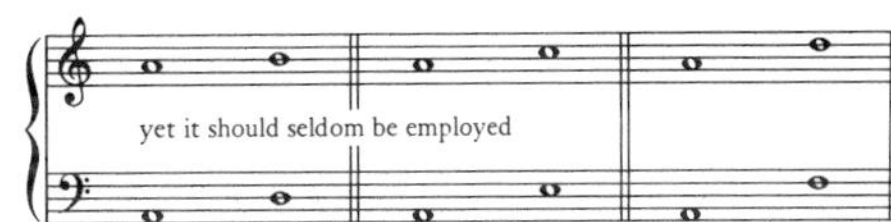

4. In contrary motion it is also correct, as: [Example 116].

EXAMPLE 116

* In M-B., these four progressions appear further below, as part of Example 113.

EXAMPLE 117

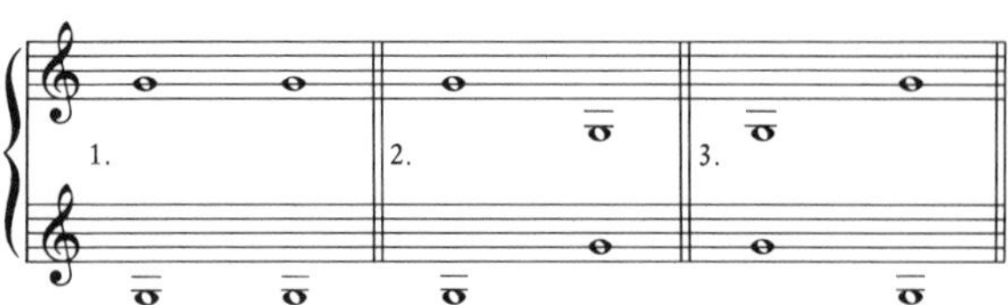

Chapter 12

Appendix concerning the Imperfect Consonances

1. In the foregoing, the use of the imperfect consonances—i.e., when such should be large or small—has at all times been left to the discretion of the composer. Even so, for the information of those eager to learn, the following rules can be kept in mind.

2. The imperfect consonances remain in their natural proportions, unless the system of the octave is altered.[21] Thus between ut and mi, and fa and la, the major third occurs, and between re and fa, and mi and sol, the minor third, as is evident from this setting of the octave, *dura* as well as *mollis*:* [Example 118].

EXAMPLE 118

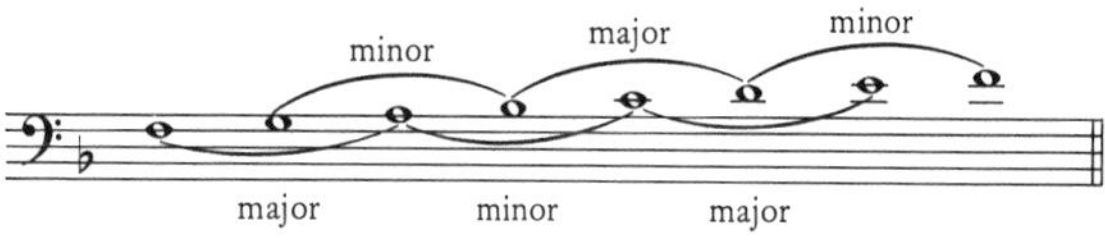

Chapter III

Of the Imperfect Consonances in General

1. Imperfect consonances are employed either in an unaltered or an altered setting of the octave.

2. The unaltered setting of the octave in *cantus mollis* features the semitones mi–fa on e and f, and again on a and b♭. In *cantus durus*, however, mi and fa are to be found on e and f, and on b♮ and c. That is:† [Example 119].

EXAMPLE 119

* "wie aus diesem Satze der *Octave* so wohl *durae* als *mollis* erhellet." This example really seems to illustrate only *mollis*, however.

† In M-B., the two scales appear as follows:

Clearly there is an error here, as both illustrate *cantus mollis*. I have made what I believe to be the most

3. The minor thirds in unaltered settings are re–fa and mi–sol. [Example 120]

EXAMPLE 120

4. The major thirds in unaltered settings are ut–mi and fa–la. [Example 121]

EXAMPLE 121

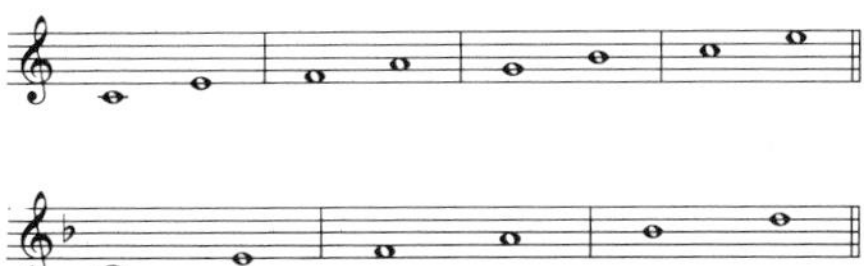

5. The minor sixths in unaltered settings are re–fa, mi–sol and mi–fa. [Example 122]

EXAMPLE 122

6. The major sixths in unaltered settings are ut–la, re–mi and fa–sol. [Example 123]

EXAMPLE 123

---

plausible change. The reader will note that here, as in the examples below (and elsewhere), Bernhard uses solmisation syllables from the *three* traditional hexachords to designate degrees of the *two* diatonic scales which these hexachords may be said to generate.

3. The alteration of such a system occurs through the displacement of the semitone from its position.

4. The reason for such an alteration is either necessity or the preference of the composer.

5. It occurs through necessity because of a step progression, a leap, or a final cadence.*

6. Because of a step progression of a second,

a) in order that this should not be larger than is natural. For example: [Example 124].

EXAMPLE 124

must therefore become:

b) if, in *cantus durus*, one would go from a to b♮ and no higher; or, in *cantus mollis*, from d to e and no higher. [Example 126]

EXAMPLE 126

hence must stand:

Exceptions are made if the b♮ or e are part of a cadence, or if a third situated below would not tolerate a change. [Example 128]

7. The alteration of the octave occurs either through necessity or through preference.

8. It occurs through necessity because of a step progression, a leap, or a cadence.*

9. Because of a step progression, if the second would be too large. [Example 125]

EXAMPLE 125

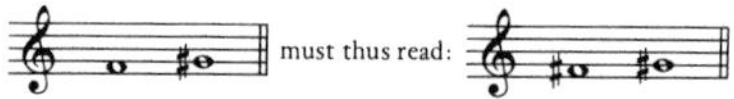

10. Or if one would go no higher than ♮ mi in *cantus durus*, or than *e* mi in *cantus mollis*. [Example 127]

EXAMPLE 127

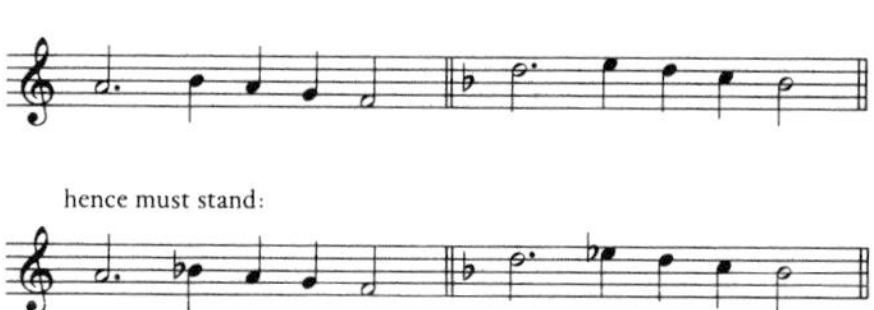

Exceptions are made in the case of cadences, wherein it would remain unaltered; also, if a third would otherwise be too small, as: [Example 129].

* "wegen eines Ganges, Sprunges oder Schluss-*Cadentz*," in the *Tractatus*. In the *Bericht*, "*Cadenz*" instead of "Schluss-*Cadentz*."

EXAMPLE 128

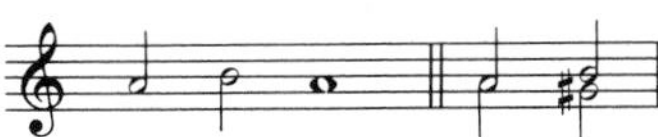

7. Because of a step progression through a fourth, in order that the fourth should not be too large. For example: [Example 130].

EXAMPLE 130

I say a step progression through a fourth, because in step progressions beyond a fourth no change is called for, as: [Example 132].

EXAMPLE 132

8. The system is altered because of a leap, if

a) an augmented fourth would occur. [Example 134]

EXAMPLE 129

11. Likewise, if a step progression through a fourth would be too large, as: [Example 131].

EXAMPLE 131

Even so, it is to be noted that such fourths are only forbidden when the notes that produce them are on strong beats.* When they do not occur on strong beats, but only slip by, then one should not change the octave from its natural setting for this reason. The following sort of example is therefore good: [Example 133].

EXAMPLE 133

12. The octave must be altered because of a leap if, in ascending, an augmented fourth, a diminished or augmented fifth, or a diminished or augmented octave would be induced. In ascending, this is forbidden: [Example 135].

* "wenn die Noten so die *quarta* machen, anschlagen."

EXAMPLE 134

b) an augmented or diminished fifth in ascending, or an augmented fifth in descending, is to be avoided: [Example 137].

EXAMPLE 137

thus becomes (better):

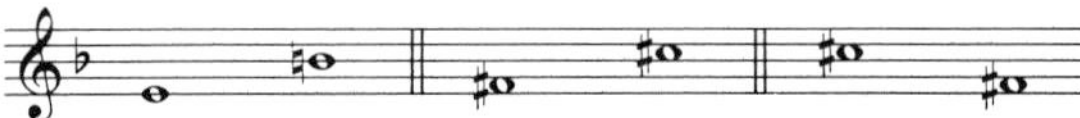

N.B. *i*) diminished fourths, both ascending and descending, are occasionally tolerated—as is, nowadays, the descending diminished fifth; *ii*) in recitative style one indeed finds the forbidden leaps mentioned above.

9. The octave is changed because of a cadence when, to suit the latter, a minor third must be changed to major, a diminished fifth to perfect, or a minor sixth to major.

10. But since there are distinct types of cadences, there are also distinct ways in which these changes occur.

11. A cadence is either a *bass cadence* or a *tenor cadence*.

EXAMPLE 135

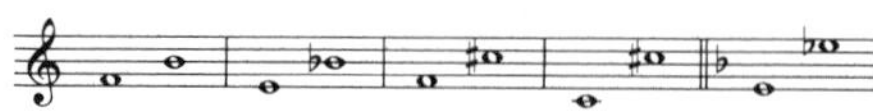

In descending, this is forbidden: [Example 136].

EXAMPLE 136

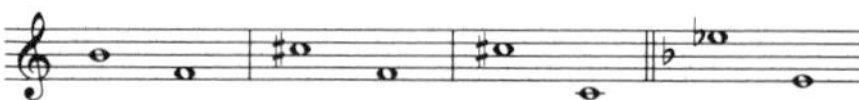

Diminished fourths are, however, permitted, both ascending and descending. Also, descending diminished fifths are accepted nowadays: [Example 138].

EXAMPLE 138

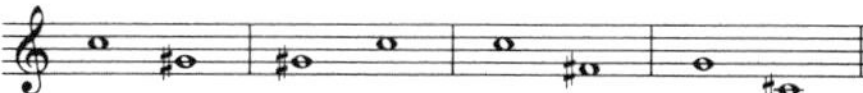

One finds others of the leaps mentioned above as well, especially in recitative style.

13. The octave is altered because of a cadence when, instead of a minor third or minor sixth, the major is taken.

14. A cadence is an elegant ending, and is formed in the lowest voice in two ways, as this voice makes either a *bass cadence* or a *tenor cadence*.*

* "entweder *Bassiret* oder *Tenorisiret*."

12. *Bass cadences* fall and rise either harmonically or arithmetically.*

13. Harmonically, when they divide the octave harmonically, making either an upward leap of a fourth or a downward leap of a fifth. This is the best sort of cadence. As: [Example 139].

EXAMPLE 139

14. These cadences always seek to have a major third above their initial note,† and

15. *Bass cadences* of the lowest voice are either perfect or imperfect.

16. The perfect ones are those which fall a fifth or rise a fourth. [Example 140]

EXAMPLE 140

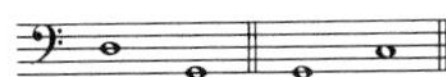

17. The imperfect ones are those which fall a fourth or rise a fifth. [Example 141]

EXAMPLE 141

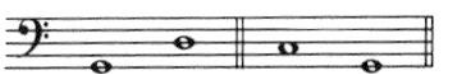

18. *Tenor cadences* of the lowest voice are either common or uncommon.

19. The common ones fall a second, as: [Example 142].

EXAMPLE 142

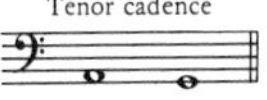

20. The uncommon ones are all others not described above, and are never used, except in a selection which has an unadorned chorale as its lowest part, as: [Example 143].

EXAMPLE 143

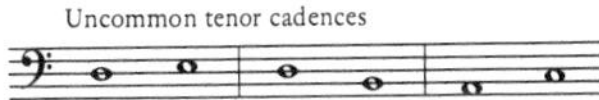

21. In perfect cadences, all thirds must be major, except in the middle of a

* See *Tractatus* note 13.

† "über der ersten Noten." (*sic*) In Bernhard, the "initial note" of a cadence is always the penultimate note, the "second note" the final one.

most of the time above their second note as well, especially at all endings, and generally also in the middle of a composition. Hence, when the system does not supply one, one must change the minor third to major through a sharp or natural sign. The diminished fifth is dealt with similarly. [Example 144]

EXAMPLE 144

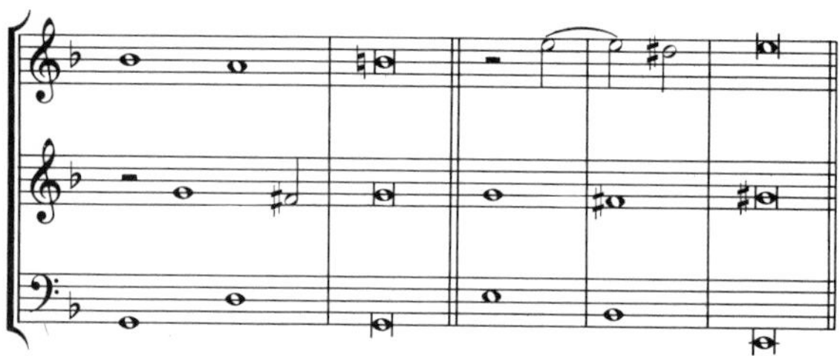

N.B. Yet, when the bass falls or rises to re or mi in the middle of a composition, the third should not always be major;* at the end, however, very much so.

15. Arithmetically, when they divide the octave arithmetically, making either an upward leap of a fifth, or a downward leap of a fourth, as: [Example 146].

EXAMPLE 146

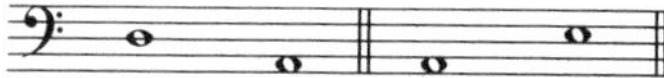

16. Such cadences in general leave the third over their initial note as they find it, but sometimes change b♮ to b♭, or e to e♭, since they prefer the minor third to the major third over their initial note. On the other hand, over their second note, and

selection, in those cadences wherein the bass ends on re or mi. In the last-mentioned, the last third can be minor. At the end, however, it must of necessity be major. [Example 145]

EXAMPLE 145

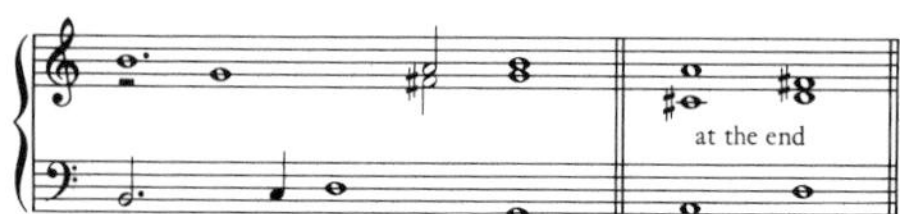

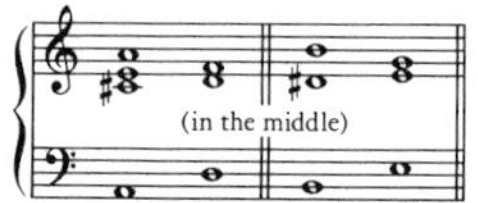

22. In imperfect cadences the third over the initial note remains as it stands in the setting of the octave; the third over the second note will, however, become major, as: [Example 148].

* "darff die *Tertia* nicht allemahl *major* seyn."

indeed always at endings, they prefer a major third. [Example 147]

EXAMPLE 147

17. *Tenor cadences* are of two kinds: usual and unusual.

18. The usual ones fall a second, and desire to have a major sixth over their first note. As to the third, it generally is left, over the first note, as found. Even so, when the lower voice falls from g to f in *systema durum*, or from c to b♭ in *molle*, the first third becomes minor, due to the false relation that would otherwise result. Over the second note, the third generally, but not always, seeks to be major. The fifth is only employed in many-voiced pieces; and if a seventh occurs in syncopation, over half of the first note.† [Example 150]

EXAMPLE 148

It sometimes happens that a third over the initial note which is major by nature will intentionally be changed to minor, as:* [Example 149].

EXAMPLE 149

23. In common tenor cadences a major sixth must be employed over the first note, a major third over the second note. Even so, one is free, in the middle of a piece, to use a minor third over the second note, if the cadence ends on re or mi. [Example 151]

* In M-B., the two natural signs in the third measure of the first progression appear as sharps. The sharp, in Bernhard's time, still meant that any note, whether natural or flat, should be raised by a half step.

† "Die *Quinta* wird nur in vielstimmigen Sachen und wo die *Septima syncopata* ist, über der ersten Note Helffte gebraucht."

EXAMPLE 150

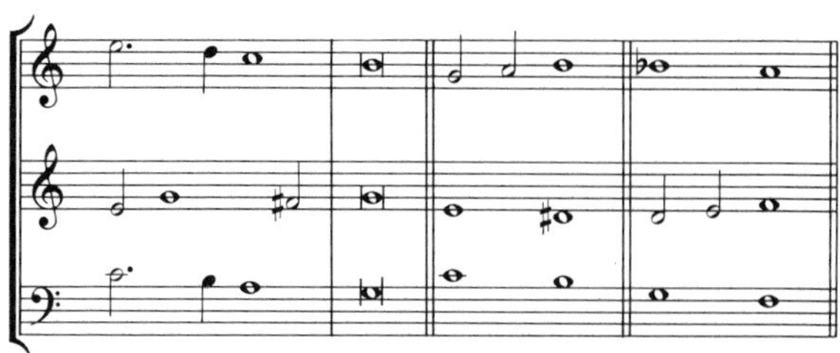

19. The unusual ones [tenor cadences] rise a second and generally leave the system without any appreciable change.

20. No cadences but these are used, unless one should choose to compose upon a chorale (which may occasionally end with a descending third, rarely with an ascending third).22 That person would above all have to realize that the remaining voices must be given a particularly elegant close. This the mode* and the judgment of the person himself will readily suggest.

21. The preference of the composer may occasionally dictate a partial or complete change of system: a complete change, when the semitones are transposed a second or a third upward or downward from their cus-

* "der *Tonus*." See ch. 44.

EXAMPLE 151

24. Uncommon cadences are to b avoided, since they do not sound to good. If, however, one chooses to tak as the lowest voice a chorale which en in such a fashion that it is necessary t employ these uncommon cadences, then it is, above all, to be arranged th at least the other voices make a fin formal close, which the mode* [or th content of the piece] will readil suggest.

25. The octave is altered out c preference, either when a whole piece transposed upwards or downwards by second, etc., or when one steps out of th setting of the octave in the middle of

tomary positions throughout a whole composition; a partial change, if this is only done where it seems most comfortable.

Chapter 13

Appendix concerning Forbidden Leaps

1. Forbidden leaps occur when, in going from one consonance to another, progressions are produced which make unpleasant harmony.*

2. They are of two kinds, for sometimes only one voice leaps, but occasionally both, as is clear from the foregoing examples, and hence unnecessary to repeat here.

3. Such leaps should be avoided diligently. Even so, this rule has its exceptions:

a) One should not adhere to it too strictly in a piece with many voices, since the succession of consonances therein required provides an excuse. Even so, one should avoid the afore-mentioned leaps in the outer voices, and also not use them in the middle voices before having made certain that successions of consonances other than the forbidden ones are not to be found. And even though certain people forbid only some leaps in a two-part piece or in a three-part piece, and a few leaps in a four-part piece, and so forth, yet he who would follow me will abstain from all such leaps in a four-part piece, will use them discreetly in more parts, and will give them more readily to instruments than to singers; for

* "eine unangenehme *Harmonie*."

piece. Since this occurs through choice, it cannot be set down in rules, and is better learned through the imitation of good composers.

Chapter IX

Of Forbidden Leaps

1. Forbidden leaps occur when, in going from one consonance to another, motion is produced which makes unpleasant harmony.*

2. They are of two kinds, for sometimes only one voice leaps, sometimes both, as is to be seen in the foregoing examples.

3. Such leaps are to be diligently avoided. Even so, this rule allows certain exceptions: 1) One should not pay too much attention to it in a piece with many voices, since the succession of consonances therein required provides an excuse. Yet one should by all means avoid the afore-mentioned leaps in the outermost voices—namely the soprano and the bass, or whatever parts would stand in their place. And even though certain people would like to see various leaps avoided in a two-part piece, others in a three-part piece, certain ones in a four-part piece, and so forth, yet he who would follow me will intentionally eschew all such leaps in a piece with no more than four voices. In pieces with a greater number of voices he should conceal such, infrequently, in the middle

vocal parts in particular should sound well, and proceed comfortably for the singers.

b) Some would have it that one might tolerate such leaps to suit a *fugue.** I do not agree, but rather am of the opinion that one can readily find countersubjects to a fugue such that no bad leaps will be contained between the two. Nevertheless, each person is free to hold his own opinion.

c) Furthermore, in the style of the present day, both *communis* and *comicus*, they are employed in some ways and excused. An industrious student of composition will not find it unprofitable to prepare a table of the above-mentioned forbidden successions and to have the same always at hand, both to avoid them more readily in his own compositions, and to examine the works of others in this regard.

voices, and preferably burden the alto and tenor instruments therewith. 2) Some would admit them in *fugues.** He who chooses can do this. I, however, hold that one can readily fashion countersubjects to a fugue such that it will not have to contain bad leaps. 3) Today many forbidden leaps are found against the bass in solo pieces,[23] and are excused on the ground that the thorough-bass (struck by an organist in four parts,† so that a five-part piece results from a solo) conceals them. Nevertheless, my advice is that this should also be avoided.

4. The situation is different in recitative style, where these leaps may be admitted to suit certain affects.

Chapter 14

Of Contrapunctus Inaequalis and Dissonances in General

1. Up to now we have dealt with *contrapunctus aequalis.* Now follows *inaequalis*, the description of which in chapter 3 should be reviewed.

2. This sort of counterpoint is far more agreeable than the first, because of the steady alternation which occurs therein between longer and shorter notes, and between dissonances and consonances.

3. Although this counterpoint permits dissonances also, nevertheless it requires consonances more often, and not infrequently takes a long note and divides it into two or more distinct consonances.

4. And although it indeed employs dissonances, yet it does not allow all dissonant sounds, but only those which are suited to the harmony.

* By "fugue" Bernhard means what we call "canon." See *Tractatus* note 7.

† "den ein Organist mit vieren schläget."

Chapter X

Of Dissonances

1. Dissonances are intervals which cause a disagreement or discord* between two voices.

2. They are of two types, for either a dissonance remains a dissonance all the time, as the second, fourth, fifth, and seventh;[24] or it occasionally becomes a consonance, as was reported above concerning the fourth.

5. These dissonances are divided into those which are always dissonant, and those which occasionally appear as consonances. The first kind includes the major semitone[25] and the tone (both of which are subsumed under the name "second"), and the minor and major seventh (both of which are subsumed under the common designation "seventh"). The other kind is the fourth, partly discussed in chapter 4, paragraph 7, also the diminished fourth and augmented fourth.

N.B. Diminished and augmented fifths have a similar character. They are only dissonant with respect to the lowest voice; among the upper voices they pass for consonances, according to the usage of practicing musicians.

6. The major semitone is the difference between mi and fa in any system. Also, whenever a sharp is applied to a degree of the scale, the note found immediately above is a major semitone higher. And when the b♮ in *durum* or the e in *molle*† is lowered by a flat, the note immediately below is a major semitone lower. [Example 152]

EXAMPLE 152

* "eine Misshälligkeit oder Miss-Laut verursachen."

† "♮ *durum* oder *e molle*."

7. The tone is the difference between ut and re, re and mi, fa and sol, and sol and la. Also, whenever a sharp is affixed to a degree of the scale, the note below is a tone lower; similarly, when a flat in *systema molle* is canceled by a sharp.* [Example 153]

EXAMPLE 153

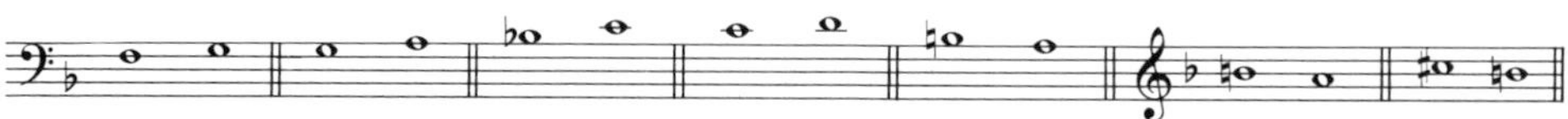

8. The diminished fourth occurs between the following degrees—namely, when ut, prefaced by a sharp, has fa a fourth above. [Example 154]

EXAMPLE 154

9. The augmented fourth occurs when mi has fa a fourth below, or when the upper note has a sharp, as: [Example 155].

EXAMPLE 155

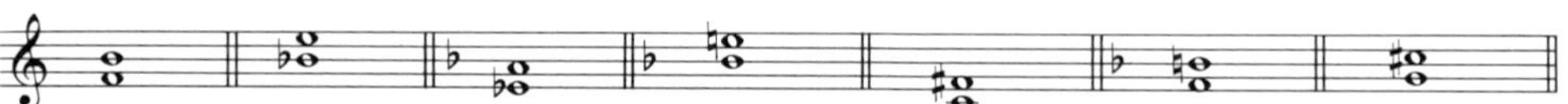

10. The diminished fifth occurs when fa stands a fifth above mi; also, when the lower of two voices, otherwise a perfect fifth apart, has a sharp, or the upper one a flat. [Example 156]

EXAMPLE 156

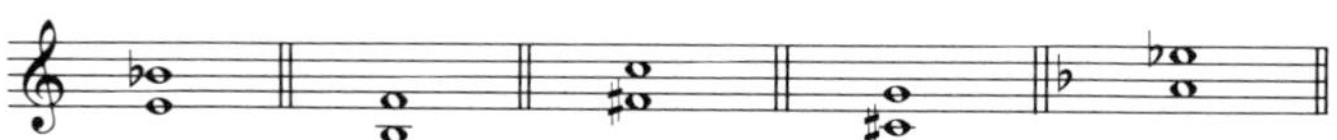

11. The augmented fifth occurs when the higher of two voices, otherwise a perfect fifth apart, receives a sharp, as: [Example 157].

EXAMPLE 157

12. The major seventh occurs when a semitone is lacking in the completion of the octave, either in the upper or in the lower voice, as: [Example 158].

* See footnote on p. 69 for *Bericht*, ch. III, para. 22. I give the example exactly as found in M-B.

EXAMPLE 158

13. The minor seventh occurs when a tone is lacking in the completion of the octave, either above or below, as: [Example 159].

EXAMPLE 159

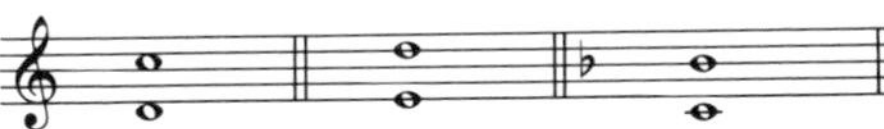

14. The fourth is an interval consisting of two tones and a semitone, and is to be found between ut and fa, re and sol, and mi and la, as: [Example 160].

EXAMPLE 160

Chapter 15

Of the Fourth

1. Since we are considering dissonances in general, it is necessary to mention the fourth, which we (to follow practicing musicians) have counted as a dissonance, although it is much more a consonance, as can be verified by the authority of former ages and by many rational arguments, if our established order would allow such.

2. Practicing musicians count the fourth as a dissonance only when it is against the lowest voice, but not when it is against the others. This perhaps is so because they note that the fourth does not divide the octave harmonically with respect to the lowest voice, but only arithmetically, so that they are inclined to admit it as consonant above more than below.

3. Hence they have also granted the fourth greater privileges against the lowest voice than those granted to other dissonances, such as permitting the formation of the following kind of syncopation, which could not occur if the fourth were at all times considered dissonant.* [Example 161]

* In connection with this example, see ch. 19, paras. 5 and 6.

EXAMPLE 161

4. And if one indeed finds the second and seventh employed in the same manner in the works of some today, this still does not make the fourth a dissonance, or the second and seventh equal to the fourth, for it has not yet been established that such a thing is well done, and may therefore be permitted. These are the examples*: [Example 162]. He who would follow me will not use the like.

EXAMPLE 162

5. Beyond this, those privileges which some have granted the fourth in the style of the present day will be treated below in the proper place. There it will also become clear that the fourth is not to be regarded as altogether similar to the other dissonances.

6. So much for the nature of the fourth. The properties of the remaining dissonances require no special elucidation. They will be clearly observable in our examples of the figures.

7. It is, however, to be remarked that composite dissonances† have the same nature as simple ones (as was also observed above in connection with consonances). This after the rule of the *musici*: *De octavis idem est iudicium.*

Chapter 16

Of Stylus Gravis

1. So far we have spoken of *contrapunctus inaequalis* in general. Now follows its first subdivision, *contrapunctus gravis.*

* The lower voice of the second progression is written a fifth lower in M-B.—clearly a mistake.

† "*Dissonantiae compositae,*" i.e., dissonant intervals greater than an octave.

2. And as it has been observed, in the description of it above in chapter 3, paragraph 8, that this style does not use every sort of figure, so it is necessary to know what a *figure* is.

3. *Figure* I call a certain way of employing dissonances, which renders these not only inoffensive, but rather quite agreeable, bringing the skill of the composer to the light of day.

4. The following figures are employed in *stylus gravis*: a) *transitus*; b) *quasi-transitus*; c) *syncopatio*; d) *quasi-syncopatio*.

Chapter X

3. One might indeed think that discords should be outlawed as enemies of music, which has pleasing euphony as its goal. Yet dissonances, when artistically employed, are indeed the noblest ornament of a work, and therefore should be avoided only when they are without a basis in musical rules, and hence unacceptable.

4. To this end—namely, to exhibit the use of dissonances that much more clearly—I have sought out certain figures, which hopefully will not be without service.

5. This time, however,* I divide them into *fundamental figures* and *superficial figures*.

6. I call those figures *fundamental* which are to be found in fundamental composition,† or in the old style, no less than in styles employed today.

7. There are two such: *ligatura* and *transitus*.

* Seemingly, in contrast to what he did in the *Tractatus*.

† "in der *fundamental Composition*." See p. 5 of my preface.

Chapter 17

Of Transitus

1. *Transitus*, which can also be called *deminution*,[26] takes place when, between two notes on odd-numbered beats, both consonant with respect to the *subject*,[27] a dissonant note slips by, as it were, on the even-numbered beat, on the tone immediately above or below.*

2. Hence all odd parts of the measure should consist of consonances. In half-beats, the first half should be good; in quarter beats, the first and third quarters; in notes with tails,† the first, third, fifth, and seventh. The even-numbered ones may be dissonant. In *tripla*, the first beat must be good, following which the second or third (not both) may be dissonant. Nevertheless, in hemiolias‡ the first note in *tripla* may also be dissonant, although it is then more like syncopation than *transitus*.

3. After the consonance, the dissonance should appear on the degree immediately below or above. The latter should in turn be followed by a consonance on a neighboring degree.

Chapter XII

Of Transitus

1. *Transitus*, which I have also called *deminution*,[26] takes place when, between two good notes, a false one is found on a neighboring tone.*

2. It is of two kinds: regular or irregular; i.e., in accordance with the rules or contrary to them.

3. *Transitus regularis* occurs when the note on the beat is consonant, but the other one dissonant.

4. In this type of *transitus* it is to be observed that all odd parts of the measure should consist of consonances, for thus I call the notes on the beat. Odd parts of the measure are the first half; the first and third quarters; the first, third, fifth, and seventh eighths, etc. In *tripla* the first note must be good; the second and third (one of the two, not indeed both) may be dissonant.

A dissonance must follow the consonance on a neighboring degree; and the dissonance must then in turn be followed by a consonance on a neighboring degree: [Example 163].

EXAMPLE 163

* "im nächsten *Intervallo* oben oder unten," in the *Tractatus*. In the *Bericht*, "im nächsten *Intervallo*."

† "geschwäntzten Noten," i.e., eighth-notes.

‡ "Rückungen."

EXAMPLE 163 (*continued*)

N.B. From this example it is clear that the first note of a measure can also be false in *tripla*, if it is the middle note of a hemiolia, wherein two measures are fashioned out of three notes.

4. The other voice, against which *transitus* occurs, should have slow-moving notes, i.e., a consonance and a dissonance should together be equal to a single note of such a voice (which I have, in paragraph 1, abusively called the *subject*).

5. *Transitus* was designed to adorn the unison or the leap of a third in a voice. All will become clear through the following examples: [Example 164].

EXAMPLE 164

N.B. 1) The diminished fourth and augmented fifth are hardly to be encountered in two-part pieces, but in pieces with more voices they are quite readily found, as when the ending of a piece should stand as: [Example 165].

EXAMPLE 165

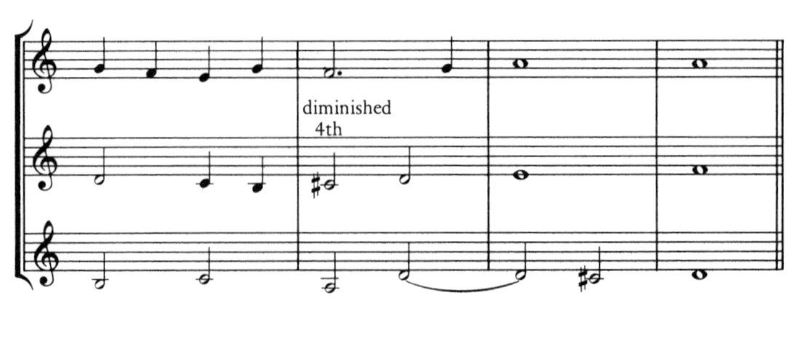

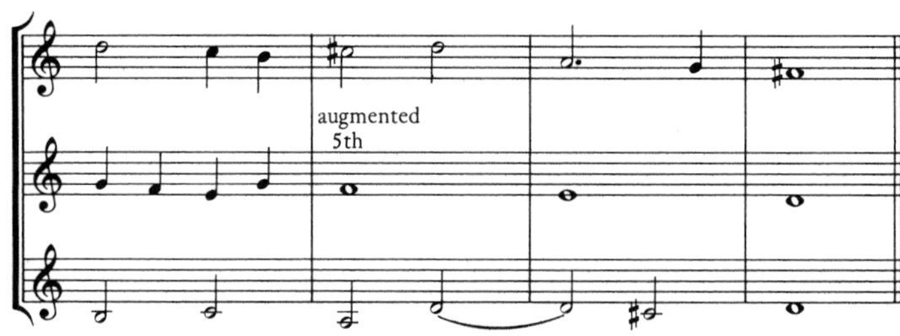

N.B. 2) These are indeed not examples of *transitus* of the diminished fourth or augmented fifth. Also, it would have been better to omit the sharp, as men in former times often did at cadences, for fear of a false relation.

Examples of *Transitus* of the Diminished Fourth and Augmented Fifth. [Example 166]

EXAMPLE 166

Examples of *Transitus* in Tripla.* [Example 167]

* The B in the second-last measure appears as a black semibreve in M-B.

EXAMPLE 167

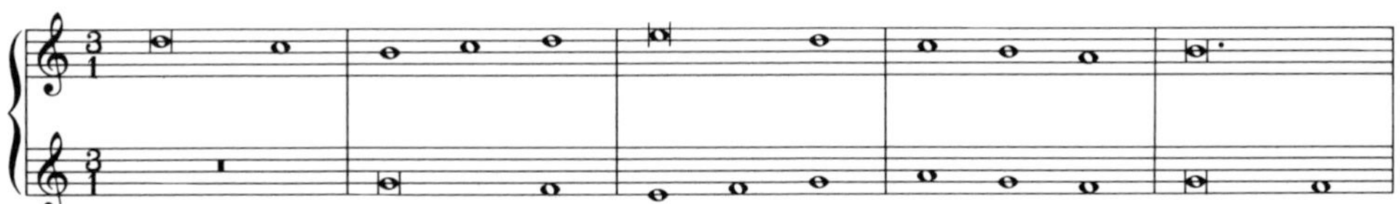

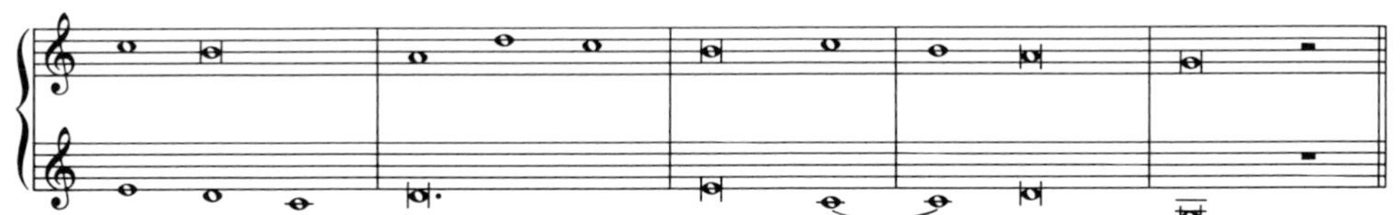

6. Certain examples from Palestrina are to be noted: [Example 168].

EXAMPLE 168

Chapter 18

Of Quasi-Transitus

1. *Quasi-transitus* occurs when a false note stands on an odd beat,[28] contrary to the above rules of *transitus*.* [Example 169]

Chapter XII

5. *Transitus irregularis* occurs when the note on the beat is false, but the following note is good.

EXAMPLE 169

* In M-B., the upper voice of the last progression of Example 169 is written a fifth higher than I give it. (A soprano clef holds sway instead of an alto clef.) Comparison with the last progression of Example 170 clearly shows this to be an error.

EXAMPLE 169 (*continued*)

2. *Quasi-transitus* was designed to adorn leaps of a third in general, leaps of a fourth almost exclusively in descending, and unisons. The above examples would naturally have stood thus: [Example 170].

EXAMPLE 170

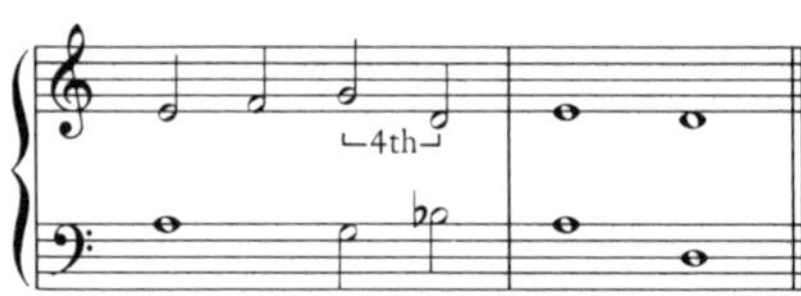

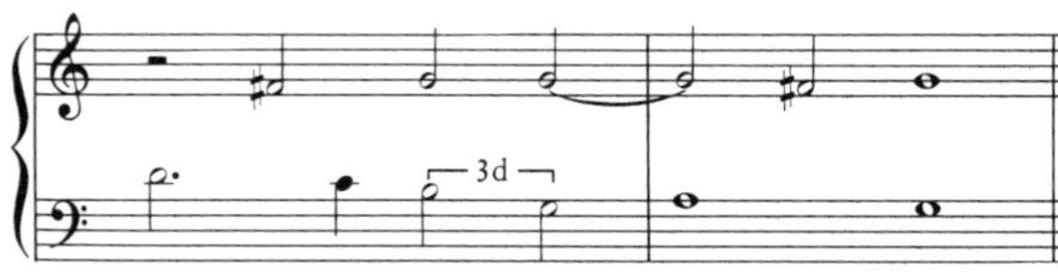

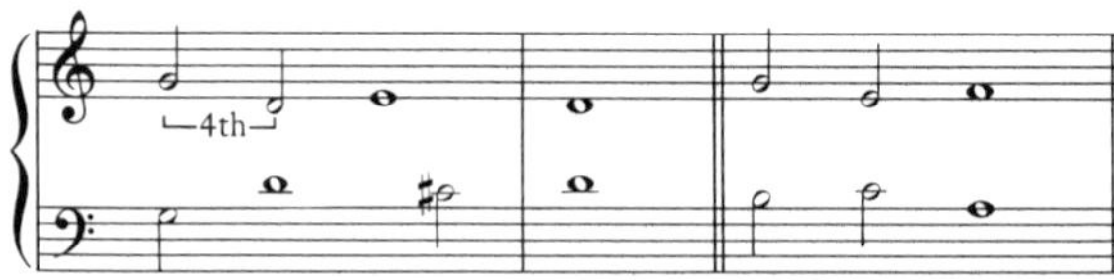

6. *Transitus irregularis* should b
used infrequently. Notes which a
divided* in *transitus irregularis* shou
go only down, but not up. A short fal
note should be on the beat; howeve
another one equal to it, falling a secor
below, should then make it goo
[Example 171]

EXAMPLE 171

Hence it is to be seen that fallin
thirds and fourths may be reinforced
this way.

* "verkleinerten Noten."

3. Some examples might be noted, of which the following are by Palestrina: [Example 172].

EXAMPLE 172

4. *Quasi-transitus* is also sometimes employed elliptically,* to avoid something false in the descent of the fourth, as the following example of Palestrina shows: [Example 173].

EXAMPLE 173

* "*ellipticè*," i.e., with one of the passing tones omitted. The example shows a cambiata being used to avoid parallel octaves.

EXAMPLE 173 (*continued*)

This *quasi-transitus* would naturally stand thus:

5. He who is eager to learn can take and examine other examples of this kind from established composers, which may or may not be worthy of imitation.

6. *Quasi-transitus*, even when in accordance with the rules, should seldom be used. But still less frequently should those specimens be employed which depart somewhat from the rules, especially those wherein dissonances are struck together on a strong beat.*

Chapter 19

Of Syncopation

1. *Syncopation*, called *ligatura* by some, takes place when a driving note[29] stands against a consonance and a dissonance.

N.B. Notes extended through a dot are also to be regarded as driving notes.

2. A driving note should have a consonance occurring against its first part, a dissonance against its second part.

Chapter XI

Of Ligatura

1. *Ligatura*, also called *syncopation*, takes place when a driving note[29] is to be found against a consonance and a dissonance.

2. In *ligatura*, the following is to be observed: 1) there must be a driving note; 2) half of it must be good, the other half bad; 3) the note following the driving note must stand a second below it.

* "diejenigen, wo die Dissonantzen mit einander anschlagen."

3. The syncopation may occur openly, as:* [Example 174].

EXAMPLE 174

4. Or it may be understood through a dot standing after the note, as one will be able to perceive in the examples.

3. In triplets, it is immaterial whether the first or second part,† or both, contain a dissonance; the third part must be consonant.

5. In *tripla*, it is immaterial whether the first or the second part of the measure be false; the third must be good.

4. The note following the driving note must fall a second and be consonant.

6. Examples of the Syncopated Second:‡ [Example 175].

EXAMPLE 175

5. The fourth, in those places where it is encountered between two thirds, or between a fifth and third, is to be taken as consonant

7. Examples of the Syncopated Fourth: Here it is to be noted that when the upper voice is driving, the lower one must stand still or fall an octave; when,

* In M-B., all but the last note of the passage in *tripla* are black breves and semibreves. He gives $\frac{3}{2}$ as the time-signature.

† Comparison with the parallel passage in the *Bericht* clearly shows that Bernhard is using "part" to mean "part of the measure" in this paragraph, unlike in the preceding paragraph.

‡ In M-B., black breves and semibreves occur in the passage in *tripla*, in bar 6 of the upper voice, and in bars 5 and 6 of the lower voice.

in its first part, as dissonant in its second part.

6. Examples of the Fourth:* [Example 176].

EXAMPLE 176

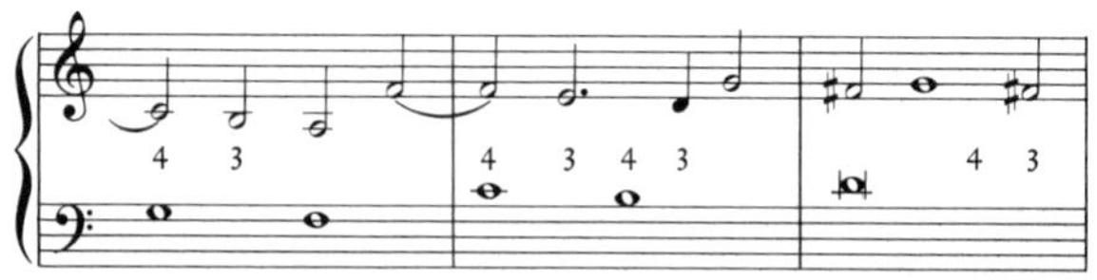

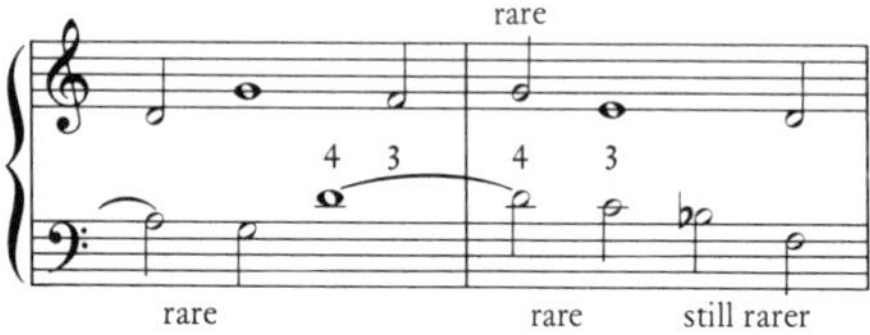

however, the lower one is driving, the upper one must climb a second: [Example 177].

EXAMPLE 177

8. Thus the following examples are to be avoided as false: [Example 178].

EXAMPLE 178

7. From these examples, the following rule could be formulated: that when the driving note is in the upper voice, the lower voice should stand still, when it comes across the dissonance, until the latter has been followed by a consonance. When the lower voice is driving, the upper one should

* All figures and comments are given as they appear in M-B.

climb a second after the dissonance. Even so, the following example, wherein the lower voice indeed falls an octave, is also good: [Example 179].

EXAMPLE 179

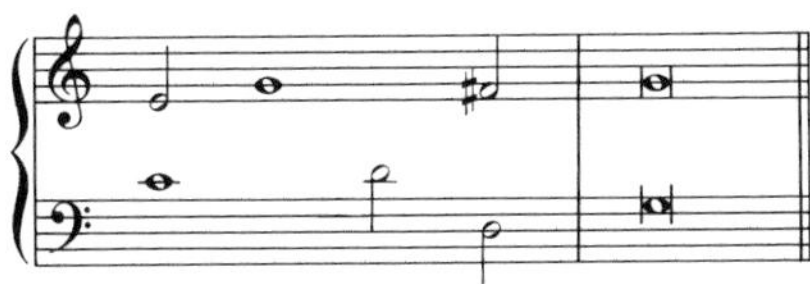

8. Examples of the Second, both Minor and Major:* [Example 180].

EXAMPLE 180

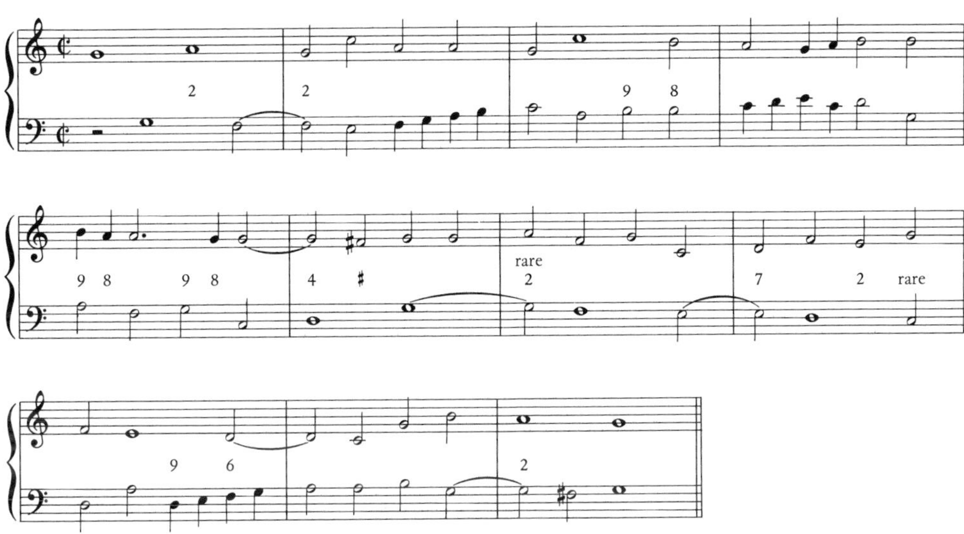

9. The following rule comes from these examples: The free voice should stand still against the driving note and its fall, rarely fall or rise a third, better climb a fourth or fall a fifth.

10. Examples of a diminished fourth against the lower voice are hardly to be found; but they are often found between the middle and upper parts, where it is then employed as are other fourths by practicing musicians.

11. The augmented fourth (which indeed is often used against the lowest voice) likewise follows the rules for properly proportioned fourths.

* The first figure of the eighth measure reads "2" in M-B. instead of "7"—clearly a mistake.

12. The diminished fifth is only used when the upper voice is driving and the lower one is free, the former falling a minor second, the latter rising by the same extent. [Example 181]

EXAMPLE 181

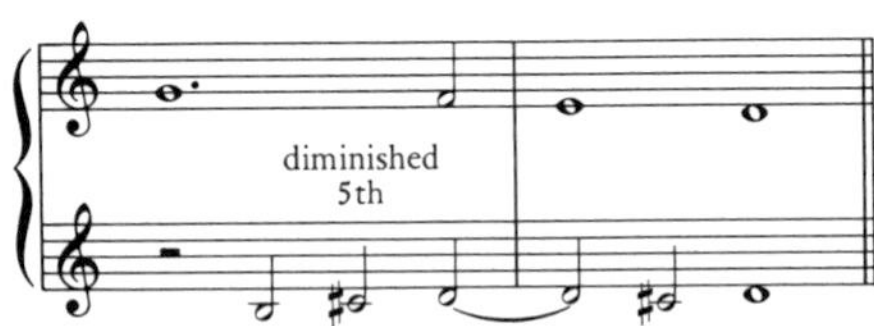

13. The augmented fifth is not employed in syncopation.

14. Examples of the Seventh, Minor as well as Major: [Example 182].

EXAMPLE 182

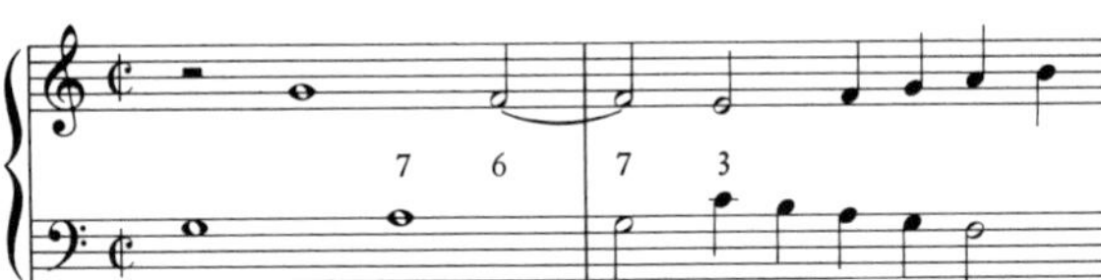

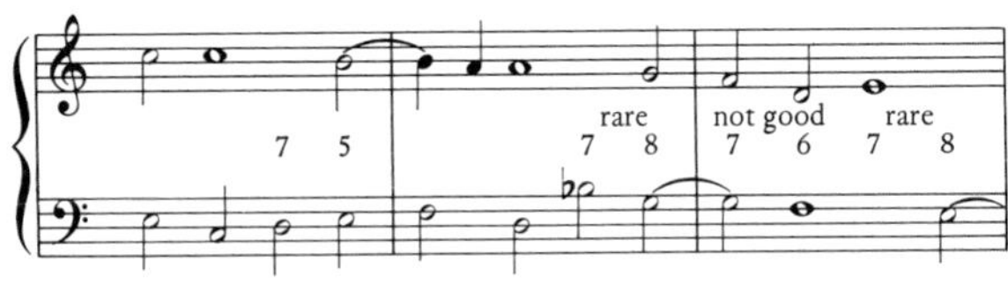

9. Examples of the Syncopated Seventh: [Example 183].

EXAMPLE 183

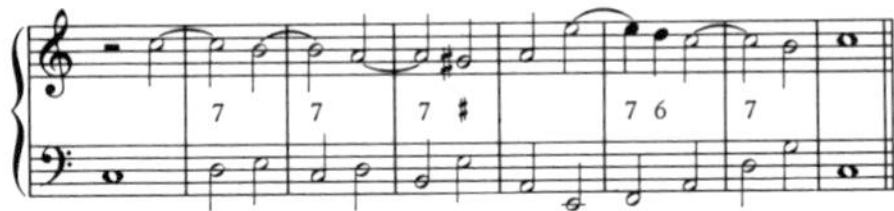

10. N.B. The seventh can be tied only in the upper voice.*

11. There follow certain examples of syncopation which break the above rules, yet are often used.† [Example 184]

EXAMPLE 184

* "lässt sich alleine in der Oberstimme binden."

† In connection with Example 184, see ch. 15, para. 4 of the *Tractatus*.

EXAMPLE 182 (*continued*)

15. From these examples flows the following rule: When the upper voice is driving, the free voice should either stand still, climb a second or fourth to a consonance, or fall a fifth, rarely a third. But if the lower voice is driving, then the upper voice best stands still until the dissonance is over.

N.B. In all syncopation, the leap of an octave is also included under "standing still"; but better downwards than upwards, and in the lower voices rather than in the upper.

Chapter 20

Of Quasi-Syncopatio

1. *Quasi-syncopatio* is the release of a tied or driving note.[30]

2. It follows the rules of *syncopation* at all times, and has no place where syncopation cannot occur.

3. It is, however, seldom employed, and then mostly in connection with the fourth, as this interval does not partake of the nature of a dissonance so completely. [Example 185]

EXAMPLE 185

4. Even so, one will find more instances where the dissonance is struck only once, than where it allows itself to be heard twice. Hence the first is better than the second: [Example 186].

EXAMPLE 186

Chapter 21

Of Stylus Luxurians Communis

1. The second subdivision of *stylus inaequalis* is *luxurians*. I call it by this name because of its many sorts of dissonance treatment, which others call *licentiae*,* since these do not seem to find justification as do the figures previously described.

Chapter XIII

Of the Superficial Figures in General[31]

1. So far we have dealt with the fundamental figures. As men of former times did not depart from these, therefore these alone should be employed in their genres of composition.

2. Since then, it has been observed that artful singers as well as instrumentalists, when such works were to be done,† have digressed somewhat from the notes here and there, and thus have given cause to establish an agreeable kind of figure; for what can be sung with reasonable euphony might indeed be written down as well.

3. Accordingly, composers in the last epoch[32] already began to set down one thing or another which was unknown to men of former times, and which seemed unacceptable to the unenlightened, but charming to good ears and the *musici*.

4. Until the art of music has attained such a height in our own day that it may indeed be compared to a rhetoric,[33] in view of the multitude of figures, par-

* See also ch. 3, para. 9, and *Tractatus* note 11.

† "wenn dergleichen Sachen zu machen gewesen," i.e., when pieces in *stylus gravis* were to be performed.

ticularly in the newly founded and, up to this present moment, ever more embellished recitative style.

5. Such figures and works, however, have the old masters as their foundation, and what cannot be excused through them must rightly be weeded out from composition as an abomination.

2. As was mentioned in chapter 3, it is of two kinds: *communis* and *theatralis*.

3. *Communis*, to be discussed here, is called thus because it is found nowadays in vocal works—both church and table music—as well as in instrumental pieces.*

4. Others also refer to this style as *modernus*, or the new style, since it was brought into being more recently than the previously discussed *stylus gravis*.

5. This style possesses the figures of the preceding, and more frequent examples of these, which otherwise occur rather rarely.

6. Besides these it has other figures as well, but not as many as *stylus theatralis*, which will be discussed in its proper place.

7. Such figures to be found in *stylus luxurians communis* are: a) *superjectio*; b) *anticipatio*; c) *subsumtio*; d) *variatio*; e) *multiplicatio*; f) *prolongatio*; g) *syncopatio catachrestica*; h) *passus duriusculus*; i) *saltus duriusculus*; j) *mutatio toni*; k) *inchoatio imperfecta*; l) *longinqua distantia*; m) *consonantiae impropriae*; n) *quaesitio notae*; o) *cadentiae duriusculae*.

6. Superficial figures include the following:† a) *superjectio*; b) *subsumtio*; c) *variatio*; d) *multiplicatio*; e) *ellipsis*; f) *retardatio*; g) *heterolepsis*; h) *quasi-transitus*; and i) *abruptio*.

* "weil derselbe nunmehro in singenden, sowohl Kirchen als Taffel-Sachen, ingleichen denen *Sonaten* gefunden wird." See also ch. 3, para. 10.

† The last five figures listed here are the ones which in the *Tractatus* belong to *stylus theatralis* rather than *communis*. See also *Tractatus*, ch. 35, para. 12.

Chapter 22

Of Superjectio

1. *Superjectio*, otherwise generally called *accentus*,* occurs when a note is placed next to a consonance or dissonance, a step above.† This happens most often when the notes should naturally fall a second.

2. *Superjectio* takes place in connection with all consonances, likewise next to *transitus*, *syncopatio*, *quasi-transitus*, and *quasi-syncopatio*, as: [Example 188].

EXAMPLE 188

This example would naturally stand thus:

Chapter XIV

Of Superjectio

1. *Superjectio*, generally called *accentus*,* occurs when a note is placed in the next degree above† a consonance or dissonance, as:‡ [Example 187].

EXAMPLE 187

2. This *accentus* is employed when a voice moves or leaps downward.

* See also *Art of Singing*, paras. 15 to 18, and *Art of Singing* note 6.

† "im nächsten *Intervallo* drüber."

‡ In M-B., the second note of the upper voice and the twelfth note of the lower voice are B♮'s—obvious mistakes. It is also likely (cf. the parallel example in the *Tractatus*) that the third note of the lower voice should be an E♭.

3. This figure derived its legitimacy from the practice of singers and instrumentalists, who at times employed an *accent** in *stylus gravis*. Composers afterwards found this to be good, and accordingly copied it in their works.

3. Nevertheless it should be remarked that, just as the foundation of composition† will not permit a leap to be made out of a dissonance, even so one cannot adorn, or excuse, such a disagreeable leap with an *accentus*.

Chapter 23

Of Anticipatio Notae

1. *Anticipatio notae*‡ occurs when a voice, moving a step up or down, begins the next note earlier than the natural setting would actually allow.

2. To this end, part of the value of the antecedent note is taken away and placed before the consequent.

3. *Anticipatio notae* occurs more often when the preceding note is a consonance than when it is a dissonance,§ more in descending *transitus* than in ascending.|| [Example 189]

EXAMPLE 189

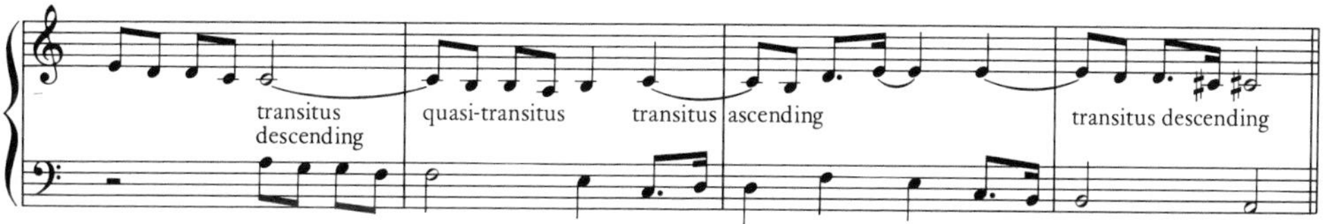

This would naturally read as follows:

4. This figure also was ushered in through the practice of singers and instrumentalists.

* "einen *Accent*." See also *Art of Singing*, paras. 17 and 18, and *Art of Singing* note 8.

† "das *Fundament* der *Composition*," i.e., *stylus gravis*. See also ch. X, para. 6, found opposite ch. 16, para. 3 of the *Tractatus*, and my preface, p. 5.

‡ Cf. *anticipatione della nota*, in *Art of Singing*, paras. 21 and 22. Also, see *Bericht*, ch. XV, para. 4, given on p. 94 and also note 34.

§ "hat mehr statt in *praecedentibus Consonantiis* als *Dissonantiis*."

|| The example is given exactly as it appears in M-B. The last two identifications, "transitus ascending" and "transitus descending" seem wrong, however, as syncopation is clearly involved in both cases.

Chapter 24

Of Subsumtio

1. *Subsumtio** occurs when I take something away from a natural note† that is followed by one a step higher, and append this to the given note a step below.

2. *Subsumtio* is more properly used in places where two consonances follow each other than anywhere in *transitus* or *syncopation*. [Example 190]

EXAMPLE 190

This must stand naturally as follows:

Chapter XV

Of Subsumtio

1. *Subsumtio*, called *cercar della nota** by the Italians, occurs when I append something to a note, in the next degree below.

2. It is of two kinds, for one can affix something underneath at either the beginning or the end of the note.

3. When one affixes something underneath at the beginning, it could be referred to as *subsumtio praepositiva*,‡ as in this example: [Example 191].

EXAMPLE 191

[it is just as if it stood thus]:

4. When one affixes it at the end of the note, it could be referred to as *subsumtio postpositiva*. In vocal works it is sometimes called *anticipatione della sillaba* by the Italians,[34] and sometimes *cercare*, as: [Example 192].

EXAMPLE 192

* Cf. *cercar della nota* in the *Art of Singing*, paras. 23 and 24. But see also final footnote on this page.

† "einer natürlichen Note," i.e., a note free of any figures or ornaments. See my preface regarding the use of "natural" in general.

‡ This kind of *subsumtio* corresponds to *quaesitio notae*, discussed in ch. 33 of the *Tractatus*.

EXAMPLE 192 (*continued*)

5. From this example it can be seen that *subsumtio postpositiva* only occurs when the notes fall or rise a second.

6. *Subsumtio praepositiva*, on the other hand, is also often found in connection with intervals that leap.[35] [Example 193]

EXAMPLE 193

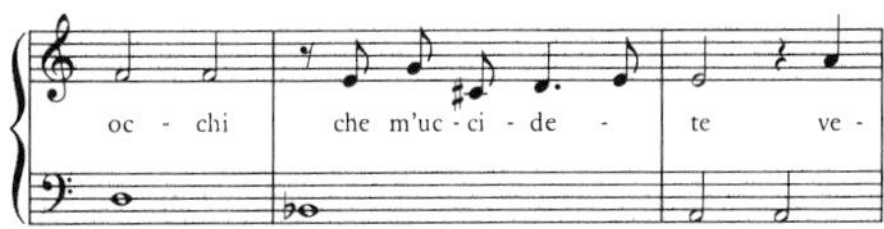

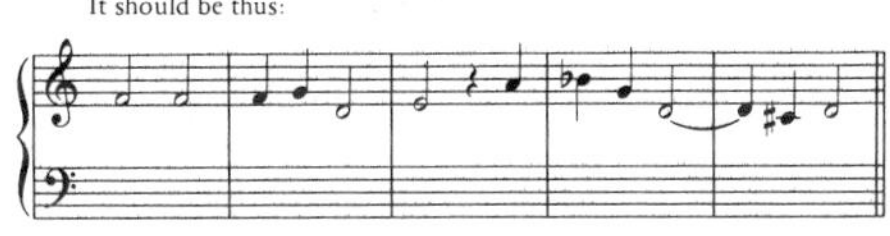

7. The following example and other similar ones also belong here.[36] [Example 194]

EXAMPLE 194

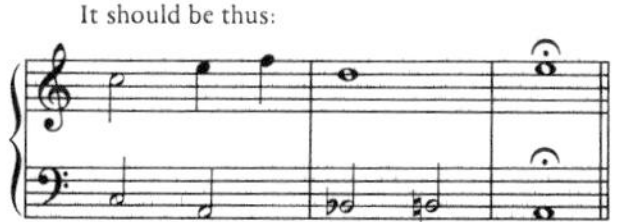

3. What was said with regard to the two preceding figures, namely, that their origin stems from the usage of singers, is also true regarding *subsumtio* and most of the following figures. This fact is therefore mentioned here, and is to be understood as applying to the kinds to come.

4. A knowledgeable person will indeed perceive when he might apply this figure in a dissonant context, especially when a suspended fourth resolves to a sixth.

Chapter 25
Of Variation

1. *Variation*, called *passaggio** by the Italians and *coloratura* in general,[37] occurs when an interval is altered through several shorter notes, so that, instead of one long note, a number of shorter ones rush to the next note through all kinds of step progressions and skips.

2. This figure is so fertile that it is impossible to exhibit all its examples.

3. Even so, the interval through which one proceeds to the following note is either a second, a third, a fourth, a fifth, a sixth, or an octave; rarely, however, a seventh.

4. Example of *variations* upon the ascending second. [Example 195]

EXAMPLE 195

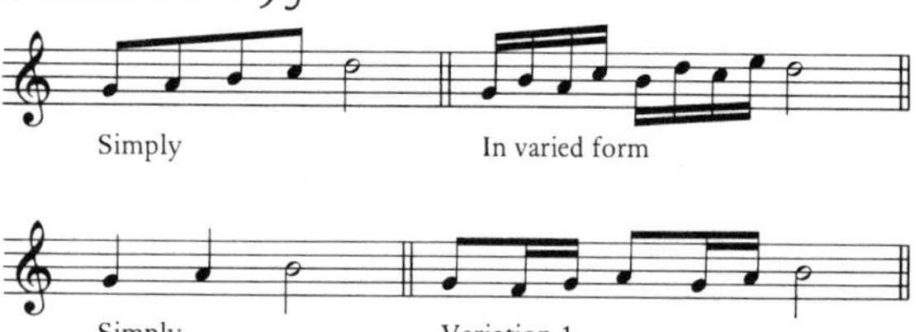

Chapter XVI
Of Variation

1. *Variation*, as a rule called *passagio*,* occurs when, in place of one long note, a number of shorter ones on different degrees are heard, rushing to the next note.

2. There are innumerable such, and hence it is not possible to write down all examples.

3. The most fashionable ones upon the second are the following: [Example 196].

EXAMPLE 196

* Cf. "*cantar passagiato*," in the *Art of Singing*, paras. 35 to 40. The spelling in the *Bericht* is given as found in M-B.

EXAMPLE 195 (*continued*)

5. Example of *variations* upon the descending second. [Example 197]

EXAMPLE 197

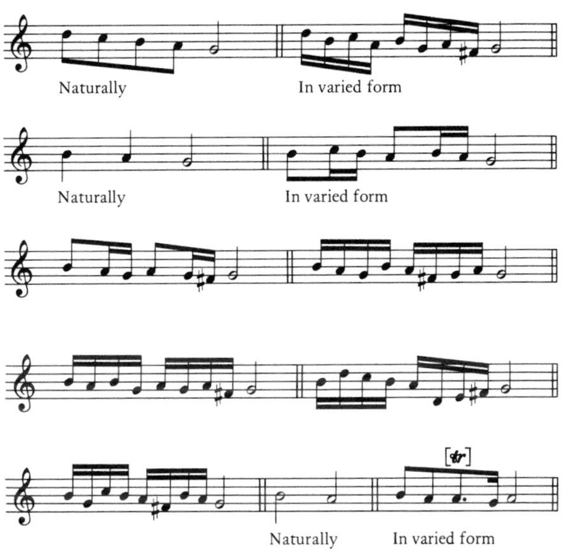

6. Example of the ascending and descending third. [Example 198]

EXAMPLE 198

* The plural is indeed found in M-B.

EXAMPLE 196 (*continued*)

4. The following are* the most fashionable upon the third. [Example 199]

EXAMPLE 199

N.B. From this example it is clear that *variation* upon the third is nothing other than *transitus.*

7. Example of the ascending and descending fourth. [Example 200]

EXAMPLE 200

N.B. It is clear from this that *variation* upon the fourth originated from *quasi-transitus.*

8. The rising or falling fifth, since it is naturally composed of two thirds, therefore is varied in the same manner as thirds are—i.e., with bona fide *transitus.*

9. The sixth is a third plus a fourth. Hence *variation* upon it involves both of these intervals, and therefore both *transitus* and *quasi-transitus.*

10. The octave is composed of a fifth and a fourth, therefore it follows that this interval will undergo *variation* like that of the fifth in one of its halves, and like that of the fourth in the other.

11. The seventh occurs rarely, hence *variation* upon it will be rarer still. If, however, someone should wish to employ it in

N.B. It may be seen from this that such a *variation* is actually *transitus.*

5. Upon the fourth one makes *variations* through *transitus irregularis,** e.g.: [Example 201].

EXAMPLE 201

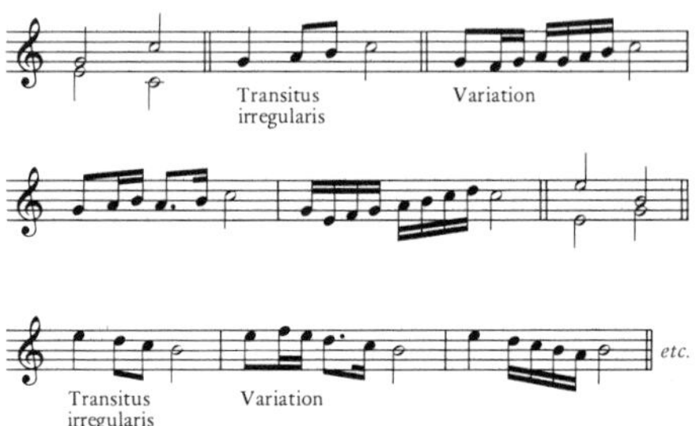

6. The fifth is varied through *transitus regularis,* just as the third above.

7. The sixth through *transitus regularis* and *irregularis.*

8. The seventh and octave in the same way.[38]

* I give the latter half of this example as found in M-B., but suspect that it should read a third lower, especially in view of the parallel example in the *Tractatus.*

varied form,* he must observe carefully whether it allows itself, in the place in question, to be divided through *variation* better into two fourths or into a fifth and a third.

12. The above examples are just a few. Further ones may be garnered from practice and from other good authors.[39]

9. Further examples of all sorts of *variations*, upon all kinds of intervals, are to be found; [they can] also be examined by writing out works in score form,[40] whereto a composer should be directed.

13. In devising such *variations*, a composer must: a) take care lest he choose kinds that are too old-fashioned—something which it is easy for a skilled [*musicus*] to know; b) not employ the same sort of *variations* everywhere, but rather take care that those which he would like to employ can go well against the remaining voices.

14. These *variations* can themselves be varied still further through smaller notes; and one who is knowledgeable will readily see, without my pointing it out, that *transitus* and *quasi-transitus* achieve the noblest effects in passage-work, *accentus* is added now and then, occasionally also *subsumtio* and other previously mentioned figures.

15. From time to time it also happens that two voices undergo *variation*. This should not occur often if the *variations* are dissonant against one another, as:[41] [Example 202].

EXAMPLE 202

* "Da aber jemand solche *passagieret* setzen wolte."

EXAMPLE 202 (*continued*)

Naturally:

Chapter 26

Of Multiplication

1. *Multiplication* is the splitting of a dissonance (be it in *syncopation* or *transitus*) into two or sometimes more parts. Examples in *transitus*: [Example 203].

Chapter XVII

Of Multiplication

1. Multiplication is the division of a dissonance into several notes on the same degree.

2. It is of two kinds: standard and prolonged.*

* "Die Rechtmässige und die Verlängerte."

EXAMPLE 203

Naturally:

Examples in *syncopation*:[42] [Example 206].

EXAMPLE 206

Naturally:

3. The standard one is that which derives from *transitus regularis* or *syncopation*, and which does not last longer than the preceding consonance. [Example 204]

EXAMPLE 204

4. The prolonged one is that wherein the dissonances last longer than the preceding consonances. [Example 205]

EXAMPLE 205

Chapter 27

Of Prolongation

1. *Prolongation* occurs when a dissonance has a longer duration than the preceding consonance, in *transitus* as well as in *syncopation*.

2. In *transitus* we have the following, but infrequently. [Example 207]

EXAMPLE 207

It would naturally be thus:

3. In *syncopation* it is used more often, but especially in connection with the fourth. [Example 208]

EXAMPLE 208

Naturally:

Chapter 28

Of Syncopatio Catachrestica

1. *Syncopatio catachrestica* occurs when a *syncopation** is not resolved through a subsequent consonance a step below, as the rule demands.

* Throughout this translation, "*syncopation*" is to be understood in the restricted sense of ch. 19.

2. It is of three kinds: The tied voice may indeed fall a second, but not to a consonance. This happens when a seventh is resolved through a false fifth,* as: [Example 209].

EXAMPLE 209

3. Another type occurs when the first part of the driving note is not fully consonant. [Example 210]

EXAMPLE 210

4. Or the note following the driving note may not fall a second,† as: [Example 211].

EXAMPLE 211

Chapter 29

Of Passus Duriusculus

1. In chapter 2, paragraph 6, it was already observed that one should beware of unnatural step progressions.

2. Nevertheless, it will not be amiss to make further mention of them at the present time, especially since such progressions may be found either within a single voice, or in one voice over against another.

3. *Passus duriusculus* within a single voice occurs when a voice rises or

* "die falsche *Quinte*." Surely the diminished fifth is meant (almost) exclusively here.

† The figure described in this paragraph can also be regarded as a type of *heterolepsis*. See ch. 41, para. 7.

falls a minor semitone.* [Example 212] Some have held such progressions

EXAMPLE 212

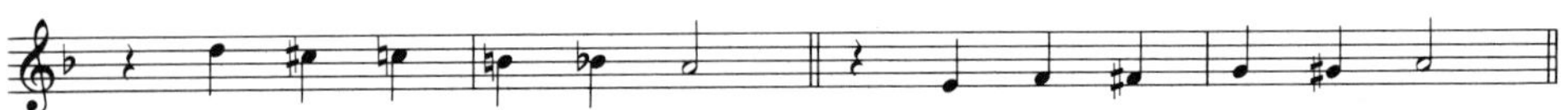

to be passages of a chromatic kind; for what reasons, however, let them fight out among themselves.[43]

4. Or when a step progression of a second is augmented, or one through a third is diminished, or one through a fourth or fifth is augmented or diminished.† The augmented second.‡ [Example 213]

EXAMPLE 213

Im - pi - è im - pi - è fe - ci - mus.

The diminished third.§ [Example 214]

EXAMPLE 214

In hac la - cry - ma - rum val - le.

5. Nevertheless, the step progressions and leaps here described should be used infrequently in *stylus communis*.

6. Ascending and descending step progressions through a diminished fourth, descending ones through a diminished fifth, and ascending ones through an augmented fourth, are permitted nowadays.||

7. *Passus duriusculus plurium vocum* may be seen in chapter 2, paragraph 12.#

* The chromatic semitone, usually 25:24, is meant here. See note 25.

† Bernhard writes "zu gross" and "zu klein," respectively, for "augmented" and "diminished."

‡ "*Secunda abundans.*"

§ "*Tertia deficiens.*" I give the words as they are underlaid in M-B., but suspect that the final syllable should be reserved for the final note.

|| The account in ch. 2, para. 6 is slightly, but perhaps significantly, different.

\# "Paragraph 6" in M-B., but surely para. 12 is meant.

Chapter 30

Of Saltus Duriusculus

1. Above, in chapter 2, paragraph 6, it was said that one should beware of unnatural step progressions and leaps. However, in *stylus luxurians communis* some of them are permitted.

2. The leap of a minor sixth was not in use among composers of former times, except between re and fa, or between mi and fa. Today, however, the following are also allowed: [Example 215].

EXAMPLE 215

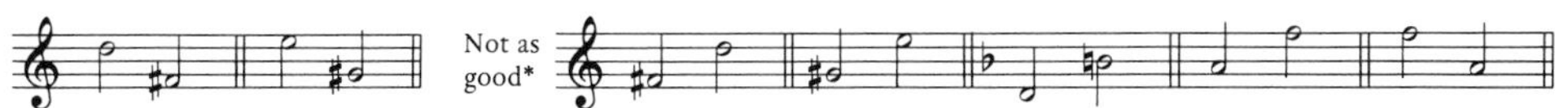
Not as
good*

3. Ascending and descending leaps of a diminished fourth, and descending ones of a diminished fifth, are also permitted nowadays.

4. The leap of a diminished seventh,† which consists of a minor sixth and a major semitone, is also occasionally encountered, although almost exclusively in music for solo voice,‡ and only in descending. [Example 216]

EXAMPLE 216

Und dein Hertz falsch______ falsch ge - we - sen ist.

5. Leaps of a regular seventh,§ as well as of a ninth and other intervals greater than the octave, are also employed more boldly today than in the past, especially in bass parts, which might indeed leap two octaves downwards.

Chapter 31

Of Mutatio Toni, Inchoatio Imperfecta, and Longinqua Distantia

1. In chapter 2, paragraph 7, it was recommended that every voice should conform to one of the twelve modes. Contemporary composers depart from this rule not infrequently, insofar as they not only mix an

* The third leap is given exactly as it appears in M-B.

† "*Septimae irregularis.*"

‡ "in *Soliciniis.*" See note 23.

§ That is, major or minor.

authentic mode with its own plagal (which composers of former times also did) but also jump from one authentic or plagal mode to another in the middle of a composition. This will be considered more fully when we discuss the modes.*

2. In the same chapter [paragraph 11] it was said that perfect intervals should begin a work. This also is not enforced so rigorously today, and as a result *inchoatio imperfecta* is formed.[44]

3. Above, in paragraph 13 of the same chapter, the wide separation of one voice from another was forbidden. However, it was already explained there that this occurs not infrequently today, and I call it *longinqua distantia.*

4. The last two figures, *inchoatio imperfecta* and *longinqua distantia*, are both permitted as a result of the thorough bass, inasmuch as the organist is supposed to play a genuine four-part structure† atop the given bass line whenever possible. Thus the perfect interval missing at the start of the composition will be supplied by the organist; and his middle voices will intervene between the high voice of the composition and its deep bass in such a way that the ear will not notice the great distance so much.

Chapter 32

Of Improper Consonances

1. The improper consonances include all three species of fourth, the diminished and augmented fifths, the diminished seventh, and the augmented second.[45]

2. The first species of fourth, namely the perfect, which consists of two tones and a semitone, is privileged by today's composers and treated as a consonance insofar as it can also be used on an uneven beat‡ from time to time. However, a) it must then be approached by step rather than by leap;§ b) the deepest voice must stand still before the fourth begins, and until another consonance, also approached by step, is finished; c) the sixth must be employed above it,[46] as: [Example 217].

* See ch. 56 in particular.

† "ein richtiges *Quatuor.*"

‡ "*loco impari.*"

§ "nicht in *saltu* sondern in *gradu* sey."

EXAMPLE 217

3. Some also are accustomed to introducing the fourth in such places by skip,* if there are many voices. Loreto Vittori.[47] [Example 218]

EXAMPLE 218

4. Some also enlist the help of the second, so that the fourth may stand between the second and the sixth.[48] [Example 219] But since the fourth is

EXAMPLE 219

* "*in saltu* zu gebrauchen."

not yet regarded by practicing musicians as a full-fledged consonance, I do not know how to condone its leaping, much less the use of the second, due to which two dissonances are produced on top of one another on an uneven beat. Nevertheless, if someone should have a mind to introduce shawms, trumpets, etc., this would not be held against him, seeing that he would thereby exhibit the characteristic use of such instruments that much more tellingly.[49]

5. Regarding both diminished and augmented fourths and fifths, it has already been mentioned above, in chapter 14, paragraph 5,* that these pass for consonant in middle voices.†

6. One may also encounter examples of the diminished fifth, employed as a consonance between the lowest and another voice in the following ways: [Example 220]. The first type illustrates not only the rule mentioned

EXAMPLE 220

above, but also that two fifths such as occur there may follow one another. The second type also belongs to the *syncopationes catachresticae*.‡

7. The diminished seventh and augmented second§ are only admitted in *stylus theatralis*, which will be described below.

Chapter 33

Of Quaesitio Notae

1. *Quaesitio notae*|| occurs when part of a note is cut off, so that this may be placed in front of the following note in the degree immediately below. In this way, the second note is being sought out, as it were.

2. It is applied rather frequently to descending notes, seldom in ascending, however—and then only in passage-work. For example:[50] [Example 221].

* The reference in M-B. reads "ch. 17, para. 5." This, however, is clearly an error.

† "in Mittelstimmen." But surely Bernhard includes the uppermost voice as well.

‡ More precisely, the second-last progression of this example. See ch. 28.

§ "*Sexta superflua* und *Tertia deficiens*." See note 45.

|| Cf. *cercar della nota*, in paras. 23 and 24 of the *Art of Singing*. Also see ch. XV of the *Bericht*, especially paras. 3–6 given on pp. 94–95. (Ch. XV of the *Bericht* is given opposite ch. 24 of the *Tractatus*.)

EXAMPLE 221

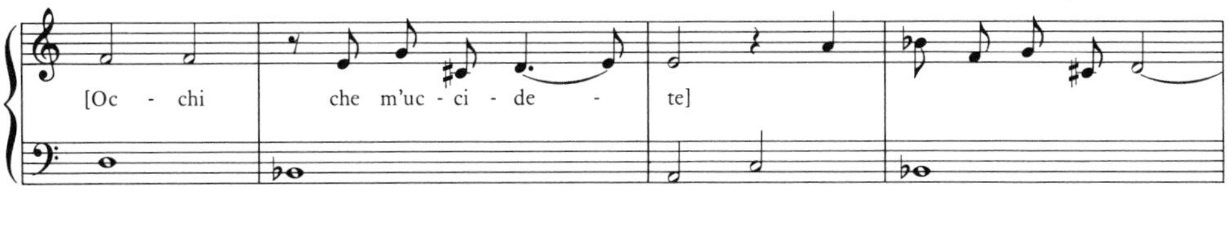

Naturally it stands thus:

Chapter 34

Of Cadentiae Duriusculae

1. Cadences that feature rather strange dissonances before the final two notes are called *duriusculae.*

2. Such are found almost exclusively in works for a solo singer, and most often in arias and in sections in triple meter.*

3. But should a few be encountered in [works] for more voices, the remaining voices will be composed in such a way as to permit no discord to be felt.

4. The examples of this figure, which I have taken from among others, might serve in place of further rules, especially since it is at all times better, as far as I am concerned, to avoid these completely. [Example 222]

* "in *Arien* und *Tripeln.*"

EXAMPLE 222

5. In the arias and other works of certain composers, the same harsh sounds also occur apart from preparations for cadences. Then they should be employed with great caution. And it would be impossible to embody in rules the quite disagreeable licenses which all composers take from time to time. One will be satisfied, in *stylus communis*, with what has been said. Beyond that, I leave each person free to accept a bit more as good, or to reject everything [as] bad.

Chapter 35

Of Stylus Theatralis

1. The other subdivision of what I have called *stylus luxurians* is *stylus theatralis*.* It derives its name from the place where it is used the most.

2. It is also at times called *stylus recitativus* or *oratorius*, since it was devised to represent speech in music, and indeed not too many years ago. Although it was at first (as everything else) rather rough, today it has been admirably refined and polished through the efforts of considerable talents, so that I hardly believe that the ancient Greeks possessed this species of music (to which they applied themselves most of all) in better form.

3. And since language is the absolute master of music in this genre,† just as music is the master of language in *stylus gravis*, and language and music are both masters in *stylus luxurians communis*, therefore this general

* Cf. *Bericht*, ch. XIII, paras. 2–6, given on pp. 90–91; also *Bericht*, ch. XXII, N.B., given on p. 116.

† "Und weil in diesem *Genere* die *Oratio Harmoniae Domina absolutissima* . . . ist."

rule follows: that one should represent speech in the most natural way possible.[51]

4. Thus one should render joyful things joyful, sorrowful things sorrowful, swift things swift, slow things slow [etc.].

5. In particular, that which is heightened in ordinary speech should be set high, that which passes unemphasized set low.

6. Similar observations should be made in connection with texts wherein Heaven, Earth, and Hell are mentioned.

7. Questions, according to common usage, are ended a step higher than the penultimate syllable, as the examples will show.*

8. Textual repetition should be employed either not at all, or just in those places where elegance permits.[52]

9. Musical repetition† occurs when two successive utterances are similar in subject matter.

10. Musical repetition a step higher occurs in connection with two or more successive questions, when their words correspond in subject matter,‡ and when the last seem to be more forceful than the first.

11. *Omnium rerum satietas.* Thus one should observe how an aria is occasionally injected into a recitative, as at the close of periods in sentences.§ Hence a poet should bring many songs|| into his theatrical work.

12. The figures belonging to *stylus theatralis*, over and above those mentioned before, might be designated as follows: a) *extensio*; b) *ellipsis*; c) *mora*; d) *abruptio*; e) *transitus inversus*; f) *heterolepsis*; g) *tertia deficiens*; h) *sexta superflua*.

13. I do not make special mention of leaps otherwise forbidden but permitted here, since I have already dealt with these sufficiently from time to time.

Chapter 36

Of Extension

1. *Extension* is the rather sizable lengthening of a dissonance.#

2. It is generally combined with *multiplication*.

* There are none to be found in this treatise.

† "Die Wiederhohlung der Noten." Obviously the repetition of entire musical phrases is meant.

‡ "in . . . Gleichheit der Worte an der *Materie*."

§ "als in *Sententiis* bey Schlüssen der *Periodorum*."

|| "viel Lieder," i.e., many portions of text regular and song-like enough to be set as arias.

\# "einer *Dissonanz* ziemlich lange währende Veränderung." Cf. *prolongation*, in ch. 27.

3. Whenever this figure (or the following ones) is encountered, the organist should play middle or upper voices with it which accompany the dissonances with nothing but consonances. For a voice above the bass* is written [to it] with this in mind: that it should not accord itself, as regards consonances, solely with the bass, but also often with the upper voice. Let this be recalled here once and for all. Examples of *extension*.[53] [Example 223]

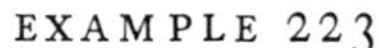

EXAMPLE 223

Chapter 37

Of Ellipsis

1. *Ellipsis* is the suppression of a normally required consonance.

2. It arises through the alteration of either *syncopation* or *transitus*.

3. *Ellipsis* arising from *syncopation* occurs quite commonly when a fourth should be resolved through a subsequent third in

Chapter XVIII

Of Ellipsis

1. *Ellipsis* means omission, and is the suppression of a consonance.

2. It occurs in two ways: first, when a rest replaces the consonance and is followed by a dissonance. [Example 224]

* "die Stimme über den Bass."

cadences, but either the third is left out altogether or another consonance is taken in its place. [Example 225]

EXAMPLE 225

It should stand thus:

4. *Ellipsis* arising from *transitus* is the omission of the consonance which is normally required in *transitus* before a dissonance. [Example 227]

EXAMPLE 227

EXAMPLE 224

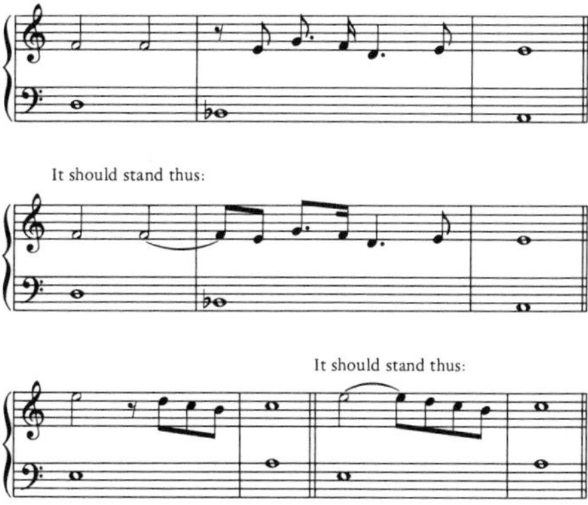
It should stand thus:
It should stand thus:

3. Also, when a fourth is not resolved through a third at a cadence, rather standing still, as: [Example 226].

EXAMPLE 226

N.B. This derives from *cercar della nota*, discussed in Rule 24 of the *Manier*.[54] For the singer must resolve it below.*

* "Denn der Sänger muss es unten *resolviren*." The connection between the thought of this last sentence and that of the previous one is unclear.

EXAMPLE 227 (*continued*)

It should stand thus:

Chapter 38

Of Mora

1. *Mora* is an inverted *syncopation*, in that the consonance following the driving dissonance does not fall a second, but rises one instead.

2. Example of a second resolved through *mora*. [Example 228]

EXAMPLE 228

3. Example of a seventh resolved through *mora*.* [Example 230]

EXAMPLE 230

Chapter XIX

Of Retardation

1. *Retardation* is a lingering, when a note should climb a second but waits too long before climbing.

2. It was invented, however, in imitation of *syncopation*, with this difference: that whereas *syncopation* resolves itself downwards, *retardation* does this upwards. [Example 229]

EXAMPLE 229

* The second bass note in the example is indeed F♮ in M-B. While somewhat unlikely, especially in view of the parallel example in the *Bericht*, it is nonetheless a possible and stimulating reading.

4. Example of a diminished fifth. [Example 231]

EXAMPLE 231

Chapter 39

Of Abruptio

1. *Abruptio* occurs when, in place of a consonance anticipated as a necessary resolution, the vocal line is either ruptured or broken off altogether.

2. Ruptured in the middle of a phrase, if a rest is written down instead of a dot. [Example 232]

EXAMPLE 232

instead of:

3. Broken off altogether at a cadence, indeed in such a way that the upper voice ends on a fourth before the bass grasps the last note of the cadence, for example: [Example 233].

Chapter XXII

Of Abruptio

1. *Abruptio* means tearing off. It occurs when one ends on the fourth of a cadence, which should first be resolved through the third before the bass finishes the cadence, as: [Example 234].

EXAMPLE 233

which should stand thus:

Chapter 40

Of Transitus Inversus

1. *Transitus inversus* occurs when the first part of a measure in *transitus* is bad, the second part good.‡

2. This is permitted in recitative style, since the measure is not kept there§ and one therefore does not perceive where its first half is, or its second.

3. Nevertheless, this figure is never encountered without *multiplication*. [Example 236]

EXAMPLE 234

It should be thus:

N.B. The above-mentioned superficial figures, such as *ellipsis*, *retardation*, *heterolepsis*, *quasitransitus*, and *abruptio*, are admitted almost exclusively in recitative style, and are not to be employed otherwise.*

Chapter XXI

Of Quasitransitus

1. *Quasitransitus*† occurs when a dissonance is struck on a strong beat, counter to the rule of *transitus*. It is allowed only in recitative style, since no beat is observed there,§ as: [Example 235].

EXAMPLE 235

* Bernhard mentions precisely those five superficial figures here that are classified under *stylus theatralis* in the *Tractatus*. See also *Tractatus*, ch. 35, para. 12.

† Cf. *quasi-transitus* as defined in the *Tractatus*, ch. 18.

‡ Bad = dissonant; good = consonant.

§ "weil darinnen kein *Tact* gebraucht wird," in the *Tractatus*; "weil daselbst kein *Tact observiret* wird," in the *Bericht*.

EXAMPLE 236

Pur si ra-du-na e non sò co-me il co-re.
[rav-vi-va]

This would correctly stand:*

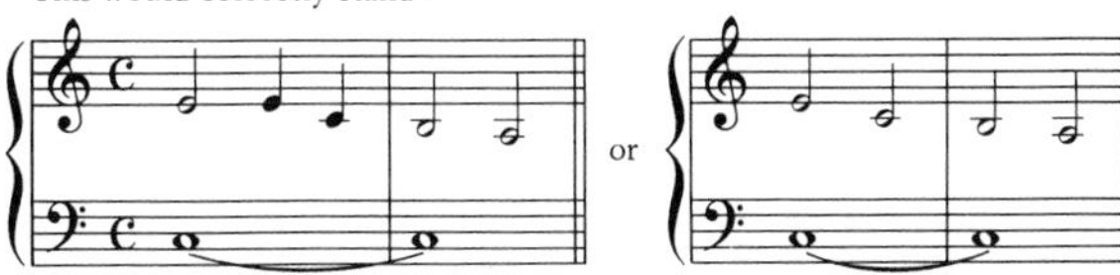
or

This would correctly stand: †

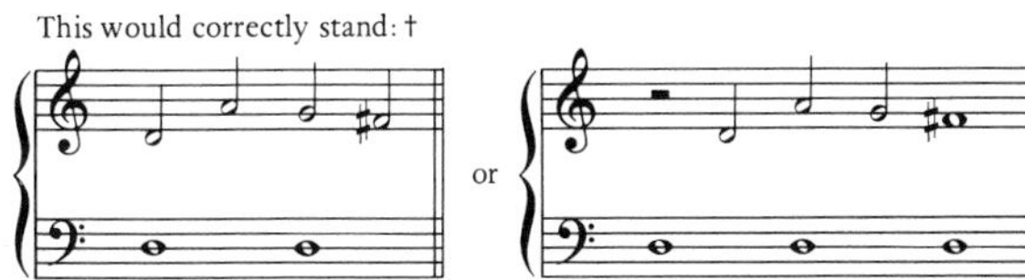
or

This would correctly stand: †

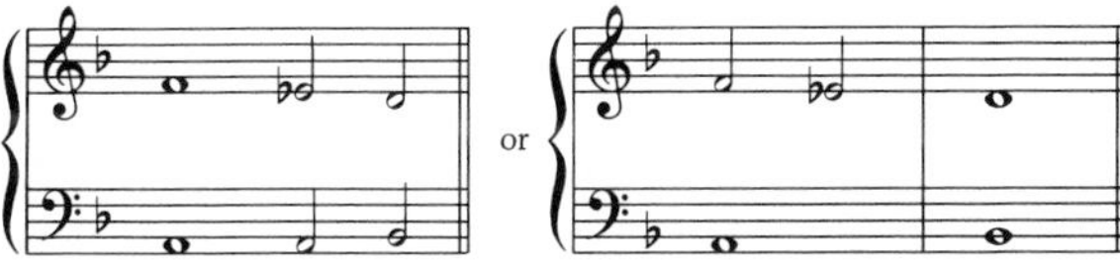
or

* Actually, both of these "correct" versions still feature a dissonance in the first half of the measure, and so leave something to be desired. Cf. the next two progressions and the following footnote.

† Only the second of these "correct" versions actually eliminates the dissonance in the first half of the measure. Bernhard is, typically, peeling off successive layers of figuration in these two versions.

Chapter 41

Of Heterolepsis

1. *Heterolepsis* is the seizure of a second voice, and is of two kinds.

2. First, when I leap or step into a dissonance after a consonance, if this* could have been done in *transitus* by another voice.

3. Example of *heterolepsis* of the second in *transitus*. [Example 237]

EXAMPLE 237

The other voices would stand thus:‡

4. Example of *heterolepsis* of the seventh in *transitus*. [Example 239]

EXAMPLE 239

The other voices would stand thus:§

Chapter XX

Of Heterolepsis

1. *Heterolepsis* means taking hold of another voice, and occurs, first, if I move from a consonance [into a dissonance], if this* could have been done in *transitus* by another voice, as:† [Example 238].

EXAMPLE 238

* Moving to the dissonance.

† The middle system of the example shows both of the voices implied in the top line: the "original" voice and the voice whose domain is suddenly taken over.

‡ That is, the B is understood to come from either the A or the C.

§ I give this progression exactly as it appears in M-B.

5. Example of *heterolepsis* of the fourth in *transitus*. [Example 240]

EXAMPLE 240

The other voices would stand thus:*

6. Second, when the lower voice is syncopated and the one above, having grasped a fourth, does not rise a second, but rather falls a third. [Example 241]

EXAMPLE 241

It should be thus:

7. N.B. The kinds of *syncopatio catachrestica* illustrated in chapter 28, paragraph 4, could also be regarded as *heterolepsis* arising from *syncopation*, especially when these examples are combined with *multiplication*.†

2. Second, such a seizure occurs in connection with a syncopated fourth, when the lowest voice is resolved but the upper one falls a third instead of climbing a second. [Example 242]

EXAMPLE 242

* In M-B., G appears instead of A in the first chord of the second measure, an obvious misprint. The material in the first measure also bears strikingly little relationship to the ornamented version, but I give it as found in M-B.

† The lower voice in the second progression is written a third higher in M-B. Comparison with the related progression in ch. 28, para. 4 clearly shows this to be an error.

[Example 243] The last two are examples of

EXAMPLE 243

syncopated *heterolepsis* with the upper voice [driving], just as the first was an example of syncopated *heterolepsis* with the lower voice driving.*

Chapter 42

Of the Augmented Second [and the Diminished Seventh]

1. The augmented second is an interval which is not quite a minor third,[55] and which stands in the following degrees: [Example 244].

EXAMPLE 244

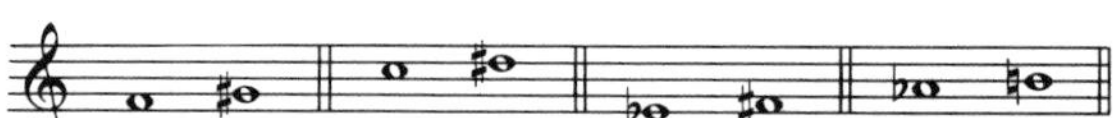

2. Examples of how it is used. [Example 245]

EXAMPLE 245

* "Dass also die letzteren beyden Exempel *Heterolepseos syncopatae parte superiore* [*ligata*] wären, wie das erste *Heterolepseos syncopatae inferiore parte ligata.*" By the "last two" examples Bernhard means the two progressions given in the present paragraph; by the "first," the one given in ch. 41, para. 6 above.

EXAMPLE 245 (*continued*)

3. The diminished seventh is a minor sixth with a major semitone added,[55] and stands in these degrees: [Example 246].

EXAMPLE 246

4. Example. [Example 247]

EXAMPLE 247

Chapter 43

Concerning Emulation

1. Until now we have talked about the use of consonances, both when these are encountered by themselves in *stylus aequalis*, and also when they are encountered in *stylus inaequalis* next to dissonances; and about the various figures which have been invented to mitigate dissonances* in *stylus gravis* as well as *luxurians*, and in the two subdivisions of the latter, namely, *stylus communis* and *theatralis*.

2. If an industrious student of composition should find something else, beyond the above-mentioned, in the works of good composers, this will either be easily reducible to the figures described above, or it will be left to his judgment whether he should imitate it or not.

3. For the emulation of the most distinguished composers is no less

* "zur *Temperirung* der *Dissonantzen*."

profitable—indeed necessary—in this profession than in any other art, as a part of one's practice, without which all precepts are useless.

4. But since an aspiring composer might easily err in his choice of models, and seeing that it is impossible and, beyond that, fruitless [to set] them all down in score,* he who would heed my counsel should avail himself of the following eminent people.† Nevertheless, I do not want thereby to take anything away from the reputation merited by other people who are not mentioned here, but on the contrary am well aware that many other excellent composers are more worthy of being emulated. But I have desired to propose these few, whose works are easily accessible, without doing prejudice to others. Beyond that, I leave it to the opportunity of each person, what composers he can set down in score, or wishes to.

5. In *stylus gravis*, the man from Praeneste,‡ whom the Italians call Palestrina after the present name of his birthplace, is especially to be imitated, in my judgment. After him SORIANO,[56] his pupil, and Morales, whose Magnificats are particularly esteemed. Among earlier composers, Adrian Willaert; Josquin; and Gombert, Kapellmeister for Charles V; yet since the text is somewhat more difficult to apply in the works of these men,[57] they might lead astray more than aright. Among more recent composers, especially in pieces sung by more than one chorus, the two Gabrielis, PRIOLI, Orazio Benevoli, Lorenzo RATTI, etc., are worthy of emulation.

6. In *stylus luxurians communis* we have the following: Monteverdi, who indeed invented and elevated this style (praise is not denied others who attempted something similar before him); his successor, ROVETTA; Cavalli; BERTALI; Stefano FABRI; Francesco PORTA; TURINI; RIGATTI; CASSATI; Carissimi; Vincenzo ALBRICI; Marco SCACCHI; BONTEMPI; PERANDA; etc.; and among the Germans, Herr Schütz; Caspar KERLL; Herr FÖRSTER; and a few more.

7. In *stylus [luxurians] theatralis*, the following have shown themselves to great advantage: Monteverdi, Rovetta, Cavalli, Carissimi, TENAGLIA, Vincenzo Albrici, Bontempi, Luigi (Rossi); and contemporary Roman

* "alle *in Partitura* [zu setzen]." See note 40.

† See note 56 for brief biographies (in alphabetical order) of those composers listed in paras. 5, 6, and 7, whose names are printed in small capitals.

‡ "*Praenestinus.*"

musicians would well-nigh take the prize from the others. We Germans up to now have been sorely lacking in charming poems such as are suitable for this genre. Therefore I, in my humble station, also have tried my hand at it, in prose and in verse.[58]

Chapter 44

Of the Musical Modes in General

1. Above, in chapter 2, paragraph 7, it was mentioned that every composition should conform to one of the twelve modes.

2. "Mode," called "tone" by most and "trope" by a few, refers in this context (for in other places these words [occasionally] mean something else)[59] to a certain form and mold of harmony,* viewed in one of the seven species of octave, after this has been divided through the fifth or fourth.†

3. Thus it is the octave and the sounds comprehended therein which form the basis of a mode; and such an octave, with its member sounds, is called *ambitus* by the *musici.*

4. This *ambitus* is of two kinds. Either it may span the octave exactly; or it may not reach an octave, or indeed overstep it. From the first kind arise the *proper tones*,[60] from the second the *improper*, called *deficient* and *superfluous*, respectively. For example:

5. A mode said to be proper in this sense is illustrated in these hymns:

Nun lob, mein' Seel', den Herren
Vom Himmel hoch da komm' ich her
O Herre Gott, dein göttlich Wort
Helft mir Gott's Güte preisen

6. A mode said to be improper and indeed defective‡ appears in the following hymns:

Nun komm, der Heiden Heiland
Allein Gott in der Höh' sei Ehr'

* "eine gewisse *Forme* und Beschaffenheit einer *Harmonie*."

† What is meant here is made clear in ch. 45, para. 2.

‡ "*defectivus*." Clearly the same as "deficient" (*deficiens*).

Jesus Christus unser Heiland, der den Tod überwand
Erstanden ist der heilige Christ
Komm, Gott Schöpfer, heiliger Geist
Der Du bist Drei in Einigkeit
Nun lasst uns Gott dem Herren

7. A superfluous mode occurs when the octave is overstepped—that is, when a second or even a third is found either above or below the same, as in the following hymns:

Vater unser im Himmelreich
Wir glauben all' an einen Gott
Gelobet seist Du, Jesu Christ
Der Tag, der ist so freudenreich
Christus der uns selig macht
Christ ist erstanden
Christ lag in Todesbanden
Nun freut euch, Gottes Kinder all'
Komm, heiliger Geist

8. To the superfluous modes belong also the *mixed modes*, which occur when a tenor not only overshoots the octave by a second or third,[61] but indeed goes as far as a fourth beneath it, or as far as a fifth above it. I indeed do not remember encountering this in our hymns;[62] in figural music, however, it does occur occasionally. They are called mixed because the authentic and plagal modes, which will be defined shortly, may both be perceived therein.

9. As far as the sounds comprehended in the octave are concerned, they are either *principal* or *subordinate*.* The principal sounds are the fourths and fifths, as well as the semitones, whose differing location forms the basis of distinction between the modes. The remaining sounds are subordinate and demand no special consideration.

10. The fifth has as its basis the finalis,† its lower limit. Its other limit lies above.

* "*dominantes* oder *servientes*."

† "*clavem finalem*."

11. There are four species of fifth, ut-sol, re-la, mi-mi, and fa-fa, as is clear from the location of the semitones.

12. The fourth has as its basis either the upper or lower limit of the fifth.

13. And has three species, ut-fa, re-sol, and mi-la, as again is clear from the location of the semitones.

14. From the different ways of joining fourths and fifths arises the distinction between authentic and plagal modes.

15. A mode is *authentic* if the fourth is found above the upper limit of the fifth. [Example 248]

EXAMPLE 248

16. A mode is *plagal* if the fourth is found below the lower limit of the fifth. [Example 249]

EXAMPLE 249

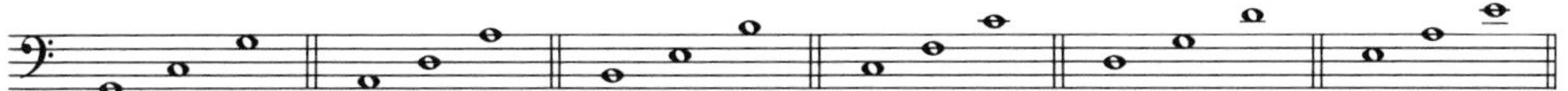

17. Since the semitones are found to be different in any one mode than in all the others, they can best be shown during our demonstration of individual modes.

Chapter 45

*Of the Number and Ordering of the Musical Modes and of Their Interrelations**

1. The *musici* have not always been of the same mind regarding the number of modes. But it is sufficient to establish that there are not more than twelve of them, and also not less.

2. Now there are only as many modes as there are ways that the octave can be divided into different kinds of fifths and fourths; there are that many modes—no more and no less—as is to be seen from the definition of the modes. But such a thing can happen in twelve ways. Ergo, as: [Example 250].

* "und von ihren Affectionibus." See para. 5 of this chapter.

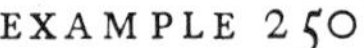

EXAMPLE 250

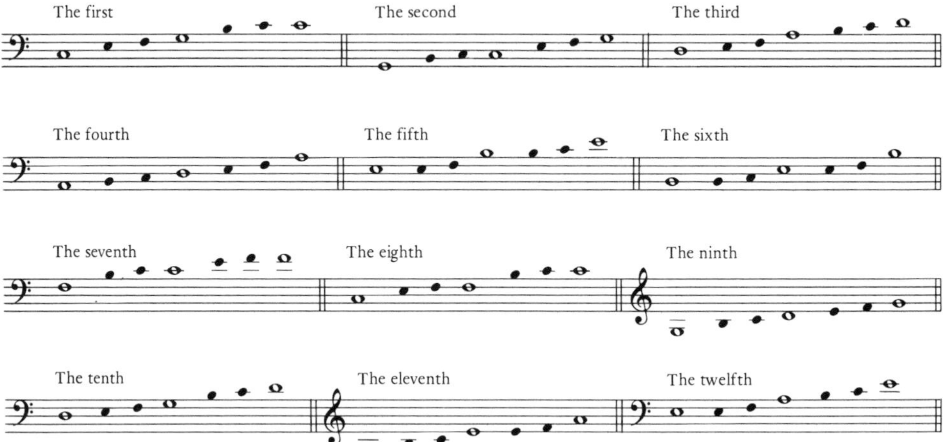

The following are spurious because of false fourths and fifths: [Example 251].

EXAMPLE 251

N.B. If, however, one should choose to render these false fourths and fifths perfect by means of a sharp, then the resultant kinds of fifth and fourth, with their semitones, would already have been encountered in another mode, and so no new modes would be created thereby. That is: [Example 252].

EXAMPLE 252

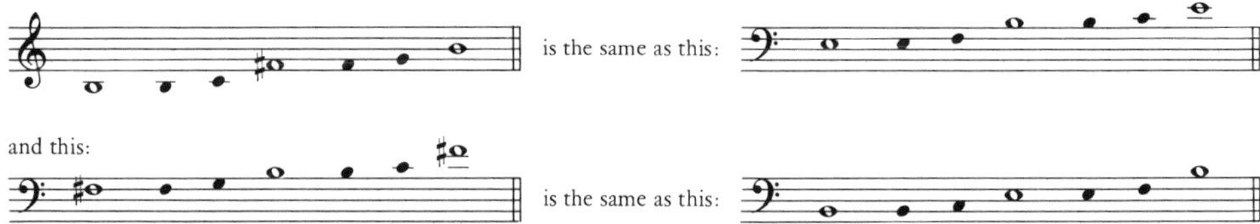

3. The *musici* are also still in disagreement over the ordering of the modes, in that certain of them hold the C-mode to be the first,[63] others the D-mode. The former have the more persuasive arguments, however, which may be seen in their writings. It is not fitting to dispute the matter here.

Nonetheless, over and above the arguments which they draw upon, this one also can be adduced: that the C-mode must be the first since all the others arrange the completion of their closes according to this one,[64] as I have visibly demonstrated to my disciples.[65]

4. For the rest, although I have my own opinion regarding the further ordering of the modes, yet will I save such thoughts for a special treatise,* God willing, and will here abide by the generally accepted ordering.

5. The interrelations of the modes are these: a) *Transposition*; b) *association*; c) *equalization*; d) *extension*; e) *alteration.*

Chapter 46

Of the Authentic First Tone and Its Plagal, the Second

1. The first tone is that which ordinarily ends on C in the bass,[66] whose octave, C–c, is divided by g, and which is composed of the first species of fifth and the first species of fourth.†

2. Examples of this from our hymns are:[67]

Gott der Vater wohn' uns bei
Vom Himmel hoch da komm' ich her
Wie schön leuchtet der Morgenstern

3. Its final close is on C, its principal confinalis on G, its lesser confinalis on E. Irregular closes occur on A and F.[68]

4. This mode is cheerful, and suitable for war, dancing [etc,].

5. The second tone is that which properly ends on C, whose octave, G–g, is divided by c in the tenor,‡ and which also is composed of the first species of fourth and the first species of fifth.

6. Examples from hymns are:

Nun lob, mein' Seel', den Herren
Es spricht der Unweisen Mund wohl
O Herre Gott, dein göttlich Wort

Yet these and most other examples are transposed.[69]

* Apparently never realized.

† Species of fifth are enumerated in the order given in ch. 44, para. 11; species of fourth are enumerated in the order given in ch. 44, para. 13.

‡ See also ch. 44, para. 8, and note 61.

7. Its closes are the same as those of the first tone.

8. This mode is somewhat more languid and sorrowful than the preceding, but nevertheless also cheerful and suitable for many things.

Chapter 47

Of the Authentic Third Tone and Its Plagal, the Fourth

1. The third tone is that whose bass properly ends on D, whose octave, D–d, is divided in the tenor by a, and which is composed of the second species of fourth and the second species of fifth.

2. Examples of this are:

Es wird schier der letzte Tag kommen
Jesus Christus unser Heiland, der von uns etc.
Wir glauben all' an einen Gott
Christ lag in Todesbanden
Ich heb' meine Augen sehnlich auf

3. Its regular closes are on D, f, and a, its irregular closes on G and b♭.

4. This mode is indeed closely related to the eleventh, since its b♮ is often changed to b♭ above the fifth, which is good to note.

5. Its nature is indifferent, gay, and sorrowful, hence convenient for meditation.

6. Its plagal is that whose bass properly ends on D, and whose octave, A–a, is divided in the tenor by d.

7. Examples of it are:[70]

Helft mir Gott's Güte preisen
Wenn mein Stündlein vorhanden ist

8. Its closes are the same as those of the preceding tone.

9. Its nature is doleful and submissive, hence good to employ for grief and misery.

Chapter 48

Of the Authentic Fifth Tone and Its Plagal, the Sixth

1. The fifth tone is that whose bass ordinarily ends on E, whose octave, E–e, is divided in the tenor by b♮, and which is composed of the third species of fifth and the third species of fourth.

2. Examples are:

Aus tiefer Not schrei' ich zu Dir
Mensch, willt du leben seliglich
Mag ich Unglück nicht widerstahen
Erbarm' dich mein, o Herre Gott
Christus der uns selig macht

3. Its regular closes are E, G, and B♮, its irregular closes a and c.

4. This one also has great affinity with the above-mentioned eleventh, particularly when the close on a is often heard therein, due to the fact that the close on b♮ is not fully acceptable, or else demands substantial alterations in the semitones.

5. It is melancholy and inclined toward sad things.

6. Its plagal is that whose bass also properly ends on E, and whose octave, B♮–b♮, is divided in the tenor by e.

7. Its closes are the same as those of the preceding.

8. And its sounds* are indeed also compatible with doleful words.

9. It is indeed very closely connected with the twelfth mode, just as its authentic counterpart is associated with the eleventh, so that these can hardly be distinguished from one another save at the end. They both† prefer those closes which fall a fourth or climb a fifth, for all the others would falsify the tone.

Chapter 49

Of the Authentic Seventh Tone and Its Plagal, the Eighth

1. The seventh tone is that whose bass properly ends on F, whose tenor

* "seine *Harmonie*."

† Seemingly this last statement refers to the fifth and sixth modes, rather than to the sixth and twelfth modes.

divides the octave F–f at c, and which is composed of the fourth species of fifth and the first species of fourth.

2. Examples are not easy to find among our hymns, but may indeed be found among the old Gregorian hymns and responsories, such as the hymn *Spoliatis Aegyptis*,[71] which the Roman Church sings on the feast day of St. Francis.

3. Its regular closes are F, c, and a. Its irregular ones are on G and d.

4. It is hardly used at all by composers today, due to the fourth, F–b♮, which frequently occurs therein. When this is altered through a flat, the mode transforms into the first.

5. There is little to say regarding its nature, although some maintain that it is modest and cheerful.

6. Its plagal, the eighth mode, is that whose bass likewise ends on F, and whose octave, C–c, is divided in the tenor by F.

7. It is found just as rarely among our hymns as its authentic counterpart, although the Roman Church uses it very often in its Gregorian chant.

8. Its closes are the same as those of the preceding.

9. It is said to be neither too cheerful nor too sweet, and therefore, in the opinion of men of former times, suited to devotion. That remains to be seen.

Chapter 50

Of the Authentic Ninth Tone and Its Plagal, the Tenth

1. The ninth mode is that whose bass properly ends on G, whose octave, G–g, is divided in the tenor by d, and which is composed of the first species of fifth and the second species of fourth.

2. Examples of this tone, so easy to recognize, need not be cited. Let this also be said concerning the following one.

3. Its regular closes are G, b♮, and d; b♮ rarely, however. The irregular ones are c, a, and e.

4. Its nature is that it is rather joyous, but at the same time dignified.

5. The tenth mode, plagal of the foregoing, is that whose bass likewise ends on G, and whose octave, D–d, is divided in the tenor by g.*

* In M-B., "a" instead of "g"—surely a misprint.

6. Its closes are identical with the preceding ones.

7. This mode is very gracious and sweet; it fills the hearts of listeners with a particular joy because of the high fifth g–d, and with pleasure because of the low fourth d–g. Therefore texts with delightful, yet dignified subjects are suited to this tone; and joyful prayers in particular. Hence this mode is indeed much in use.

Chapter 51

Of the Authentic Eleventh Tone and Its Plagal, the Twelfth

1. The eleventh mode is that whose bass properly ends on A, whose octave, A–a, is divided in the tenor by e, and which is composed of the second species of fifth and the third species of fourth.

2. Its final close is on A. Its principal confinalis is E. Its lesser confinalis is C. Uncommon closes occur on D and G.*

3. Above, in connection with the third tone, we have already remarked that the latter tone has a great affinity to this one, which is to be understood not only from their step progressions and melodic turns, but also from the nature of both of them.

4. The twelfth mode is that whose bass properly ends on A, and whose octave, E–e, is divided in the tenor by a.

5. Its nature is not very different from that of the fourth and sixth [modes], since its harmonic and melodic make-up† is not very different.

6. Its closes are the same as those of the preceding.

7. I have called the closes arising from the mediation of tones "principal confinales,"[72] seeing that it is not customary to give a piece in two or three sections a close on the finalis‡ at the end of every section, but also at times one on the confinalis. Thus, in pieces with two sections, the first section should close on the confinalis, but the second on the finalis. In pieces with three sections, the first and the last have a close on the finalis, but the middle one a close on the confinalis. Hence, in a Mass in the first tone, the *Kyrie* should end in C, the *Christe* in G, the *Kyrie* in C. Similarly, the *Et in terra* in G, the *Qui tollis* in C.

* "die frembden sind D, G." Bernhard does not use the designation "frembden" anywhere else.

† "ihre *Harmonie* und *Modulation*."

‡ "*clausulam finalem*."

Chapter 52

Of the Transposition of Modes

1. Since the tones are not all constituted in such a way that they can lie in the tenor comfortably, the *musici* have remedied this inconvenience through the transposition of their semitones, fourths, and fifths, and have increased their charm quite a bit.

2. Such a transposition is either common or uncommon.

3. The common kind is effected through a transformation of *cantus durus* into *cantus mollis*, by means of a lift of a fourth or a drop of a fifth, as: [Example 253].

EXAMPLE 253

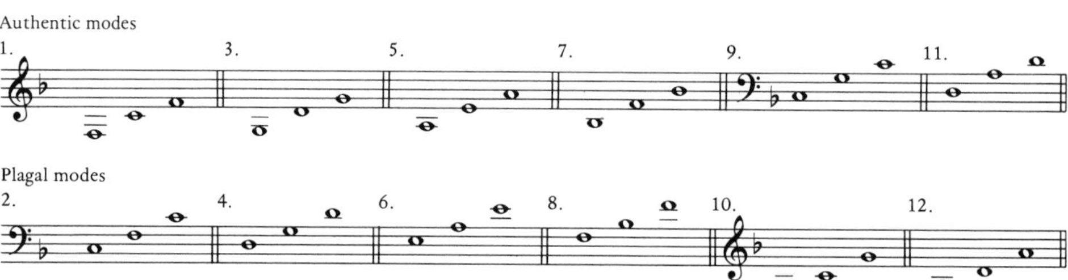

4. The rarer kind is effected by lifting *cantus durus* a second or a third into sharp keys, or by dropping it a second into a flat key,* or however else one desires. Only this should be remembered: that the fourths and fifths must keep semitones at the same distances as before. One example will suffice for all: [Example 254].

EXAMPLE 254

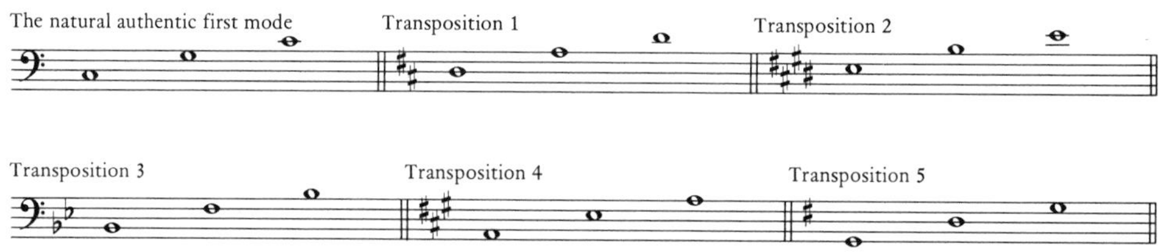

* "Die seltenere geschieht durch eine Erhebung des *Duri* in *durum per Secundam et Tertiam Superiorem* oder in *mollem per Secundam inferiorem*."

Chapter 53

*Of the Association of Modes**

1. From the discussion up to now, it can be seen, among many other things, that the tenor is actually the voice upon which one should chiefly base one's decision regarding the tone of a composition. Now it is necessary to tell how the remaining voices should be judged or arranged.

2. Seeing that the remaining voices, especially alto and bass, cannot be of quite the same mode as the tenor, because of the height or depth of the tone and its singability or awkwardness, therefore it has been necessary to assist them through association.

3. The *association of modes* is the union of an authentic mode with its plagal, or of a plagal mode with its authentic counterpart, maintained in two, three, or more voices over against one another.

4. Association differs from the mixing of modes, mentioned above in chapter 44, paragraph 8, in that mixing occurs within the tenor or some other single voice, but association occurs in more than one.

5. Since the soprano is an octave away from the tenor, both of these almost always have the same tone.

6. On the other hand, since the alto and bass differ from the tenor by a fourth or a fifth, but have the distance of an octave between each other, these generally are in a different tone than the tenor, but themselves are both in the same tone, so that:

7. If the tenor is in the first tone, it shares this with the soprano; the bass, however, is in the second tone, and the alto also. If, on the other hand, the tenor is in the second tone, then the soprano agrees with it, while the other two are in the first tone.

8. Association is the best way to bring fugues† into all the voices in accordance with the tone, especially if the subjects do not overstep a fourth or fifth, and have a comfortable skip.[73]

9. To this end the fourth is transformed into a fifth; the fifth, however, into a fourth. Whenever possible, semitones are preserved, as well as those notes which are principal sounds,‡ as we can see from the following examples, which cover all the tones.

* "Von der Consociation derer Modorum."

† See note 7 for the meaning of "fugue" in Bernhard; also see ch. 57.

‡ "*Soni dominantes.*" See ch. 44, para. 9, and its footnote.

10. Examples of the first tone.[74] [Example 255]

EXAMPLE 255

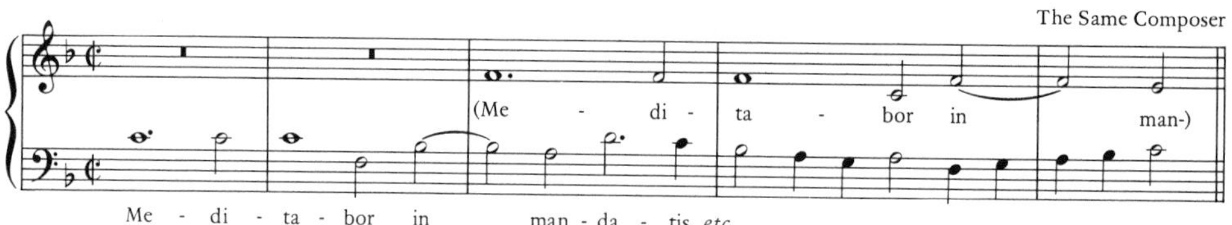

11. Examples of the second tone. [Example 256]

EXAMPLE 256

EXAMPLE 256 (*continued*)

The Same Composer

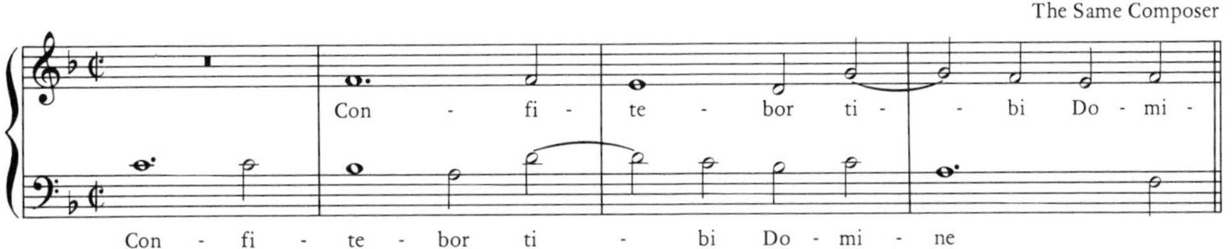
Con - fi - te - bor ti - - bi Do - mi -
Con - fi - te - bor ti - bi Do - mi - ne

[C. B.]

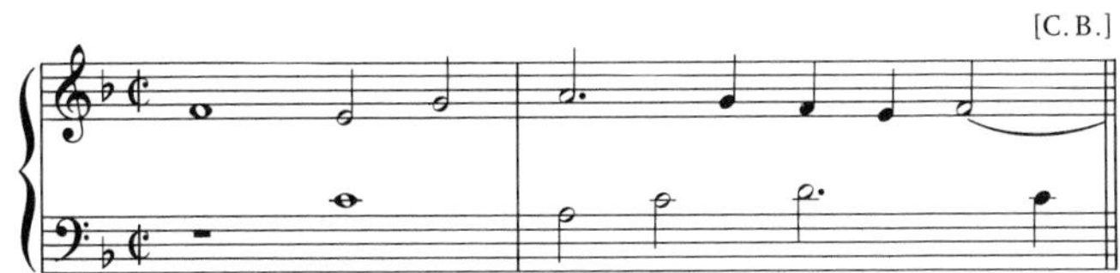

12. Examples of the third tone.[75] [Example 257]

EXAMPLE 257

Palestrina

Stel - la quam vi - de - rant
Stel - la quam vi - de - rant

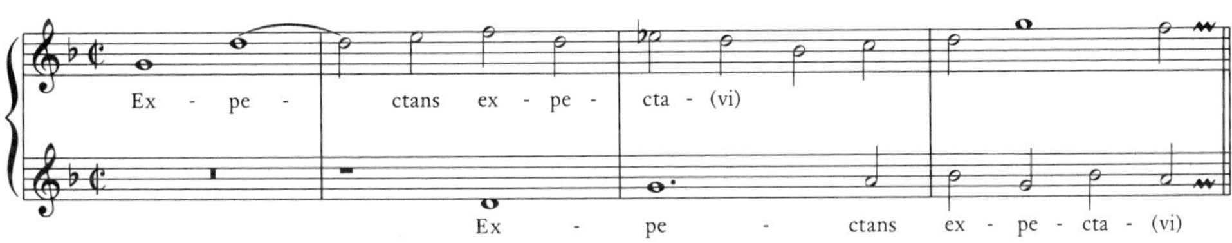
Ex - pe - ctans ex - pe - cta - (vi)
Ex - pe - ctans ex - pe - cta - (vi)

[C. B.]

EXAMPLE 257 (*continued*)

13. Examples of the fourth tone. [Example 258]

EXAMPLE 258

14. Examples of the fifth tone, which undergoes fugue in almost the same way as the eleventh tone. [Example 259]

EXAMPLE 259

15. Examples of the sixth tone, which best undergoes fugue in a way similar to that of the twelfth. [Example 260]

EXAMPLE 260

16. Examples of the seventh and eighth tones are hardly to be found. Yet one might wish to look at these: Seventh tone. [Example 261]

EXAMPLE 261

Eighth tone. [Example 262]

EXAMPLE 262

17. Examples of the ninth and tenth tones. The ninth tone. [Example 263]

EXAMPLE 263

Tenth tone. [Example 264]

EXAMPLE 264

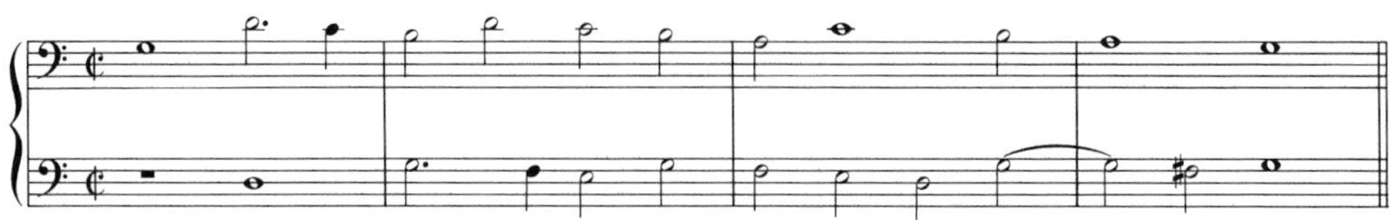

18. Examples of the eleventh tone.* [Example 265]

EXAMPLE 265

19. Examples of the twelfth tone.† [Example 266]

EXAMPLE 266

* In M-B., the second passage of this example also appears (in exactly the same form) in the following paragraph, as an illustration of the twelfth mode. Surely Bernhard does not regard this passage as belonging to two different modes simultaneously, but it is difficult to ascertain which mode is in fact the correct one. Hence I give it in both paragraphs.

† See the preceding paragraph and the preceding footnote.

EXAMPLE 266 (*continued*)

20. At the beginning,* one should not depart too readily from applying the figures in this way.[76] On the other hand, rules are not so exactly observed in the middle, and the following procedure is more often employed there.

Chapter 54

Of the Equalization of Modes

1. I call it the *equalization of a mode*† when the second voice of a fugue, to preserve a fourth, fifth, sixth, or octave, does not proceed in the most closely related mode,‡ but rather in such a one§ as is similar to the first only by virtue of its fourth or fifth.

2. Yet this type of fugue is used more often in stepwise motion than in leaping, more often in the middle than at the beginning.

3. As can be gathered from its description, fourths remain fourths in restatements, and fifths fifths; and therein is it actually distinguished from the previous kind, namely association.

4. In equalization, the first and second tones undergo fugue in such a way that a fourth or a fifth is kept both in the leading and in the following voice: First tone.|| [Example 267]

EXAMPLE 267

* Of a composition.

† "*Aequationem Modi.*"

‡ That is to say, the plagal or authentic counterpart of the mode of the first voice.

§ "in einem solchen *Tenore.*" See note 61.

|| In M-B., the staff of the lower voice is indeed left blank in bars three and four of the first passage.

EXAMPLE 267 (*continued*)

Second tone. [Example 268]

EXAMPLE 268

5. It is done in the same way in the remaining tones, such as the third and fourth. Third tone. [Example 269]

EXAMPLE 269

Fourth tone.* [Example 270]

* In M-B., the lower voice has three C♮'s in the third measure of the first passage. While I indeed give it this way, it nonetheless seems likely that at least the last C should have a sharp before it, and very possibly the second one also.

EXAMPLE 270

6. Fifth tone. [Example 271]

EXAMPLE 271

Sixth tone. [Example 272]

EXAMPLE 272

7. As the seventh and eighth tones are not very common, examples that are appropriate here are also not readily to be found. Yet these could pass for examples: Seventh tone. [Example 273]

EXAMPLE 273

Eighth tone. [Example 274]

EXAMPLE 274

8. The ninth and tenth tones are often encountered as, for instance, in the works of Palestrina:* Ninth tone. [Example 275]

EXAMPLE 275

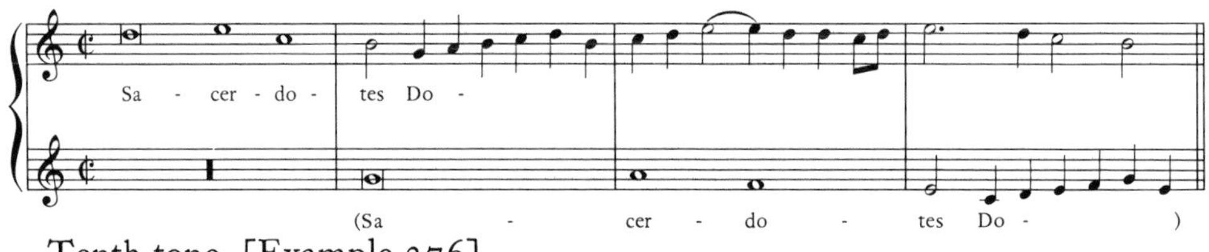

Tenth tone. [Example 276]

* In M-B., the two passages illustrating the tenth mode are printed before the two illustrating the ninth. Identifications of mode and composer in Examples 275 and 276 are given as in M-B.; however, both passages illustrating the ninth mode are by Palestrina.

EXAMPLE 276

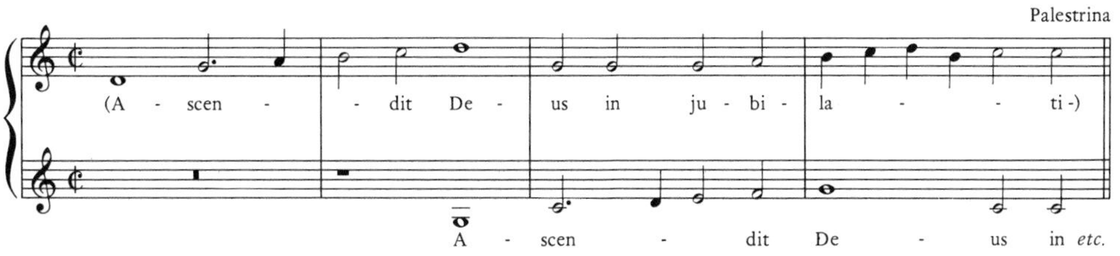

9. Examples of the eleventh and twelfth tones.* Eleventh tone. [Example 277]

EXAMPLE 277

* In M-B., none of the following passages is associated with the twelfth mode. The B♮ in the first passage and the B♭ in the third passage are mine. The last passage in this group (on p. 144) is also by Palestrina. The words appearing before it point to the fact that the two given voices are the lowest voices in this piece, so that they assume the roles of tenor and bass, respectively, even though their ranges are those of an alto and a tenor.

EXAMPLE 277 (*continued*)

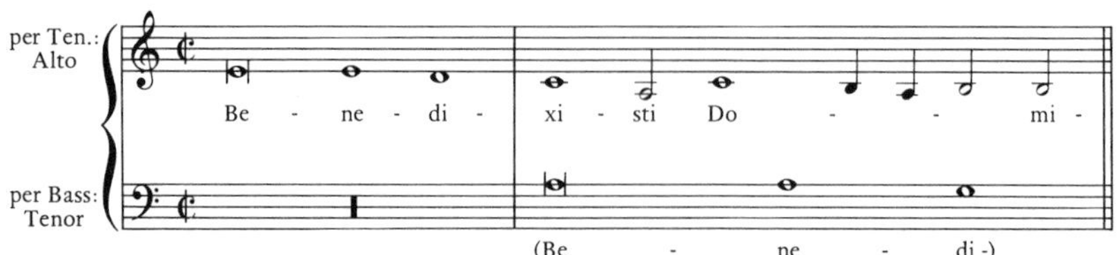

10. All these examples illustrate not only that a fifth is answered by a fifth, and a fourth by a fourth, but also that the fifth ut–sol is generally answered by ut–sol, and re–la by re–la, the fourth ut–fa, by ut–fa, re–sol by re–sol, and mi–la by mi–la.

Chapter 55

Of the Extension of Modes

1. The *extension of a mode* is the stretching out of a composition, after its tone has been sufficiently established, over all the sounds of the octave, especially the principal ones.[77]

2. And it is left to the judgment and opportunity of the composer, how soon he should employ extension, and for how long he should remain outside the proper framework of the mode by means of it.

3. To cite examples of extension in all the modes would be too wearisome, and moreover fruitless. Therefore we will content ourselves with one, and leave the rest to the diligence and talent of our pupils. We take it from the motet *Ad te levavi animam meam* by Palestrina,* in which the fourth mode is formed in the following way at the beginning. [Example 278].

EXAMPLE 278

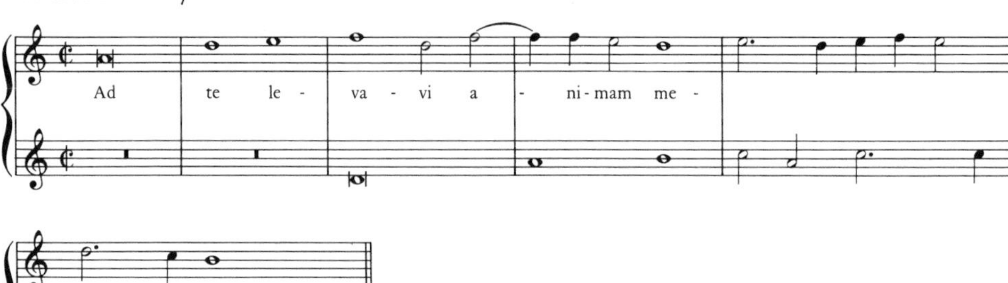

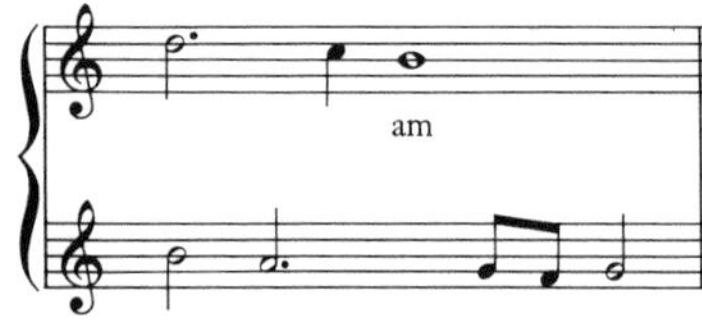

* This motet is from the Offertories a 5.

4. The first extension takes place through a and e, as follows:* [Example 279].

EXAMPLE 279

5. The second is also through a and e. [Example 280]

EXAMPLE 280

6. The third is through d and a, likewise d and g, likewise a and e.[78] [Example 281] And the subject is employed in still other ways.

EXAMPLE 281

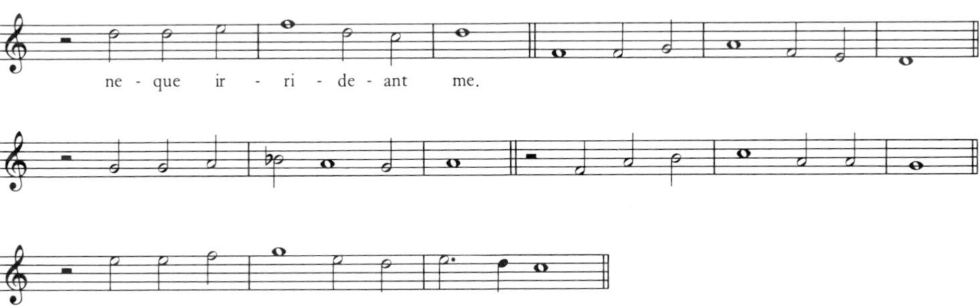

* The example is given exactly as in M-B., except that the third note of the lowest voice is B♮ there, not B♭.

7. The fourth is through c and g. [Example 282]

EXAMPLE 282

8. The fifth features a chordal entrance—with an imitation, however, on F.[79] *Etenim*, etc.* We need not write it down here.

9. The sixth, and last, is through e and a, likewise through other degrees, as can be perceived below. [Example 283]

EXAMPLE 283

10. From this it can be seen that all degrees and sounds in this tone are introduced through subjects. An industrious score-lover will also find this in other works, and know how to imitate it.

Chapter 56

Of the Alteration of Modes

1. *Alteration of mode* takes place when a piece begins in one tone, but ends in another.

2. Such alterations occur quite often in the fifth and sixth tones, which

* The text at this point reads "Etenim universi qui te exspectant."

transform at the end into the eleventh; also, in the eleventh and twelfth, inasmuch as both end in the fifth tone quite frequently.

3. Seldom does a piece begin in the fourth mode and end in the eleventh.

4. Even less frequently does the eighth (which, like its authentic counterpart, is rare in any case) change into the first.[80]

5. Occasionally the first changes into the tenth.

6. The second does not often change into the ninth.

7. Similarly for the ninth to change into the second.

8. And the tenth into the first.

9. We have taken examples of this from Palestrina's Offertories a 5. This seems to be in the first tone, but ends in G, the tenth tone:* [Example 284].

EXAMPLE 284

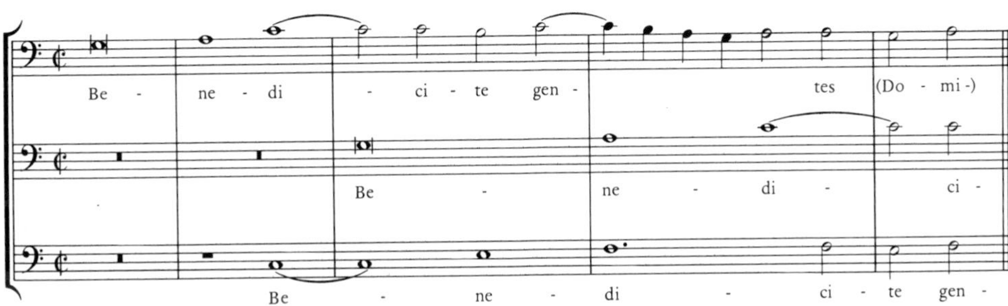

This seems to be in the second tone, but ends in G, the ninth tone: [Example 285].

EXAMPLE 285

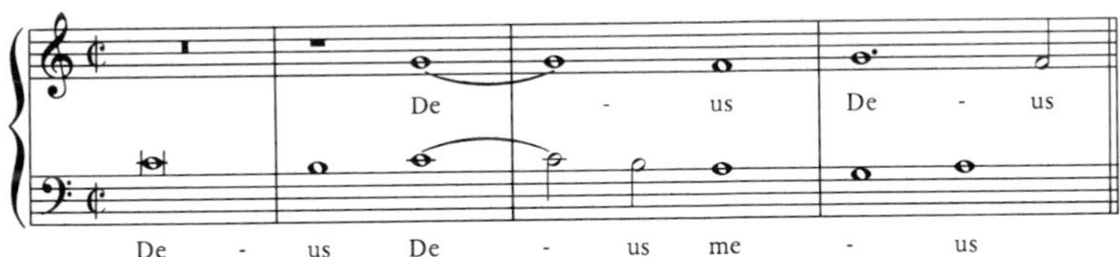

All these seem to be initially in the second tone; at the end, however, they are in the ninth mode: [Example 286].

* Bernhard's comments pertaining to individual examples in this series appear sometimes before these examples, sometimes after, sometimes partly before and partly after. Here comments will consistently be placed before the examples to which they apply.

EXAMPLE 286

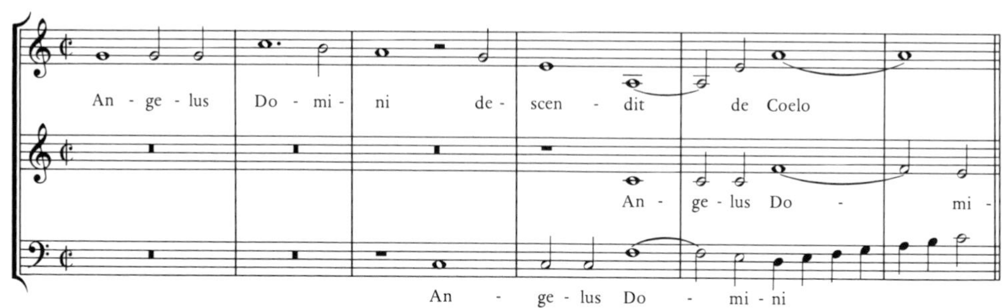

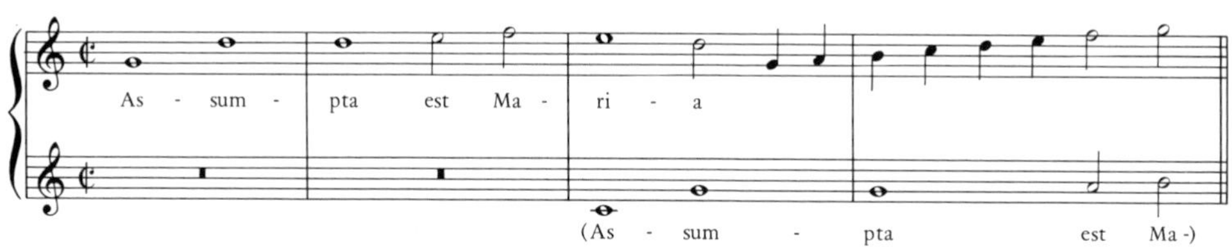

On the other hand, the following seem at first to be in the fourth mode: yet all end in A, the eleventh mode. [Example 287]

EXAMPLE 287

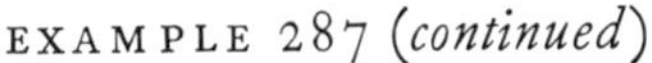
EXAMPLE 287 (*continued*)

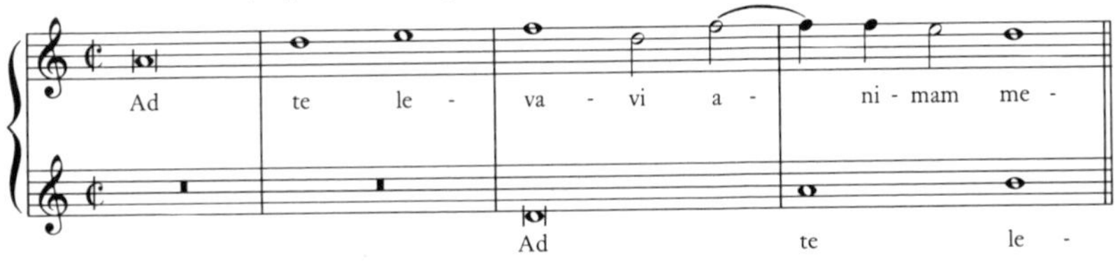
Ad te le - va - vi a - ni - mam me -
Ad te le -

Re - cor - da - re me - i Do -
Re - cor - da -

Similarly, the following is at first in the eighth mode—as this extract shows—yet closes in F, the first tone. [Example 288]

EXAMPLE 288

Be - ne - di - ctus es Do - mi - ne
Be - ne - di - ctus es Do -

In like manner, the following start as if they were in the ninth tone, but end in D, the fourth tone.* [Example 289]

EXAMPLE 289

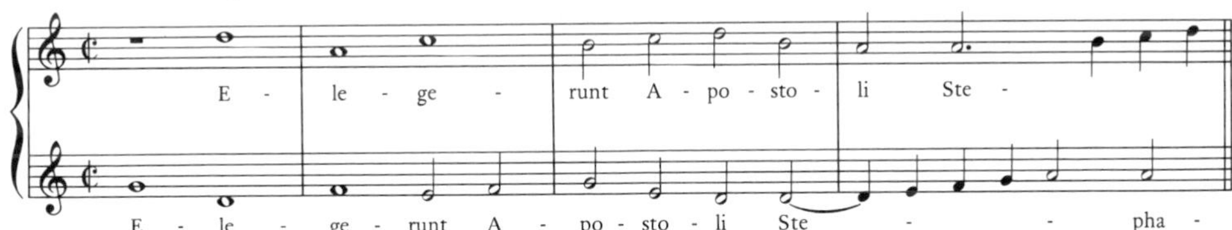
E - le - ge - runt A - po - sto - li Ste -
E - le - ge - runt A - po - sto - li Ste - - pha -

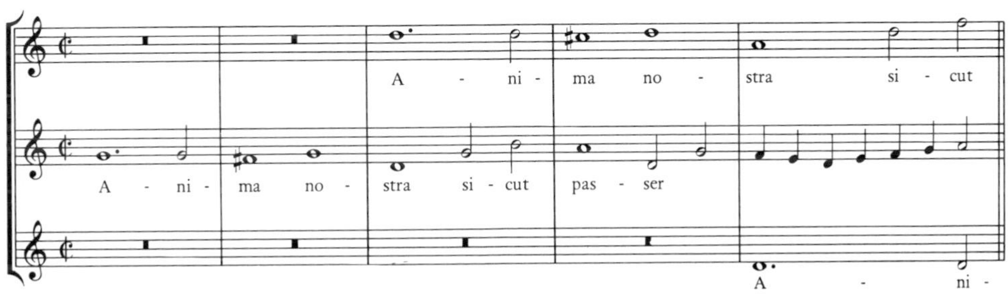
A - ni - ma no - stra si - cut
A - ni - ma no - stra si - cut pas - ser
A - ni -

* In M-B., "D *Secundi Toni*"—clearly an error. The fifth note of the lower voice in the third excerpt is indeed a B♮ in M-B., as in the Palestrina complete edition; thus we give it this way, though we consider it likely that B♭ would be substituted for it in performance.

EXAMPLE 289 (*continued*)

Furthermore, these two seem to incline toward the tenth tone, yet end in the first tone. [Example 290]*

EXAMPLE 290

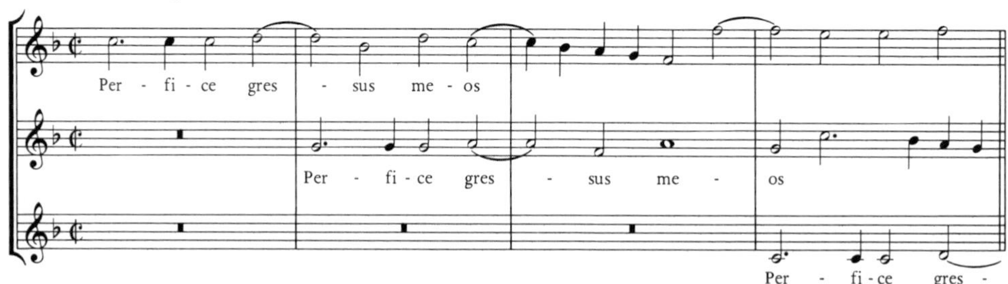

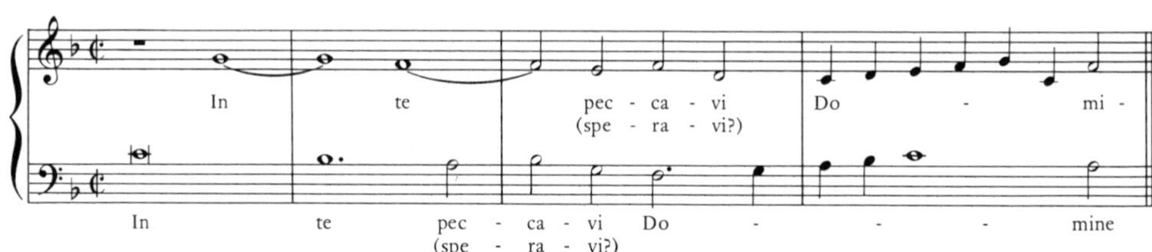

This one, however, seems to incline toward the eleventh tone, yet ends in E, the fifth tone. [Example 291]

EXAMPLE 291

In the same way, the following initially tend toward the twelfth tone, but close in the fifth. [Example 292]

* The material in parentheses is an editorial comment on the part of M-B.

EXAMPLE 292

10. From these it can also be seen that equalization and alteration merge from time to time.

Chapter 57

*Of Fugues in General**

1. Above, in the general rules, chapter 2, paragraph 8, it was mentioned that one should not often repeat the same kind of melodic configuration. But fugues are not prohibited thereby.

* See note 7.

2. The restatement of a melodic configuration through fugues, far from being forbidden, is in fact a valuable asset for a composition.

3. And even if a composition were worked out in accordance with all the rules of counterpoint, the ear would nevertheless judge that it lacked the greatest adornment of all, if there were no fugue to follow therein.

4. But fugue is the restatement of a melodic configuration introduced in a preceding voice.

5. Such a restatement or fugue is either partial or total.

6. *Fuga partialis* is also called *soluta* by some, and is the restatement of only a part of a melodic configuration that had previously been stated in another voice.

7. Examples of such partial fugues have already been given, and belong either to the association or the equalization of tones. From the description of total fugues, the differences of partial fugues from these will become clear, as will their own characteristics. Thus we see no need to dwell on them any further here.

8. *Fuga totalis* [called *ligata* by some] is the restatement of all of a melodic configuration heard in a foregoing voice.

9. Hence: a) a space of time should elapse,[81] and the other voice or voices then follow in good order; b) this time-space should be indicated by a certain sign; c) the first voice alone should be written out, with the others following it at the proper interval according to the indications given at the beginning and at the time-space; d) the ensuing voice should also have a sign as to when it should stop, unless the fugue be a perpetual one; e) the *canon* (that is, the title and instructions, as it were, written at the top) should convey the time-space, the interval, and the type of motion.*

10. This type of fugue is called "canon" by some—a name which nevertheless does not belong to it, pertaining only to its heading, as indicated above. Hence canon and fugue are distinguished from one another in the same way as the title [of a thing] and the thing itself.

11. In such a heading, the number of voices, the interval, and the time-space are expressed. More is generally not required, unless the fugue be in contrary motion, in augmentation, in diminution, or perpetual. More will be said concerning these.

* "das . . . *Motum,*" i.e., whether the fugue proceeds in similar or contrary motion.

12. The sign for the time-space is ·S· at the beginning, and 𝄐 at the end.

13. *Fuga totalis* is either simple or mixed. If simple, with regard to intervals it may be *aequisona*, *consona*, or *dissona*; with regard to time, *aequalis* or *inaequalis*; with regard to duration, perpetual or nonperpetual.*

14. *Mixta* is a combination of two or more of the kinds mentioned above.[82]

Chapter 58

Of Fugae Aequisonae

1. *Fuga aequisona* is a restatement of a melodic configuration,† in which the ensuing voice follows the preceding one at an equisonant interval.

2. I call the unison (which indeed can only be termed an interval abusively) and the octave, both upper and lower, equisonant intervals.

3. Examples: Canon in two voices at the unison, after a tactus.[83] [Example 293]

EXAMPLE 293

* "*Fuga totalis* ist *Simplex* oder *Mixta, Simplex ratione Intervalli,* ist entweder *aequisona* oder *consona,* oder *dissona, Ratione Temporis* ist sie *aequalis* oder *inaequalis, ratione durationis* ist sie *perpetua* oder *non perpetua.*" In typically careless fashion, Bernhard omits the choice between similar and contrary motion here.

† "eine wiederhohlte *Modulation.*"

EXAMPLE 293 (*continued*)

4. Canon in two voices at the upper octave, after a semibreve. [Example 294]

EXAMPLE 294

5. Canon in two voices at the lower octave, after a tempus.* [Example 295]

EXAMPLE 295

Chapter 59

Of Fugae Consonae and Dissonae

1. *Fuga consona* is a restatement of a melodic configuration, in which the ensuing voice follows the preceding one at a consonant interval.

2. I call the fourth and the fifth, which are very well suited for it, consonant intervals; likewise the third and the sixth, which, however, are not too well suited for it.

3. Canon in two voices at the upper fourth, after a semibreve. [Example 296]

* A tempus always has the value of a breve in these examples.

EXAMPLE 296

Solved:

4. Canon in two voices at the lower fourth, after a semibreve. [Example 297]

EXAMPLE 297

Solved:

EXAMPLE 297 (*continued*)

5. Canon in two voices at the upper fifth, after a tempus. [Example 298]

EXAMPLE 298

6. Canon in two voices at the lower fifth, after a semibreve. [Example 299]

EXAMPLE 299

EXAMPLE 299 (*continued*)

Solved:

7. Those at the third or sixth are not very common; even so, an industrious composer can also try his hand at them, and will find that they are easy to make.

8. *Fuga dissona* is a restatement of a melodic configuration in which the ensuing voice follows the preceding one at a dissonant interval, e.g., a second or a seventh. These are rare, except in contrary motion, which will be discussed forthwith.

Chapter 60

Of Fugae Rectae and Contrariae

1. *Fuga recta* is a restatement of a melodic configuration, in which the ensuing voice follows the preceding one in all steps and leaps, climbing whenever these go up, falling whenever they go down.

2. *Fuga recta* is assumed in the canon at all times when contrary motion is not indicated. Appropriate examples of it have already been given.

3. *Fuga contraria*, which is also called *per arsin et thesin*, is an inversion of the melodic configuration of the preceding voice, so that the ensuing one sings everything downward that had gone upward, and everything upward that had gone downward.

4. One can fashion these at all intervals. We will be satisfied here with only a few, however.

5. Canon at the unison in contrary motion, after a semibreve. [Example 300]

EXAMPLE 300

6. Canon at the upper octave, *per arsin et thesin*, after a semibreve. [Example 301]

EXAMPLE 301

EXAMPLE 301 (*continued*)

7. Canon at the lower fifth in contrary motion, after a semibreve. [Example 302]

EXAMPLE 302

Solved:

8. Canon at the upper seventh in contrary motion, after a semibreve. [Example 303]

EXAMPLE 303

EXAMPLE 303 (*continued*)

9. Canon at the lower second in contrary motion, after a tempus. [Example 304]

EXAMPLE 304

Chapter 61

Of Fugae Aequales and Inaequales

1. *Fuga aequalis* is a restatement of a melodic configuration, in which the

time values* of the preceding voice are at all times preserved in the ensuing one.

2. Examples include all of those already given above, and it is assumed in the canon at all times when neither diminution nor augmentation of note-values is mentioned.

3. *Fuga inaequalis*, on the other hand, is a restatement of a melodic configuration, in which the ensuing voice either augments or diminishes the note-values of the preceding one.

4. These also can occur at all intervals. For the sake of brevity, however, we will present only two.

5. Canon in two voices in augmentation, at the lower fourth, after a semibreve. N.B. In the second voice the notes have double value.[84] [Example 305]†

EXAMPLE 305

(sic!)

Solved:

(sic!) (sic!)

(sic!)

* "der *valor*."

† The example (including "*sic*'s") is given exactly as found in M-B.

6. Canon in two voices in diminution, at the lower fourth, after four tempora. N.B. In the second voice, all notes possess only half as much value as in the first.* [Example 306]

EXAMPLE 306

Chapter 62

Of Nonperpetual and Perpetual Fugues

1. *Nonperpetual fugue* is a restatement of a melodic configuration in which the ensuing voice does not imitate the preceding one all the way to the end, but only up to the sign 𝄐 or ·S·.

2. Examples of it include all those up to now.

3. *Perpetual fugue*, on the other hand, is a restatement of a foregoing melodic configuration, which could be started anew after its end is reached, and repeated, as it were, *ad infinitum*.

* The slight, inconsequential inaccuracy in the solution was found in M-B.

4. These are of two kinds, for either one starts the fugue again, at its conclusion, in the tone previously employed, or in another.

5. An example of the first kind: Perpetual canon in four voices at the unison, after a semibreve. [Example 307]

EXAMPLE 307

6. The second kind is again twofold, for one can, after the end, start either a second higher or a second lower.

7. Perpetual canon in two voices at the lower fifth, after a breve.* [Example 308]

EXAMPLE 308

8. Perpetual canon in two voices at the upper fifth, after a tempus. [Example 309]

EXAMPLE 309

* Accidentals in the solution are given exactly as in M-B.

9. Other kinds of perpetual fugues can also be found, which a diligent composer will as readily discover in his own work as in that of someone else.

Chapter 63

Of Mixed Fugues

1. Mixed fugue is defined in the chapter concerning fugues in general.
2. Example of *fuga inaequalis et contraria*. Canon in two voices at the unison, in contrary motion and augmentation, after a semibreve. [Example 310]

EXAMPLE 310

3. Example of *fuga perpetua et contraria*. Canon in four voices at the unison, upper octave and lower octave. He who will hit upon it is a good contrapuntist.* [Example 311]

* "*Qui invenerit bonus Symphoniurgus est.*" The clefs and starting notes of the four voices are given here as found in M-B. M-B. does not state whether these were found in the manuscripts, though I would conjecture that they were not. I keep this example in the original clefs, contrary to my usual practice, because of that special indication.

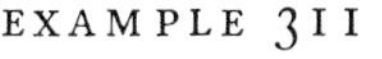

EXAMPLE 311

[The translator's solution follows.]

N.B. Retrograde [fugues?] must be discussed.*

The play of genius portraying the genius of play.† In three voices. Two voices, of which one proceeds in contrary motion at the octave, after a tactus. The third will lie concealed, going by equal steps.‡ [Example 312]

EXAMPLE 312

* "*De retrogradis dicendum.*" The bracketed material is mine. M-B. informs us that a half page is empty in the manuscripts following this remark, probably intended for a discussion of retrograde fugue.

† "*Lusus ingenii genium Ludi exprimens.*"

‡ "*à 3. Duae voces quarum una in motu contrario per Diapason procedit post tactum. Tertius, aequali graditur per sorte, latebit.*" The first voice and the comments concerning the third voice (including the "N.B.'s") are given as found in M-B.

EXAMPLE 312 (*continued*)

[The translator's solution follows.]

APPENDIX ON DOUBLE COUNTERPOINT

Chapter 64

Of Double Counterpoint in General

1. Double counterpoint is an ingenious type of composition in which, after the proper transformation of the lower voice into the upper and of the upper into the lower, an entirely different harmonic structure* is heard than had been heard before.

2. It is of two kinds, for either mi and fa will appear in their former places† after the transformation, or they will not.

3. When mi and fa appear in their former places after the transformation, the counterpoint is at the octave.

4. When, however, mi and fa do not appear in their former places after the transformation, then the counterpoint is again of two kinds, that is, either at the tenth or at the twelfth.

* "eine gantz andere *Harmonie*."

† That is, the semitones will remain in their former places in the melodic lines.

Chapter 65

Of Counterpoint at the Octave

1. Counterpoint at the octave is composed in such a way that the lower voice can be moved an octave higher, and the upper one an octave lower.

2. To do this, one should never employ the fifth in the original setting,* for it would result in a fourth after the transformation, which is not a consonance in a piece in two voices. Let us show examples: [Example 313].

EXAMPLE 313

Transformation:

Chapter 66

Of Counterpoint at the Tenth

1. Counterpoint at the tenth is that in which the lower voice of the original setting can be placed an octave higher, and the higher voice a tenth lower.

* "in der Haupt *Composition*."

2. This can happen when two consonances of the same kind are never set next to each other,[85] even if one be major, the other minor.

3. There must be no syncopation involving dissonances.*

4. The voices should not readily stand more than a twelfth from one another.[86] [Example 314]

EXAMPLE 314

5. One could also alter things in such a way as to put the lower voice a tenth higher and the upper one an octave lower. [And one has to choose between these two transformations, as to which is the more attractive.] For example: [Example 315].

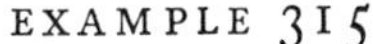
EXAMPLE 315

6. One can also fashion this counterpoint in three parts in the following way: if in the original setting a third voice is created a tenth above the lower voice, and if in the transformation it stands a seventeenth (two

* "Es soll keine Rückung aus *Dissonantzen* bestehen."

octaves plus a third) below the upper voice. Indeed, the voices will not all come off too well against one another, but that is not a consideration in such compositions.* [Example 316]

EXAMPLE 316

Transformation:

* As given in M-B., the fifth and sixth-last notes of the parallel voices in the original setting have the rhythm 𝅗𝅥. ♩, instead of 𝅗𝅥 𝅗𝅥. This is clearly a mistake, if only in view of the transformation.

Chapter 67

Of Counterpoint at the Twelfth

1. Counterpoint at the twelfth is that in which the lower voice is placed an octave higher than in the original setting, and the higher one a fifth lower.

2. To do this, one must first of all not employ the sixth, unless it be used in the manner of a dissonance.[87]

3. Also, one must completely renounce the syncopated seventh, when this is resolved through the sixth. The other resolutions can be employed.[88]

4. The voices should never stand [more than] a twelfth from one another.

5. The upper voice should, moreover, never go beneath the lower, or the lower one above the upper.

6. The octave or twelfth (compound fifth) should never be placed after the minor tenth in the original setting, or the unison or fifth after the minor third.[89]

[7. The original setting should not readily introduce a cadence.[90] 8. The false fifth is also to be avoided.]

7. Thus it happens that the twelfth of the original setting becomes a unison in the transformation, and the fifth an octave. From the sixth a seventh is obtained in the transformation, and from the seventh a sixth, as:[91] *Aus tiefer Not schrei' ich zu dir.* [Example 317]

EXAMPLE 317

Another example. [Example 318]

EXAMPLE 318

EXAMPLE 318 (*continued*)

Transformation:

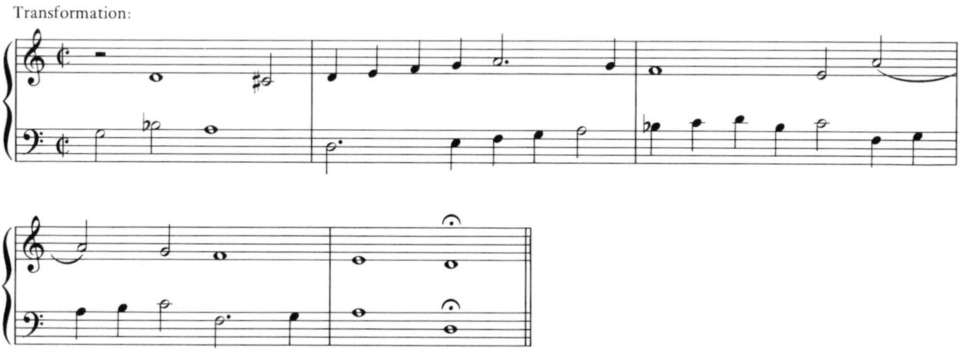

8. N.B. An intelligent composer will readily see where he should, from time to time, write fa in the transformation instead of mi.*

9. For the sake of greater variety, this counterpoint could also be transformed in such a way that the higher voice would come an octave lower, and the lower one a fifth higher, e.g.: [Example 319].

EXAMPLE 319

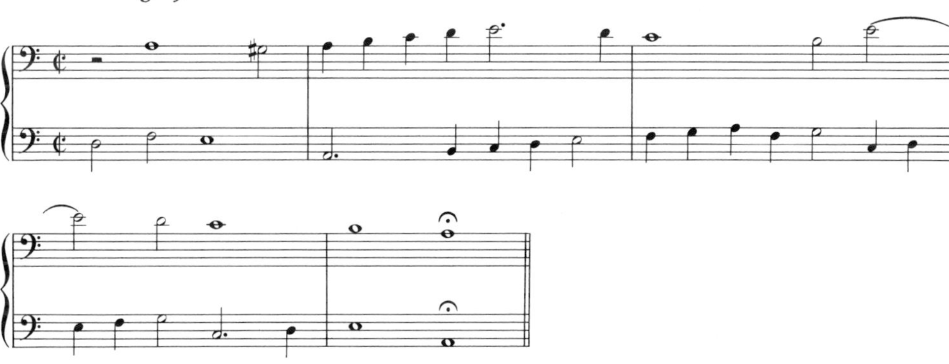

* That is, change the position of the semitones.

Chapter 68

Of Double Counterpoint in Contrary Motion

1. Counterpoint in contrary motion is that in which both voices can be inverted, so that where they had previously fallen, they [now] rise [in the inversion], and where they had previously risen, they fall.

2. In this, no syncopation involving dissonances must be employed.[93]

3. Also, a tenth should not go before the octave, nor a third before the unison, if the voices rise together.[94]

4. One can indeed begin in various ways, but not with a fifth. The most reasonable way to begin is with an octave, as: [Example 320].

EXAMPLE 320

To find the altered version, the lower voice must be placed a seventh higher, and the upper one a ninth lower.[95] [Example 321]

EXAMPLE 321

5. The lower voice can also be transposed a seventh higher, and the upper voice a tenth lower.[96] Let this be an example. [Example 322]

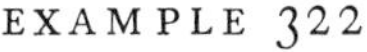
EXAMPLE 322

Chapter 69

Of That Counterpoint Which Fashions a Quartet Out of a Duet

1. To make this, one must use only two consonances: the third and the octave.[97]

2. Dissonances can be employed in *transitus*, but not in *syncopation*. [Example 323]

EXAMPLE 323

3. New voices are now set a third above the upper voice, and also a third above the lower voice. For example: [Example 324].

EXAMPLE 324

4. Two consonances of the same kind must not follow one another, save in contrary motion.

5. One should take pains that the voices of the original setting go in contrary motion as much as possible.

Chapter 70

Of Quadruple Counterpoint

1. Quadruple counterpoint is a type of composition whose reply* converts the bass into the soprano and the alto into the tenor. There are three kinds: ordinary;† in contrary motion; in retrograde motion.

2. To fashion the first kind, a) the bass and soprano must be in counterpoint at the octave; b) the fifth must not be employed in the middle parts against the soprano other than as a dissonance.‡

3. The voices should be placed as close to one another as possible, and not over or under their staff lines.

4. A fourth in the middle voices against the soprano is good, for it becomes a fifth in the reply.

5. In the reply, the soprano drops an eleventh, the alto a fourth; the tenor climbs a fifth, the bass a twelfth.§ [Example 325]

EXAMPLE 325

* "*Replica.*"

† "Der *schlechte.*" See also *Art of Singing*, para. 5, and *Art of Singing*, note 2.

‡ That is, it must be in *transitus* or *syncopation* against the soprano.

§ The fourth-last note of the alto in the original setting reads D in M-B. This is obviously an error, in view of the two replies and the rule given in para. 2.

EXAMPLE 325 (*continued*)

Or the soprano falls a twelfth, the alto a fifth; and the bass climbs an eleventh and the tenor a fourth. [Example 326]

EXAMPLE 326

The second kind, in contrary motion, is made as follows: a) The bass and soprano are in counterpoint at the twelfth, free of syncopations, and in contrary motion as much as possible, so that too many forbidden leaps do not result in the inversion. These leaps, however, must be permitted in any case, in such a difficult form of composition. b) The alto should not have two thirds or sixths against any voice, nor begin with a fourth against the soprano; it admits no fifth against the soprano, and is in counterpoint at the twelfth against the bass. c) Tenor and soprano can have no fourths between them. d) Leaps of fourths and fifths are not always good in the reply.* e) In the reply, the soprano falls an eleventh and becomes bass, the alto falls a ninth and becomes tenor, the tenor begins in the same degree as

* That is, their counterparts in the reply are not always acceptable (see Example 327!).

before* and becomes alto, and the bass moves a twelfth higher and becomes soprano. Thus the upper voices and the bass must commence in such a way that they do not go too high or too low in the reply. The soprano should begin on G, f, or a and the bass an octave beneath, and the bass should not climb higher than where it had begun, as:[98] [Example 327].

EXAMPLE 327

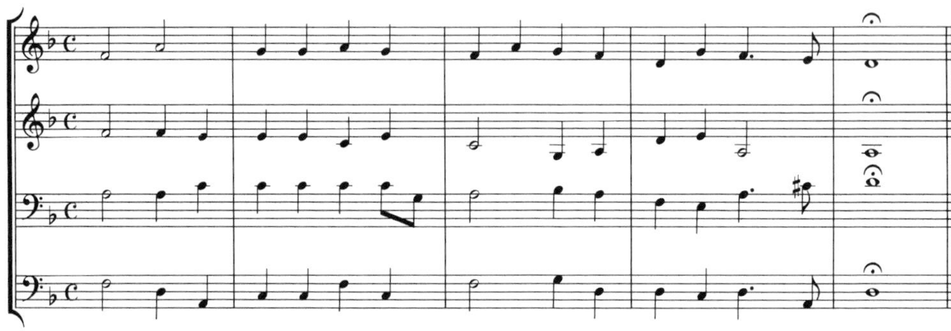

The third kind, retrograde counterpoint, is fashioned in two different ways: first, so that the voices can merely be sung backwards, without preserving the previous lines and spaces. The foregoing would be [examples], except that one must employ no dissonances or dots in them.[99] For example: [Example 328].

EXAMPLE 328

* "im *Unisono*."

EXAMPLE 328 (*continued*)

Or one keeps the notes in their former lines and spaces in the reply. To make this kind: a) above all, no dot or dissonance must be used; b) the soprano and bass must be in counterpoint at the twelfth; c) the middle voices must have no fourth against the soprano; d) at the end, the clef of the soprano must be written before the bass, the clef of the alto before the tenor, and so on. For example:* [Example 329].

EXAMPLE 329

* Example 329 is given exactly as found in M-B., except that the sixth-last note of the alto appears as an F there, and the ninth note of the tenor as a B—both obvious errors.

NOTES FOR THE *Tractatus* AND THE *Bericht*

1. By "General Rules" Bernhard seems to mean especially the material given in chs. 2 to 4; by "Special Rules" the material given in subsequent chapters—especially the detailed accounts of individual intervals found in chs. 5 to 11.

2. "sich wohl singen lasse." Singability was always a principal consideration for Italian composers. Zarlino, *Istitutioni harmoniche* (Venice, 1573), pp. 216–17, already emphasized its importance as a criterion.

3. "deren eine jede wohl singe." Müller-Blattau (henceforth referred to as M-B.) discards this clause, found only in one manuscript, as redundant. I, however, have decided to retain it on the grounds that it helps to clarify the thought of the sentence.

4. "nach einer richtigen *Mensur* bestehen." The reader should recall that a time signature in the seventeenth century still often had a double function: the indication of meter and the indication of a proportional relationship between the tempo of the section under consideration and the tempo of the section preceding it. Hence "*Mensur*" probably refers to this combination of ideas.

5. "Wovon in der Singe-Kunst mehr Bericht gegeben wird." Seemingly, a reference to the *Art of Singing* (para. 36 in particular?), implying prior existence of that work. But a variant from one manuscript, "mit mehreren Bericht gegeben werden soll," might be taken to imply rather that the *Tractatus* antedates the *Art of Singing.*

6. *Falsobordone*, in sixteenth- and seventeenth-century Italy (and *fabordon* in sixteenth- and seventeenth-century Spain), was a simple chordal style of setting chant (especially psalm tones). In such settings, the same chord would often be repeated several times in succession without any change in disposition, if the chant itself remained on the same degree for several syllables.

7. "*Fugen* und *Imitationes.*" In treatises of the sixteenth and early seventeenth centuries, e.g., Zarlino's *Istitutioni* and Thomas Morley's *A Plain and Easy Introduction to Practical Music*, R. Alec Harman, ed. (New York, Norton, 1963), "fuga" ("fugue" in English) always covers the species of imitation that we call "canon." But the term also frequently extends to less rigorous forms of imitation, including the type found in the expositions of what we ourselves call "fugues." Bernhard deals with the term in this more all-embracing sense in ch. 57, referring in particular (in para. 7) to the "association" and "equalization" of modes—our "tonal" and "real answers," in effect—under its heading. Then, in chs. 58 to 63, he concentrates on examples of fugues in the former, more restricted sense.

"*Imitatio*" may have either a broad meaning, covering everything that our own "imitation" covers (when "fugue" is also interpreted in its broadest sense, the two terms then become more or less synonymous), or else may denote forms of imitation looser than fugue (when the meaning of the latter is somewhat restricted). Zarlino reserves "fuga" for canonic passages at perfect intervals, wherein half and whole steps are (with rare exceptions) faithfully preserved (p. 257); he applies "imitatione" to canonic passages at intervals other than the perfect ones, where changes between half and whole steps are usually much more frequent, as well as to those canonic passages at perfect intervals wherein changes of this kind are, for one reason or another, unusually prevalent (p. 262). Moreover, either "fuga" or "imitatione" may be "strict" or "free," according to Zarlino: "strict" if the correspondence persists for a long period of time, "free" if it is dropped soon after the voices have entered (p. 257 and p. 262). For Bernhard's use of "canon," see ch. 57, paras. 9–11.

I have chosen to translate "fuga" or "Fuge" with its English cognate (or leave it in its Latin form), since no other English word exactly covers the domain of meanings which it has in Bernhard. Thus "fugue" is consistently to be understood in the sense of that epoch rather than in our more modern sense.

8. "sollen alle *Consonantzen* wo möglich ... anzutreffen seyn." By "all consonances" Bernhard surely means all the pitch-classes in a particular chord; thus he seems in particular to be barring triads with the third or fifth missing.

9. "*Semidiapente.*" In Example 19, the diminished octave is labelled "Semidiapason." These designations for intervals already appeared in Zarlino, as did many others used by Bernhard.

10. Dialogues are duets, generally for soprano and bass, with instrumental accompaniment. A popular genre in the seventeenth and early eighteenth centuries, their texts would often feature a series of questions and answers. Among the earliest known examples are the *Dialoghi* of Orazio Vecchi (1608) and the *Dialogo di Ninfa e Pastore* by Marco Gagliano (1611). The Germans adopted the genre toward the middle of the century, notably for sacred purposes, the dialogue now often consisting of a conversation between a Soul and God. Andreas Hammerschmidt's "Dialogues between God and a Faithful Soul" (1645) constitute a good example of this. Nearly one hundred years later, Bach still availed himself of the idea, e.g., in his Cantatas 32, 60, 140, and 152.

11. "*Licentiae*" are "liberties," or "licenses," which the composer takes in employing dissonances. See chs. 16 ff. for a presentation of the various "licenses" or "figures." Bernhard is exceptional, for his time, in considering the question of figures from a purely musical point of view—that of dissonance treatment— rather than from the standpoint of text-music relationships (as the word "*melopoeticae*" might suggest). See *Bericht*, ch. XIII, para. 4, given on pp. 90–91; also, note 33.

12. "*intra Senarium comprehensis.*" The *senario*, or first six partials of the overtone series, is given particular prominence in the writings of Zarlino (though he does not yet acknowledge an overtone series as such, but just the mathematical proportions existing

between the various notes). See Zarlino, pp. 31–32; also his *Sopplimenti musicali* (Venice, 1588), p. 88.

13. The *arithmetic* division of a string is into sections of equal length:

$$\frac{n}{n}, \frac{n-1}{n}, \ldots, \frac{2}{n}, \frac{1}{n}.$$

In *harmonic* division, sections of the string become progressively shorter, the numerator of all fractions being 1, while the denominator assumes all positive integral values in increasing order: $\frac{1}{1}, \frac{1}{2}, \frac{1}{3}, \ldots, \frac{1}{n}, \ldots$

Let us now assume that the entire length of a string gives the lower note of the octave of which Bernhard is speaking. Then its upper note is given by exactly one half of the string length. In saying that a fourth divides the octave only arithmetically, Bernhard obviously is speaking of a disposition wherein the fourth is underneath the fifth, for in such a disposition the division of the octave indeed occurs at the midpoint of the octave length—i.e., one fourth of the way up the string. On the other hand, if the fourth were on top of the fifth, harmonic division would result, as the division point in question would be one third of the way up the string. Thus Bernhard is relating the more dissonant nature of a fourth when it is found against the bass to the less "natural" form of intervallic division involved. See also ch. 15, para. 2.

14. "*quia datur numerus, harmonice utrumque dividens,* 3.4.5." The number is 4, and the major sixth is divided into a fourth (below) and a major third (above). Successive integers are involved in this division, so it is a harmonic division in the purest sense. Zarlino reasoned exactly the same way (*Istitutioni*, p. 192).

15. "*quia datur numerus utrumque harmonicè dividens,* 5.6.8." The number is 6, and the minor sixth is divided into a minor third (below) and a fourth (above). Here successive integers are not involved (although 6:8 can be reduced to a ratio of successive integers), and Bernhard is in effect broadening his concept of harmonic division to establish the minor sixth as a consonance. Zarlino also had to employ special, somewhat unconvincing reasoning to derive this interval from the *senario* (p. 193).

16. M-B.'s judgment is that the absence of a comment concerning any particular progressions in the examples that follow (e.g., nos. 1–4 of Example 29) implies that these progressions are acceptable. This seems, in general, to be a sound interpretation.

17. "*Systema durum*" denotes the diatonic scale consisting of all the white notes on the keyboard, and hence including b♮ (♮ durum) and the "hard" hexachord.

18. "*Systema molle*" denotes the diatonic scale containing the six white notes c–a and b♭ (♭ *molle*). It thus includes the "soft" hexachord.

19. "und dass sie zu ihrer Vermittelung die *Tertie* erfordert." Here, as elsewhere, Bernhard certainly means the "first inversion" of a triad rather than the "second

inversion," since the fourth is considered dissonant against the bass. See also ch. 10, para. 2.

20. "in ermeldete *Claves*." Seemingly Bernhard is speaking of altered degrees which had already been introduced, and to some extent established, prior to the moment under consideration.

21. "Die *imperfecten Consonantzen* bleiben in ihrer natürlichen *proportion*, es werde denn das *Systema* der *Octave* verändert." By "system of the octave," or "setting of the octave" ("Satz der *Octave*"), Bernhard seems to mean the particular way in which the tones and semitones are arranged in a given octave—i.e., in a given mode. By "altering the system of the octave," "changing the octave," etc., he then means changing the positions of the tones and semitones within it. The "natural proportion" of an imperfect consonance is its size (major or minor) in the unaltered octave. Here again, as elsewhere, "natural" is employed to mean "devoid of artifice." See my preface for a consideration of Bernhard's use of this word in general.

22. The chorale, *Nun komm, der Heiden Heiland*, furnishes one of the rare examples of this situation, its second line ending with the drop of a third. It is interesting to observe how Bach handles this spot in his organ prelude, BWV 661.

23. "*Soliciniis*." The term "*solicinium*" seems to denote a piece for solo voice with instrumental accompaniment—almost surely in recitative style.

24. In listing the "fourth" and "fifth" under this category of dissonances, Bernhard might possibly be referring to the augmented fourth and the diminished and/or augmented fifth. But even this would not square completely with the parallel passage in the *Tractatus*. Most likely a mistake, pure and simple.

25. By "major semitone," Bernhard evidently means the diatonic semitone, 16:15. Chromatic semitones are generally smaller, hence "minor," e.g., 25:24 or 135:128.

26. This spelling, an earlier form of the word, is found in both treatises. *Transitus* is seen to be a form of diminution, in so far as long notes are divided up into shorter notes.

27. The "subject" is the voice against which *transitus* occurs: in a sense, the "given" voice. See ch. 17, para. 4.

28. The meaning of *quasitransitus* in the *Bericht* is quite different from what it is here. See ch. XXI of the *Bericht*, given on pp. 116–17.

29. "eine rückende Note"; i.e., a note tied over a strong beat. Morley consistently used the term "driving note" for this in his *A Plain and Easy Introduction*.

30. "der gebundenen oder rückenden Stimme Aufflösung." By this, Bernhard means that the syncopated note is articulated anew on the strong beat, rather than just held. As Artusi's specific objections to passages in the Monteverdi madrigals clearly demonstrated, this rearticulation—meaning that both portions of the dissonance are now attacked at once—was regarded as a major departure from the older style.

31. The superficial figures, as defined in this chapter of the *Bericht*, comprise

figures from both of the subdivisions of *stylus luxurians* (*communis* and *theatralis*) which are mentioned in ch. 21 of the *Tractatus*. Hence there are passages in this chapter of the *Bericht* which correspond with passages in ch. 35 of the *Tractatus*. (See ch. XXII, N.B. and its footnote, given on p. 116.) It is especially interesting to compare the account offered here of the genesis of the superficial figures with the account given in the *Tractatus*, ch. 35, paras. 2 and 3. I have given all of this chapter at this point in order not to break it up too much.

32. "in vorigem *Seculo*." Seemingly, the last two or three decades of the sixteenth century and the very beginning of the seventeenth are meant here.

33. Most of the German theorists of the early seventeenth century indeed viewed the figures primarily from the standpoint of their rhetorical functions—i.e., the special ideas or feelings which each was capable of illustrating. Joachim Burmeister, Johannes Lippius, Johannes Nucius, Andreas Herbst, and Athanasius Kircher are examples of this trend.

34. See also *Art of Singing*, paras. 19 and 20. The ornamental notes in the first and fourth measures of Example 192 actually seem instances of *anticipatione della nota*, as described in paras. 21 and 22 of the *Art of Singing* and in ch. 23 of the *Tractatus*, rather than of *anticipatione della sillaba*.

35. In this example, mixed in with bona fide instances of *subsumtio praepositiva*, we also find cases of *subsumtio postpositiva* (first E of the second measure) and of *anticipatio notae* (second E of the second measure). The staff for the bass line in the latter part of this example is indeed empty in M-B., having been found so in the manuscripts, according to his editorial note. Essentially the same example is given by Bernhard in ch. 33 of the *Tractatus*, for *quaesitio notae*. See also *Bericht*, ch. XVIII, paras. 2 and 3, given on pp. 112–13.

36. The G in the first measure is indeed an instance of *cercar della nota*, as described in the *Art of Singing*, para. 24, but can hardly be referred to as *subsumtio*, as defined in the present chapter.

37. The term "*coloratura*" is used somewhat differently in the *Art of Singing*. See paras. 38 and 39 of *Art of Singing* and note 15 in particular.

38. That is, by first breaking these intervals up into component thirds and fourths, and then applying *transitus regularis* to each of the former and *transitus irregularis* to each of the latter. See the parallel passage in the *Tractatus*.

39. "*Authoribus*." Possibly theorists are meant here, more than composers. Generally, however, Bernhard seems to mean composers when he uses this word.

40. "[können] auch durchs *Spartiren observiret* werden." Different voices of a composition for more than one performer were still commonly written on separate sheets at this time. Hence students of composition usually had to write all the parts under

one another in score form themselves, before they could examine vertical relationships in any detail.

41. The numbering of successions in Example 202 is mine. Otherwise I give the example exactly as it appears in M-B. "Natural" versions do not appear for nos. 5 and 6, or for the latter half of no. 4. A B♭ signature appears only at the very outset in M-B., but is certainly intended for both versions of nos. 1 and 2—and certainly *not* intended for nos. 4–6.

42. In a variant reading indicated by M-B., the upper voice has two eighth notes at the start of the fourth measure, instead of the quarter note. Pitches are not given for these notes, but surely they repeat the E heard at the end of the previous measure. It is uncertain whether the first of these eighth notes would be tied over from the previous measure or not.

43. This almost sounds like a jab at some rival musician(s). The reference, however, is obscure. In any case, the use of the adjective "chromatic" for the minor semitone (see footnote for ch. 29, para. 3) was certainly standard by this time. Bernhard's objection to using the same adjective to denote progressions such as the two given above seems based on the fact that they contain diatonic semitones as well as chromatic semitones. Morley makes exactly the same objection in connection with the latter of these two progressions, saying that it is a "bastard point patched up of half Chromatic and half Diatonic" (p. 103).

44. Both here and in ch. 21 above, "*imperfectae*" is sometimes found in one manuscript source as a variant of "*imperfecta*." Clearly there is no great difference of meaning involved here, since, by ch. 2, para. 11, it will always be less than perfect for voices to begin a work with entrances at distances other than perfect intervals.

45. Bernhard calls the last two intervals "*Sexta superflua*" and "*Tertia deficiens*," respectively; but from the account given in ch. 42, it is clear that the diminished seventh and augmented second are actually the intervals under discussion, rather than the augmented sixth and diminished third. Bernhard's classification of these intervals as consonances seems in line with his regarding them as types of sixth and third, respectively. I thought it best to call them by the names that we commonly give to them, to avoid our confusing them with what *we* call augmented sixths and diminished thirds.

46. The "sixth" mentioned here is to be measured upward from the bass, and may occur at any octave above it. The bass-oriented continuo player in particular will regard it as "above" the fourth, quite irrespective of whether its actual pitch is higher or lower than that of the fourth. The first progression below verifies that it may indeed be lower in pitch.

47. This two-part progression appears in M-B. directly after the four-part progression of para. 4. This is where it was found in one manuscript, according to a comment in

M-B.'s *Revisionsbericht.* This same comment also speaks, however, of a N.B. in the other manuscript which asserts that it should appear *here*, at the end of para. 3, rather than in para. 4. Neither placement is ideal: the leap into the fourth makes it seem appropriate for the present paragraph, the mention of "many voices" inappropriate. However, there appears to be no compelling reason at all why it should appear under para. 4; hence I choose to include it here.

In M-B., the name "Loretto Vittorii" appears alongside the four-part example of para. 4. In his *Revisionsbericht*, however, M-B. speaks of the "two-part example of Loretto Vittorii," suggesting rather that the name should appear in connection with the present example. My conjecture is that the latter is more likely, since the composer in question was a prolific exponent of the modern, dramatic style.

Loreto Vittori (pseudonym "Olerto Rovitti") was born in Spoleto in 1604, died in Rome in 1670. A castrato, he studied with Soriano and G. B. Nanini at Rome, then became a member of the papal chapel after 1622. His fame derived not only from his operas (the biographical article in *MGG* lists three), oratorios (likewise three), plays with music, and libretti, but even more from his fantastic soprano voice. An especially noteworthy account of his vocal powers is given in Manfred Bukofzer, *Music in the Baroque Era* (New York, Norton, 1947), p. 66. His oratorios in particular pursued the monodic premises of Cavalieri's works (*ibid.*, p. 124).

48. Nothing is implied, regarding the specific vertical arrangement of the sixth, fourth, and second, by the word "between." As in ch. 32, para. 2 above, Bernhard is speaking from the standpoint of a continuo player, measuring everything upward from the bass and equating upper octaves (see note 46). See note 47 regarding the appearance of the name "Loretto Vittorii" next to Example 219 in M-B.

49. Perhaps Bernhard's thought was that these instruments were often used to underscore important points in the musical structure by their entries, and that these entries would tend to be all the more striking if such a combination of dissonances was featured. An unusual dissonance in a part for trumpet might also have been excused because of the limited number of pitches available on that (then) valveless instrument.

50. In M-B., words are given only for the first half of the first passage. Substantially the same passage, and a similar "natural" version, appear in the *Bericht*, ch. XV, para. 6 (given opposite ch. 24 of the *Tractatus*). I give the second passage (and its "natural version") exactly as found in M-B., but suspect that the lower voice should read a third higher.

51. "dass man die Rede aufs natürlichste *exprimiren* solle." It is interesting to compare the account given in the subsequent paragraphs with that in paras. 30–34 and 40 of the *Art of Singing*.

52. This paragraph reads as follows in M-B.: "Die Wiederhohlung des Textes soll entweder garnicht, oder nur an den Orten, wo es die Zierligkeit zulässt im *Unisono* gebraucht werden." According to the *Revisionsbericht*, however, the phrase "im

Unisono" is only found in one manuscript source; and I feel that the sentence makes more sense when it is left out.

53. In a variant reading mentioned in M-B.'s *Revisionsbericht*, the tenor has the following note values in the second-last measure of the upcoming example: ♩ ♩ ♩. ♪. This version may be deemed more "correct" from the standpoint of dissonance treatment, but is certainly less attractive. The flat signature is missing from the lower system throughout this example in M-B. As a consequence the tenor has a B♮ in the second-last measure. While the resulting cross-relation is pleasing in its own way, it is highly doubtful that it was intended here.

54. The reference is to para. 24 of the *Art of Singing*. This confirms that the *Bericht*, at any rate, was written after that treatise.

55. Throughout this chapter the augmented second is referred to as "*tertia deficiens*," the diminished seventh as "*sexta superflua*." (See note 45.) Bernhard's statement that the "*tertia deficiens*" is "not quite" a minor third is correct, for a major third minus a diatonic semitone is less than a minor third. $\left(\frac{5}{4} \times \frac{15}{16} = \frac{75}{64} < \frac{6}{5}.\right)$

56. The following are brief biographical sketches (in alphabetical order) of the lesser-known composers mentioned in ch. 43, paras. 5, 6, and 7.

Vincenzo Albrici was born in Rome in 1631 and died in Prague in 1696. He took up residence at the Swedish court in 1650, as director of the queen's Italian opera house; then he entered the Dresden chapel in 1654. With his brother Bartolomeo, he went to London in 1664, where the two were chapel composers until 1667. That year he was appointed Kapellmeister back at Dresden, a position which he held through 1680, except for a stay in Paris from 1672 to 1676. He was organist at St. Thomas Church, Leipzig, in 1681–82, then became church Kapellmeister at Prague. Albrici's compositions include three Te Deums for chorus and orchestra, and numerous Masses, cantatas, and instrumental works. An item of special interest in his works is a setting of the Lord's Prayer in Swedish, "which is the first important vocal composition with words in that language" (*Grove's Dictionary of Music and Musicians*, 5th ed., I, 98).

Antonio Bertali was born in Verona in 1605 and died in Vienna in 1669. He was Viennese court violinist starting in 1637, and in 1649 was made Kapellmeister there. His compositions, numbering over 600 in all, include twelve operas, two oratorios, and much church and chamber music. A dissertation on his dramatic works was written by Christopher Laroche (Vienna, 1919, unpublished).

Giovanni Andrea Bontempi (real name Angelini) was born in Perugia in 1624 and died there in 1705. A castrato, he was in the choir at St. Mark's, Venice, in 1643, then held posts as *maestro di cappella* in various Roman and Venetian churches. He came to Dresden to head the court chapel in 1651, and during his tenure there published a treatise, *Nova quatuor vocibus componendi methodus* (1660), and produced *Paride* (1662), the first Italian opera to be performed in that city. Two German operas followed, both produced there in collaboration with Peranda (*q.v.*), as well as an oratorio. He returned to Italy in 1680, writing two more treatises, one of them a history of music. Bontempi was celebrated for his mastery of both the *stile antico* and the *stile moderno*, and also acquired fame as a theatrical architect.

Gasparo Cassati (Casati) was born in Pavia early in the seventeenth century. A Franciscan monk, he was named *maestro di cappella* at the cathedral of Novara in 1635, then died there prematurely in 1641. He wrote Masses, psalms, and motets in one to four voices, under the influence of the monodists.

Stefano Fabri was born in Rome in 1606 and died there in 1658. A pupil of Bernardino Nanini, he was *maestro di cappella* at various churches in his native city, and wrote Magnificats, motets, and concerted psalms.

Kaspar Förster, the younger, was born in Danzig in 1616 and died in Oliva (near Danzig) in 1673. A pupil of his father, Kaspar Förster, the elder, who was cantor at St. Mary's in Danzig, and later of Marco Scacchi at Warsaw, he was employed as a baritone and as choral director at the court chapel in Warsaw, then traveled to Venice and Copenhagen between 1652 and 1655 to fulfill similar roles. In 1655 he came back to Danzig to become cantor at St. Mary's himself, retaining that post until 1657. In 1660–61 he again went to Copenhagen, later in 1661 to Dresden, still later to Hamburg. He spent his last years in the monastery of Oliva. His works include six trio sonatas and numerous cantatas and concerted church works.

The elder Förster was a celebrated defender of the *stile moderno*, although we know of no works of his in that style. He engaged in constant polemics over the matter with Paul Siefert, the organist at St. Mary's, who stood against the newer ways. For more on this controversy, see my preface, pp. 2–5.

Johann Caspar Kerll ("Kerl" in M-B.) was born in Adorf, Saxony, in 1627 and died in Munich in 1693. He studied organ with Valentini at Vienna, then went to Rome to study with Carissimi (and possibly Frescobaldi). During these student years he was thoroughly converted to the Italian vocal style, both new and old, and also was struck by the bold, expressive instrumental idiom of Frescobaldi and his followers. Entering the service of the Bavarian elector in 1656, he soon gained a reputation as an outstanding organist; in 1674 he moved to Vienna, where he became organist of St. Stephen's in 1677 and court organist in 1680. He returned to Munich in 1684. Kerll produced at least ten Italian operas during his earlier stay at Munich, plus numerous sacred works. He is best known, however, for his keyboard works, which, like those of his contemporary, Froberger, are remarkable for their daring use of dissonance, and which won the attention of both Bach and Handel years after his death.

Marco Giuseppe Peranda was born in Rome ca. 1625 and died in Dresden in 1675. Bernhard brought him to Dresden for his alto voice between 1651 and 1656. He then became Vice-Kapellmeister there in 1663, Kapellmeister in 1666. His compositions include concerted Masses, motets and madrigals, a Christmas story, and a Passion according to St. Mark; also instrumental music. With Bontempi (*q.v.*) he produced *Dafne*—"eine Deutsche Musicalische Opera"—at Dresden in 1671, and *Jupiter und Jo* in 1673.

Francesco della Porta was born in Monza around the start of the seventeenth century and died in Milan in 1666. He held posts as *maestro di cappella* and organist at various churches in the latter city. Three books of his motets, for two to five voices, were published in Venice and Antwerp between 1645 and 1654, and some of his psalms appeared in Venice in 1656 and 1657. He wrote a number of *ricercari* for organ.

Giovanni Prioli (Priuli) was born in Venice between 1575 and 1580 and died in Vienna in 1629. A composer-organist, he was a pupil of Giovanni Gabrieli and worked at St. Mark's between 1607 and 1612, assisting his aging teacher. In 1615 he became Hofkapellmeister at Graz, and in 1619 went to the imperial court at Vienna. His works include three books of madrigals (the last book partly in concerted style), as well as canzonas, sonatas, motets, psalms, and Masses (again, some of these concerted). Two secular concerted works are found in *Denkmäler der Tonkunst in Österreich*, Bd. 77, 89 ff.; a *Domine labia me* appears in *Caecilia* (1843), p. 128.

Lorenzo Ratti ("Laurentius Rattus" in M-B.) was born in Perugia in 1590 and died in Loreto in 1630. He was a boy-singer in the Cappella Giulia in Rome between 1599 and 1601, and was organist at Perugia between 1614 and 1616. Later he held the position of *maestro di cappella* at various religious establishments at Rome. He wrote two books of madrigals, and many motets, most of them a cappella. His *Sacrae Modulationes* (1628), a collection of works on texts from the Proper, were very popular in the smaller Roman churches during the seventeenth century. An opera of his, *Il Ciclope*, was produced in Rome in 1628.

Giovanni Antonio Rigatti (Rigati) was born in Venice in 1615 and died there in 1649. A priest, he was appointed *maestro di cappella* at Udine in 1635, and *maestro del coro* at the Venetian Conservatorio degli Incurabili in 1646. His works include concerted Masses, psalms, and motets, and also works for solo voice with basso continuo, both sacred and secular.

Giovanni Rovetta was born ca. 1596 (site unknown) and died in Venice in 1668. The son of an instrumentalist at St. Mark's, he himself was employed there for most of his life: first as a choirboy; then as a bass, starting in 1623; then as vice-*maestro di cappella*, starting in 1627; and finally as *maestro di cappella*, succeeding Monteverdi at that position in 1644. Two operas by him, as well as several books of psalms, concerted madrigals, motets, and Masses are known. Bukofzer (p. 35) mentions him as having excelled in his continuo madrigals.

Marco Scacchi was born in Gallese (near Rome) in 1602 and died there ca. 1685. A pupil of G. F. Anerio, he was Kapellmeister and court composer at Warsaw between

1628 and 1648. He wrote five operas, an oratorio, a twelve-part Mass, four-part Masses, and five-part concerted madrigals; also a treatise, *Breve discorso sopra la musica moderna* (Warsaw, 1649), and several important letters and tracts dealing with the features and relative merits of the old style and the new. For more information concerning these letters and tracts, as well as his alleged influence on Bernhard, see my preface.

FRANCESCO SORIANO (Suriano) was born in Viterbo (Suriano) in 1549 and died there in 1621. He was *maestro di cappella* at various churches at Rome, including St. John Lateran, Santa Maria Maggiore, and St. Peter's, and for a time was also in Mantua, as master of the duke's private chapel. His works include three books of madrigals, and much sacred music; an eight-voiced *Ecce sacerdos magnus* is found in *Musica Sacra*, Vol. XXV, ed. by F. Commer (Berlin, 1884); two Masses are found in *Selectus novus Missarum*, ed. by C. Proske (Regensburg, 1855–61); a Passion is given by Fr. X. Haberl in *Kirchenmusikalisches Jahrbuch* X (1895); various sacred works appear in *Musica Divina* III, ed. by C. Proske (Regensburg, 1859). With Felice Anerio he took part in preparing the "Editio Medicaea" of the Gradual (1614).

ANTONIO (or Giovanni) FRANCESCO TENAGLIA was born in Florence early in the seventeenth century and died after 1661 in Rome. He had two operas produced at Rome, in 1656 and 1661, and wrote over fifty cantatas, as well as numerous madrigals and arias.

FRANCESCO TURINI was born in Prague in 1589, the son of an Italian musician there, and died in Brescia in 1656. The pupil of his father, Turini became court organist at Prague at the age of twelve. After holding various other posts, he was named organist at the cathedral of Brescia in 1624, a post which he retained for the rest of his life. He wrote solo madrigals and motets under the influence of Monteverdi and the monodists, as well as many other concerted vocal works, both sacred and secular, and also trio sonatas. Bukofzer (p. 70) says that he was highly skilled in the *stile antico* as well as in the new style. An example of his skill in the former is a four-part Mass, written wholly in canon.

57. "doch weil bey ihnen der *Text* etwas schwerer zu *appliciren*." Bernhard is probably referring to the fact that text-underlay was often not very accurate in that earlier period.

58. "*in prosa et ligata*." Three poems by Bernhard are included in Christian Dedekind's song anthology, *Aelbianische Musenlust* (Dresden, 1657). This same poet wrote of Bernhard, after the latter had died, that he was an artist "to whom words and music were one and the same" ("dem Text und Ton war einerlei"). See Gerhard Bittrich's dissertation *Ein deutsches Opernballett des siebzehnten Jahrhunderts; ein Beitrag zur Frühgeschichte der deutschen Oper* (Leipzig, Frommhold and Wendler, 1931) for an attempt to establish Bernhard as the author of a French-style opera-ballet entitled "Die sieben Planeten," which was produced in Dresden ca. 1680.

59. "Modus" denoted one of the proportional relationships in mensural notation. "Tonus" can mean a specific recitation formula for a psalm, Magnificat, etc., and, of course, the major second. "Tropus," while most often used to mean a textual or musical addition to a pre-existent chant, can also denote one of the various alternative endings of a psalm tone (otherwise called "differentiae").

60. "*Toni proprii.*" The subsequent three kinds are called, respectively, "*improprii*," "*deficientes*," and "*superflui*" by Bernhard. "*Tonus*" and "*Modus*" both appear time and again in the upcoming discussion, seemingly interchangeably. I will, wherever possible, translate each one with its English cognate.

61. Here and in the sequel, the exact meaning of "tenor" is not always clear, and in any case seems to vary somewhat. Sometimes the word appears to refer to a principal melody line, be it a *cantus firmus* or a freshly composed line; sometimes to a voice with tenor range. In view of the importance of the tenor voice as a frequent carrier of *cantus firmi* in German Renaissance polyphony—whose traditions and precepts remained alive throughout the Baroque—the word may also on occasion denote both these things at once. (In connection with this point, see the quote from Folengo given in *Art of Singing*, note 16.) As used here, it seems to carry the first meaning; in ch. 52, para. 1 and ch. 53, para. 1, the second meaning seems paramount; in ch. 46, para. 5, both may well be intended.

62. There are clear examples of mixed modes in plainchant, however—e.g., the Easter sequence, *Victimae paschali laudes.*

63. When Bernhard speaks of the mode "aus dem C," he clearly is referring to the *pair* of modes, one authentic and the other plagal, which have C as finalis.

64. "weilen die übrigen alle ihrer Schlüsse *Perfection* nach diesem richten." Bernhard apparently is referring to the fact that final cadences in any mode end on a major triad, even if an accidental is needed to bring it about.

65. "wie ich meinen *Discipeln oculariter demonstriret.*" Perhaps a reference to the discussion of cadences found in ch. 12 above.

66. In M-B., some of the pitch names in this discussion of modes are capitalized, others appear in lower case. Although choices of upper or lower case seem too inconsistent to suggest any serious attempt on Bernhard's part to designate specific octaves, they will nonetheless be preserved in this translation.

67. The first chorale mentioned here has the range of a ninth. Hence it appears that Bernhard is not limiting himself to instances of "proper modes" here.

68. I generally translate "*cadentia*" by "close" in this discussion, since it is clear that many of the stopping points referred to are relatively minor ones, and as Bernhard appears to use "*cadentia*" and "*clausula*" interchangeably. The four different types of cadence-degrees mentioned in this paragraph are called "*Cadentia finalis*," "*Confinalis principalis*," "*minus principalis*," and "*Irregulares*," respectively, by Bernhard. Each

represents a lower rank in the hierarchy of pitch-classes within a mode than its predecessors. The *confinalis principalis* would normally be called the "dominant" by us; there is more discussion of it in ch. 51, para. 7.

69. A melody from G to G would not lie within the comfortable register of most voices. The most common transposition is, of course, a fourth upward or a fifth downward. (See ch. 52, para. 3.)

70. When Bernhard mentions *Wenn mein Stündlein vorhanden ist* here, he obviously is not referring to the tune most often associated with this text, which is in the second mode (according to his numbering). The melody that he probably means may be found in Michael Praetorius, *Musae Sioniae*, Vol. VIII of *Gesamtausgabe der musikalischen Werke*, ed. by Friedrich Blume (Wolfenbüttel–Berlin, Kallmeyer, 1932), pp. 116–17.

71. The hymn referred to by Bernhard is *Proles de caelo prodiit*, *Novus* . . ., sung at first vespers for the feast day of St. Francis of Assisi. Its second stanza begins "Spoliatis Aegyptis. . . ." The fact that the second stanza is given instead of the first suggests that some form of alternatim performance took place. The melody may be found in Bruno Stäblein, *Monumenta Monodica Medii Aevi* (Kassel, 1956), I, 443. The text is found in Franz Joseph Mone, *Lateinische Hymnen des Mittelalters* (Freiburg, 1855; reprint 1964), III, 308. Zarlino also gave this particular chant as an example of this mode (p. 404).

72. Here Bernhard seems to use "tones" in the sense of psalm tones. The *mediation* of a psalm tone is the close which comes halfway through any line of recitation in that tone. The "recitation tone," around which the mediation centers, very often happens to lie a fifth above the finalis of the related mode, but not always. When Bernhard identifies the *confinalis principalis* of a mode specifically (distinguishing it from other *cadentiae regulares*), it indeed always is a fifth above the finalis; however, it should be observed that he does not actually specify the *confinalis principalis* for every mode.

73. "einen bequemen Sprung haben." It is possible that Bernhard actually is talking about the total range of a fugal subject here—i.e., that this should not be too large.

74. In the subsequent series of examples, I give pitches and note values exactly as found in M-B. (except where I indicate the contrary). In the quotes from Palestrina, note values often differ slightly from those found in the editions of his complete works. Most of the Palestrina excerpts are from his Offertories a5; most often beginnings of pieces are chosen.

75. The two passages by Bernhard feature chorale tunes in the upper voice: *Wir glauben all' an einen Gott* and *Vater unser im Himmelreich.*

76. "Von dieser Art die *Figuren* anzubringen." Here Bernhard seems to be talking about "figures" more in the sense of characteristic melodic turns—such as are found in subjects for points of imitation—than in his customary sense.

77. "geschehend durch alle *Sonos* der *Octave.* Zumahl durch die *Dominantes.*" As

the following examples will show, this statement refers to the fact that in *extension* points of imitation may begin on any degree of the mode, not just finalis and dominant. See ch. 44, para. 9 concerning the "principal sounds" (*Dominantes*).

78. The second excerpt appears a third too high in M-B. It should be as I give it: an entry on F, not A. The next pair of entries mentioned by Bernhard, on D and G, respectively, actually occur simultaneously (in parallel fourths most of the way); in M-B. only the G-entry is given, and its fourth note appears as a B♮. The first note of the second "A-entry" is indeed F; in M-B., however, it appears as an A. In the examples of this chapter in particular, first and last notes of excerpts often are given different time values than appear in the motet itself.

79. "Die fünffte ist durch ein *Tutti*, doch mit einer *Imitation* im F." All but one of the voices enter together in chordal fashion for this phrase. The remaining voice enters immediately afterwards, imitating the top voice of the chordal structure. It enters on F.

80. In M-B., the word "sixth" appears instead of "eighth." The case for the latter is a strong one: The seventh and eighth modes have repeatedly been referred to as rare; and these modes, as the first, feature the major triad, while the fifth and sixth feature the minor. Moreover, the seventh and eighth modes differ from the first only in the fourth degree, which is augmented in the case of the former, and hence particularly susceptible to alteration.

81. "ein *Spatium* einer Zeit," i.e., a time interval. Bernhard reserves the term "Intervallum" for a pitch interval, and I will follow suit.

82. "*Mixta* ist aus zweyen oder mehreren der vorhergesagten Arten vermenget." Bernhard clearly misrepresents his conception of "mixed fugue" here. As ch. 63 will confirm, such a fugue entails a combination of two or more of the *more unusual* options mentioned in para. 13, such as diminution, augmentation, and perpetual fugue—as well as contrary motion (not mentioned in para. 13) and special tricks such as are illustrated in ch. 63. The more normal options mentioned in para. 13, such as *aequisona*, *aequalis*, etc.—seemingly also *dissona*—almost certainly should *not* be counted as contributing factors; else we would have a host of trivial cases of mixed fugue.

83. "*Canon a 2. in Unisono post Tactum.*" The headings for all the subsequent fugues also are given in Latin in M-B., with consistent use of the word "canon" rather than "fuga." The tactus obviously has the value of a breve here, unlike elsewhere in the Bernhard treatises.

84. As M-B. observes, this fugue simply does not work. The second voice of the solution was not written out in one manuscript source.

85. Obviously Bernhard means two thirds or two sixths here. Cf. Morley's discussion of counterpoint at the tenth (pp. 191–92) and Zarlino's (pp. 269–70), which are very similar to Bernhard's.

86. Of two variant readings, "*Duodecimam*" and "*Decimam*," M-B. prefers the

latter. I choose the former, because both Zarlino (p. 269) and Morley (p. 191) give the twelfth, rather than the tenth, as the limit. Note, however, that the original setting of Bernhard's example actually includes a thirteenth at one point.

87. That is, in *transitus* or *syncopation*. Cf. Morley's discussion of counterpoint at the twelfth (pp. 188–90) and Zarlino's (pp. 267–69), which are very similar to Bernhard's.

88. Certain of the less common resolutions of the syncopated seventh indeed work in this kind of counterpoint: e.g., the lower voice climbing a fourth (or falling a fifth) while the upper voice falls a second. However, "*Resolutiones*" probably refers here to the other chief kinds of suspensions—the second, the fourth, and the ninth, all of which go nicely if resolved in the normal way. Zarlino (p. 267) quite explicitly outlaws all syncopations involving the seventh.

89. Bernhard's objection to an octave after the minor tenth, or to a unison after the minor third (when the voices go in contrary motion) is clear, for tritones are induced between the voices in the transformation. His reason for banning a twelfth after the minor tenth, or a fifth after the minor third, is less clear, but may have something to do with the long-standing principle that perfect intervals should be preceded by *minor* imperfect intervals (the third and tenth would both be major in the transformation) when two voices approach one another by step. In any case, both Morley (p. 189) and Zarlino (p. 267) also forbid the latter kind of progression.

90. "Auch soll die Erste Partey nicht leicht einen Schluss machen." Elsewhere in this chapter, Bernhard uses the word "Partey" to mean an individual voice; here "Erste Partey" seems to mean the original setting of the double counterpoint as a whole. Morley (p. 189) specifically forbids cadences in the original setting which feature the syncopated seventh (see this chapter, para. 3), so this may again be what Bernhard has in mind here.

The present rule and the following one are found in one all-inclusive set of brackets in M-B., just in the location where I give them, and seem to have been readings found in one manuscript source only. They clearly break the thought of the rest of the chapter and to some degree constitute redundancies; nonetheless, I include them because they do seem to add some substantial matter to the discussion.

91. This last sentence has a bracket at its start in M-B., again suggesting a variant reading. Note that the first example is hardly a good illustration of the thought contained therein, since no sixth appears in the original setting.

In Example 317, the lower voice of the original setting indeed states the first line of *Aus Tiefer Not*. Meanwhile the upper voice has the first line of another chorale, *Ach Gott vom Himmel sieh' darein*. An ingenious combination!

92. This is an alternative transformation, analogous to the alternative transformation for counterpoint at the tenth mentioned in para. 5 of the preceding chapter. A

formulation for it is given below in this chapter, para. 9. By "octave lower," Bernhard only seems to point to the obvious but not particularly noteworthy: namely, that the upper voice of the original setting is lowered an octave in this transformation, rather than a fifth.

93. "keine *Syncopation* aus *Dissonantzen*." Zarlino gives exactly the same rule (p. 271). Cf. Morley's discussion of double counterpoint in contrary motion (pp. 195–197), and Zarlino's (p. 271).

94. Morley (p. 196) gives the same rule, except that he writes "descend together" instead of "rise together." Zarlino, on the other hand, agrees with Bernhard, directing the rule to ascending voices (p. 271).

95. This rule, given by Morley (p. 196) and Zarlino (p. 271) also, works splendidly if the voices start an octave apart, as was advised in the preceding sentence; for then all intervals are preserved in the transformation. It can lead to disastrous results, however, not only if the voices start a fifth apart—as was prohibited above—but also if they start at other intervals, such as a third, sixth, fourth, etc.; for then the correspondences between intervals in the original setting and their counterparts in the transformation are in no way controlled by rules given here.

Again, the choice of seventh and ninth as the intervals by which initial notes should be transposed seems very appropriate in the present example, whose original setting begins with two D's, for the position of the semitones is then preserved in the transformation (with the aid of a B♭ in the signature); but if the original setting began with two E's, for example, then it would be impossible to preserve the position of the semitones even by introducing a flat or sharp in the signature of the transformation. Hence the choice of seventh and ninth as intervals of initial transposition (as opposed, for example, to sixth and tenth, or, indeed, an octave for each voice) seems arbitrary even when it is assumed that the voices will start an octave apart.

96. This rule, like the one given in para. 4, works beautifully in the example which Bernhard gives to illustrate it, but breaks down if the interval between the first notes of each voice, the mode of the original setting, or any one of a number of other factors is different than it is here. Note that the lower voice of the original setting is actually "transposed" up a fourteenth rather than a seventh. The top voice of the original setting states the first line of *Vater unser im Himmelreich.*

M-B. indicates that one source gives two additional paragraphs for this chapter after Example 322, which reintroduce the material of ch. 66, paras. 5 and 6. There seemed to be no need to give that material here.

97. Why the sixth is prohibited is unclear, unless this rule can be traced back to the non-quartal style prevalent ca. 1500. (A sixth would of necessity induce a fourth in the transformed version.)

98. I give both the original setting and the reply exactly as found in M-B. (including all accidentals). Bernhard dramatically illustrates his own observation that leaps of fourths often will not turn out well in the reply! As in ch. 68, paras. 4 and 5 (which also happen to deal with double counterpoint in contrary motion), Bernhard has given unsatisfactory rules here. The conditions for the alto and tenor are insufficient; and everything breaks down if the alto starts a sixth below the soprano, or the tenor in unison with the bass (possibilities which the rules seem to allow). Also, the bass in Bernhard's example is "transposed" up a fifth—not a twelfth, as he himself had required.

99. "Dass die Partheyen nur können zurücke gesungen werden, ohne die Erhaltung der vorigen Linien und *Spatiorum*, und sind die vorigen, nur dass man darinnen keine *Dissonantz* und *Puncta* gebraucht." The bracketed word in the text is mine. The following two passages are retrograde versions of the replies found in the two earlier examples of this chapter (in the case of the first example, the second reply), with changes in both rhythm and pitch to make them more palatable. These changes are clearly in keeping with the provision that there be no dissonances or dots anywhere, but obviously Bernhard did not change enough. (I give both passages exactly as found in M-B.) When Bernhard says that the "previous lines and spaces" are not preserved, it seems that he is comparing the present versions with the original settings of those two earlier examples, and remarking that notes of those original settings and these retrograde versions do not "preserve lines and spaces" in the special sense found in the subsequent kind of retrograde counterpoint.

Haydn's Elementarbuch

A DOCUMENT OF CLASSIC COUNTERPOINT INSTRUCTION

ALFRED MANN

THE RECENT publication of Thomas Attwood's studies with Mozart in the *Neue Mozart-Ausgabe* has called new attention to the eminent place that contrapuntal instruction held in the work of the Classic Viennese composers. Far from being indifferent to formal studies, the masters of the Viennese school showed a keen interest in the contrapuntal discipline and a thorough acquaintance with its details. This predilection for the craft was a Viennese heritage. The study of counterpoint had been codified in Johann Joseph Fux's *Gradus ad Parnassum* (1725), which had crowned the career of the Viennese *Altmeister*. Mozart must have become acquainted with this work in his early years, for Leopold Mozart owned a copy (preserved in the Mozart Museum, Salzburg) and Padre Martini owned a copy (preserved in the Liceo Musicale, Bologna). It is likely, however, that Mozart's thorough exploration of the *Gradus* exercises, which speaks from the pages of the Attwood studies, was prompted by discussions with Haydn.

Haydn, who had sung under Fux as a choirboy at St. Stephen's, acquired Fux's treatise probably in 1750, at the age of eighteen, when he had first achieved a sufficient measure of economic and artistic independence to "enable himself through a serious study of theory to bring order (which he loved above all, as we already know) into the outpourings of his soul." [1]

[1] *Biographical Account of Joseph Haydn, according to his spoken narration drawn up and edited by Albert Christoph Dies*; English edition in Vernon Gotwals, *Joseph Haydn, Eighteenth-Century Gentleman and Genius* (Madison, University of Wisconsin Press, 1963), p. 95.

Unlike Leopold Mozart's and Martini's *Gradus* copies, Haydn's copy of the work has not survived; it formed part of the Esterházy collection which was destroyed by fire during World War II. There is a detailed description of this copy in Pohl's Haydn biography with an account of some of Haydn's marginal notes,[2] and by good fortune Pohl transferred these notes with meticulous care into another copy of the work which passed from Pohl to Eusebius Mandyczewski and eventually to the Archives of the Gesellschaft der Musikfreunde in Vienna.

The comparison of this copy of Fux's work with those formerly owned by Leopold Mozart and Martini is striking. Leopold Mozart's and Martini's copies, too, contain marginal notes, but while these attest to a careful use of the text, they are sporadic and for the most part concerned with the correction of minor errors not contained in Fux's own (and rather extensive) errata listing. For instance, Martini corrects "8" to "10" (Example 1) in the second of two examples comparing differently introduced 9-8 resolutions; Leopold Mozart corrects the tenor clef to the alto clef in an example given erroneously in Fux's text (Example 2).[3]

EXAMPLE I

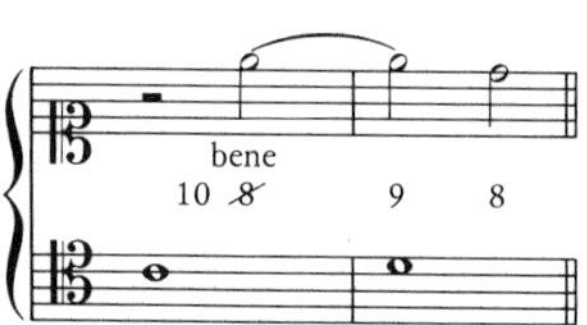

EXAMPLE 2

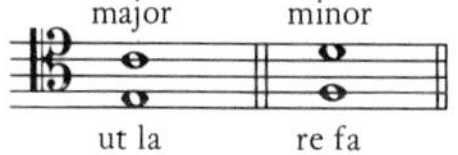

One of these two misprints seems to have escaped Haydn, but there are hardly any others that he failed to note—in fact, there is hardly a single problematic spot in the 280 folio pages of Fux's work that does not show

[2] C. F. Pohl, *Joseph Haydn* (Leipzig, Breitkopf and Härtel, 1878), I, 176.

[3] See *Gradus ad Parnassum* (facsimile edition) in Johann Joseph Fux, *Sämtliche Werke*, Series VII, Vol. I, edited by Alfred Mann (Kassel, Bärenreiter, 1967), pp. 71 and 38.

the most exacting and thorough commentary by Haydn, written (with one or two exceptions), like the original text, in Latin.[4]

Haydn's annotations range from minute emendations and clarifications to the most penetrating criticism and challenge of principles presented by Fux. He rewrites rules and examples, and he detects misprints in portions of Fux's own work quoted at the end of the book. He finds errors in Fux's own errata listing, to which he adds a complete page of his notes. There is no doubt that a large part of Haydn's commentary was made when he was a student first acquainting himself with the study of counterpoint. But he must have returned to the text again and again. His various references to Kirnberger could not have been entered before the 1770s, presumably twenty years after his first marginal notes were written.[5]

We know that Haydn took a strong interest in teaching during the 1770s. Ignaz Pleyel, staying at Haydn's house, studied with him for five years, and among various other pupils were Carl Maria von Weber's two older brothers, Fritz and Edmund (Carl Maria received his first formal instruction from Haydn's brother Michael).

The highly systematic exposition of Fux's study of counterpoint by Mozart in the Attwood papers is the account of Classic counterpoint instruction closest in spirit to Haydn's *Gradus* annotations that has come down to us, and it shows significant parallels with these (for instance, in the fashioning of variant patterns for four notes against one not covered in Fux's text).[6] Mozart moved to Vienna in 1781 and, in the course of the following decade, discussions of didactic questions must have taken place between the two masters.[7]

[4] A choice of Haydn's annotations directly concerned with the revision of the text has been published in the Critical Notes of the new edition of Fux's works, see footnote 3. Cf. also the present writer's articles "Eine Textrevision von der Hand Joseph Haydns" in *Musik und Verlag, Karl Vötterle zum 65. Geburtstag*, edited by Richard Baum and Wolfgang Rehm (Kassel, Bärenreiter, 1968), pp. 433–37, and "Haydn as Student and Critic of Fux" in *Studies in Eighteenth-Century Music, A Tribute to Karl Geiringer on his Seventieth Birthday*, edited by H. C. Robbins Landon in collaboration with Roger E. Chapman (London, Allen and Unwin, 1970), pp. 323–32.

[5] The first volume of J. P. Kirnberger's *Die Kunst des reinen Satzes* appeared in 1771 (reissued in 1774); the second volume appeared in three sections in 1776, 1777, and 1779, respectively. Haydn mainly compares the two writers' views on parallel (though interrupted) progressions of octaves or fifths occurring between one accented beat and the next.

[6] See *Thomas Attwoods Theorie- und Kompositionsstudien bei Mozart* in W. A. Mozart, *Neue Ausgabe sämtlicher Werke*, Serie X, Supplement, Werkgruppe 30, Band I, edited by Erich Hertzmann and Cecil B. Oldman, completed by Daniel Heartz and Alfred Mann (Kassel, Bärenreiter, 1965), pp. 53 ff.

[7] A letter from the year 1784 shows that Haydn tried to obtain a second *Gradus* copy, see footnote 18. Attwood studied with Mozart from 1785 to 1787.

A document which gives evidence of Haydn's teaching activity during these years has been preserved in the Esterházy Archives.[8] Entitled *Elementarbuch der verschiednen Gattungen des Contrapuncts aus den grösseren Wercken des Kappm. Fux, von Joseph Hayden zusammengezogen*, it is an abstract—unfortunately fragmentary—of Fux's treatise on counterpoint as presented in the manuscript of Haydn's student F. C. Magnus, possibly taken down from Haydn's dictation, but more likely transcribed from a rough copy prepared by Haydn himself.

The manuscript is dated 1789, two years after Attwood had completed his studies with Mozart. Aside from its own documentary value and its proximity—both in time and in details of formulation—to the Attwood studies, this text, published below for the first time, is of great interest since it is also connected with Beethoven's study under Haydn. Gustav Nottebohm has suggested that Haydn formulated a similar abstract for each of his students. In his monograph dealing with Beethoven's studies, he presents a reconstruction of the *Elementarbuch* that may have been used by Beethoven.[9] No such original manuscript has been preserved, and Nottebohm's presentation of the *Elementarbuch* text is introduced by the following note: "Beethoven's copy of the *Elementarbuch* has been lost. The present rendition is based upon two sources of which one is fragmentary and the other unreliable. Thus our presentation of the text can lay no claim to accuracy or completeness."

It is much to be regretted that Nottebohm was not more specific about describing his sources. From Pohl's work, published five years after Nottebohm's, we learn that one of the two was indeed the *Elementarbuch* prepared by Magnus. Being fragmentary, this then is the first source of which Nottebohm speaks. But what was the nature and origin of the other source? Nottebohm describes it as "unreliable." Nevertheless, he must have used it exclusively for approximately half of his reconstructed text, for the abstract written by Magnus breaks off at the beginning of the chapter dealing with the third species of counterpoint, whereas the text presented by Nottebohm covers the entire discussion of two-part counterpoint.

[8] Now in the National Széchényi Library, Budapest, class mark Ha I 10.

[9] Gustav Nottebohm, *Beethoven's Studien. Erster Band. Beethoven's Unterricht bei J. Haydn, Albrechtsberger und Salieri* (Leipzig and Winterthur, J. Rieter-Biedermann, 1873), pp. 21 ff.

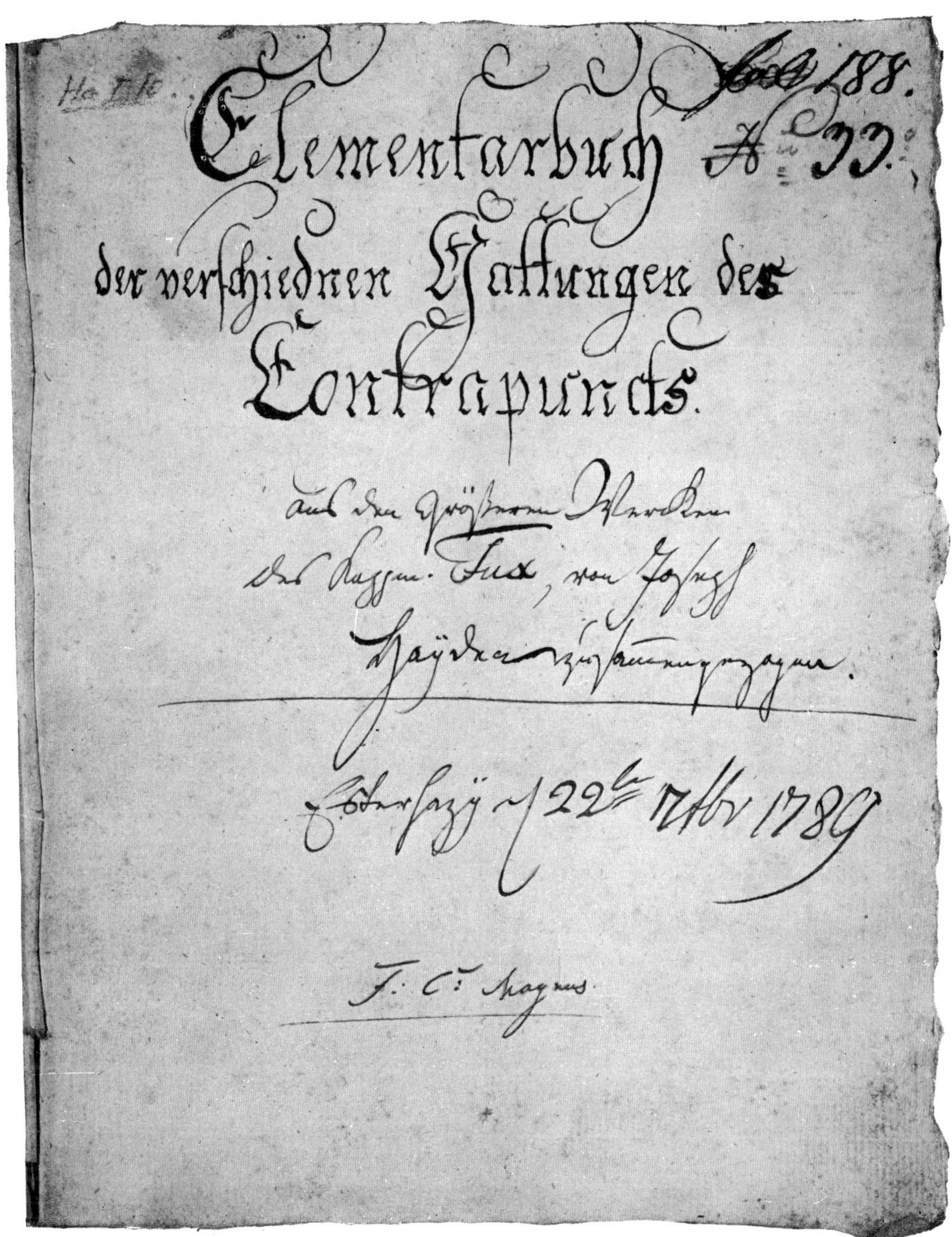
188.

Elementarbuch No 33.

der verschiednen Gattungen des

Contrapuncts.

aus den grösseren Werken

des Kappm. Fux, von Joseph

Haydn zusammengezogen.

Esterhazy 22ten 7ber 1789

F. C. Magnus

Title page from the *Elementarbuch*.

This illustration and those on page 203 are reproduced, and the entire text of the *Elementarbuch* is presented, with the kind permission of the National Széchényi Library, Budapest. Grateful acknowledgment is made to Dr. István Kecskeméti, director of the library's music division.

Thus, aside from the Magnus copy, we have no reliable account of the material that Beethoven may have used as a guide for his counterpoint lessons with Haydn. We do have a document, however, from which we can draw further conclusions about the material Nottebohm presents, for Beethoven himself made an abstract of Fux's *Gradus* entitled *Einleitung zur Fuxischen Lehre vom Kontrapunkt* which was preserved among the manuscripts first published—in a highly arbitrary editorial manner—by Ignaz Ritter von Seyfried.[10] The manuscript sources were reviewed, and Seyfried's various licenses nailed down, in the exemplary account contained in Nottebohm's *Beethoveniana*,[11] which includes Beethoven's *Einleitung* in excerpt.

The situation is further complicated by the fact that a number of examples and text portions from the Magnus copy do appear, in slightly altered form, interwoven in Seyfried's haphazard account of Beethoven's studies[12]—suggesting that the Magnus text, or a copy of it, was among Beethoven's manuscripts at the time Seyfried prepared his edition. Of this, however, Nottebohm makes no mention, and there is no doubt that at the time of his writing, forty years after Seyfried's edition, the manuscripts of Haydn's and Beethoven's *Gradus* abstracts had been separated.

Nottebohm was able to date a portion of Beethoven's manuscripts, and the date at which he arrived, 1809, supports his assumption that Beethoven compiled his *Einleitung*, together with other parts in the group of manuscripts, for Archduke Rudolf, one of his foremost patrons, with whose instruction he was concerned at the time. As Nottebohm points out, we are dealing almost throughout with a text which Beethoven merely copied, not formulated or paraphrased himself, from various theoretical works available in print.[13]

[10] Ignaz Ritter von Seyfried, *Ludwig van Beethoven's Studien* (1st German ed.: Vienna, T. Haslinger, 1832; French ed.: 1833; 2d German and 1st English ed.: Leipzig, Hamburg, and New York, Schuberth, 1853, reissued in facsimile: Hildesheim, Georg Olms, 1967).

[11] Gustav Nottebohm, *Beethoveniana* (Leipzig, J. Rieter-Biedermann, 1872), pp. 154 ff.

[12] Seyfried, 1832 ed., pp. 76–83; 1853 ed., pp. 68–74.

[13] As sources for the *Einleitung*, Nottebohm actually identifies not only Fux's text in the German translation by Bach's student Lorenz Mizler—Johann Joseph Fux, *Gradus ad Parnassum; oder, Anführung zur regelmässigen musikalischen Composition* (Leipzig, im Mizlerischen Bücherverlag, 1742), but also C. P. E. Bach's *Versuch über die wahre Art das Clavier zu spielen* (Berlin, im Verlag des Auctoris, gedruckt bey C. F. Henning, 1753); J. P. Kirnberger's *Die Kunst des reinen Satzes*; J. G. Albrechtsberger's *Gründliche Anweisung zur Komposition* (Leipzig, J. G. I. Breitkopf, 1790); and D. G. Türk's *Kurze Anweisung zum Generalbassspielen* (Leipzig, Schwickert, 1791).

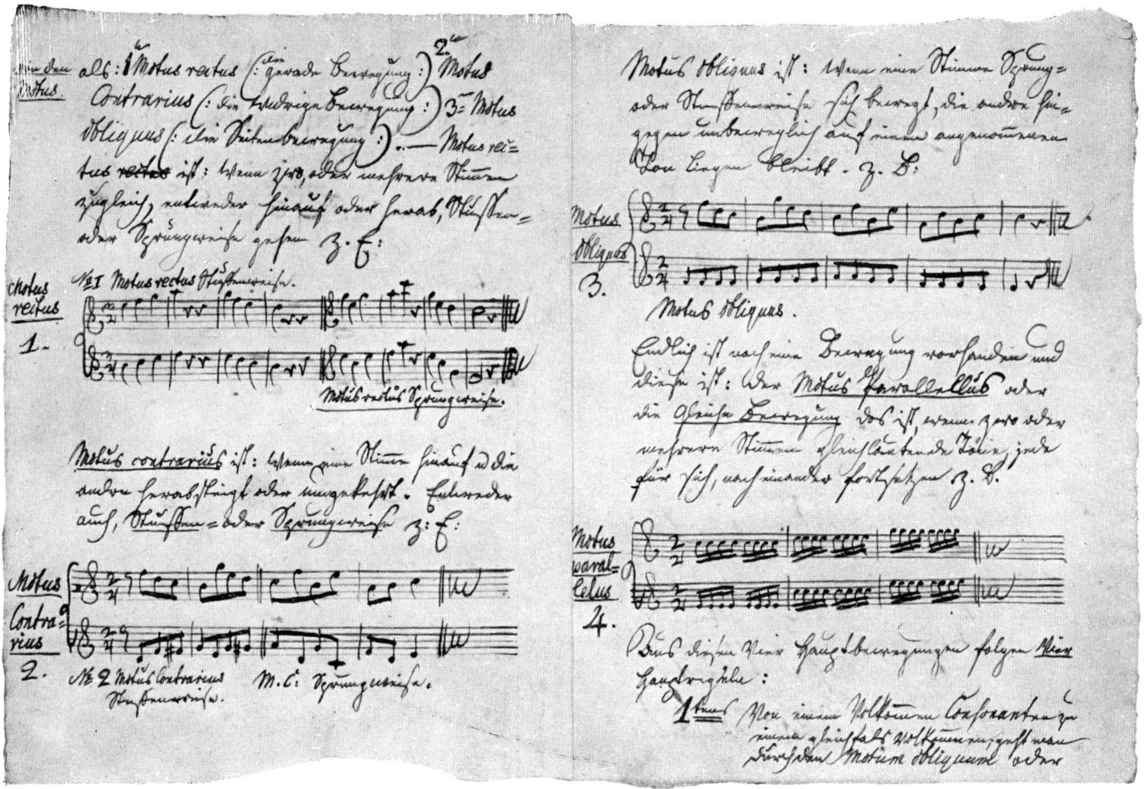

The fourth and fifth pages from the *Elementarbuch.*

Even a casual comparison of the text of Beethoven's *Einleitung* with the text which Nottebohm presents as Haydn's *Elementarbuch* for Beethoven's use shows common characteristics. For instance, Nottebohm traces the first paragraph of the *Einleitung* to the text of Türk. The first paragraph of the reconstructed *Elementarbuch* shows the same wording. It is likely that Türk's study served only Beethoven, not both Beethoven and Haydn, as a source: it was not represented in Haydn's library.[14] Was the second *Elementarbuch* compilation of which Nottebohm speaks made by

[14] O. E. Deutsch, "Haydns Musikbücherei," in *Musik und Verlag* (see footnote 4), pp. 220–21.

Beethoven rather than by Haydn, and did it date from a later period than Beethoven's study with Haydn?

These questions receive added importance because our information about Beethoven's study with Haydn is incomplete: we know Beethoven's side of the story better than Haydn's. In surveying the evidence Nottebohm has assembled in his *Beethoven's Studien*, it may be difficult to argue with his judgment that Haydn's counterpoint instruction was "inadequate." Yet, if we hold Nottebohm's wording "Haydn was not systematic, not thorough, not conscientious as a teacher" against the evidence of Haydn's meticulous, searching, and methodical manuscript annotations upon Fux's text, the evaluation of Haydn's didactic interest and activity grows more complex.

It is against this background that the fragmentary Magnus copy of the *Elementarbuch* gains special significance. Dating from a period close to Beethoven's arrival in Vienna (1792), it shows the same concern for pedagogical detail that we find in the annotations of the *Gradus* copy Haydn acquired forty years earlier. Haydn's interest in contrapuntal theory had remained strong. Having had to revise our judgment about the role of the didactic process in Mozart's work on the basis of the Attwood studies, we may also have to reappraise the influence of Haydn's didactic activity and its role in the rise of the Classic Viennese style.[15]

While the Magnus copy is unique as a text especially prepared for Haydn's teaching, it must be considered with some reservation. Doubtless we are dealing with Haydn's own formulations, but various errors suggest that some of these formulations were garbled by the copyist and that Haydn did not check the copy. The greatest interest the manuscript has for us lies in a general style of presentation, which is both more expansive and more stimulating than the text Nottebohm has given and, at the same time, is closer to a treatment of the material we can identify as characteristic of Haydn on the basis of the *Gradus* annotations Pohl has preserved.

The manuscript, written with great care and embellished with a title and chapter headings in elaborately printed Gothic letters, gives the impression that Magnus was entrusted with the preparation of a special fair copy. Haydn spoke of him as "a poor but well-educated and well-bred young

[15] A paper dealing with Beethoven's contrapuntal studies under Haydn was read by the present writer, after this article had gone to press, at the musicological congress held in observance of the Beethoven bicentennial at Bonn in 1970; it appeared in enlarged form in the special issue, published for the bicentennial, of *The Musical Quarterly* (October 1970), pp. 711–26.

man from Livonia, to whom I give composition lessons free of charge because of his extraordinary diligence."[16] For reasons unknown (Magnus continued his studies with Haydn at least until the following year), the task was not completed: the manuscript ends at the bottom of the seventeenth page, leaving blank the majority of pages in the neatly bound book. The text is a free paraphrase of excerpts from the sections covering pp. 41–66 of the *Gradus ad Parnassum*, in which Haydn's own translation of Fux's wording is combined with passages drawn from Mattheson's *Der vollkommene Capellmeister* (1739).[17] Unlike Beethoven, Haydn seems to have worked for the most part from the original text of Fux's work without referring to Mizler's German translation.[18] An exception is the opening of the second chapter, especially the second paragraph of page 11, in which portions of sentences are identical with Mizler's wording.

The present copy follows the original arrangement of pages and lines and the original punctuation and spelling with the following minor exceptions: Words in which the doubling of a consonant is indicated by a line (e.g., *zusam̄engezogen*) have been spelled out. The umlaut invariably placed, according to eighteenth-century spelling, over the letter *y* has been omitted. (The spelling for Haydn's name appears on the title page as *Haÿden.*) The German double consonant *sz* (ß) has been rendered as *ss*. The abbreviated form for *und* (u.) has been spelled out.

The original text appears in German script, except for some derived words and terms (*perfect*, *Tritonus*) which are written in Latin script. Underscoring has been indicated as in the original. Errors in copying, crossed out in the original manuscript, have been so rendered in the present copy and in the translation whenever an obvious change of meaning is involved. Corrections essential to the understanding of the text have been indicated in the footnotes. The original pages, measuring 15 × 20 cm., were not numbered. The wording of the title, referring to "Fux's larger works" is likely Magnus' own.

16 Haydn's letter to Friedrich Jacob van der Nüll, June 7, 1790. See H. C. Robbins Landon, *The Collected Correspondence and London Notebooks of Joseph Haydn* (London, Barrie and Rockliff, 1959), p. 103.

17 Johann Mattheson, *Der vollkommene Capellmeister* (Hamburg, Christian Herold, 1739); facsimile reprint (Kassel, Bärenreiter, 1954).

18 In his letter of April 8, 1784, Haydn requested Artaria to obtain a copy of Mizler's translation for him (see Landon, p. 46), but in Haydn's library only the original Latin edition was preserved.

[TITLE PAGE]

Elementarbuch
der verschiednen Gattungen des
Contrapuncts.

aus den grösseren Wercken
des Kappm. Fux, von Joseph
Hayden zusammengezogen.

Esterhazy d. 22ten 7tbr 1789

F: C: Magnus.

[PAGE 2 BLANK]

[TITLE PAGE]

A Compendium of the different species of Counterpoint

Condensed from the larger works of Kapellmeister Fux by Joseph Haydn

---

Esterhazy, September 22, 1789

F. C. Magnus

[PAGE 2 BLANK]

[PAGE 3]

Regeln des Contrapuncts.

Von den Consonanten oder Wolklingenden Tönen.

Unis, Terz, Quinte, 6te, Octave.

Cons: Consonanten sind 5 als:

mit ihren Compositis (zusammengesetzten)
Unter diesen sind einige Volkommen oder perfect;—

Volkommen sind:

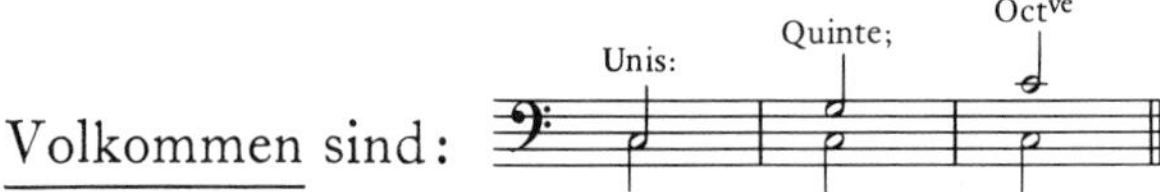

volkommen und unvolk:

Unvolkommen sind:

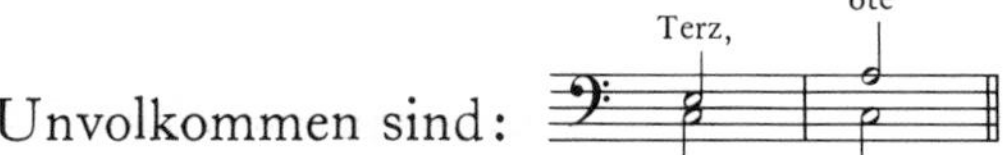

weil sie nach belieben, verringert, oder vergrössert werden können—Die übrigen als die

Secunde, Quarte, Quinta falsa 7tima 9ne

und der Tritonus, sind Dissonanten oder übellautende Töne. Aus diesen musikalischen Elementen, besteht die ganze Composition, theils durch ihre Versetzung oder Veränderung; theils durch ihre Bewegung; wenn ich von einem Intervall zum anderen übergehe. Diese Bewegung oder Motus ist dreyfach, als:

[PAGE 3]

Rules of Counterpoint.

Of Consonances or Agreeable Sounds.

CONS.: There are five consonances, namely: [example]
unison, third, fifth, sixth, octave

or the intervals made up of these and the octave (compound consonances).

Some of these consonances are perfect:—

perfect Perfect are: [example]
unison, fifth, octave

and

imperfect Imperfect are: [example]
third, sixth

because they can be diminished or augmented, as may be desired*—the remaining intervals,

namely [example]
second, fourth, diminished fifth,† seventh, ninth

and tritone, are dissonances or incompatible sounds. These musical elements determine the entire art of part-writing, both through the various ways in which they may be placed and the various ways in which they may move in the progression from one interval to another. Such motion or motus is threefold, namely:

* The description of imperfect consonances as those which "can be diminished or augmented as may be desired" is added to Fux's text.

† The example for "Quinta falsa" (probably given as c–g♭) is crossed out in the original almost beyond recognition, reducing the number of examples given for dissonances to those formed diatonically on the tone c.

[PAGE 4]

von den Motus

als: 1^{ns} Motus rectus (:die gerade Bewegung:) 2^{ns} Motus Contrarius (:die widrige Bewegung:) 3^{ns} Motus obliquus (:die Seitenbewegung:).—Motus rectus ~~rectus~~ ist: wenn zwo, oder mehrere Stimmen zugleich, entweder hinauf oder herab, Stufen- oder Sprungweise gehen z.E:

Motus rectus 1.

N°1 Motus rectus Stufenweise.

Motus rectus Sprungweise.

Motus contrarius ist: wenn eine Stimme hinauf und die andere herabsteigt oder umgekehrt. Entweder auch, Stufen- oder Sprungweise z: E;

[PAGE 4]

THE MOTIONS

namely: 1. Motus rectus (:direct motion:) 2. Motus contrarius (:contrary motion:) 3. Motus obliquus (:oblique motion:).—Motus rectus occurs when two or more parts move up or down by step or skip, e.g.:*

Motus rectus 1.

[example]
N° 1 Motus rectus occurring by step.

[example]
Motus rectus occurring by skip.

Motus contrarius occurs: when one part moves up and the other down, or vice versa. This may again occur by step or skip, e.g.:

Motus Contrarius 2.

[example]
N° 2 Motus Contrarius occurring by step.

[example]
M.C. occurring by skip.

* With minor exceptions, the examples appearing in the *Elementarbuch* are not taken from Fux's text. As in Fux's text, separate examples are given for direct motion by step and by skip, but no mention of these two manners of progression is made by Fux.

[PAGE 5]

Motus obliquus ist: wenn eine Stimme Sprung- oder Stufenweise sich bewegt, die andere hingegen unbeweglich auf einem angenommenen Ton liegen bleibt. z. B:

Motus obliquus 3.

Endlich ist noch eine Bewegung vorhanden und diese ist: der Motus Parallellus oder die Gleiche Bewegung das ist, wenn zwo oder mehrere Stimmen gleichlautende Töne, jede für sich, nacheinander fortsetzen z.B.

Motus parallelus 4.

Aus diesen vier Hauptbewegungen folgen die Hauptregeln:

1^{tens} Von einem Volkommen Consonanten zu einem gleichfals volkommen, geht man durch den Motum obliquum oder

[PAGE 5]

Motus obliquus occurs when one part moves either by skip or step whereas the other remains stationary on a given tone, e.g.:

Motus obliquus [example]

Motus obliquus.

3.

There is still another motion, which is: Motus Parallelus* or Even Motion and which occurs when in each of two or more parts the same tones are repeated several times, e.g.:

Motus parallelus [example]

4.

From these four principal motions are derived the principal rules:

1. From one perfect consonance to another perfect consonance one must proceed by oblique motion or

* The category of *motus parallelus*, important from the point of view of the Classic style, is added from Mattheson (p. 249), which accounts for the varying references to "the three motions" or "four principal motions." Contrary to Pohl's statement (p. 177), however, no examples are taken from Mattheson's text.

[PAGE 6]

Motum contrarium.

2[tens] Von einem Volkommen Consonanten zu einem Unvolkommen, geht man durch alle drey Bewegungen.

3[tens] Von einem Unvolkommen zu einem Volkommen Consonanten geht man durch den Motum obliquum oder Contrarium.

4[tens] Von einem Unvolkommen zu einem ebenfals unvolkommen, geht man durch alle 3 Bewegungen.

Aus diesen vier Hauptregeln wird man bemerken, das unter allen vier Fortschreitungen der Motus obliquus und Contrarius die Brauchbarsten sind. Der Motus rectus hingegen ist nur blos dann anzunehmen, wenn man von einem Volkommen zu einem unvolkommen oder umgekehrt, von einem unvolkommen zu einem volkommen Consonanten geht.

Aus diesen dreyen Bewegungen hängt (:um den Ausdruck des Kapm: Fuchs beyzubehalten:)

[PAGE 6]

by contrary motion.

2. From a perfect consonance to an imperfect consonance one may proceed by any of the three motions.

3. From an imperfect consonance to a perfect consonance one must proceed by oblique or contrary motion.

4. From one imperfect consonance to another imperfect consonance one may proceed by any of the three motions.

It will be noticed from these four principal rules that oblique and contrary motion are the most useful of the four motions.* Direct motion, on the other hand, can be applied only in going from a perfect to an imperfect consonance, or conversely, going from an imperfect to a perfect consonance.

Upon these three motions depends: (:to adopt the wording used by Kapellmeister Fux:)

* After presenting the four rules, Fux (p. 42) singles out oblique motion as the only motion suited for all situations of part-writing. As in many similar instances, Haydn completes the explanation. At the end of this paragraph appears the most striking error contained in the manuscript ("or conversely, going from an imperfect to a perfect consonance").

[PAGE 7]

das ganze Gesetz der musikalischen Propheten zusammen.

Vom Contrapunct

Das Wort Contrapunct heisst nichts anderes als Punkt gegen Punkt. Dieser Ausdruck ist eine genaue Darstellung der Art, wie unsere Vorfahren Componirt haben. Sie bedienten sich nehmlich im Choralgesange in den ältesten Zeiten, bloss der Punkte ohne Striche; da wir hingegen unseren Punkten oder Noten, Striche auf und abwerts hinzufügen. Wenn sie also zu einer Reihe von Punkten noch eine andere darunter fügten, so nannten sie diese gegeneinander stehenden Punkten Contrapunct, folglich: Punkt gegen Punkt.

Dieser Contrapunkt nun, hat verschiedene Eintheilungen oder Gattungen, als:

1^{tens} der Gleiche oder Einfache.

2^{tens} der Ungleiche oder Gerade.

[PAGE 7]

the entire law of the musical prophets.*

Of Counterpoint

The term counterpoint means nothing else but point against point. It describes precisely the manner in which our elders used to compose. In writing chant they originally used merely points without stems, whereas we add stems going up or down to our points or notes. Thus when they placed one series of such points below another one, they called these combined series of points counterpoint—point against point.

Counterpoint comprises several subdivisions or species, namely:

1. Equal or simple counterpoint.
2. Unequal or plain counterpoint.†

* Fux's wording of the concluding sentence reads: "Ab hac triplicis motus cognitione, usuque pendet (ut dicere solemus) Lex, & Propheta."

† The old distinction between equal and unequal counterpoint, first given by Tinctoris (*Liber de arte contrapuncti*, 1477), is not mentioned in Fux's text. Mattheson (p. 246 f.) uses *gleich* (note against note) and *ungleich* (several notes against one note). The latter is also named *schlecht* (plain) in Mattheson's text (corresponding to Haydn's *gerade*) in distinction to *figürlich*. To this last category belong, according to Mattheson, not only contrapuntal settings with individual rhythmic motion in all parts, but also settings written in invertible counterpoint (*doppelter oder mannigfaltiger Kontrapunkt*).

[PAGE 8]

3^{tens} der fügerliche, doppelte oder manigfal-
tige Contrapunct.
Nachdem nun die Kunst so hoch gestiegen ist,
dass unter vielen Stimmen eine jede derselben
ihre eigene Mensur und eignen Gesang hat; eine
der andrn untergeordnet ist und demnach zu
gleicher Zeit alle herschen; so ist aus dem
gleichen oder Einfachen Contrapunct nicht
nur der ungleiche, sondern auch der fügurliche
doppelte, und aus dem doppelten der Viel-
fache Contrapunct entstanden. Im
Gleichen oder Einfachen Contrapunct, sind
alle übereinander stehende Noten, einerley
Geltung und haben keine Dis- sonder lauter Consonanten. Die Erste
Gattung des Contrap: ist die Einfachste Zu-
sammensetzung zweyer oder mehrer
Stimmen aus lauter Consonanten (:sie
mögen, ganze, halbe oder viertelnoten seyen:)
~~entstanden~~

Wir machen also den Anfang
mit ganzen Noten in zweyen Stimmen (:a Due:)

[PAGE 8]

3. Figural,* double, or multiple counterpoint.

When the art of part writing had reached a level where each of several parts had its own meter and melody, each part following and at the same time determining the other, there arose from equal or simple counterpoint not only unequal but also figural counterpoint, double counterpoint, and (from double counterpoint) multiple counterpoint. In equal or simple counterpoint, all notes placed one above the other are of the same duration and form no dissonances but only consonances. The first species of counterpoint is therefore the simplest consonant combination of two or more parts (:which may consist of whole notes, half notes, or quarter notes:)†

Let us begin with whole notes in two parts (:a due:)

* Magnus corrects his misspelling of *figürliche*, only in part, eight lines later—"*fügurliche*."

† For this paragraph, cf. Mattheson's wording (p. 246): "Nachdem nun die Kunst so hoch hinausgewollt hat . . ."

[PAGE 9]

Es muss demnach in dieser Gattung des Contrap: in der Oberstimme einer jeden Note ein Consonans, entweder ein Volkomner oder Unvolkomner gegeben werden; mit dieser Ausnahme, dass die allererste und letzte Note ein Volkommner seyn muss. z. E:

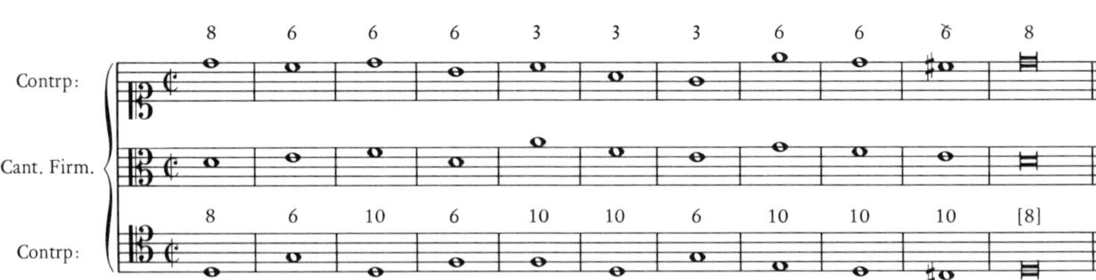

Hiebey müssen die 3 Motus wol beobachtet werden, auch ist es besser und sicherer, wenn man öfter den Motum obliquum und Contrarium gebraucht weil diese zwey Motus wenigern Fehlern unterworfen sind. Viel behutsamer aber muss man mit dem Motu rectu oder der graden Bewegung verfahren, weil man bey dieser mehr der Gefahr Fehler zubegehen ausgesetzt ist; Wie aus den Beyspielen zuersehen seyn wird.

Hauptsächlich muss man beobachten, dass wenn der Cantus Firmus unten steht, die vorletzte

[PAGE 9]

According to this species of counterpoint each note must be accompanied in the upper part* by a consonance, either perfect or imperfect, except that the very first and last notes must form perfect consonances; see the example:

[example]

Counterpoint
Cantus firmus†
Counterpoint

Here the three kinds of motion must be kept well in mind; it is better and safer to use mostly oblique and contrary motion since these two motions are less likely to lead to error. Much greater caution is needed in using motus rectus or direct motion which is more likely to result‡ in mistakes, as will become evident§ from the examples.

Above all, in placing the cantus firmus below, it is important to observe that the next to last

* *in der Oberstimme* follows Fux's text (p. 45), in which the assignment of placing the counterpoint in the lower part is treated separately.

† The Dorian cantus firmus is the same as used for Beethoven's studies with Haydn (see G. Nottebohm, *Beethoveniana*, p. 172); two separate two-part exercises are contained in the example.

‡ "*zubegehen*" should read "*zu begehen.*"

§ "*zuersehen*" should read "*zu ersehen.*"

[PAGE 10]

die vorletzte Note in der Oberstimme die 6te major,
wenn aber der Cant: Firm: ~~unten~~ oben steht
in der Unterstimme oder dem Contrapunct
die Terz Minor zu machen sey.

NB. In dieser Gattung des Contrap: sind die vielen Unisoni und Octaven zuvermeiden. Weil sie der Harmonie zu wenig Abwechslung verschaffen. Ausgenommen, am Anfang und am Ende eines Tonstücks, wo sie zu dulden sind.

Von der zweiten
Gattung
des
Contrapuncts

[PAGE 10]

the next to last* note of the upper part form a major sixth; in placing the cantus firmus ~~below~~ above, that the lower part or counterpoint form a minor third.

NB. In this species of counterpoint one should avoid† using many unisons or octaves. They yield too little variety of sound. Excepted are the beginning and end of a piece, where they can be more easily accepted.‡

Of the Second Species of Counterpoint

* The first two words are repeated from the preceding page. Magnus uses such a repetition in the manner of a *custos* or guide also on pp. 3, 4.

† "*zuvermeiden*" should read "*zu vermeiden.*"

‡ The concluding note in this chapter departs in two respects from Fux's text: Fux refers to the use of all perfect consonances (p. 46), and he singles out the use of the unison as suited only for the beginning and end (pp. 53 f.).

[PAGE 11]

Diese Gattung des Contrapuncts besteht darin, dass zwey halbe Schläge oder Noten, auf einen ganzen Schlag oder Note gesetzt werden. Von diesen zweien Schlägen, oder halben Noten heisst der Niederschlag Thesis und der Aufschlag Arsis, welcher zweyer Wörter wir uns bey dieser Übung bedienen werden. Jene halbe Note so in Thesi zu stehen kommt muss allezeit ein Consonans seyn, die andere hingegen in Arsi, kann auch eine Dissonans seyn, nehmlich die 2, 4, 7 u.s.w. wenn sie von einer Note zur ander Stufenweise geht; schreitet sie aber durch Sprünge fort so muss sie auch ein Consonans seyn.

Es kann also in dieser Gattung des Contrapuncts kein Dissonans anders statt finden, als wenn man den Raum oder Interval, welcher zwischen den Noten ist ~~so~~ die einen Terzsprung von einander liegen, ausfüllt z.E:

N° I

[PAGE II]

This species of counterpoint consists of placing two half beats or half notes against one whole beat or whole note. Of these two beats or half notes the downbeat is called thesis and the upbeat arsis, which two terms we shall use in our exercise.* The half note placed on the thesis must always be consonant; the other one, placed on the arsis, may be dissonant, forming a second, fourth, seventh etc., if the approach from one note to the other† occurs stepwise; if the approach occurs by skip, it must also be consonant.

Thus a dissonance cannot appear in this species of counterpoint except in filling out the space or interval between two notes that are a third apart, e.g.:

N° I [example]

Counterpoint
Cantus firmus

* Haydn's wording "*bey dieser Übung*" follows that of Fux, in whose text "*Exercitium*" is regularly used as a heading.

† "*zur ander*" should read "*zur anderen.*"

[PAGE 12]

Diese Ausfüllung oder diese Note ~~in unserm Exempel~~ in Arsi, kann auch zuweilen ein Consonans seyn, wie wir bey der vorletzten Note in unserm Exempel sehen werden, wo also die erste Note eine

Siehe N° II Quinte, die Zweite die 6te major ist. NB wenn der Cant: Firm: ~~mus~~ unten steht; Befindet sich der oben, so muss die erste Note eine 5te die zwote eine kleine Terz seyn z. E: N° 3

N° 3

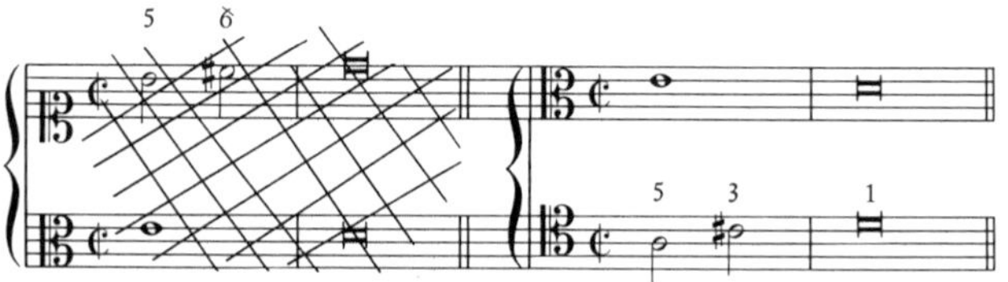

N° II

Es ist deswegen allezeit besser vorhero auf das Ende zu sehen. Um in diese Gattung zuerleichtern ist ~~in~~ der Contrapunctstimme erlaubt anstat der ersten Note in Thesi, eine halbe Pause zu setzen. Auch ist erlaubt, wenn beyde Stimmen zu enge zusammen kommen, durch einen Sechst- oder Octavensprung

[PAGE 12]

This intervening note on the arsis may at times also be consonant, as we shall see from the next to last note in our example,
See in which the first note forms a fifth and the second a major
N° II sixth—NB if the cantus firmus is placed below. If it is placed above, the first note must form a fifth and the second note a minor third, see N° 3*

N° 3 [example]

N° II [example]

For this reason it will always be better to consider the end ahead of time. In order to make this species easier† one may use a half rest in place of a first note occurring on the thesis. It is also admissible, whenever the two parts have moved too close together, to separate them through a skip of a sixth or of an octave.

* The examples for cadential patterns are taken from Fux's text, but the linear succession of two consonances, which is stressed in Haydn's discussion here and again in the following species, is not mentioned there.

† "*zuerleichtern*" should read "*zu erleichtern.*"

[PAGE 13]

von einander zu gehen. Endlich muss man hauptsächlich darauf sehen das man in dieser Gattung von Composition zwey aufeinanderfolgende 5ten und 8ven ~~nicht mache~~ mit einem Terzsprung nicht mache; welche verboten sind z.E.

N° 4

N° 4

Erstens weil die Noten die in Arsi steht, so angesehen wird, als wäre sie nicht vorhanden. z.B. N° 4 siehe oben. Zweitens weil solche nicht wegen Kürze der Zeit und des Raums verhindern kann dass das Ohr die übeln Verhältnisse zweier schnell aufeinander folgender 5ten und 8ven vernehmen solte. Eine ganz andere Beschaffenheit hat es mit einem Sprung, welcher einen grösseren Raum ausfüllt

z.B.

[PAGE 13]

Finally one should give particular attention in this species of composition not to connect two successive fifths or octaves by the skip of a third, which is not permissible, see the examples:

Fifths connected by the skip of a third*

N° 4 [example]

N° 4 [example]

For one thing the note occurring on the arsis might in effect be considered absent, see example N° 4, above. For another, its small duration and distance cannot obviate the disagreeable effect which the ear will perceive from the close succession of two fifths or octaves. A totally different situation would arise from the skip of a larger interval, e.g.

* The examples designated "bad" and "good" are taken from Fux's text. The last example, designated "more tolerable" and based on a principle not mentioned by Fux, was added by Haydn. Cf. the rule stated in the Attwood studies (p. 54) for similar patterns in the third species: "If in y[e] preceding bar there is an octave on whatever part of it, & in the following the first Note of it is an octave 'tis all ways as bad as two octaves," with the added remark: "Here is no octave." (The second of the two octave intervals in question occurs on the light beat.)

[PAGE 14]

mit der 4te, 5te, oder 6te durch welche Sprünge die Ohren nicht so beleidigt werden. Was endlich die verschiedenen Bewegungen oder Moti anbetrieft, so hat man sie bey dieser Gattung sowol als bey allen ~~vorherge~~ nachfolgenden genau zu beobachten.

Von der dritten Gattung des Contrapuncts

Die 3te Gattung des Contrp.

Die dritte Gattung des Contrapuncts ist, wenn vier viertelnoten auf eine ganze Note gesetzt werden. Dieses kann auf verschiedene Art geschehen. 1.) kann eine jede viertelnote ein Consonans seyn z.B. N° 1

[PAGE 14]

the fourth, fifth, or sixth, through which the ear would be less offended. So far as the different motions are concerned, their use will have to be carefully observed in this species as well as in all ~~preced~~ succeeding ones.

Of the third Species of Counterpoint

The third species of counterpoint

The third species of counterpoint arises when four quarter notes are placed against one whole note. This may occur in different ways. 1.) Each quarter note may be consonant,* e.g. N° 1

* The first pattern here listed for four notes against one marks a departure from Fux's discussion which is prompted by a new, harmonically oriented approach to this species expressed also in Attwood's examples and Mozart's corrections (see p. 61 in the Attwood studies).

[PAGE 15]

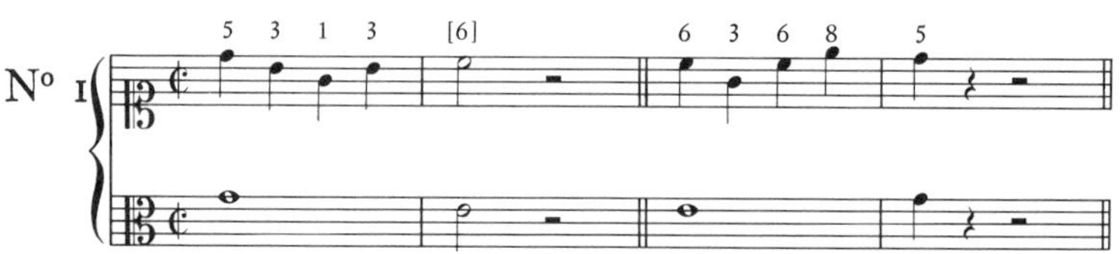

2^{tens} Wenn fünf Viertel im herauf und herabsteigen Stufenweise auf ein ander folgen, so muss die erste Note ein Consonans, die zwote aber ein Dissonans seyn. z.B.

3^{tens} Wenn die zweite Note eine Dissonans ist, so muss die dritte ein Consonans seyn z.B. wie oben bey N° 2.

4^{tens} Kann auch die zweite und vierte Note ein Consonans die dritte aber ein Dissonans seyn, z.E. N° 3

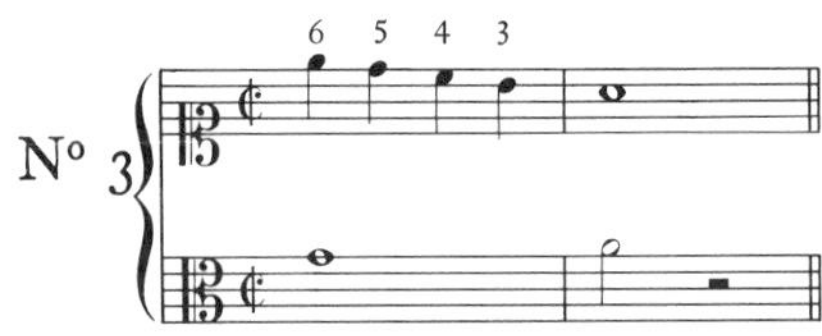

5^{tens} Kann auch die 1te, 3te und 4te ein Consonans, ~~seyn~~ die 2te aber ein Dissonans seyn. Siehe N° 2 Fig. 2.

[PAGE 15]

N° 1 [example]

2. In a stepwise succession of five quarters up or down, the first may be consonant and the second dissonant, e.g.

N° 2 [example]

3. If the second note is dissonant, the third must be consonant, see example N° 2, above.

4. The second and fourth notes may be consonant and the third dissonant, see example N° 3.

N° 3 [example]

5. The first, third, and fourth notes may be consonant and the second dissonant, see Fig. 2 in example N° 2.*

* The rules given on page 15, and summarized somewhat differently on page 17, are stated more fully than those appearing in Fux's text.

[PAGE 16]

Wenn der Cantus Firmus unten steht, so kann man von der Septime als einer Dissonans, einen Terzsprung herab in die Quinte machen, die Note aber vor der Septime mus allezeit eine Oktave seyn z.B. N° 4

N° 4

Ist aber der Cantus Firmus oben, so kann man von der 4[te] einen Terzensprung herabmachen in 6[te] machen z.B. N° 5

N° 5

Wohlzumerken; die 7 time und Quarte heisst man Wechselnoten oder (:Nota cambiata:) z: B: N° 6

N° 6

[PAGE 16]

If the cantus firmus is placed below, one may descend by the skip of a third from the seventh, a dissonance, to the fifth. The note preceding the seventh, however, must always form an octave, see example N° 4.*

Counterpoint

N° 4 [example]

Cantus firmus

If the cantus firmus is placed above, one may descend by the skip of a third from the fourth to a sixth, see example N° 5.

Cantus firmus

N° 5 [example]

Counterpoint

Observe that the seventh and the fourth are called changing notes (:Nota cambiata:), see example N° 6

N° 6 [example]

* This point is not stressed in Fux's text.

[PAGE 17]

Es können also, erstens in dieser ~~ein~~ Gattung alle vier Noten Consonanten seyn, zweitens die ersten 3 können Consonanten und die Vierte kann eine Dissonans seyn; drittens kann die erste und dritte ein Consonans ~~seyn~~ die zweite und vierte aber eine Dissonans seyn. Viertens, kann die 1te, 2te und 4te Note ein Consonans, die 3te aber eine Dissonans seyn.—die Beyspiele hierbey werden die Sache mehr erleichtern und aufklären.

Wenn der Cantus Firmus unten steht, muss der vorletzte Tackt folgendergestalt seyn z: B: N° 7

N° 7

Steht aber der Cantus Firmus oben ~~so~~ so muss der Vorletzte Tackt wie bey N° 8 seyn.

N° 8

[PAGE 17]

Thus in this species there can be, firstly, four notes which are all consonant, secondly, three notes which are consonant followed by a fourth note which is dissonant, thirdly, a first and a third note which are consonant and a second and a fourth note which are dissonant, fourthly, a first, a second and a fourth note which are consonant, and a third note which is dissonant.—The examples will make this clearer and more understandable.*

If the cantus firmus is placed below, the next to last measure must be as follows in example N° 7.

N° 7 [example]

If the cantus firmus is placed above, the next to last measure must be as in example N° 8.

Cantus firmus

N° 8 [example]

Counterpoint

* In his *Gradus* annotations for this chapter, Haydn points out the linear sequence of two dissonances, occurring in the middle of the measure, as a case not covered by Fux.

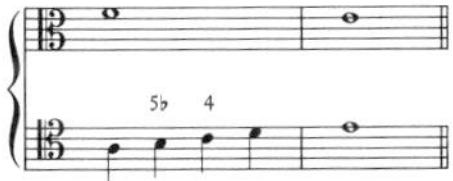

Conversely, in the present text Haydn deals with the linear sequence of two consonances occurring at the beginning or end of the measure (see page 15). Like his marginal annotations, Haydn's additions to Fux's text contained in the *Elementarbuch* are typical of his concern for completing and clarifying explanations, for the explicitness and "order which he loved above all."

Bach's Fugue in B$^\flat$ Major, Well-Tempered Clavier, Book I, No. XXI

CARL SCHACHTER

IN PRINCIPLE the analysis of a fugue should present no problems essentially different from those encountered in other types of music. Fugal procedures, after all, grow out of the contrapuntal and harmonic elements fundamental to tonality. And two fugues by the same composer may well differ by at least as much as two rondos, two sonata movements, or two nocturnes.

Unfortunately what we might expect in principle does not always coincide with what we find. As it happens the analysis of fugues involves difficulties which, if not fundamentally new, are often unusually intractable. There are, I think, several reasons for this. The first and most important is that masterpieces of fugue tend to be dense, tightly knit webs of voice leading which concentrate into relatively short musical spans a fantastic number of contrapuntal, harmonic, and motivic relationships.

Furthermore in the fugue (and in other genres based upon imitation), important thematic elements constantly shift from voice to voice; this can make it difficult to determine the controlling outer-voice structure. A solution to this latter problem is often blocked if we hear the various elements of fugal design—subject, countersubject, episodes, etc.—as entities separable from the fugue as a whole. All too often a conventional theoretical training in fugue tends to bring about this unproductive approach to hearing. A study of the enormous literature on fugue will show

how infrequently the fugal theorists have been able to reassemble into some kind of connected whole the *disjecta membra* produced by their analyses.[1]

PRELIMINARIES

FUGUE XXI (WTC I) is in three "voices," each with a range of about two octaves (soprano, c^1–c^3; alto, e♮–f^2; bass, E♭–f^1). It fills forty-eight bars and is in through-composed form. The subject begins on the fifth step of the scale; the answer, therefore, is tonal. There are two countersubjects; both, especially the second, often undergo minor changes owing to contrapuntal, harmonic, or instrumental exigencies. Only two episodes occur (bars 19–22 and 30–35); the second contains a free contrapuntal inversion of the first. The accompanying chart (see Example 1) shows at a glance the clear and simple design. Note that the subject and answer enter alternately and in pairs throughout the piece, and that these entrances shift from voice to voice with complete regularity.

LINEAR—HARMONIC CONTENTS

ONE MIGHT well begin such a study with an analysis of detail and end it with a comprehensive view of the whole piece. Two considerations led me to follow a different course. First, the linear–harmonic contents of the Fugue do not reflect the simplicity of its formal design. The reader, I think, will find it easier to follow the section-by-section analysis of detail if he can relate it to a larger framework. My second reason was my wish to counteract the prevalent (though usually unstated) assumption that a fugue is pieced together out of its parts and that these parts are independent entities, intelligible when separated from each other and from the work as a whole. For these reasons I shall begin with a discussion of background and of the more remote levels of middleground. I shall then proceed to a section-by-section analysis of the foreground. The article will conclude

[1] To be sure, the published literature on the fugue, although largely a desert, contains a number of oases. The classical treatises quoted and discussed in Alfred Mann, *The Study of Fugue* (New Brunswick, Rutgers University Press, 1958), present much valuable information. The writings of Donald Francis Tovey, though restricted to the musical foreground, can be remarkably insightful. And Heinrich Schenker left us an indispensable essay, "Das Organische der Fuge," *Das Meisterwerk in der Musik* (Munich, Drei Masken Verlag, 1926), II, 57–95. Schenker's essay contains an exhaustive analysis of the Fugue in C Minor, *WTC* I; although the analysis as such is not, in my opinion, completely convincing, it nonetheless remains immeasurably superior to any other fugal analysis known to me.

EXAMPLE 1

					5					10					15	
top voice	S				CS 1				CS 2				A			
middle voice					A				CS 1				CS 2			
bass									S				CS 1			

(Exposition)

				20					25					30		
top voice	from bars	S, 3, 4	from	S, bar	3	CS 1				CS 2				from	S, bar	1
middle voice	from	CS 1	(rests)			S				CS 1				(filling	voice)	
bass	from	CS 2	from	S, bar	1	CS 2				A (modified)				from	S, bar	3

(Extension) (Episode 1) (Middle Group of Entrances) (Episode 2)

			35					40					45			
top voice	from bar	S, 3	from	CS 2	S				CS 1				from	CS 2		
middle voice	from	S,	from bars	S, 1, 2	CS 1				A				from	S, bar	3	
bass	bar	1	from	CS 1	CS 2				CS 2				from	CS 1		

(Incomplete Entrance) (Closing Group of Entrances) (Final Cadence)

with a more detailed middleground graph which, I hope, will help the reader to unify the distant and the immediate perspectives.

The subject drives so surely to d² (bars 4 and 5), and the d² functions so clearly as the beginning of the Fugue's large-scale melodic progressions, that the fundamental structure seems hardly open to question. It consists of a melodic line falling a third from d² through c² to b♭¹, this line supported by a harmonic progression I–V–I. Example 2a shows the first level of prolongation and, although still very abstract, begins to indicate the Fugue's individual profile. Of particular importance is the neighboring tone e♭² supported by subdominant harmony; strictly speaking this is an incomplete neighbor, as the d² following it functions as a passing tone. Note that the indicated register of the top voice is the one in which it actually unfolds in the piece.

In Example 2b, the middle-voice tone, b♭¹, of the preceding graph becomes activated and forms part of the melodic line; the vertical third and fourth become unfolded into the horizontal dimension. Note the bass arpeggio b♭–g–e♭, which subdivides into two thirds the progression from I to IV. The melodic passing tone, d^2, is now shown as part of a cadential $^6_4$ over the V.

Example 2c adds considerably more detail; this graph should be the primary source of orientation for the detailed analyses to follow. Note that the unfolded third and fourth of the preceding graph have become step-

EXAMPLE 2

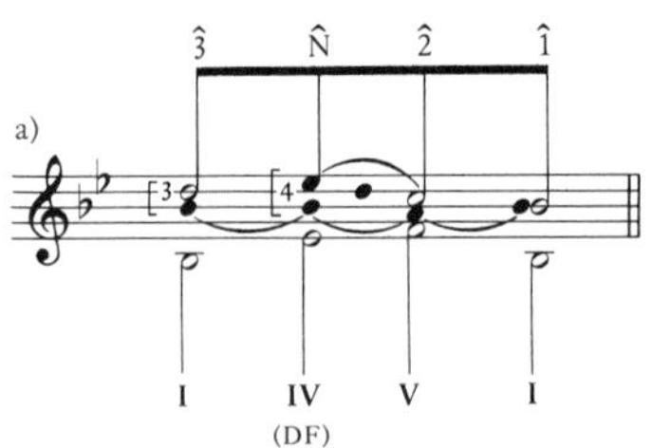

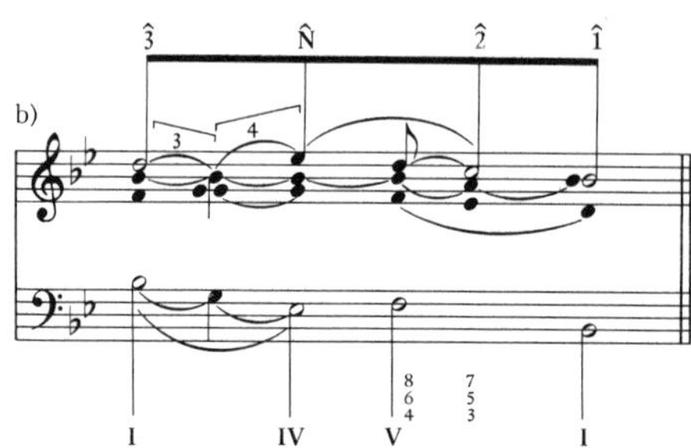

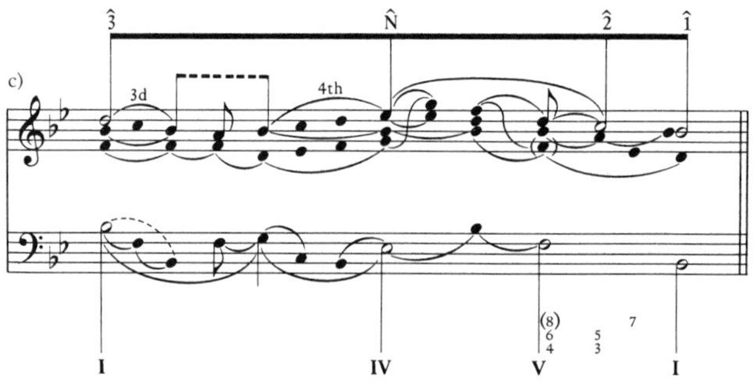

wise linear progressions. The third is supported by a harmonic elaboration of the tonic; the bass motion supporting the fourth gives rise to the C-minor coloration of bars 26–35. This graph, although more detailed than the preceding ones, is still highly synoptic; in particular, events which occur over a span of several measures are here compressed into a single chord (the very first tonic chord, for example). At this stage, obviously, the bar numbers can function only as a rough guide to the contents of the graph as they relate to the piece. Nevertheless, the graph offers a basis for understanding the inner articulations of the through-composed form.

The Fugue falls into three connected segments; the beginning of each new one overlaps the ending of the preceding one. The first segment (bars 1–19) contains the exposition plus a two-bar extension. Structurally it is governed by the descending third of the top voice supported by a prolonged tonic and a transition to G minor effected by the initial third of the bass's descending arpeggio. The second segment (bars 19–37) contains the first episode, the middle group of entrances, the second episode, and the "false," incomplete entrance of bars 35–36. This segment is unified by the linear progression of an ascending fourth in the top voice, supported by a bass motion of a third leading from G minor to E♭ major (conclusion of arpeggio). The final segment (bars 37–48) includes the closing group of entrances and final cadence. This segment contains the structural denouement of the Fugue; the top voice descends from the neighboring e♭^{2} to c^{2} and b♭^{1}, and the harmony progresses from IV to the final V and I.

FOREGROUND

First Segment (bars 1–19)

Example 3 contains a detailed graph and a somewhat reduced one of the first nineteen bars. I would suggest that the reader first consult the reduction (Example 3b), which provides an easier orientation. The bass plan and the harmonic scheme are not difficult to follow. The first entrance expresses tonic harmony; there is no bass, of course, but B♭ is clearly implied. The second entrance (answer) begins on the tonic and moves to the dominant (bars 8–9). The third entrance picks up the dominant and moves to

EXAMPLE 3

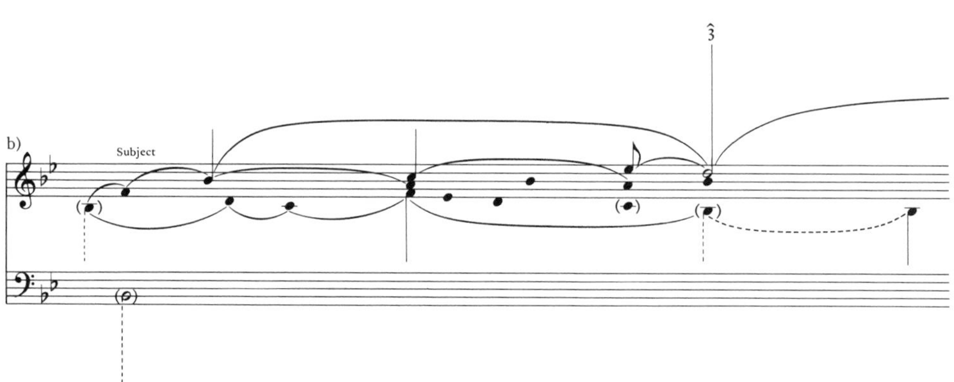

the tonic (bars 12–13). The added soprano entrance (answer) moves again to the F-chord; this F functions more importantly as a transition to the coming G minor than as a harmonic elaboration of the tonic. The motion is effected through a chromatic passing tone, f♯.

Example 4 is intended to help clarify the direction of the top voice from the beginning to bar 13. It shows the beautifully simple and ingenious

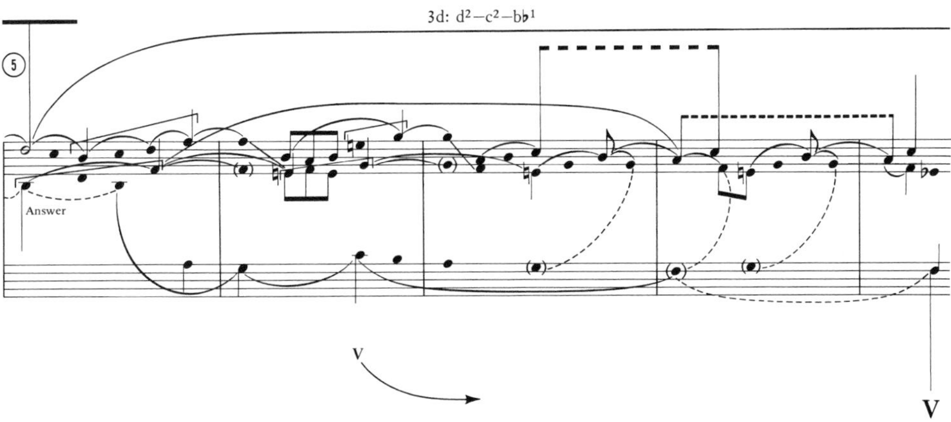

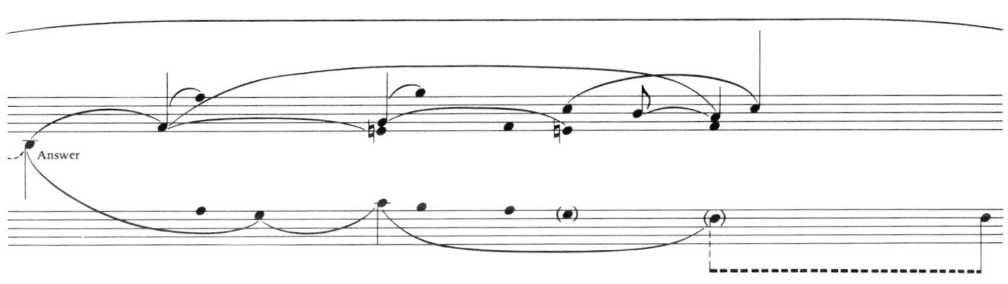

manner in which the culminating tones of the subject and two countersubjects join together to form a coherent melodic progression. The subject drives clearly and purposefully to d², the first tone of the Fugue's fundamental melodic line. The d² moves to c² at the end of the first countersubject and through that tone to the b♭¹ that ends the second countersubject. Note that Bach has composed his subject and counter-

EXAMPLE 3 (*continued*)

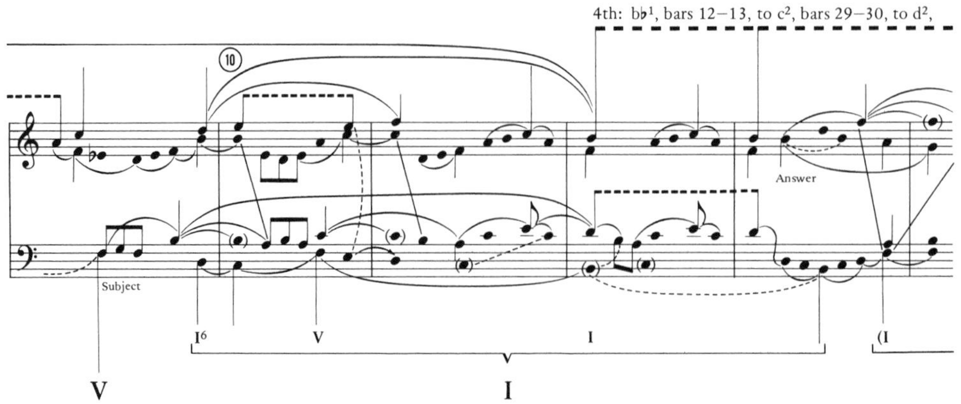

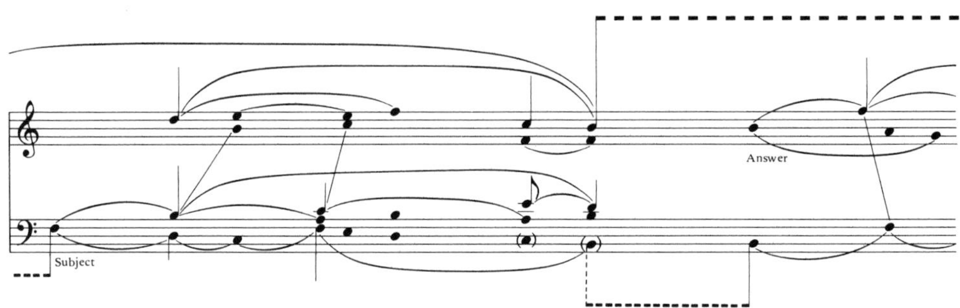

subjects so that they form both triple counterpoint when combined vertically and a large-scale melodic progression when heard one after the other.

The top voice of bars 13–19 is easier to follow and should be clear from Example 3 without additional graphs or lengthy discussion. The main point to observe is that the b♭¹ of bars 12–13 is prolonged but not in its original register; instead an upward-moving transfer of register (b♭¹–b♭²)

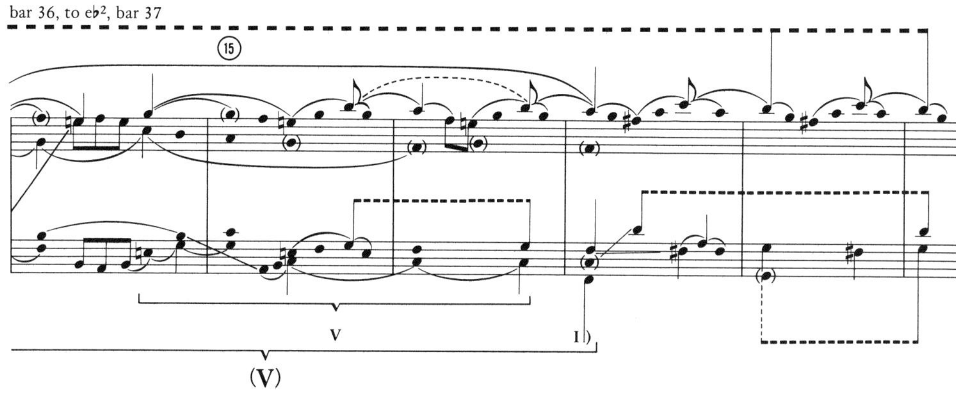

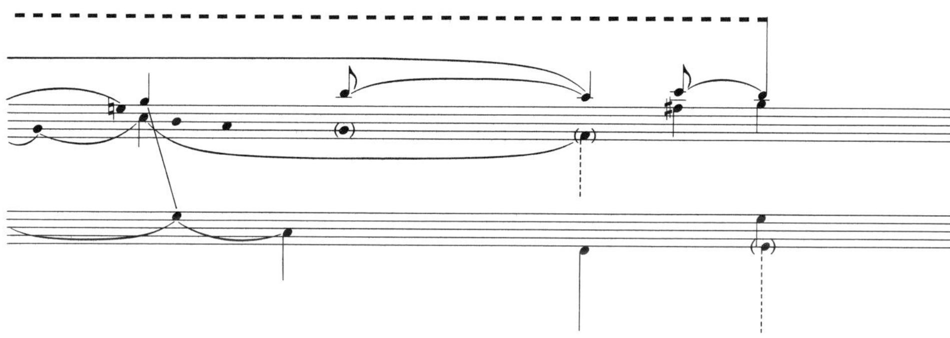

takes place, the arrival at b♭² coinciding with the appearance of the G-minor chord.

Subject. We can now proceed to an examination of the subject and of other elements of the Fugue's design. I would suggest that the reader relate these discussions of detail to the larger framework provided by Example 3; as

EXAMPLE 4

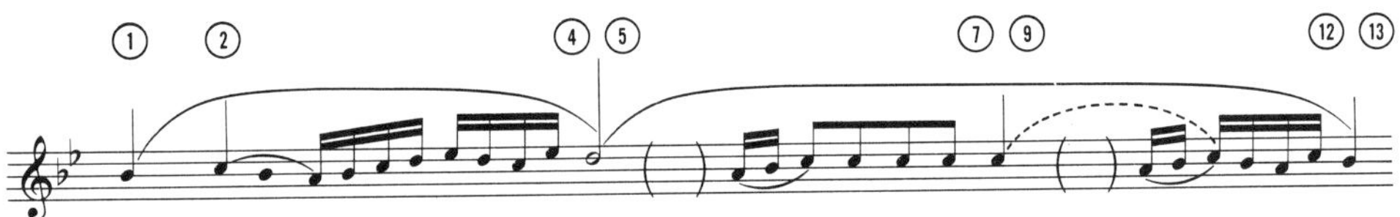

we go on, Example 3a will probably become clearer and easier to follow.

The subject is a rather complex melodic line; however its fundamental idea shines clearly through the elaborate detail. This idea is a melodic progression rising a third from $b\flat^1$ through c^2 to its goal, d^2 (Example 5a).[2] In Example 5b we see this essential motion abstracted from the subject; this example adds the clearly implied harmonic support $b\flat$–f^1–$b\flat$ (the f^1 is not implied but actually occurs as the seventh tone of bar 2).

Example 5c begins to show the development of this nucleus into the complete subject. Of particular importance is the incomplete neighbor, $e\flat^2$, whose appearance enables the goal tone to fall upon a first rather than a third beat. Comparing Example 5c with Example 2a reveals an interesting symmetrical relationship between the melodic outline of the subject and the top-voice structure of the Fugue as a whole. An incomplete neighbor on $e\flat^2$ figures prominently as an embellishment of both the ascending subject and the descending fundamental line. In the subject it leads into the goal tone; in the large structure it follows the initial tone.

Example 5c contains two other features requiring comment. In the lower "voice" the fifth f^1–$b\flat$ appears filled in by a stepwise passing motion. In addition the $b\flat^1$ and c^2 are followed by brief descending progressions which produce a counterforce to the upward urge of the subject's fundamental line. As a result the line rises in three overlapping segments (*Übergreifstechnik*) rather than in a single, unbroken curve.

As so often happens in Bach's polyphonically conceived melodic lines, our subject strongly hints at suspensions. These are shown in Example 5d by the sevenths that begin bars 2 and 3. The implied suspensions are significant for the performer; once aware of them he will play the opening

[2] Hugo Riemann maintained that the subject continues through the third note of bar 5. See his *Katechismus der Fugen-Komposition,* 1. Teil (2d ed.; Leipzig, Max Hesses Verlag, 1906), p. 144. This is certainly incorrect.

sixteenths of bars 2 and 3 as the continuation of the preceding tones, not as new beginnings. As we shall see, the first countersubject will bring into actuality these hinted-at suspensions.

Example 5e concentrates on important melodic diminutions and on rhythmic features. Observe how the neighboring figure of bar 1 is carried through into bar 2—a relationship disguised in the subject by the sixteenth-note figuration. The notes in parentheses (c^1 and b♭) represent the conclusion of the subject's lower "voice" as shown in Examples 5c and 5d. In the subject, this lower "voice" is broken off and is completed in its proper register only at the beginning of the next entrance (bar 5). However the sixteenth-note figuration conceals the missing tones in a higher register. The placement of these tones serves to prepare for the rhythmic position of the first tone of the answer (see arrows).

Example 5f shows the completed subject minus the repetition in bar 4, which will be discussed below. Only one point requires some comment. The sixteenth-notes of bar 3 are the inversion of those of bar 2. This was pointed out by Tovey, whose brief but instructive remarks about this Fugue stress the importance of melodic inversion in its design.[3] A most unusual feature of the subject is the repetition in bar 4 of the contents of bar 3. Although bar 4 brings in no new material, the repetition does make important contributions to the Fugue's design. In the first place, it creates a rhythmic balance between bars 1–2 and 3–4. In addition the repeated bar adds to the beauty of the voice leading at the next entrance. A most important feature of the second entrance is its delayed statement of b♭, the tone that completes the subject's lower "line." Now the first beat of bar 4 contains an obligatory $b\flat^1$ as part of the resolution of the diminished fifth a^1–$e\flat^2$ of bar 3. If the subject were shorter by a measure (in other words, if bar 3 were left out), the two b♭'s would come in at almost the same time to the advantage of neither one. By means of the repetition, Bach first has us hear the resolution a^1–$b\flat^1$ of bar 4. Once this has taken place, we can direct our attention to the b♭ of bar 5, whose effect is further enhanced by the bar's delay. In both countersubjects Bach has the fourth bar repeat the third; by thus emphasizing the repetition, Bach makes of it one of the salient elements of the Fugue's foreground design.

[3] See J. S. Bach, *Forty-eight Preludes and Fugues*, Book I, edited by Donald Francis Tovey (London, The Associated Board of the Royal Schools of Music, 1924), pp. 158–59.

EXAMPLE 5

Answer. As Example 6a indicates, Bach answers tonally both the first and the third tones of the subject; the second tone, however, is answered at the fifth (here, of course, the lower fourth). These changes in the answer produce an emphatic statement of tonic harmony in bar 5 (note the part interchange) that functions both as a goal for the contents of bars 1–4 and as the point of departure for the coming progression to F major (V). The second entrance, unlike the first, is not grounded in a single prolonged harmony; it consists instead of a transition from I to a tonicized V. The beginning of the answer contrasts with the subject contrapuntally as well as harmonically. The first tone does not belong to the middle but rather to the lowest "voice" of the horizontalized B♭-chord. As such it begins the lower part of the answer's implied polyphony. As before, the line and the harmonic movement are fulfilled only at the beginning of the next entrance (bass, bar 9). Example 6b gives a detailed picture of the answer.

Later Entrances. The modulatory quality of the second entrance will characterize most of the later entrances of the subject as well as the answer. Only the E♭ entrance of bar 37 expresses a single sonority. If the reader will refer to Example 3, he will see that the bass entrance of bar 9 bears a very different meaning from the opening statement of bars 1–4. The first tone now functions as the root of the F-chord and, consequently, as the harmonic goal of the preceding four measures. Although the prolongation

EXAMPLE 6

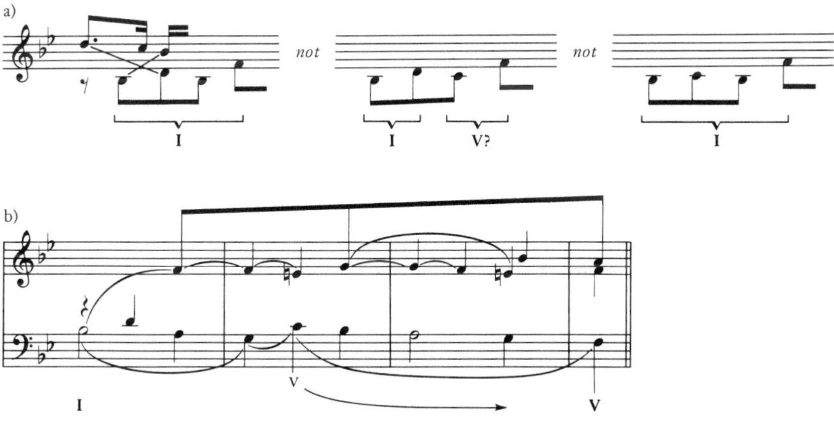

of the B♭-chord begins on the third beat of bar 9, the chord is stabilized only at the end of the subject (bars 12–13).

Countersubjects. There is no audible break between the subject and the first countersubject; the simplest and best interpretation is to regard the last note of one as the first of the other. In later entrances Bach often adjusts the beginning of this countersubject to fit the prevailing harmonic and contrapuntal conditions.

In contrast to textbook prejudices in favor of "independent" voice leading, Bach makes the first two measures of this countersubject markedly dependent upon the subject or answer (see brackets, Example 3). The most prominent features of these bars (at the second entrance, bars 6–7) are the suspended sevenths, which transform into audible reality the hinted-at suspensions of the subject. The graceful interplay of the two voices with the suspensions and their resolutions tossed from one to the other creates a beautifully light and transparent texture. As Example 3a shows, the second suspension (soprano, bar 7) is resolved only at the lower octave and in the alto voice.

The latter half of the countersubject reinforces the answer by moving in parallel thirds with it for part of its course. The repeated tones of bars 7–8, however, constitute a new and important element. They emphasize the tone c^2, here the fifth of the F-chord, and in a broader context the second step of B♭ over a prolonged dominant. If the reader will refer back to Example 4, he will recall that the c^2 forms part of the governing melodic progression of the Fugue's exposition.

In its first statement (bar 9 ff.), the second countersubject begins with a stepwise motion filling in an embellishing third above a prolonged d^2. In subsequent entrances, the corresponding measures often vary both in meaning and in melodic content. The last two measures recur without change; the line parallels the sixteenth-notes of the subject. In so doing it sounds, here two octaves higher, the "missing" c and B♭ at the end of the subject (see tones in parentheses, Example 5e).

Second Segment (bars 19–37)

This middle segment is the longest of the three and, in some ways, the most difficult to understand. As I mentioned earlier, the governing idea is a stepwise ascent in the top voice from b♭^{1} to e♭^{2}, the structural neighboring note (see Example 2c). This melodic progression is supported by a bass motion leading from submediant to subdominant (end of bass arpeggio). Example 7a attempts to give the reader a better orientation by showing him the turning points through which the melodic progression becomes manifest. The reduction of Example 7b indicates that each melodic step is embellished by its upper third, thus: $b\flat^1$–d^2, c^2–$e\flat^2$, d^2–f^2, $e\flat^2$. The general course of the bass line is clear. The tone c arrives only in bar 35, but it belongs to the entire C-minor section (bars 29–35). The primary function of this C minor is contrapuntal, to provide support for the otherwise dissonant passing tone, c^2 (Example 7c).

EXAMPLE 7

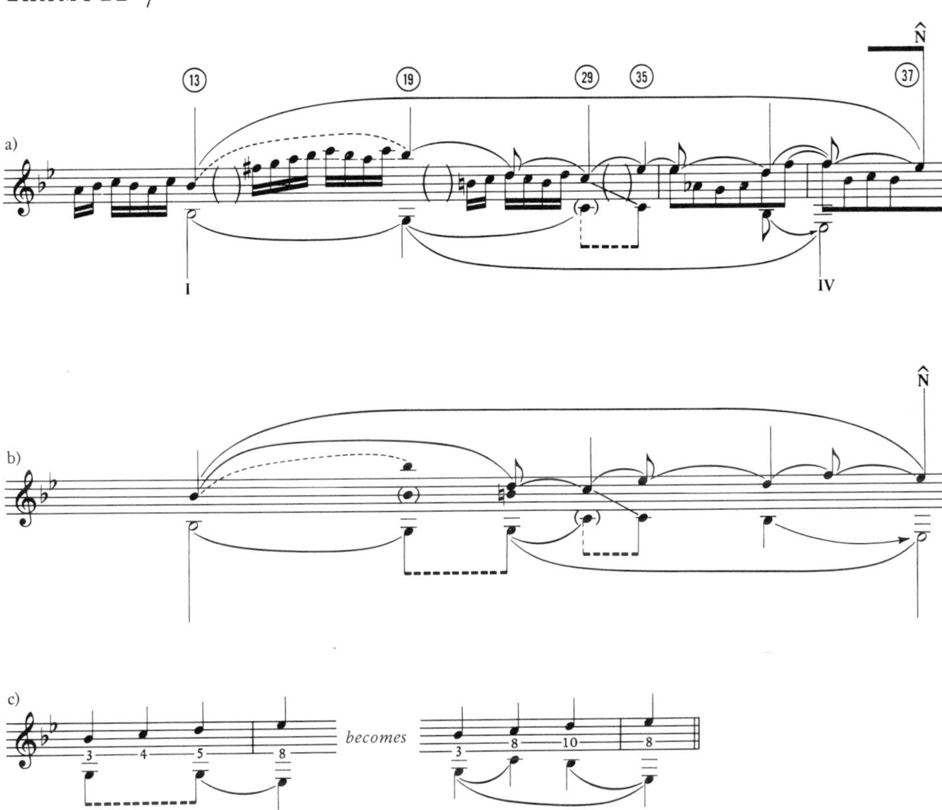

First Episode (bars 19–22). Example 8, which includes the first episode and the middle group of entrances, forms the continuation of Example 3. Smaller graphs of detail will be added as needed.

EXAMPLE 8

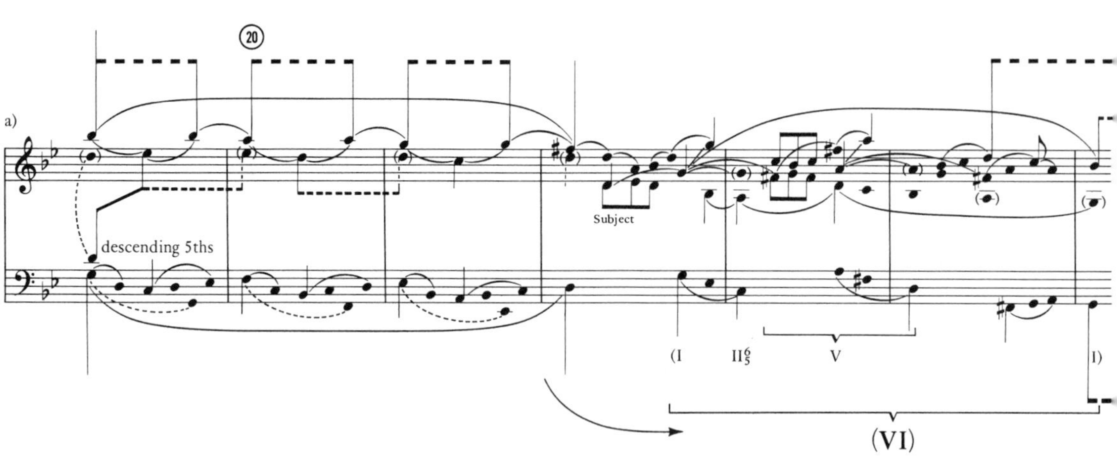

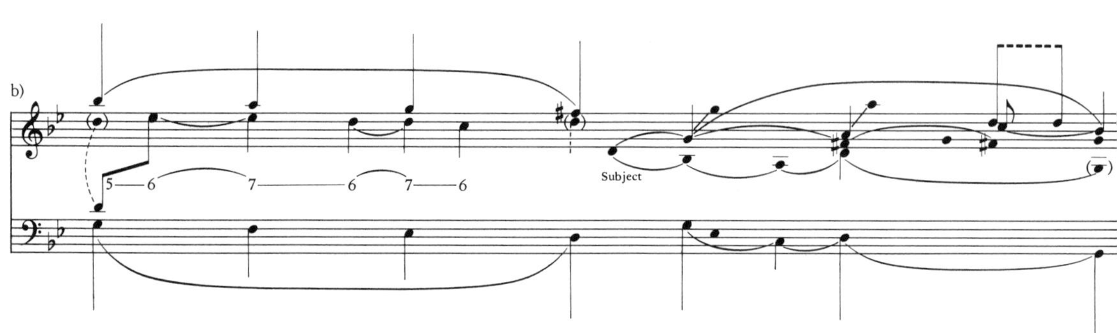

The materials of this episode derive completely from the subject, the top voice from bars 3–4 and the bass from a free melodic inversion of bar 1 (see Example 9). The harmonic function of this episode is not the usual one of leading to a new key area. G minor has already arrived in bars 18–19; however it has not been stabilized by a root-position dominant. The episode

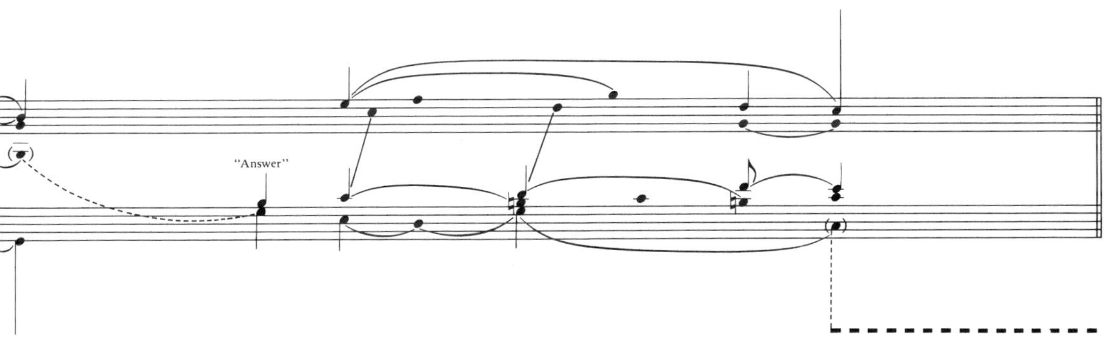

leads to just such a dominant and therefore serves to stabilize the G minor. This is an episode within a single prolonged sonority, leading from the fluid, unstable tonic (really only a potential tonic) of bars 18–19 to the explicit dominant of bar 22 and making possible the stable, confirmed tonic of bars 25–26. The voice leading of the episode, as is so frequent with

Bach, crystallizes around a suspension series, here harmonically elaborated by means of descending fifths (see Examples 8a and 8b).

EXAMPLE 9

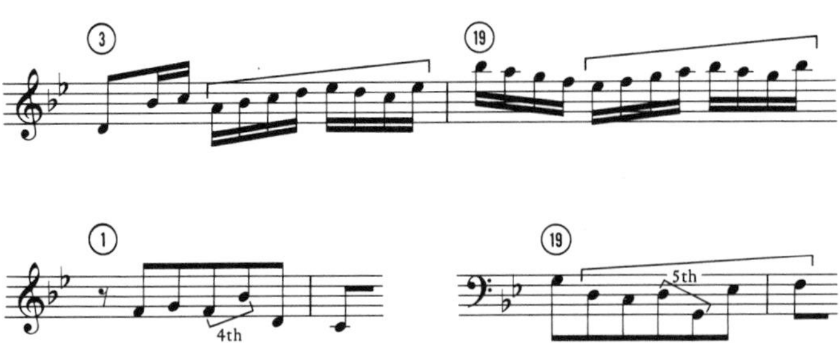

Middle Group of Entrances (bars 22–30). The G-minor entrance of bar 22, like that in B♭ (bar 9), begins over a dominant, which progresses to a tonic that becomes firmly grounded only in bars 25–26. The bass entrance of bar 26 begins with the rising third characteristic of the answer; one would expect, therefore, that the entrance would continue as in Example 10a and would lead to D minor. Instead Bach leads to C minor by lowering the melody a whole step from the fourth tone on (Example 10b). This change is necessary, creating as it does the possibility for the ascending melodic fourth which governs this middle segment of the fugue, and permitting a logical progression to the culminating E♭ entrance of bar 37.

EXAMPLE 10

The larger melodic shape and the basic voice-leading progressions of this section become clear only when considered in relation to what has gone on before. As Example 11 indicates, bars 13–19 contain the octave transfer

$b\flat^{1}$–$b\flat^{2}$ over a retained middle-voice d^{1}. In bars 19–25 the top and middle voices exchange their tones:

The d^{2} then proceeds to c^{2} in bars 29–30. Example 11a shows these events in some detail; Examples 11b and 11c offer progressive reductions and eliminate the octave transfer to point up the larger patterns of voice leading.

EXAMPLE 11

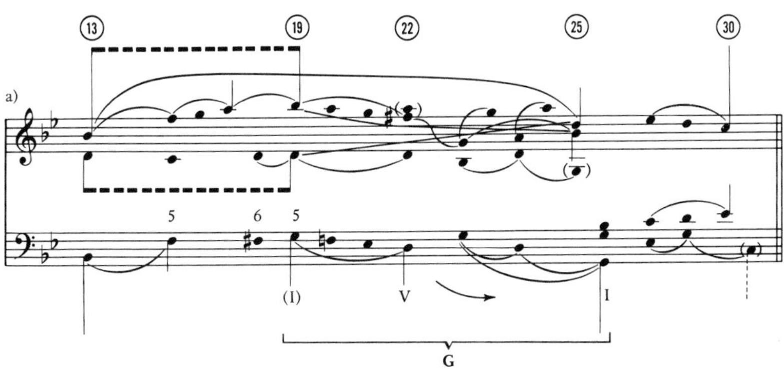

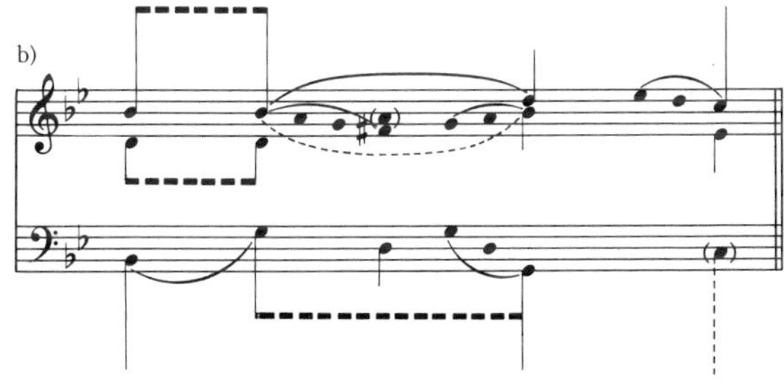

Second Episode and Incomplete Entrance (bars 30–37). The second episode falls into two parts (bars 30–32 and 33–34); the second part is based upon a contrapuntal inversion of the first. As it happens, the first part of this episode is itself a free inversion of Episode I; the bass of bars 30–32 echoes the soprano of bars 19–21 while the soprano of 30–32 resembles, but in modified form, the bass of 19–21 (see Example 12). More important than the change of melodic pattern is the changed significance of the voice leading. Instead of the descending fifths of bars 19–21, we now find a stepwise series of $^{6}_{3}$ chords, all but the first preceded by lower neighbors. In contrast to the first episode, the third eighth-note of each measure is now a neighbor rather than a chordal tone (see Example 13).

EXAMPLE 12

In bars 33–34, the sixteenth-notes, previously in the bass, move to the soprano; the left-hand part takes over the eighth-notes, distributing them between two voices, as is shown in Example 14. The contrapuntal inversion of bars 33–34 coincides with an important harmonic shift. In bars 30–33 the melodic lines have moved down the G-minor scale, thus suggesting a return to G minor as a key area. However the G-minor $^{6}_{3}$ of bar 33 is not stabilized. Instead the b♭ (bass) is inflected to a b♮ (middle voice, bar 34) leading to C minor. The G-minor chord, therefore, functions as a minor dominant within the progression I–V♭–♮–I of C minor (bars 30–35).

EXAMPLE 14

Example 15 gives a detailed picture of the whole episode. As mentioned above, the second episode, like the first one, moves within a single key area (here C minor). The structural meaning of this episode is the following. With one exception, all entrances of the subject or answer have ended in (or have been immediately followed by) a local tonic chord in root position. The one exception has been the entrance of bar 27, which has not concluded with a C-minor triad in root position. The episode provides the missing c in the bass, but only after a delay which generates a considerable tension, a tension only dissipated by the triumphant E♭ entrance of bar 37.

The arrival of c in bar 35 coincides with what would seem to be a C-minor entrance in the alto. However only the first measure really corresponds to a statement of the answer; the second measure is changed in order to point the way to E♭ major (see Example 16). As Example 15 shows, Bach leads from the C-minor chord to the V of E♭ through an F-minor seventh; this chord provides a smooth harmonic transition and breaks up parallel fifths as well. The reader will perhaps have noticed that the harmonic path of this middle segment of the Fugue traverses a series of falling fifths (G, bars 19–26; C, bars 26–35; F and B♭, bar 36; E♭, bar 37). This progression in fifths does not form the path of motion from the G-minor to the E♭-chord; it results, rather, from the harmonic elaboration of the progression given in Example 2c.

Final Segment (bars 37–48)

This last part of the Fugue poses three interpretive problems for the analyst: the melodic analysis of the E♭ entrance (bars 37–41); the structural meaning of the return to B♭ in bars 44–45; the leading of the upper voices over the cadential dominant. The reader should consult Example 17 in connection with the discussion below.

EXAMPLE 15

The E♭ statement of the subject (bars 37–41) is in itself no different from previous entrances. However its relation to immediate and distant environments requires us to give it a different interpretation. Whereas other entrances lead up to their main melodic tones in the third and fourth measures, this one states its principal tone, e♭^{2}, near the beginning (bar 37); the subsequent ascent to g^2 must be heard as an embellishment above the

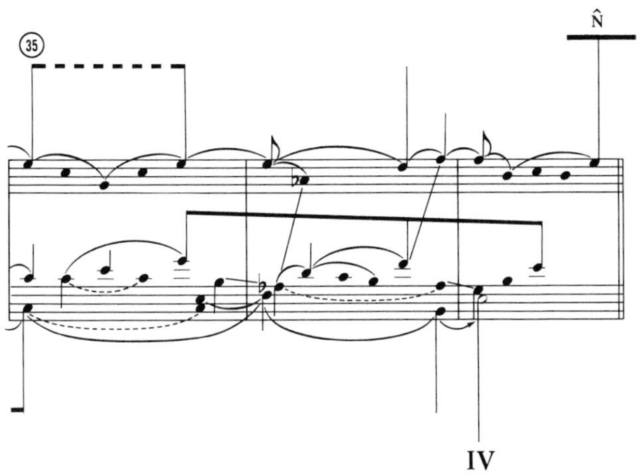

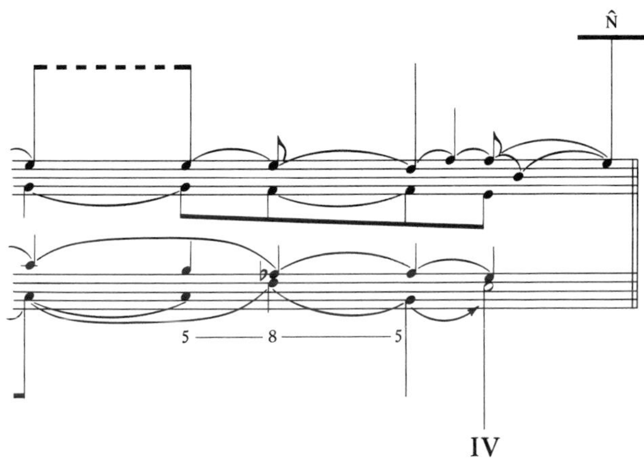

main tone. My reasons for this reading are the following. Over the long span, the e♭^{2} forms the stepwise continuation of d^2, the top-voice tone of the initial prolonged tonic; the g^2 of bars 40–41 enters into no such far-reaching connections. The immediate context also points up the importance of e♭^{2}. Unlike any previous entrance, this one is non-modulatory and begins on a chord of tonic color preceded by its dominant. As a result, the first

EXAMPLE 16

important melodic tone is grounded in a stable harmony. In addition the melodic tones d^2 and f^2 of bar 36 converge upon the e♭^{2}. Both harmonic and melodic forces make the beginning of this entrance sound like an arrival and not a point of departure.

The entrance of the answer (bars 41–45) moves from E♭ major to the B♭-chord of bars 44–45; the B♭-triad is preceded by a root-position dominant that arises out of a change in the second countersubject. Despite this harmonic emphasis, the B♭-chord is insufficiently stabilized to constitute a tonic of structural significance connected with the prolonged B♭ harmony of the exposition. Instead I read it as the upper fifth of the sub-dominant effecting a transition to the cadential dominant of bars 45–48, and awakening our expectation of the final tonic that is to appear in bar 48. I believe that if Bach had heard a structural return to the tonic in bars 44–45, he would have redistributed the entrances among the voices so that d^2 would appear in the soprano; this would have reinforced the connection with the opening tonic. (Of course such a redistribution would have a profound impact on the structure and design of the Fugue; it would have become a different piece.) As it is, the top voice of bars 44–45 is, so to speak, up in the air, continuing the embellishing g^2 of the previous entrance with f^2; only over the final dominant will the top voice take up and conclude its fundamental line. (The registral association of the tones F and G occurs in the top voice and bass throughout the Fugue: f^2–g^2–f^2, bars 5–11, top voice; F–G, bars 17–25, bass; g^2–f^2, bars 40–45, top voice. The connection with the opening of the subject is evident.)

In bar 45, the contrapuntal inversion of the outer voices creates a chord succession $^{7}_{5}$ $^{6}_{4}$ over a decorated dominant pedal in the bass. As Example 17 indicates, the $^{6}_{4}$ and not the seventh chord is the leading element here. The interchange between the outer parts transforms the B♭ $^{5}_{3}$ of bars 44–45 to a cadential $^6_4$, but one with the "wrong" tone, b♭², in the soprano. A further interchange, this time between the top and the middle voice, brings in d² (bar 47) as the delayed continuation of e♭² (bar 37) leading to the final melodic descent through c² to b♭². It is this last interchange that justifies the amusing "extra" repetition of the bass figure in bar 47.

CONCLUSION

EXAMPLE 18 (see pages 266–67) is a middleground graph important to the understanding of the whole Fugue. The reader who has gone through this article will, I am sure, be able to understand it without any further comment.

In concluding this study I would like to devote a few words to the relationship between fugal analysis and the traditional study of fugue. Many would agree, I think, that a regime of academic fugal theory would for the most part hinder rather than help us in undertaking an analysis such as the one I have presented in this article. At one time or another we have all learned (and some of us still teach our students) to construct Frankensteinian fugues, robbing one graveyard for the subject, another for the countersubject, a third for the episodes. Such exercises have a value, of course. But too many textbooks (and teachers as well, I would suspect) display their timid little monsters—or worse yet, the blueprints for assembling them—as if they were touchstones by which we might evaluate the "deviations" of a Bach or Handel.

In teaching, to be sure, it is best to confront the student with one new problem at a time. One can hardly avoid, therefore, presenting separately the different elements of fugal design: subject, answer, countersubject, episodes, etc. The mistake—and it is an avoidable one—is to transfer this approach to the analysis of fugal masterpieces; a pedagogical help in teaching the student to write fugues becomes a stumbling block to the understanding of fugues by the great composers.

I believe therefore that any course of study in fugue should include as an integral part of the approach the analysis of complete fugues in a manner that goes beyond the identification of elements and proceeds to an understanding of their function within the whole. Of course the kind of analysis

EXAMPLE 17

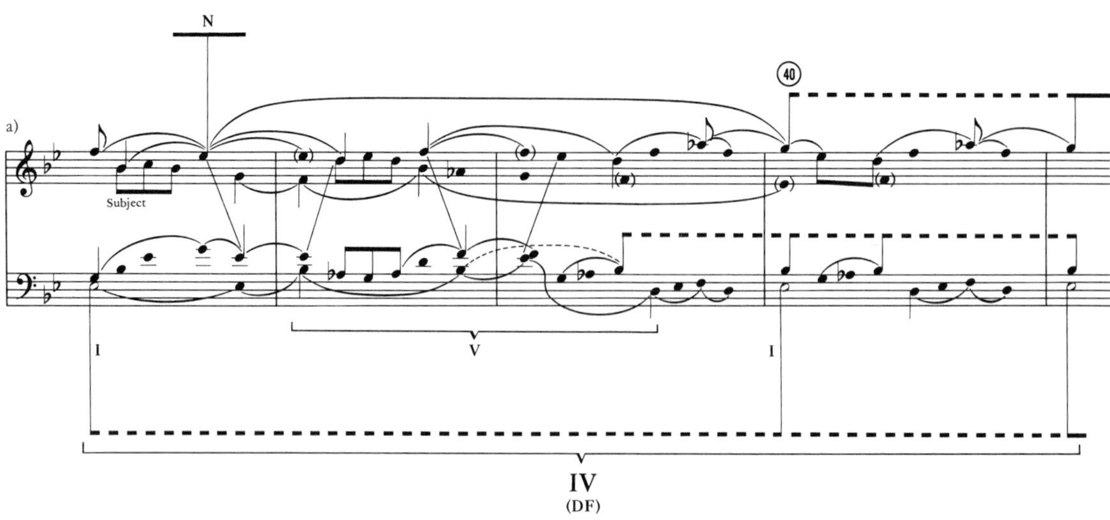

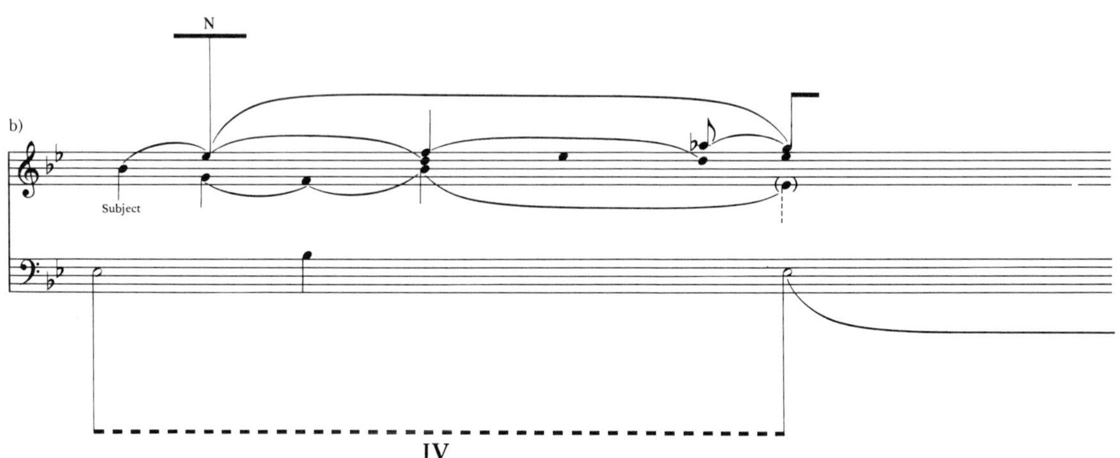

that I have attempted here makes greater demands upon student (and teacher) than conventional description does. However, many who would be unable at first to undertake such an analysis themselves would, with proper guidance, be able to hear, understand, and respond to many important features of the composition. I would maintain that if a student

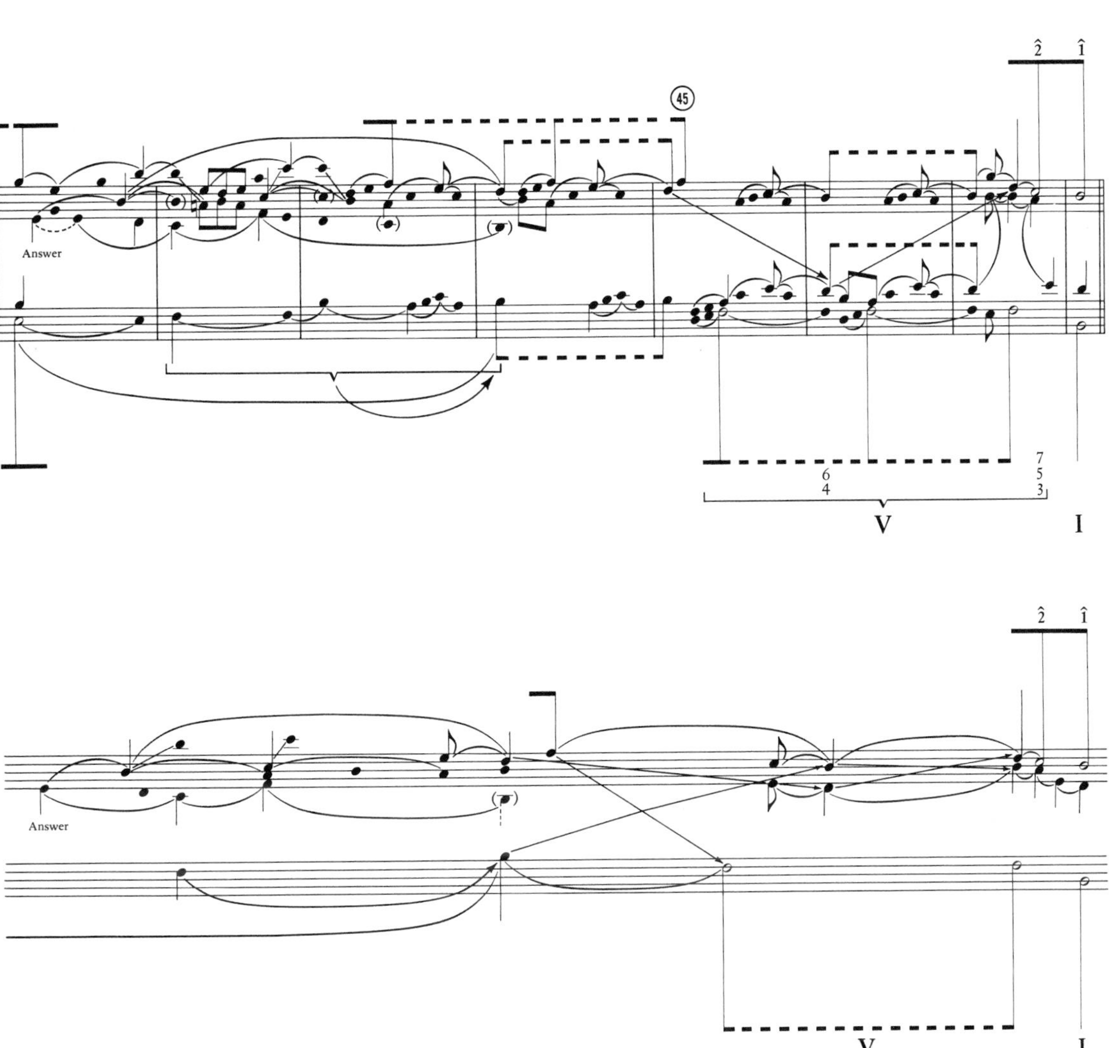

could not follow, for example, the course of the soprano voice in bars 1–13 of our Fugue, he ought not to be writing fugues at all. On the other hand the student who learns to attain a comprehensive view of such compositions—dense with meaning and rich in detail—will have strengthened his musical instincts in a way hardly to be achieved by other means.

EXAMPLE 18

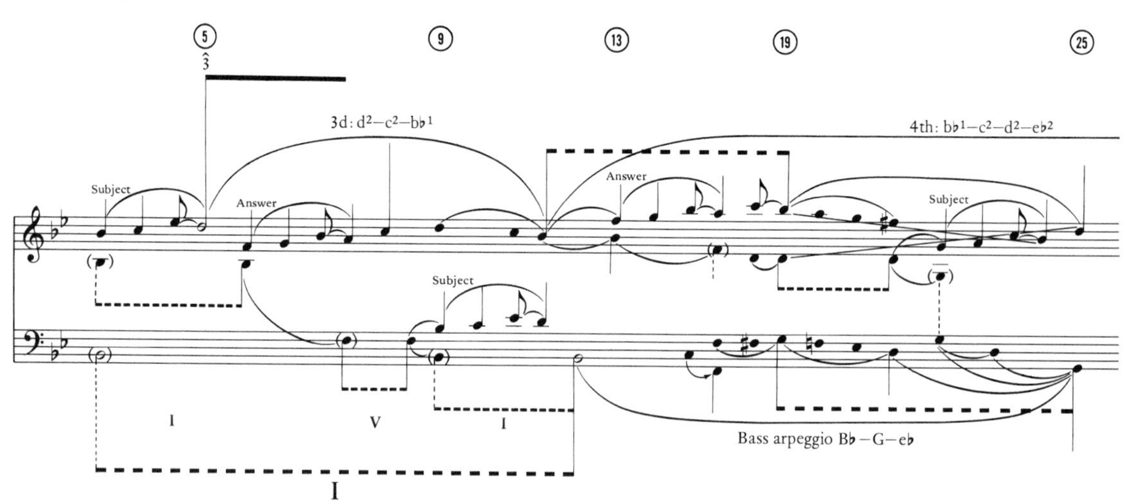
5
3̂
9
13
19
25
3d: d²–c²–b♭¹
4th: b♭¹–c²–d²–e♭²
Subject
Answer
Answer
Subject
Subject
I
V
I
I
Bass arpeggio B♭–G–e♭

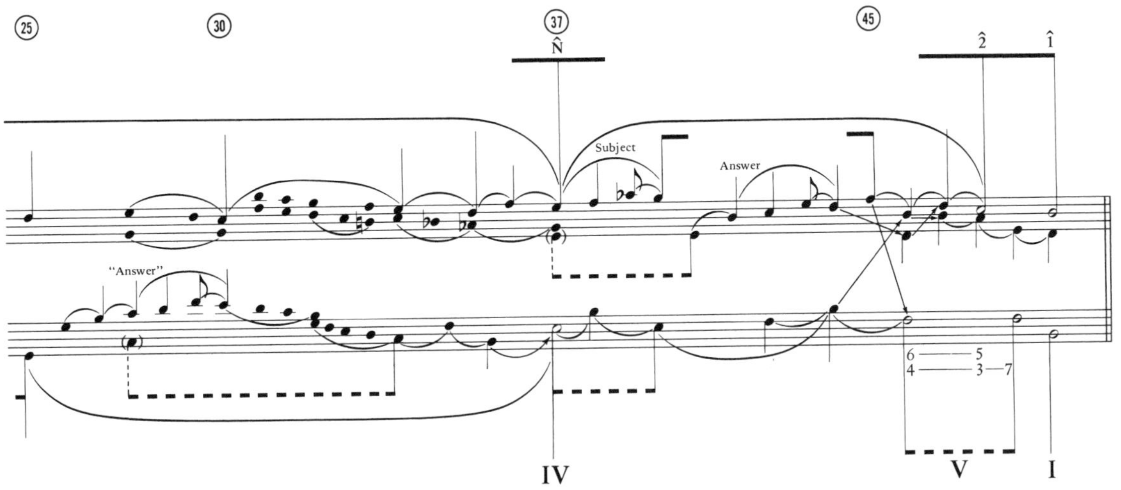

25
30
37
45
N̂
2̂
1̂
Subject
Answer
"Answer"
6 — 5
4 — 3 — 7
IV
V
I

Beethoven's La Malinconia from the String Quartet, Opus 18, No. 6

TECHNIQUES AND STRUCTURE

WILLIAM J. MITCHELL

RELATIVELY little is known about the composing of Beethoven's String Quartet, Op. 18, No. 6.[1] The Adagio which opens the final movement is extraordinary, bearing the title *La Malinconia* and instructions to perform it with the "greatest delicacy." The Allegretto quasi Allegro which directly succeeds it might well have been called "La Gioia." The contrast in expressive content is apparent, however, and hardly in need of a clarifying descriptive title.

In the absence of a biographical gloss to the title and whatever might have been a programmatic aim, one is hindered, if not blocked, from enlarging on the extra-musical significance of the piece. In any event, Beethoven's portrayal of *La Malinconia* and its contrast is infinitely more eloquent and moving than any verbal comment that might be made on it. It is proposed, here, to attempt what may turn out to be a more rewarding assignment, a representation of the musical anatomy of melancholy.

Such a task faces its own challenges, for, after a clear beginning in B♭ major, the Adagio embarks on a venturesome chromatic course that seems to leave the tonal issue in doubt until the very end. Certainly, traditional harmonic analysis, with its endless successions of chords and keys, will

1 Nottebohm, characteristically, quoted a few snippets from a Beethoven sketchbook, but only enough to whet the appetite. Nothing more has appeared to my knowledge. Cf. Gustav Nottebohm, *Zweite Beethoveniana* (Leipzig, Rieter-Biedermann, 1887), p. 60 ff.

lead us nowhere if we seek in such a procedure an informative affirmation of the encompassing properties of the tonality of B♭ major–minor. It is hoped, however, that insight may be gained into the unified career of the work by calling upon analytic techniques of a linear structural nature. A corollary of the analysis of *La Malinconia* will be an examination of the relationships between the Adagio and the following Allegretto quasi Allegro. Beethoven suggests the relationships when he introduces swatches of *La Malinconia* in bar 195 and further, and also when, in bars 272–75, he presents the main subject of the finale in a tempo, poco adagio, suggestive of the deliberateness of the beginning of the movement.

Bars 1–20. The Adagio can be divided conveniently into two parts, bars 1–20 and bars 21–44. The first part expresses a placid subject with fretful turns and sharp dynamic contrasts. In part it contains a filled in perfect fifth, b♭ to f, stated twice (bars 2–4 and 6–7). However the fifth surrenders its serenity immediately thereafter to a diminished fifth, the perfect form being regained only momentarily and much later in bars 196–198. The difference is worth noting, for the perfect fifth has a stabilizing effect as B♭ major is introduced, the diminished fifth a groping, restless one as chromaticism takes over. The various forms assumed by the fifth are represented in Example 1.

EXAMPLE I

Our primary analytic concern in bars 1–20 (21, so far as immediate levels of meaning are concerned) is the way in which Beethoven moves from the tonic of B♭ major to the dominant of as remote an area as possible, E minor. The essence of the motion is sketched in Example 2. In Example 2a, the relationship appears in a generic contrapuntal form as a 5–6–5 progression. In Example 2b, roots appear in the bass and chordal functions are indicated. In Example 2c, an illustration by C. P. E. Bach is shown,[2] which Bach introduced as part of a demonstration of modulatory connections between distant keys.

EXAMPLE 2

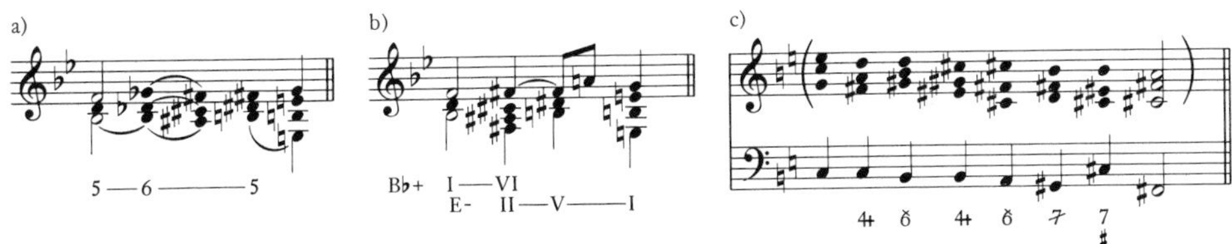

C. P. E. Bach's and Beethoven's procedures are similar in that both are offspring of the procedures of Examples 2a and 2b. But they have another feature in common in that both fill in linearly the space between the tonic chord of the key of departure and the supertonic chord of the key of arrival. Beyond this, however, there are marked differences between Bach's simple textbook illustration and the unique cast of Beethoven's chromaticism. Immediate and intermediate levels of structure are graphed in Example 3. Especially striking is the limning of the diminished fifth (bars 12–16), f♯ through a to c, with the passing tones g (bar 13) and b (bar 15) placed an octave below their normal "passing tone" register and assigned to the second violin. The cello and, in fact, all instruments contribute to this crazy quilt of successive diminished-seventh chords. Example 3b shows a normal assembly of the tones of the passage.

One detail demands examination. When the cello reaches f♯ in bar 12, its accompaniment is a $^{6}_{4}$. Those who are privy to the behavior of such a position in such a context will recognize that it represents only a delayed $^{5}_{3}$. In truth, $^{\sharp 5}_{\sharp 3}$ appears in bar 13, but it is shrouded in an elision. A

[2] From C. P. E. Bach, *Essay on the True Art of Playing Keyboard Instruments*, translated and edited by William J. Mitchell (New York, W. W. Norton, 1949), p. 436 f., figure 475, 9th illustration.

EXAMPLE 3

compression of chord successions such as this, of course, was not unknown in the eighteenth century. Testimony is provided by Mozart in the Andante, bars 91–99, of the Piano Sonata, K.533/494. The passage is presented in a reduced form in Example 4a. The identical technique of detail as employed by Beethoven is sketched in Example 4b.

EXAMPLE 4

In such a partial view as is presented in bars 1–20/21, no attempt can be made to assess the ultimate function of the motion from B♭ major to E minor. In its immediate meaning, it stands as a modulation, but its broader role in the totality of events will become apparent only at the time when remote meanings become our concern, following an analysis of the second section.

Bars 21–44. A new subject enters in bar 20 and holds sway until bar 29. Thereafter, it and elements of the initial subject alternate, with the "turn" occupying bars 29–33, the second subject, bars 33–36, and the turn once again, bars 37–42, following which the Adagio comes to an *attacca* ending. In studying the second section it will be helpful to be guided by these subdivisions.

Two factors are present in bars 21–29: brief employments of invertible counterpoint in the octave, and a motion of the bass in ascending fifths (or descending fourths) interspersed with applied dominants. Example 5a isolates the invertible counterpoint of the outer parts; Example 5b places the voices in a straightforward relationship in order to clarify the ascending nature of the successive figures of the sequence. Example 5c illustrates the ascending chromatic bass formed by the applied dominant relationships connected with the ascending fifths; Example 5d is an abstraction of the total motion and is intended to show that the result of the prolongation of ascending fifths and applied dominants is ultimately the replacement of the E-minor chord (bar 21) by a C-major chord (bar 28). Examples 5e and 5f represent the beginning and end of the bars under consideration. In Example 5e, the E- and C-chords stand in a 5–6 relationship; in Example 5f an alternate of the connection is expressed as a 5–8 relationship. This latter form agrees with the basses e (bar 21) and c (bar 28) that appear in the score of the piece. C is a consequence of the technique, represented in Examples 5c and 5d, whereby the lowest voice, starting from e, seeks out c by means of an ascending filled-in sixth.

The passage can be studied profitably for the means used by Beethoven to avoid the hazard of monotony caused by four identical statements of the sequential figure. He presents them straightforwardly, in invertible counterpoint, disguised by a stretto-like intrusion of the first violin in bar 26, and by changes in scoring and registration as the passage increases in intensity. However, these strokes by the composer can be comprehended only if the underlying bare sequence is known, as represented in the various sketches of Example 5.

EXAMPLE 5

The arrival at c in the cello (bars 28, 29) prepares the way for a striking parallelism in bars 30–33, whereby the prolonging fourth of the top voice, g to c (bars 21–27), is answered by a similar ascending fourth, a to d, in bars 29–32. The bass, starting from c, carried over from the preceding C-chord, provides the accompaniment as it rises through f♯ on the way to the terminating g of bar 33. Of special significance for an evaluation of the broad structure of the Adagio is the appearance of the high b♭ in bar 33. Its normal position, in terms of the technique employed, should be an octave lower. Both registers are indicated in Example 6, which includes Example 5d in order to juxtapose the parallel construction of bars 21–29 and 29–33. The significance of the high b♭ in the inclusive structure of *La Malinconia* will be discussed later in connection with Example 8.

EXAMPLE 6

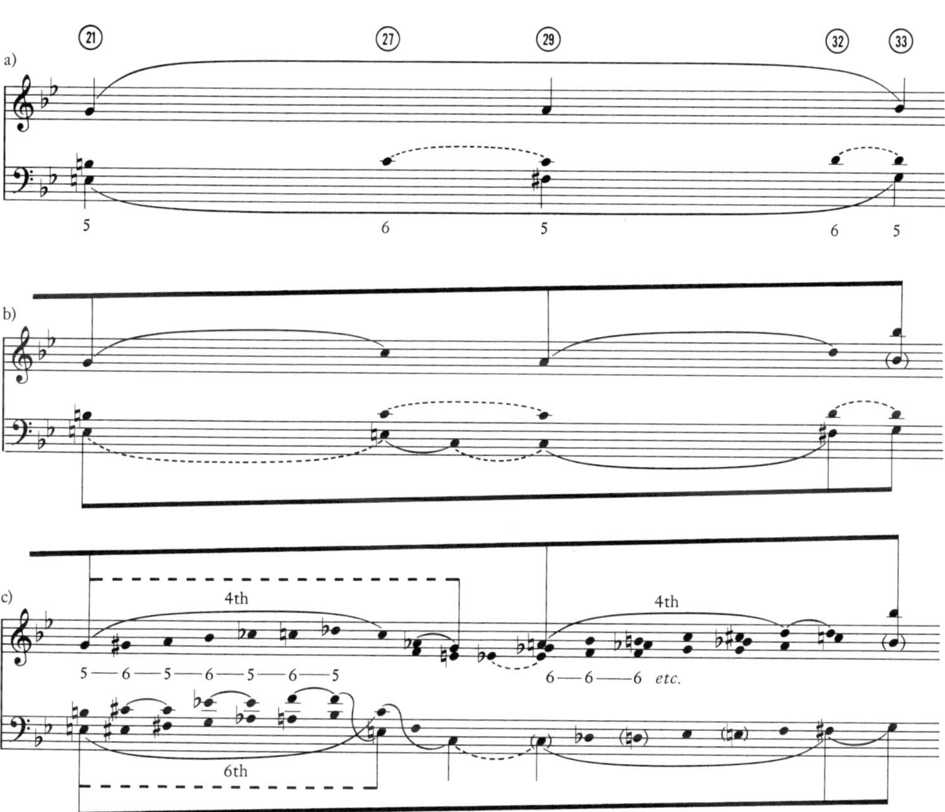

The concluding bars, 33–44, resolve the chromatic riddle posed by the Adagio. Resolution, however, must lean heavily on the inclusive contexts of the outer parts, for the inner voices present a series of shifting colors that enliven the broad frame, but in doing this they can easily mislead the unwary listener. Example 7a represents in its three sketches the intermediate meaning of the connection between the G-minor chord of bar 33 and the A-minor chord of bar 35. The technique is the same as that used by Beethoven in bars 21–29, but in this instance it leads to the connecting of b♭ and c in the upper part accompanied by the bass g to a. In Example 7b, the outer parts of bars 35–42 are represented alone, in order to reveal the arpeggiated diminished seventh chord which forms the inclusive frame, representing a function of the seventh step of B♭ major–minor. The cadence of bars 43–44 needs no graphic representation at this time.

EXAMPLE 7

In order to arrive at an inclusive view of this remarkable piece, it is necessary to regard chromatic elements, modulations, and the like, as factors concerned with immediate values and as such representatives of techniques of motion or means of emphasis and prolongation. The task in presenting the total scope of the piece in its remote meaning is to find some kind of summary graph of details from beginning to end to show their functions in terms of the complete idea, this being a dynamic, indeed a fantastic, statement of the organizing powers of the tonality of B♭ major–minor. Example 8a suggests the remote structural meaning of *La Malinconia*; Example 8b presents the first level of prolongation, an unfolding, whereby the inner voices, b♭ (accompanied by g) and c, become parts of a vaulting action in the ultimate relating of f to its neighbor g♭; Example 8c graphs the filling in technique between f (bar 8) and b♭ (bar 33), the accompaniment to which gives the first suggestion of the E-minor chord of bar 21. Example 8d is a more detailed graph of intermediate levels of activity and, as such, simply joins together the various sketches already presented separately in the preceding discussions of the sections and subsections of the Adagio.

EXAMPLE 8

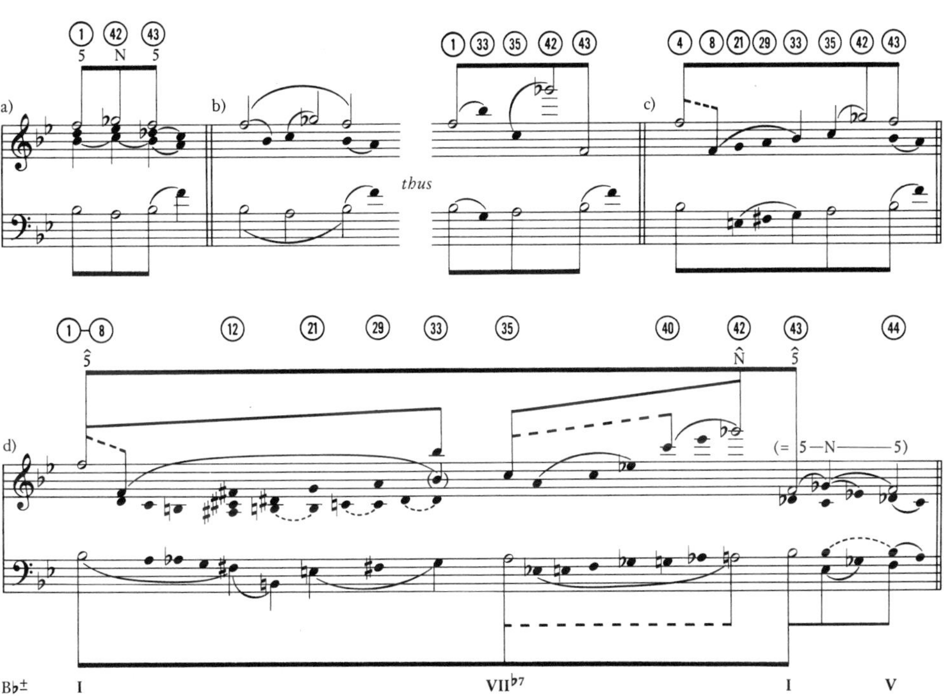

Two related matters remain to be discussed. They are the thematic relationships between the Adagio and the Allegretto, and the nature of the cadenza-like reentry of material from the Adagio in bar 195 and further, preceding the final statement of the main subject, starting in bar 221.

The general similarity of the contours of the thematic material of bars 1–4 and 44–49 is apparent and need not be dwelt on. However, the most direct thematic relationship is between the head of the motive first stated in bar 21 and the anacrusis of the principal subject of the finale in bar 44. They have been juxtaposed in Example 9. Note that it is Beethoven who underscores the relationship when, in bar 195 and further, he alternates the first subject of the Adagio and elements from the Allegretto. Moreover, in bars 271–275, he states the head of the principal subject in a tempo, poco adagio, that is strongly suggestive of the pace of *La Malinconia.* The initial nature of this element in bar 21 and further of the Adagio is searching and meditative; the second form of it, in the Allegretto, is affirmative and ebullient. The relationship is heightened by contrast—by the minor mode and deliberate pace of the first, by the major mode and active pace of the second. The relationship is, perhaps, most acutely stated in bar 204, where it is not at all certain, after the fermata, which form, slow or fast, major or minor, will enter. It turns out to be the fast form, but in minor.

EXAMPLE 9

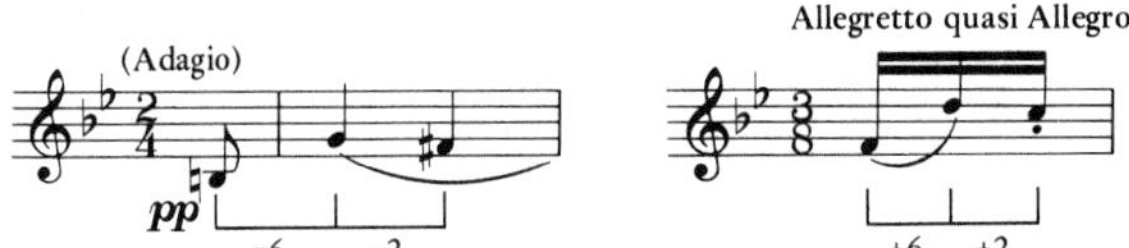

Consanguinity between the first subject of the Adagio and the continuation of the finale's principal subject can be illustrated on an intermediate structural level. Example 10a graphs the relationship which consists essentially of the expansion of the ascending fifth of bars 2–4 and elsewhere into the major sixth of bars 45–49. The middle voice of bars 48 and 49 has been included in the example, for it is this voice that takes a direct route to g, while the top voice, after an upward leap of an octave, descends to the same tone.

Example 10b portrays a relationship on a remote level in which the structural neighbor, g♭, of bars 42 and 43 is replaced by g in bar 49.

There remains an examination of the cadenza of bars 195–220 with its

EXAMPLE 10

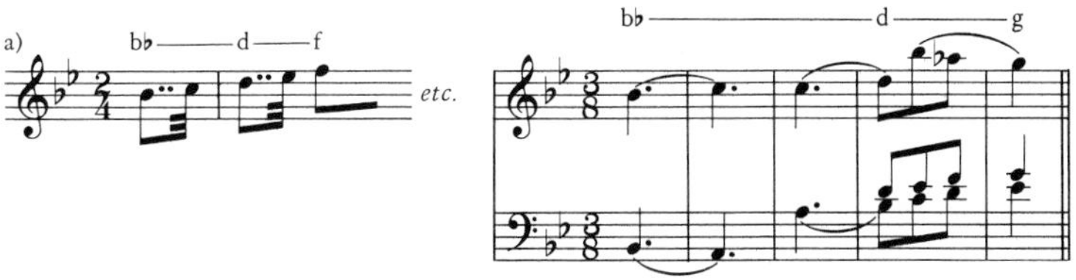

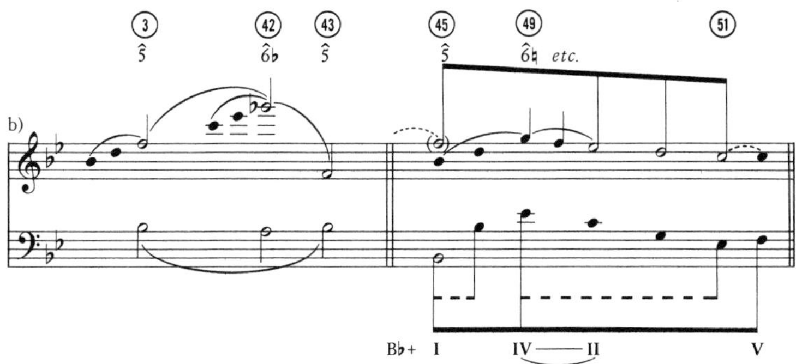

delightfully uncertain alternation of Adagio and Allegretto elements. Like so many cadenzas, the inclusive frame is the motion of $\frac{6}{4}$ to $\frac{5}{3}$ on the dominant as in Example 11a. In Examples 11b, 11c, and 11d, successive stages in the elaboration of the cadenza are shown. They consist in the introduction of b♮ (11b), the seeking of this tone from the top voice, accompanied in parallel tenths by the middle voice (11c), and a more elaborate form of the same technique, making use of applied dominants before each of the accompanying chords (11d). A new factor is the extension of each accompanying chord by means of a linear ascent (a, b♮, c, and g, a, b♮) to each of the structural tones that form the underlying prolongation. Finally, Example 11e presents a closer and at the same time a comprehensive view, bar by bar, of the working out of the entire cadenza.

EXAMPLE II

195
219
a)
b)
c)
(10)
10
10
6 — 5
4 — 3
Bb+
V

195
201
205
210
215
217
219
d)
(10)
a.d.
10
a.d.
10
a.d.

e)
Adagio
10
Allegretto
10

Adagio
Allegretto
10
Reprise
etc.

Chopin's Etude in F Major, Opus 25, No. 3

THE SCOPE OF TONALITY

FELIX SALZER

ANY ANALYTICAL investigation of Chopin's Etude in F major, Op. 25, No. 3 will sooner or later be confronted with the problem of how to understand or interpret the B-major section (bars 29–36) in a work in F major. For too long a time we have been satisfied with descriptive statements about the undoubted surprise effect or the so-called harmonic boldness of such passages, without coming to grips with the essential problem—their function and meaning within the tonal organism of the entire work.

In his analysis of Op. 25, No. 3, Hugo Leichtentritt has not only mentioned the A–B–A form of the work, but has also emphasized that a strange sound-geometry (*seltsame Klanggeometrie*) is at work in this Etude.[1] In reading the score we are in fact struck by an arresting play with tonal symmetries. In its main outline the bass moves from F to the dominant C (bar 17), from there to F♯ (bars 26–28) as dominant of B (bar 29). From B then there is tonal movement to F♯ (bar 37) and on to C (bars 46–48), the dominant of the tonic F. The latter progression is, of course, the exact retrograde of the former (see Example 1).

The Roman numerals show that the dominants C and F♯ become Phrygian supertonics (II Phr.) in their corresponding drives to B (bar 29) and to F (bar 49). This bass design supports a melodic design which is equally symmetrical and which shows a similar retrograde order. The

[1] Hugo Leichtentritt, *Analyse von Chopin's Klavierwerken II* (Berlin, Max Hesse, 1922).

EXAMPLE I

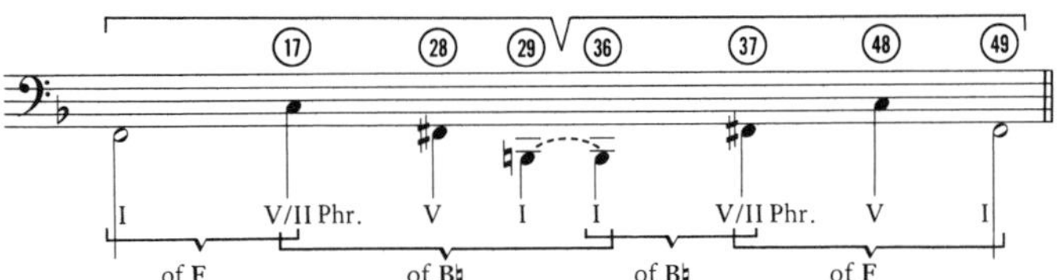

melodic design consists of three periods which are designated a–b–c; c is simultaneously the end of the first pattern and the beginning of the second, which is the reverse of the first, thus: a–b–c–b–a (see Examples 2 and 3).

EXAMPLE 2

All the foregoing may point to a binary form. For if one bases one's reading of the underlying form on those symmetric and retrograde patterns, it may seem logical to assume that the work is divided into two overlapping

EXAMPLE 3

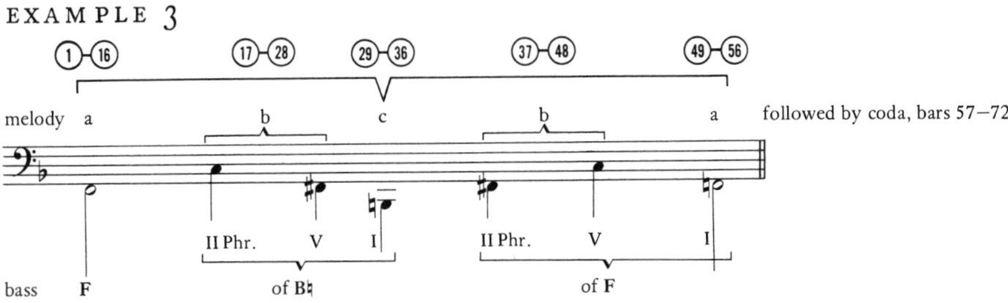

form sections; the above-mentioned harmonic drive to B major and then to F major might tend to strengthen this point of view.

To me, however, the above reading appears most unconvincing, for I believe that it draws the wrong conclusions from the symmetrical and retrograde patterns; it appears unconvincing if for no other reason than that it is not at all characteristic for Chopin to base an entire work on what one is inclined to call a clever tone game: "how to get from F major to B major and back by means of a retrograde progression." It would, however, be entirely within his conception of tonal organization to have the B-major passage act as a seeming or simulated goal. This trend then is boldly redressed by the composer, thus making the passage subordinate to a progression of higher structural order. The following analysis will show that the symmetrical patterns—while having a function and meaning—do not determine the basic form of this work which is most definitely a three-part form, A–B–A. Viewed as a whole, the work presents a clear example of a progression divided through interruption (see Example 4). This background progression expands into a three-part form through prolongation of the dividing V (section B) and through anticipation of the structural

EXAMPLE 4

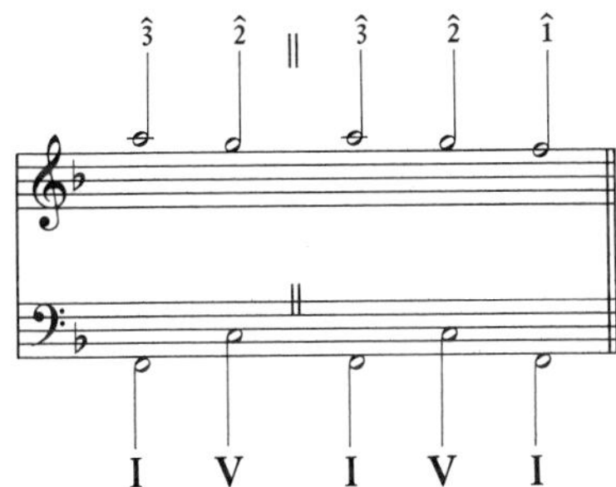

interruption by an interruption on the middleground level, showing a motion into the inner voice while the structural $\hat{3}$ is retained (see Example 5).

EXAMPLE 5

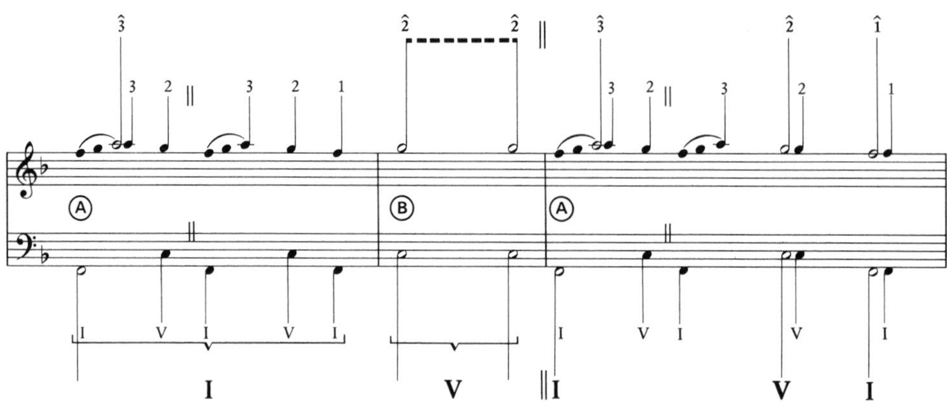

The prolongation of the dividing dominant constituting the middle section is of such daring originality and its understanding so crucial to an interpretation of the entire Etude that we will demonstrate its contents in detail and in direction from background to foreground (see Example 6). The middle section begins in bar 17 on the dominant; a downward motion develops reaching F♯ in bars 26–28. Careful study of the voice leading discloses a progression essentially moving in whole steps in both outer voices and resulting in a series of fifths. The same pattern is repeated starting from F♯ in bar 37 and reaching the C-major chord (V of F) in bars 46–48 (see Example 6b). This highly original organization of the descending octave into whole steps is imaginatively prolonged; the prolongation, of course, eliminates the parallel fifths of the middleground progression and subdivides the whole step preceding F♯ (bar 26) and the corresponding one before C (bar 46); see Example 6c. With the first subdivision (A♭–G), Chopin creates the impression that he is abandoning the whole-step progression, for he lengthens the measure group from two to four bars. The G, however, is not treated as a goal (V of C) since by moving down yet

EXAMPLE 6

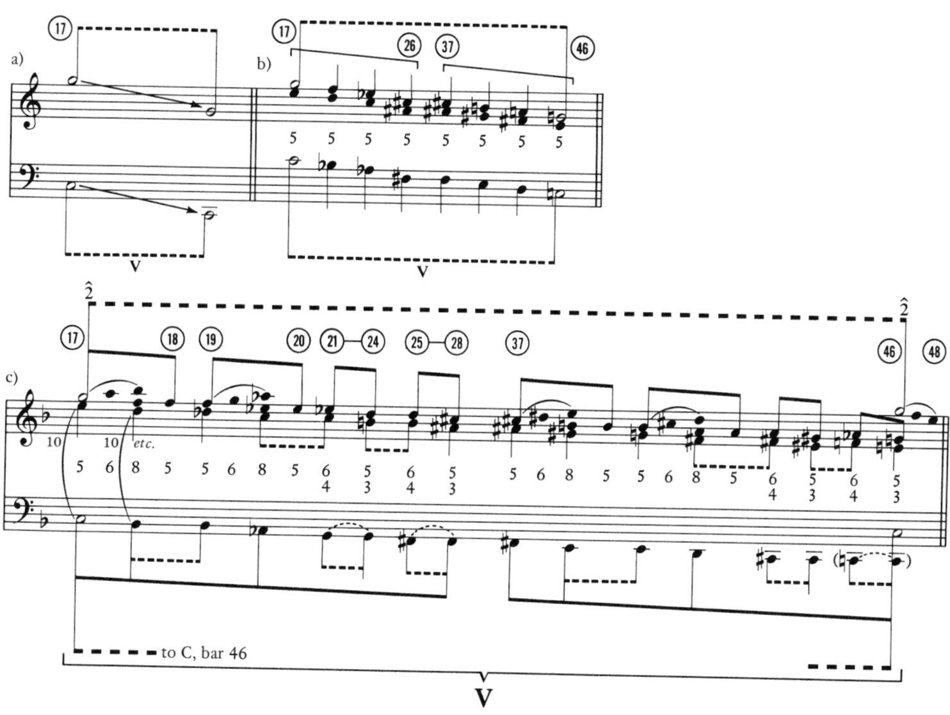

another half step, Chopin surprisingly completes the whole-step progression. Nevertheless, through transfer of registers, the original octave position of both top voice and bass is regained at the end of the entire whole-step descent (compare bar 17 with bar 46/47).

This brings us now to one of Chopin's most inspired ideas: the F♯ chord —a passing chord within the entire prolongation of the V—is momentarily made to act as a dominant. The immediate consequence is the short B-major section. Since it repeats the motivic–thematic design of the opening measures, it functions as a misleading and thus "false" recapitulation; the main course of the voice leading, the passing motion within the dominant octave (C–C) has been interrupted! However, the moment the F♯ sonority reappears in bar 37 and the motion downward is continued, any bewilderment

EXAMPLE 7

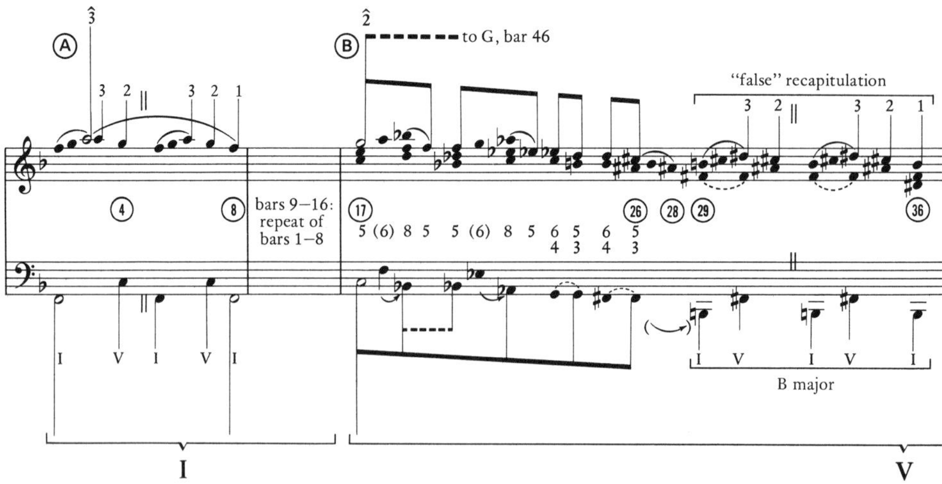

of the listener ceases.[2] The motion which began in bar 17 is resumed and leads, as explained before, to its end (bars 46–48). The true recapitulation now begins with an overpowering, jubilant logic (see Example 7).

Let us now take up again the question we posed at the beginning of this article: what is the meaning of the B-major section within this F-major composition? Some might suggest that it functions as an expansion of the lower neighboring tone of C; however, the voice leading, especially of the top voice, does not bear out such an interpretation. For the D♯ of the B-major section stands in no melodic relationship to the G which is the structural top-voice tone of the middle section. Rather, the B-major section acts as a wedge breaking the whole-tone progression into two parts: C–F♯ and F♯–C. In so doing it intensifies the symmetrical division of the

[2] When one is confronted with a succession of two sonorities of which one is a dominant of the other, one's first inclination is to regard the dominant as subordinate to the tonic. Larger connections, however, often reveal, as in this case, that the dominant has the superior structural function.

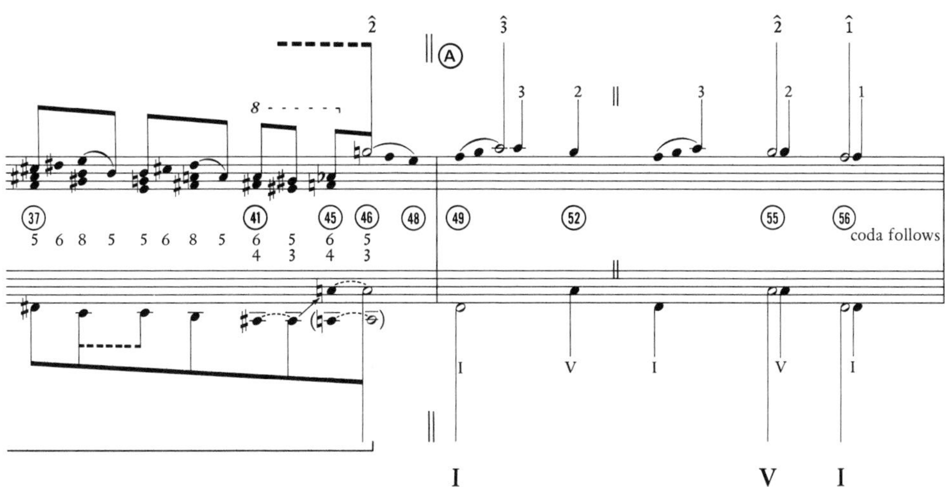

octave, and indeed causes a symmetrical pattern for the middle section and, as a consequence, for the work as a whole.

EXAMPLE 8

B
C Bb Ab F♯ F♯ E D C

F C F

Form: Ⓐ Ⓑ Ⓐ

This diagram (Example 8) can serve as a quasi corrective to Examples 1 and 3 by showing the symmetries in their hierarchical order. The B-major section, far from being a central goal is instead a false recapitulation subordinate to the whole-tone progression which itself functions as the prolongation of a structural dominant.

Example 9 presents the detailed voice leading, including the imaginative coda, of an imaginative work. (Occasionally, register changes have been omitted to show the voice leading more clearly.)

EXAMPLE 9

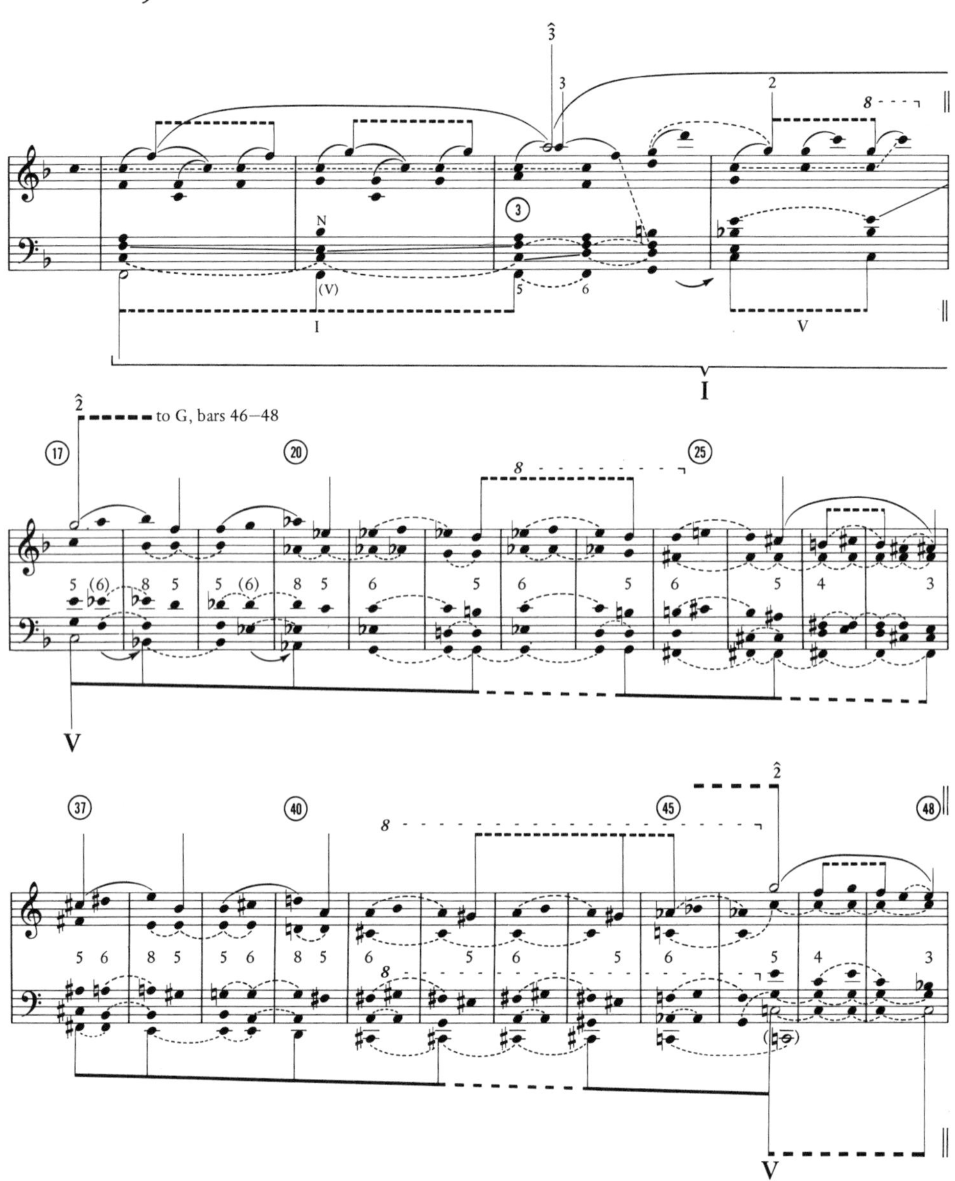

3̂
3
2
8
N
(V)
5
6
I
V
I
2̂
to G, bars 46–48
17
20
25
8
5 (6) 8 5 5 (6) 8 5 6 5 6 5 6 5 4 3
V
37
40
45
48
8
2̂
5 6 8 5 5 6 8 5 6 5 6 5 6 5 4 3
8
V

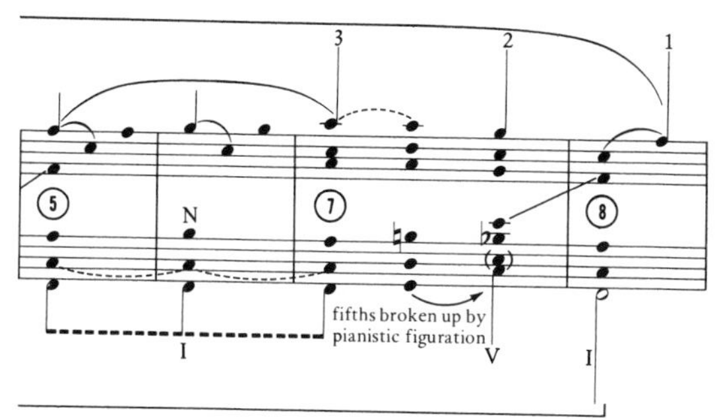

bars 9–16: figurated repetition of bars 1–8

The coda begins simultaneously with the structural completion of the voice leading in bar 56. For a few measures Chopin hesitates playfully on the tonic with the superimposed C in the top voice (cf. bar 4). Then, in bar 60, C begins to descend to F, while the middle voice (in the left-hand part) once more repeats—now dramatically prolonged—the preceding structural descent from A via G to F. Supporting this line, the bass moves in descending fifths, the opening fifth being F–B (!). How poetic is this reappearance of the B-major chord, which earlier caused so much excitement, and is now brought in as a faint and quickly passing reminiscence in a totally different context. There could be no greater contrasts between two B-major chords in a work in F major (see Example 9).

In viewing the work as a whole, we again see that once the composer is consciously or unconsciously secure in his background and middleground structure, he can be most adventurous with the foreground's possibilities of surprise and deception.

Some Unpublished Music and Letters by Maurice Ravel

ARBIE ORENSTEIN

IN THE COURSE of an article I wrote in 1967, mention was made of some five hundred pages of unpublished material by Ravel, located in various private collections.[1] The present article will discuss some of this source material, and thus, it is hoped, shed some new light on a number of areas which, of necessity, have remained obscure until now.[2]

RAVEL AND VERLAINE (Plates Ia–Id)

PAUL VERLAINE wrote the following well-known lines in his poem "Art poétique": "Music above all. . . . Music again and always!" His suggestive art beckoned the musician, and many of his poems are now inextricably linked with the name of Claude Debussy, and, above all, with that of Gabriel Fauré. Ravel once described the human voice as the "most expressive of sonorous instruments," [3] and of his creative output of some eighty compositions, about thirty, or nearly 40 percent, were written for the voice. Although he admired Verlaine's poetry, his settings of *Un Grand sommeil noir* (1895) and *Sur l'herbe* (1907) were workmanlike, but below

[1] See my article, "Maurice Ravel's Creative Process," *The Musical Quarterly* (October, 1967), pp. 467–81.

[2] It may be noted parenthetically that in 1895, at the age of twenty, Ravel's handwriting underwent some perceptible modifications, the most significant of which was his matter of writing the letter *A*. This may be observed by contrasting Plate Ia (c. 1893, the final word *sa*) with Plate IIa (*Habañera*, 1895). This and other minor changes in the composer's calligraphy make it possible to date all of his early manuscripts within a twelve-month period.

[3] Maurice Ravel, "La Sorcière à l'Opéra-Comique," *Comoedia Illustré* (January 5, 1913), p. 321.

PLATE 1a. "Le ciel est, par-dessus le toit," page 1, from Verlaine's *Sagesse*. In the piano accompaniment, most of the indications for the bass clef should be for the treble clef. The key signature is four sharps throughout.

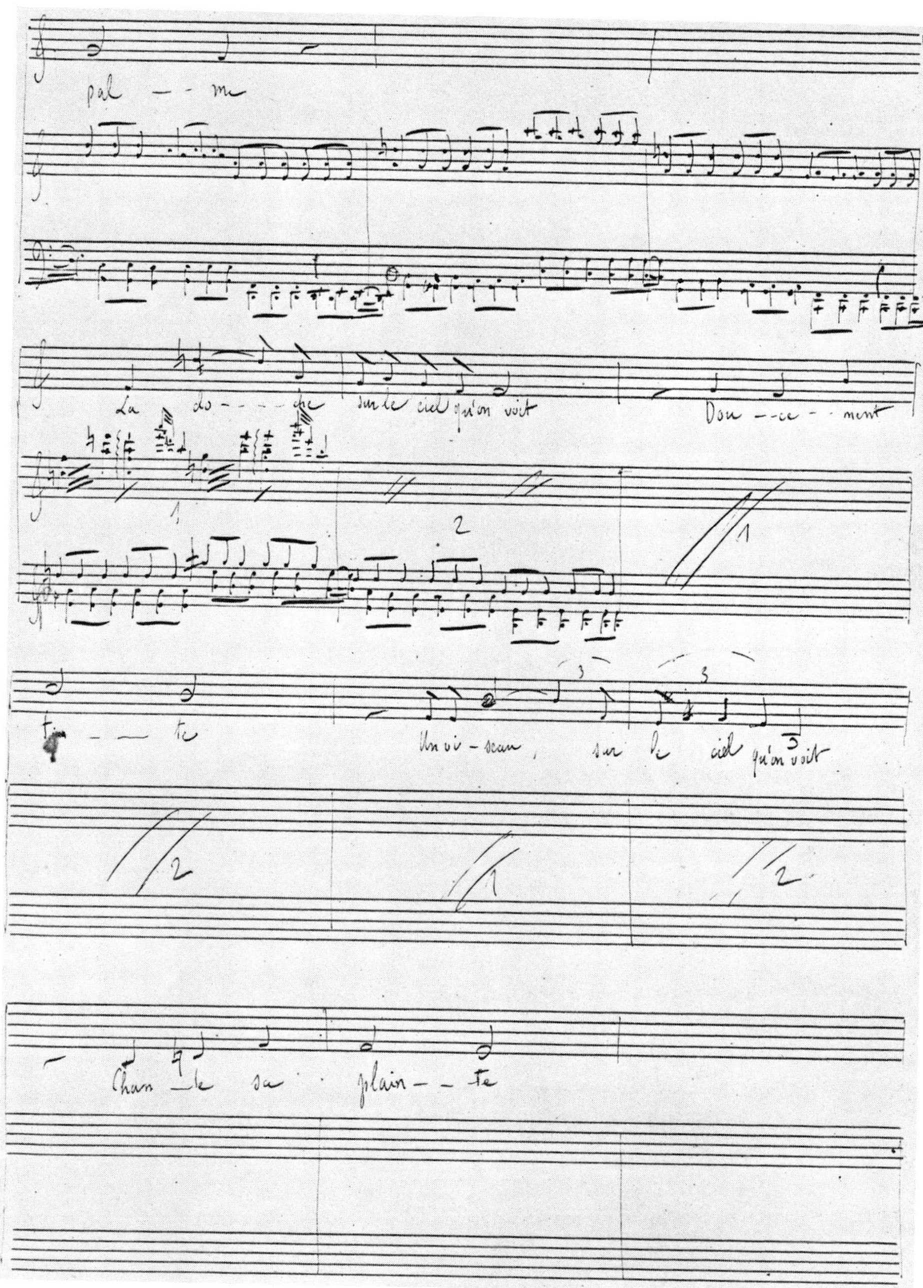

PLATE 1b. "Le ciel est, par-dessus le toit," page 2.

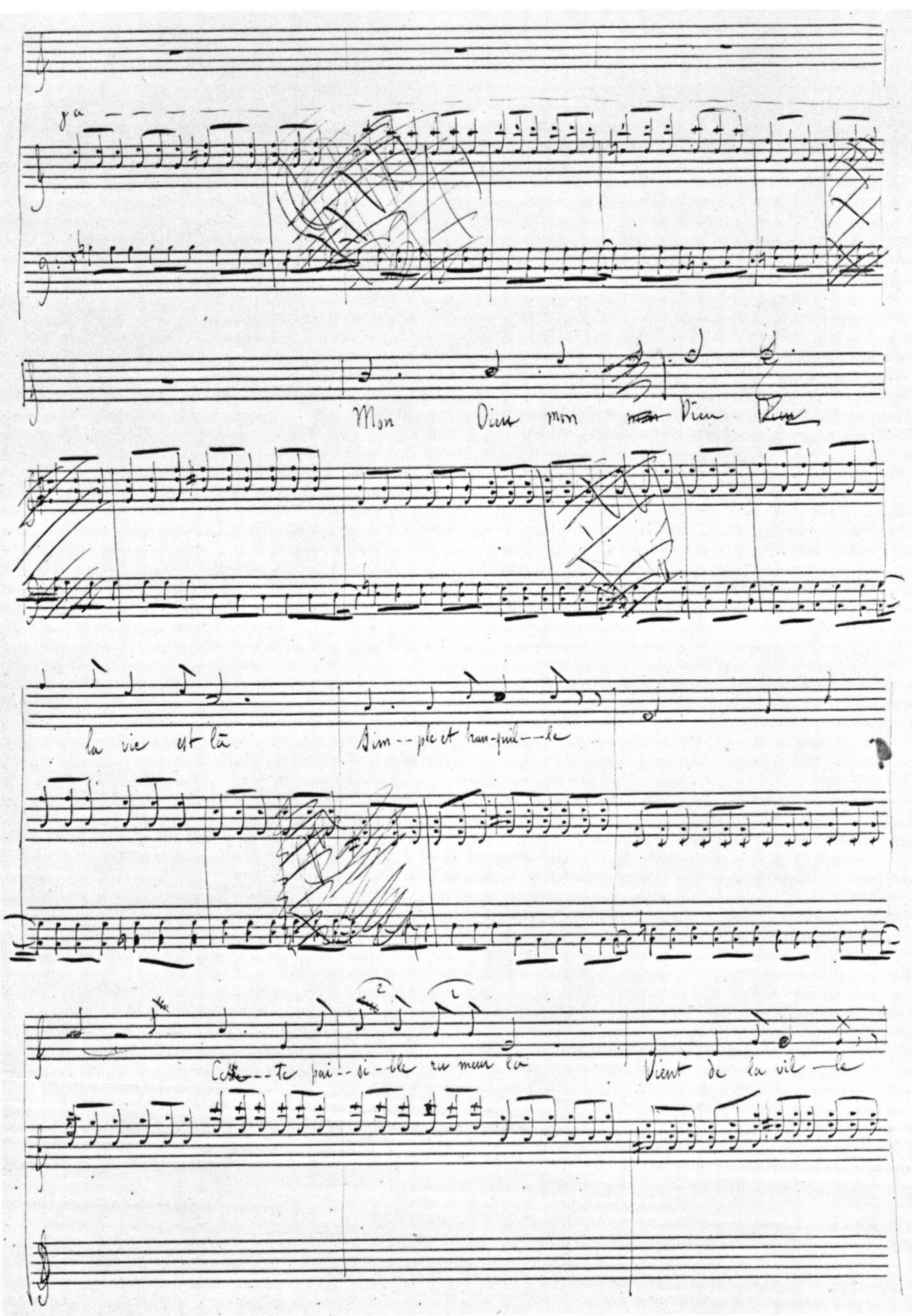

PLATE 1C. "Le ciel est, par-dessus le toit," page 3.

PLATE 1d. "Le ciel est, par-dessus le toit," page 4.

his best level. In 1907, he mentioned *Sur l'herbe* in a letter to the critic Jean-Aubry, and remarked that a bit of preciosity asserted itself, which was indicated both in the text and in the music.[4] It is apparent that the composer was not fully satisfied with his settings of Verlaine's poems. He withheld publication of *Un Grand sommeil noir*, and consequently the song first appeared posthumously in 1953. Moreover, in another letter to Jean-Aubry, written in March, 1907, he stated that among his earliest vocal works, written in the early 1890s, those that were set to Verlaine's poems were "far too juvenile" for publication.[5] It is now evident that one of these early songs was a setting of "Le ciel est, par-dessus le toit," from the collection *Sagesse*. The manuscript, consisting of four pages for voice and piano, is almost complete, save for several blank measures in the accompaniment, as well as a concluding passage. In setting the text, Ravel adopted the time-honored technique of repeating an initial rhythmic pattern in the accompaniment throughout the song. Despite a paucity of imagination, the manuscript is nonetheless an interesting example of the composer's initial difficulties in transposing poetry into song.

SITES AURICULAIRES, 1895: A WORK FOR TWO PIANOS (Plates IIa and IIb)

Sites auriculaires, consisting of two short pieces, *Habañera* and *Entre cloches*, was Ravel's first composition for two pianos.[6] Although the work remained unpublished, the *Habañera* was later incorporated virtually unchanged into the *Rapsodie espagnole* (1907).[7] The composition was performed once in public by Marthe Dron and Ricardo Viñes. Performing

[4] Unpublished letter dated September 4, 1907. Autograph in the private collection of Madame Jean-Aubry.

[5] See R. Chalupt and M. Gerar, *Ravel au miroir de ses lettres* (Paris, Robert Laffont, 1956), p. 59.

[6] A third piece, "Nuit en gondoles," was projected, but was not composed. Ravel returned to this genre but once more in composing the little-known *Frontispice*, printed in *Les Feuillets d'Art* (1919).

[7] The orchestral score (Durand edition, p. 28), indicates that the *Habañera* was originally composed in 1895. I have studied no fewer than five complete autographs of *Sites Auriculaires*. On the autograph copy belonging to Manuel Rosenthal, Ravel added an epigram, taken from Baudelaire's poem "A une dame créole": "Au pays parfumé que le soleil caresse" (In the perfumed country which the sun caresses). See Rollo H. Myers, *Ravel* (New York, Thomas Yoseloff, 1960), frontispiece. Although Ravel was deeply influenced by Baudelaire's writings, this epigram proved to be his sole direct artistic contact with the author of *Les Fleurs du Mal*.

PLATE IIa. *Habañera*, page 1, from *Sites auriculaires*, for two pianos.

PLATE IIb. *Entre cloches*, page 1, from *Sites auriculaires*, for two pianos.

from manuscripts, the pianists played the chords of *Entre Cloches* in unison which were supposed to be played in alternation. The resulting cacophony was Ravel's formal debut before the public, and it turned out to be the first of many stormy premières in his career.

RAVEL AND THE PRIX DE ROME, 1901–05
(Plates III, IV, and Va–Vd)

THE NAME of Maurice Joseph Ravel first appeared in the Conservatoire's official publications in 1891, when the sixteen-year-old pianist received a Premier Prix in the institute's preparatory division. (The second prize that year was awarded to Alfred Cortot, who soon thereafter became one of the outstanding concert pianists of his generation.) Some ten years later, Ravel began to compete for the Prix de Rome, and the jury members deemed his compositions inferior to those of the following prize winners: André Caplet, Gabriel Dupont, Aymé Kunc, Roger Ducasse, Albert Bertelin, Raoul Laparra, Raymond Pech, Paul Pierné, Victor Gallois, Marcel Rousseau, Philippe Gaubert, and Louis Dumas. After unsuccessfully attempting to win the Premier Grand Prix in 1901, 1902, and 1903, Ravel entered the competition a fourth time in 1905, and was eliminated in the preliminary round, the jury solemnly declaring that the composer of *Jeux d'eau* (1901), the String Quartet (1902), and *Shéhérazade* (1903), lacked the technical proficiency to be a finalist in the contest.[8] His disqualification was not only hotly debated by music critics, but the ensuing *affaire Ravel* turned out to be front-page news in the French dailies.[9]

In a letter to Paul Léon, director of the Beaux-Arts, Romain Rolland eloquently summed up the views of many impartial observers.

[8] The competition was conducted in two stages. In the first stage, the contestants composed a four-part fugue based on a given subject (Plate IV), and, in addition, they set a text selected by the jury for solo voice, chorus, and orchestra (Plates Va–Vd). Some twenty students generally entered this round, and of these, about six were subsequently allowed to compete for the first prize. The concluding round entailed setting a prescribed cantata text for soloists and orchestra.

[9] See *Le Matin*, May 22, 1905.

Friday, May 26, 1905

Dear Sir:
I read in the papers that there is no *affaire Ravel.* I believe it my duty to tell you (in a friendly way and just between ourselves) that this question exists, and cannot be evaded. In this *affaire* I am personally entirely disinterested. I am not a friend of Ravel. I may even say that I have no personal sympathy with his subtle and refined art. But justice compels me to say that Ravel is not only a student of promise—he is already one of the most highly regarded of the young masters in our school, which does not have many. I do not doubt for an instant the good faith of the judges. I do not challenge it. But this is rather a condemnation for all time of these juries; I cannot comprehend why one should persist in keeping a school in Rome if it is to close its doors to those rare artists who have some originality—to a man like Ravel, who has established himself at the concerts of the National Society through works far more important than those required for an examination. Such a musician did honor to the competition; and even if by some unhappy chance, which I should find it difficult to explain, his compositions were or seemed to have been inferior to those of the other contestants, he should nevertheless have been rewarded outside of the competition. . . . Forgive me for mixing into an affair that does not concern me. It is everyone's duty to protest against a decision which, even though technically just, harms real justice and art, and since I have the pleasure of knowing you, I feel I should give you—I repeat, entirely between ourselves—the opinion of an impartial musician. N.B. Isn't there any way for the State (without going against its decision) at least to prove its interest in Ravel?[10]

Other observers, however, ventured to impugn the jury's integrity, and another scandal erupted when it was disclosed that all of the six finalists were pupils of the same professor of composition—Charles Lenepveu.[11] In addition to the many personal charges and countercharges, the entire curriculum of the Conservatoire was sharply attacked, and among the concrete results of the scandals were the resignation of Dubois as director and his replacement by Fauré.[12] Several faculty members submitted their resignations as well.

10 Marguerite Long, "Souvenir de Maurice Ravel," *La Revue Musicale* (December, 1938), pp. 173, 174.

11 The seventeen students who entered the preliminary round were pupils of Widor, Fauré, and Lenepveu; among them, eight were pupils of Lenepveu. The Premier Grand Prix was awarded to Victor Gallois, whose subsequent musical activities were as undistinguished as those of his teacher.

12 The critic Pierre Lalo observed that the Conservatoire taught its students their craft, but did not

Grand Prix de Rome de 1905
en
Composition Musicale.

Concours d'Essai.

Composition de M. Ravel, Loge No 12, remise le 12 Mai, à [illegible] heures du soir

Le Conservateur,

MINISTÈRE DE L'INSTRUCTION PUBLIQUE
ET DES BEAUX-ARTS
PALAIS DE COMPIÈGNE
CONSERVATION

Le Compositeur,
Maurice Ravel

Ms. 10911 (1-2)

PLATE III. Ravel's official entry in the 1905 Prix de Rome competition.

One must differentiate clearly between two decisions made by the jury. The first was to eliminate Ravel in the preliminary round, while the second was to award all the prizes to Lenepveu's pupils. Although both verdicts evoked vigorous opposition, the latter appears particularly objectionable,

teach them their art. They were taught rules and formulas, but possessed no musical culture whatsoever. See Jean Marnold, "Conservatoriana," *Le Mercure Musical* (October 1, 1905), p. 398. Another critic, Louis Laloy, suggested that it was time to abolish the absurd notion that the Conservatoire's primary purpose was to produce opera singers and composers of operettas. In a scathing attack, he noted the resignation of two well-known "comedians," and trusted that they would be replaced by "musicians." "Les Réformes du Conservatoire," *Le Mercure Musical* (October 15, 1905), p. 453.

PLATE IV. Fugue (1905), page 1. Each part is written in a different clef, and each contrapuntal device is dutifully labeled.

and despite Lenepveu's assertions to the contrary, an impartial observer will find it difficult to believe that the jury arrived at its decision in a scrupulous manner.

Ravel's elimination has been explained by all commentators as a personal expression of the jury's hostility, but an impartial study of his choral piece shows considerable justification for his disqualification. It is curious that neither the composer's contemporaries nor present-day commentators have mentioned the choral piece, *L'Aurore*, in their discussions, and yet it is only by means of the music that his elimination is fully clarified. Although both music and text are extremely jejune, our critique is concerned exclusively with the technical proficiency of the score. In addition to numerous minor errors in the autograph, one particular passage contains seven consecutive measures of parallel octaves between the soprano and bass parts—a blatant infraction of traditional four-part writing which any first-year student at the Conservatoire would have eschewed (see Plates Vc and Vd). Even allowing for the rapidity with which the work was composed, this error is indeed puzzling. When viewing this obvious blunder as well as several other oversights, the jury members must have assumed that Ravel was either not taking his work seriously, or was disdainful of them. One juror stated that "Mr. Ravel may indeed consider us *commonplace*: he will not take us for imbeciles with impunity."[13]

To some extent, Ravel's repeated failures to win the Prix de Rome were indicative of his fundamental approach to his craft: his music could neither be rushed by arbitrary timetables nor be inhibited by trite texts.[14] He left the Conservatoire shortly after the 1905 competition, and soon after embarked upon a period of unparalleled creative activity.

13 Roland-Manuel, *Ravel* (Paris, Gallimard, 1948), p. 46.

14 Shortly after the 1903 competition, the composer received a gift copy of Jean Bénédict's book *Chansons-Proverbes*, with the following dedication: "To Maurice Ravel, for striving against the obligatory and soporific literature of the Institute's regular purveyors."

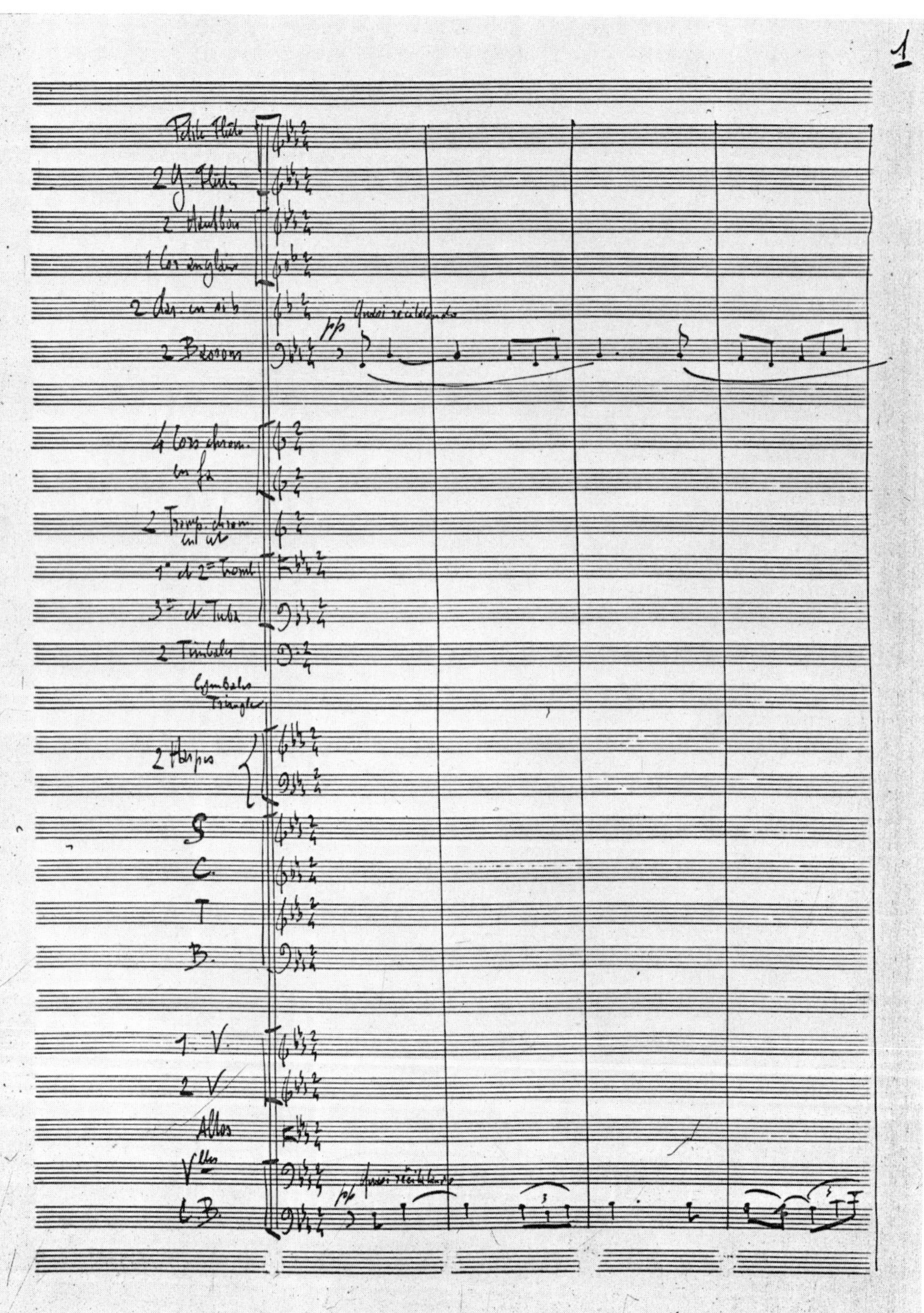

PLATE VA. *L'Aurore* (1905), choral piece, page 1.

PLATE vb. *L'Aurore*, page 2. The key signature is three flats.

PLATE VC. *L'Aurore*, page 17. The key signature is F♯.

PLATE vd. *L'Aurore*, page 18. The key signature is F♯.

SKETCHES FOR THE FIRST MOVEMENT OF THE SONATINE, 1903
(Plates VIa and VIb)

THE FIRST MOVEMENT of the *Sonatine* was completed in 1903 and entered in a competition sponsored by the *Weekly Critical Review*. Soon after, however, the contest was canceled as the *Review* rapidly approached financial collapse. Two years later the work was completed with the addition of the second and third movements. Plates VIa and VIb offer a rare opportunity to observe Ravel "in his workshop" as it were, and examine his work before it was meticulously and painstakingly polished and refined. New compositions were customarily sketched in light pencil, while more developed or final versions of a work were written in ink. The most important difference between the sketch and the printed score was the deletion of eleven bars in the passage leading to the second theme (Plate VIa, bars 11–21).[15]

The recapitulation is of particular significance (Plate VIb). The sketch (Example 1) indicates that it was originally intended to be identical to the opening measure (note the indication D.C.). Only later was the G♯ added to the melody, a subtle but effective emendation.

EXAMPLE I

Indeed, one might well sum up the composer's artistic creed by recalling Boileau's statement: "Twenty times put your handiwork back on the loom: polish it ceaselessly and repolish it; add sometimes and frequently erase."[16] In addition to influencing virtually all subsequent French literature, this seventeenth-century dictum finds its very embodiment in Ravel's art.

[15] Other changes from the printed score involve rhythmic modifications (Plate VIa, bar 3), changes in harmony (Plate VIa, staves 5 and 6 from the bottom, penultimate bar, and staves 3 and 4 from the bottom, bars 1 and 2), and the discarding of extraneous repetition (Plate VIb, bars 4 and 5). There are, in addition, several oversights with regard to accidentals.

[16] *L'Art poétique*, 1674.

PLATE VIA. *Sonatine*, first movement, page 1. The sketches are written in light pencil.

PLATE VIb. *Sonatine*, page 2.

CHANSON ÉCOSSAISE (SCOTTISH SONG), 1910 (Plate VII)

ON THE BASIS of what appears to be only a sketch, it is possible to reconstruct Ravel's Scottish song. In 1910, at the invitation of Madame Marie Olénine d'Alheim,[17] the composer participated in an international musical competition sponsored by the Maison du Lied in Moscow. The organization was founded with a threefold purpose in mind: first, to stimulate public interest in folk melodies; second, to increase the repertory of artistically harmonized folk melodies by inviting composers to enter biannual competitions; finally, to encourage young singers by giving them the opportunity to perform folk songs before the public in small recital halls. The seven prizewinning songs were published by P. Jurgenson.

Song	*Harmonization*[18]
1. Spanish	M. Ravel
2. Russian	A. Olénine
3. Flemish	A. Georges
4. French	M. Ravel
5. Scottish	A. Georges
6. Italian	M. Ravel
7. Hebraic	M. Ravel

Thus three of Ravel's harmonizations remained unpublished.

Shortly after learning of his quadruple victory, he wrote to Olénine d'Alheim: "By the same mail I am writing to Moscow in order to thank the jury for the pleasant and flattering distinction with which it has honored me. In this regard, I wish to express my sentiments of gratitude to you personally. Indeed, thanks to your kindness it was possible for me to take part in the competition."[19]

[17] Marie Olénine d'Alheim was born in Russia in 1869. Her official debut took place in Paris in 1896, and for some forty years she specialized in singing the music of Russian composers, particularly Mussorgsky, as well as folk songs from many nations. In 1908, she founded the Maison du Lied with her husband, Pierre d'Alheim. A gifted linguist, he carried out many of the organization's translation assignments.

[18] Alexander Olénine, Olénine d'Alheim's brother, was a student of Balakirev. Alexandre Georges was a minor French composer of the day.

[19] Unpublished autograph, dated November 3, 1910, in the Glinka Museum of Musical Culture, Moscow. Printed with the kind permission of Madame Olénine d'Alheim.

PLATE VII. Ravel's Scottish Song.

The seven winning songs were first performed by Olénine d'Alheim on December 19, 1910, at the Salle des Agriculteurs, a small auditorium in Paris. They were well received, and one critic wrote that when it comes to singing Mussorgsky or folk songs, Olénine d'Alheim is the artist par excellence.[20]

In order to ascertain that Ravel's sketch is indeed a complete song,[21] one must compare it with a printed copy of Alexandre Georges's prize-winning accompaniment to the same folk melody (Plate VIII). Ravel's version begins with an introduction for the piano, followed by the melody and its accompaniment. The missing text, a poem by Robert Burns,[22] may be inserted by referring to Georges's printed version. Following the completion of the first stanza, Ravel's sketch concludes with a brief postlude for piano, and one additional measure for voice and piano. This additional measure is important, as it is identical to the first measure for voice and piano. Georges's version corroborates the hypothesis that the entire melody is repeated, and thus Ravel's composition unfolds as follows:

1. Introduction (piano)
2. First stanza (voice and piano)
3. Postlude (piano)
4. Second stanza (voice and piano), the music of which is identical to 2
5. Postlude (piano), identical to 3, which draws the work to its conclusion.

Viewed in this light, the composer's sketch is seen to be an effective form of shorthand. His tasteful setting of the Scottish folk melody is a further example of his strikingly broad musical empathies.[23]

[20] M. D. Calvocoressi, "Aux concerts—Mme. Olénine," *Comoedia Illustré* (January 15, 1911), p. 245.

[21] The Roman numeral III, placed just before the words "Chanson Écossaise," suggests that Ravel's other unpublished songs were sketched in a similar manner. These sketches, unfortunately, appear to have been lost.

[22] The poem, entitled "The Banks o' Doon," was written in 1791, and exists in several versions. See Andrew Lang, ed., *The Poems and Songs of Robert Burns* (2d ed.; New York, Dodd, Mead, 1899), pp. 449–51.

[23] Ravel's setting of the *Chanson écossaise* is of greater harmonic interest than Georges's prize-winning version. The latter setting, on the other hand, shows more variety, owing to its different accompaniment for each of the poem's stanzas.

PLATE VIII. Alexandre Georges's Scottish Song.

DAPHNIS ET CHLOÉ: A LETTER TO RALPH VAUGHAN WILLIAMS (Plate IX)

Daphnis et Chloé received its world première at the Théâtre du Châtelet in Paris, on June 8, 1912, with Nijinsky as Daphnis, Madame Karsavina as Chloé, and Pierre Monteux, conductor. Ravel stated that the ballet reflected the Greece of his fantasy as depicted by late eighteenth-century French artists, and noted that the development of a few motives unified its broad canvas. Indeed, *Daphnis et Chloé* proved to be his most expansive work.[24] The choral sections, although primarily decorative in function, were the cause of a bitter dispute between Ravel and Diaghilev,[25] the latter viewing them as an unnecessary additional expense, while the composer insisting that they were an integral and significant component of the work. As a compromise, Ravel composed an alternate orchestral version of the ballet's only solo choral section, with the understanding that the choruses would be included in all major productions of the work. The controversy finally came to a head in 1914, when Diaghilev planned a production of *Daphnis et Chloé* in London without the choruses. The composer was incensed, and protested in an open letter to four London newspapers—*The Times*, the *Morning Post*, the *Daily Mail*, and the *Daily Telegraph*. In addition, he copied out an English translation provided for him and sent it to Vaughan Williams, asking him to circulate its contents as widely as possible.[26] By copying his statement into English (a language he did not understand), Ravel thus created a unique and curious document.[27]

[24] See Roland-Manuel, "Une Esquisse autobiographique de Maurice Ravel," *La Revue Musicale* (December, 1938), pp. 21, 22.

[25] Sergei Pavlovich Diaghilev, the director of the Ballet Russe, collaborated with many brilliant creative personalities, among them Nijinsky, Pavlova, Fokine, Debussy, Stravinsky, and Picasso. His company's striking impact on French cultural life was succinctly summarized in *La Liberté* on June 11, 1912: "The Russians have brought to us, this remains incontestable, a profoundly original revelation of the greatest artistic interest." Diaghilev's group dispersed following his death in August, 1929.

[26] Printed with the kind permission of Mrs. Ursula Vaughan Williams. Autograph in the British Museum.

[27] The letter has been printed by Ursula Vaughan Williams in *R.V.W.: A Biography of Ralph Vaughan Williams* (London, Oxford University Press, 1964), pp. 112, 113, with several corrections in the composer's understandably faulty version. The letter begins as follows:

My dear friend, June 7, 1914
No, alas! I will not be going to London, and the following letter, which I am addressing to the English press, will explain the reason to you.

7/6 14

Mon cher ami,

Non hélas! je n'irai pas à London. Et la lettre suivante, que j'adresse aux journaux anglais, vous en expliquera la cause:

Sir,

My most important work, Daphnis et Chloé, is to be produced at the Drury Lane Theatre on Tuesday, June I was overjoyed; and fully appreciating the great honour done to me, considered the event as one of the weightiest in my artistic career.

Now I learn that what will be produced before the London public is not my work in its original form, but a makeshift arrangement which I had accepted to write at M. Diaghilev's special request, in order to facilitate production in certain minor centres.

M. Diaghilev probably considers London as one of the aforesaid "minor centres," since he is about to produce at Drury Lane, in spite of his positive word, the new version, without chorus.

I am deeply surprised and grieved and I consider the proceedings as disrespectful towards the London public as well as towards the composer. I shall therefore be extremely thankful to offering you my thanks in anticipation. I remain dear Sir faithfully yours Maurice Ravel

PLATE IX. A letter from Ravel to Ralph Vaughan Williams.

Following World War I, it appears that Diaghilev acquiesced to some extent, and agreed to perform the ballet with its choral sections. His decision, however, was not due to any change in his viewpoint, but was simply a tactful and successful diplomatic maneuver. Ravel was appeased and agreed to compose *La Valse* for the Ballet Russe. When the score was completed, however, Diaghilev refused to stage the work, a decision which engendered a permanent rupture of relations between the two men.

LA CLOCHE ENGLOUTIE: AN INCOMPLETE OPERA (Plates Xa and Xb)

THE CRITIC M. D. Calvocoressi, who was a gifted polyglot, explained that Ravel's views of literature were highly colored due to his inability to read foreign languages. Thus, Ravel almost completed an opera based on A. Ferdinand Hérold's translation of Gerhardt Hauptmann's play *Die versunkene Glocke* (*La Cloche engloutie*), and expressed admiration for the "rhythm, color, and musical quality" of certain passages in the translation. Calvocoressi doubted that the composer's reaction would have been the same had he been able to read the original German.[28]

Ravel worked intermittently on *La Cloche engloutie* for almost a decade, until it was definitively abandoned shortly after the outbreak of World War I. Hauptmann's play, which was subtitled "Ein deutsches Märchendrama," was first performed in Berlin's Deutsches Theater in December, 1896. Some nine years later, while browsing in a Parisian bookstall, Ravel discovered Hérold's translation. Soon after, he planned to adapt the work, and explained his ideas to Hérold, who agreed to collaborate on the project.[29] Ravel responded warmly to the libretto, which was a spiritual descendant of *Der Freischütz*. The elements of fantasy and enchantment abounded, together with a generous supply of forest scenes, elves, nymphs, prayers, incantations, and dances, as well as human and supernatural beings. In a letter to his friend Maurice Delage, the composer could scarcely contain his enthusiasm: "For two weeks I haven't left the grind. I have never worked with so much frenzy. Yes, at Compiègne perhaps, but that was less

[28] M. D. Calvocoressi, *Musicians Gallery: Music and Ballet in Paris and London* (London, Faber and Faber, 1933), p. 78.

[29] Ravel's professor of counterpoint at the Conservatoire, André Gédalge, gave him a letter of introduction to Hérold, and a warm friendship soon developed between the composer and librettist of *La Cloche engloutie*. The composer's personal library at Montfort l'Amaury contains several works by Hérold, among them *Maisonseule*, and *La Vie de Bouddha*.

PLATE XA. *La Cloche engloutie*, page 1.

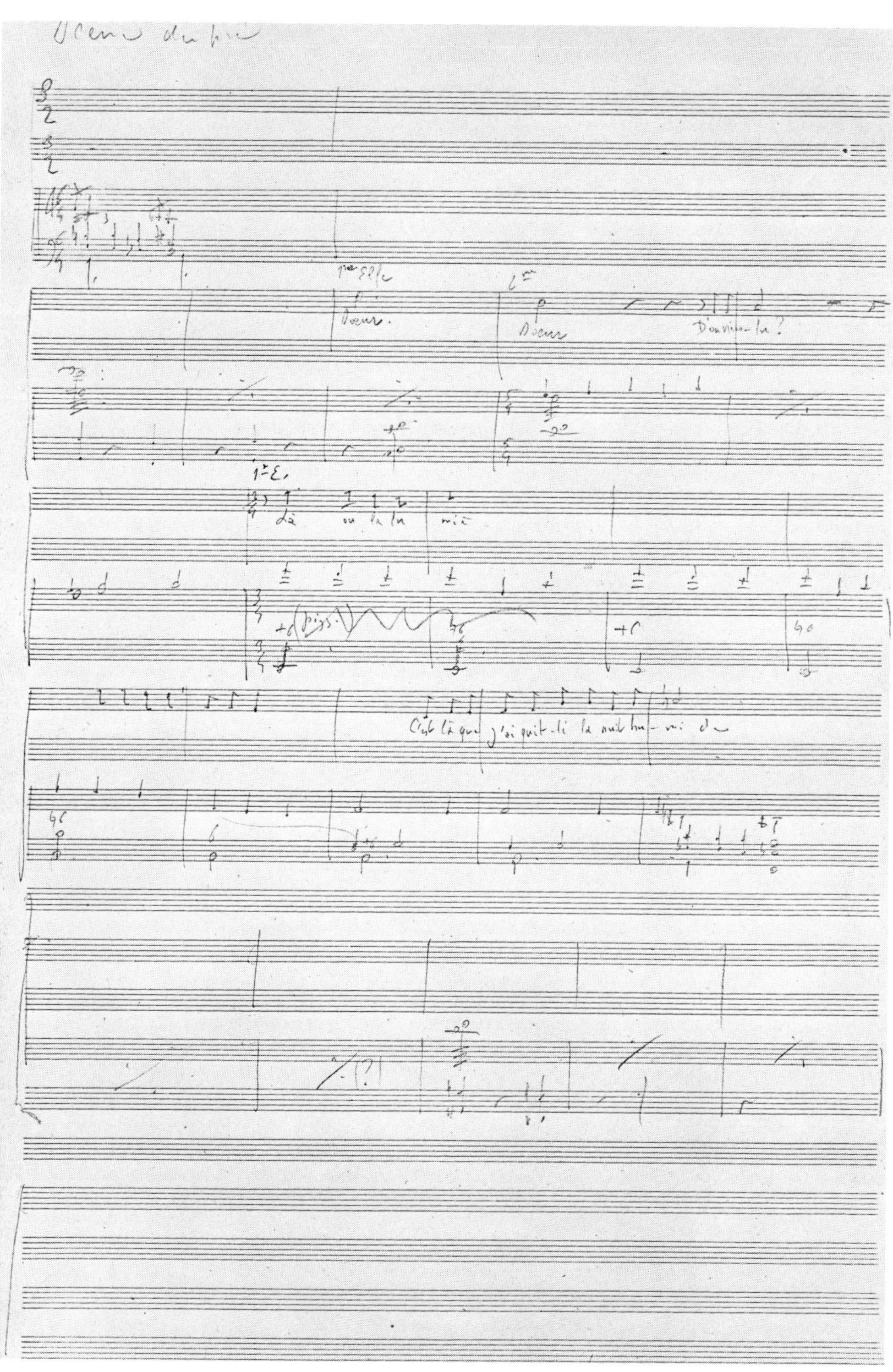

PLATE xb. *La Cloche engloutie.* Scene in the fields (Act I). The figured bass indications are of particular interest.

sportive. It is thrilling to write a work for the theater."[30] By August, 1906, the first two acts of the opera were virtually completed. On August 20, in an enthusiastic burst of hyperbole, the composer wrote to Delage: "Would you like an opera in five acts? You will have it within a week!"[31] Ravel continued to work on the opera intermittently, and in 1909 he signed a contract which stipulated the financial details of forthcoming performances of the work. The contract, dated January 15, 1909, was also signed by Auguste Durand, Hérold, and Hauptmann.[32] Some five years later, in a letter to Stravinsky, Ravel explained that he planned to finish the opera in the winter of 1914, but the outbreak of hostilities had prevented him from doing so. A few days after writing to Stravinsky, the opera was mentioned again in a letter to Roland-Manuel. Punning on the word "engloutie," the composer wrote that he now believed the project was really "sunk":

> Je fais également de la musique: impossible de continuer Zaspiak-Bat, dont les documents sont restés à Paris. Délicat de travailler à la *Cloche Engloutie*—cette fois, je crois qu'elle y est bien — et d'achever *Wien*, poème symphonique.[33]

The "delicate" matter of continuing to work on *La Cloche engloutie* resulted from an ever-increasing crescendo of Germanophobia, which rose to fever pitch during the war. Ravel realized that in the present situation, it would be impractical to adapt a theatrical work based on a text by a German playwright, and, accordingly, he set aside his libretto once more, this time never to return to it.

[30] Letter dated June 12, 1906. The Prix de Rome competitions were held at the Palais de Compiègne. See Roland-Manuel, *A la gloire de Ravel* (Paris, Éditions de la Nouvelle Revue Critique, 1938), p. 68.

[31] Chalupt and Gerar, p. 56.

[32] The document is in the archives of Durand et Cie., Paris. While the specific financial details of the contract are confidential, its nonpecuniary stipulations may be mentioned. Durand allotted a fixed sum for each of the following events: 1) delivery of the completed manuscript; 2) the first Parisian performance of the opera in a nationally subsidized theater; 3) the twenty-fifth performance in the same theater; 4) the fiftieth performance in the same theater.

In addition, the contract stipulated that the fiftieth performance was not to take place more than ten years after the first. For these initial fifty performances, two-thirds of the profits went to Ravel, and the remaining one-third was equally divided between Hauptmann and Hérold.

[33] "I am also writing music: impossible to continue *Zaspiak-Bat* [a projected piano concerto based on Basque themes, see pp. 327–28], the documents having remained in Paris. It's a delicate matter to work on *La Cloche Engloutie*—this time I think it really is [sunk] and to complete *Wien* [the original title of *La Valse*, completed in 1920] a symphonic poem." Letter dated October 1, 1914. See Roland-Manuel, *A la gloire de Ravel*, p. 127.

Some twenty-five years after their collaboration terminated, Hérold discussed the projected adaptation of his libretto.

I do not believe that Ravel composed any part of the score,[34] but he thought of it for a long time. The scenes which occur in the factory of Henry the founder were to have been of striking power. Ravel did not envision a small artisan's workshop; he imagined a huge factory, equipped like the most grandiose one sees today, and he would have utilized the innumerable sounds of hammers, saws, files, and sirens.[35]

The author's comments were eloquently confirmed by Ravel, in a letter to Delage.

On the Rhine, toward Düsseldorf, July 5, 1905

. . . This is Haum, a gigantic foundry in which 24,000 men work day and night. . . . Toward evening we went down to see the factories. How can I tell you about these great smelting castles, these incandescent cathedrals, and the wonderful symphony of traveling belts, whistles, and terrific hammerblows in which you are submerged? And everywhere the sky is a scorching deep red. . . . How much music there is in all this!—and I certainly intend to use it.[36]

From his description, the composer undoubtedly had *La Cloche engloutie* in mind.

Ravel told his colleague Roland-Manuel that parts of *La Cloche engloutie* served as a model for *L'Enfant et les sortilèges*.[37] It is clear, for example, that the beginning of *L'Enfant et les sortilèges* was adapted from the opening of the second act of *La Cloche engloutie* (Example 2).

In addition, as in *L'Enfant et les sortilèges*, it appears that the unpublished opera would have utilized a predominantly conversational type of declamation, together with several brief, lyrical episodes. In 1920, when Ravel began to study the libretto of *L'Enfant et les sortilèges*, he must have been

[34] Hérold's mistaken notion strikingly underscores Ravel's total isolation in setting his libretto. Likewise there was remarkably little collaboration between the composer and Franc-Nohain (*L'Heure espagnole*), and only slightly more with Colette (*L'Enfant et les sortilèges*). See my article, "L'Enfant et les sortilèges: Correspondance inédite de Ravel et Colette," *Revue de Musicologie*, Vol. LII, No. 2 (1966), pp. 215–20.

[35] A. Ferdinand Hérold, "Souvenirs," *La Revue Musicale* (December, 1938), p. 198.

[36] Chalupt and Gerar, p. 38.

[37] See Roland-Manuel, *Maurice Ravel et son oeuvre dramatique* (Paris, Les Éditions Musicales de la Librairie de France, 1928), p. 50.

struck by the number of similarities between Colette's libretto and Hérold's adaptation of Hauptmann's play. Although dealing with differing plots, both libretti unfolded within the realm of sheer fantasy and enchantment, and it was indeed a brief distance from the forest and dancing elves of *La Cloche engloutie* to the garden and dancing animals of *L'Enfant et les sortilèges* (see Plate Xb).[38] Thus, in the last analysis, *La Cloche engloutie* was not totally abandoned, and it proved to be the most important of the composer's numerous incomplete vocal projects.[39]

EXAMPLE 2

La Cloche engloutie, beginning of Act II

L'Enfant et les sortilèges, p. 1

AN ORCHESTRATION OF SCHUMANN'S CARNAVAL
(Plates XIa–XId)

VERY LITTLE is known about Ravel's orchestration of Schumann's *Carnaval.* Commissioned by Diaghilev, it is believed that the work was performed by the Ballet Russe in London, shortly before World War I.[40]

[38] Ravel's treatment of his operatic libretti demonstrated his essential gifts as a miniaturist—while completing two one-act operas, a projected opera in five acts remained unfinished.

[39] The sketches in my possession contain parts of Acts 1 and 2. Unfortunately, the music for the foundry scene (Act 4) is lacking. Other adaptations of Hauptmann's play were composed by Heinrich Zoellner (*Die versunkene Glocke*, 1899), and Ottorino Respighi (*La Campana sommersa*, 1927).

[40] Approximately one-third of the autograph has been recovered. It contains the following complete sections: Préamble, Valse allemande, Paganini, and Marche des "Davidsbündler" contre les Philistins.

PLATE XIa. Orchestration of Schumann's *Carnaval*, page 1.

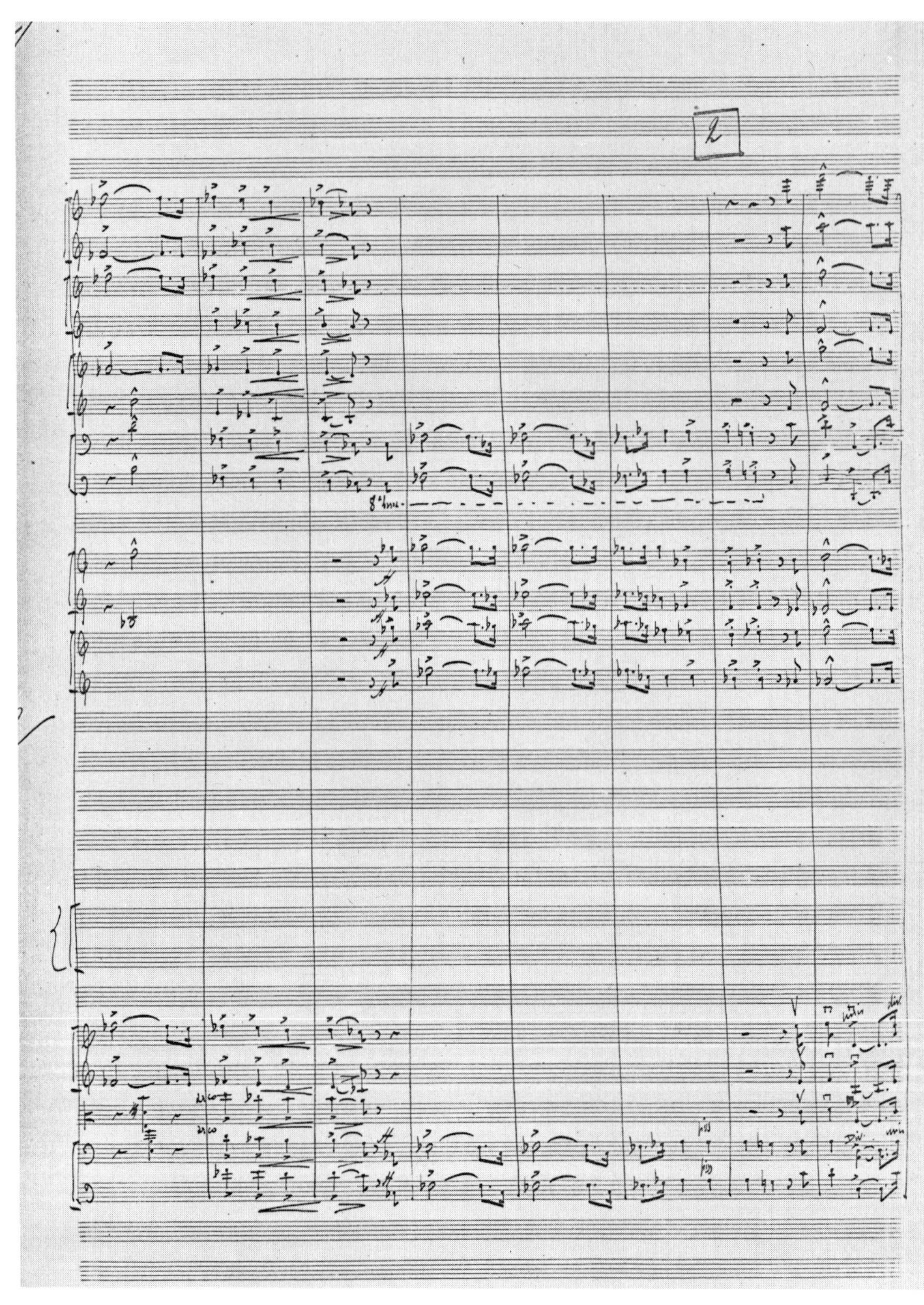

PLATE XIb. *Carnaval*, page 2.

PLATE XIC. *Carnaval*, page 6.

PLATE XId. *Carnaval*, page 93.

The indication "curtain" on page six of the autograph would suggest that the manuscript was used as a conductor's score—a fairly common performance practice of the day (see Plate XIc).

ZAZPIAK BAT: AN INCOMPLETE PIANO CONCERTO BASED ON BASQUE THEMES (Plate XII)

IN THE BAY of Saint-Jean-de-Luz, in France's Basque territory, a boulder emerges majestically above the water, bearing the following curious inscription: 4 + 3 = 1. The addition is curious, however, only to the uninitiated: the four Spanish Basque provinces together with the three French Basque provinces, form one unified Basque nation. "Zazpiak Bat" means "the Seven are One" in Basque.

It is a commonly mistaken notion that Ravel was fluent in Basque.[41] Born of a Basque mother and Swiss father in Ciboure, a small fishing village in France's Basque territory, the composer felt a warm affinity for his birthplace and frequently summered there. The Trio was completed at Saint-Jean-de-Luz in 1914, and the composer explained that its opening theme was "Basque in color."[42] At the same time he was composing the Trio, he was sketching *Zazpiak Bat.* Most commentators have suggested that the work was abandoned because Ravel found it impractical to incorporate folk melodies into the broad canvas of a piano concerto.[43] A surviving fragment of the work, part of the development section of the first movement, would suggest, however, that the folk melodies were indeed capable of development by the time-honored devices of modulation and thematic fragmentation.[44] Ravel returned to Basque folklore only once more, in the *Chanson épique*,[45] which is based on the rhythm of the Zortzico, a Basque dance.

[41] He was fluent only in French. In his letters he delighted in using phrases in foreign languages, such as Basque, Italian, Polish (to his friends the Godebskis), and in English. He knew a little Spanish and a few words of German, but never studied the classics.

[42] Roland-Manuel, "Une Esquisse autobiographique de Maurice Ravel," p. 127.

[43] See, for example, Myers, pp. 47, 48.

[44] The fragment contains alternations of $\frac{3}{4}$ and $\frac{2}{4}$ (forming measures of $\frac{8}{4}$), a characteristic of Basque folk melodies.

[45] From the song cycle *Don Quichotte à Dulcinée* (1932).

PLATE XII. *Zazpiak Bat*, a fragment sketched in light pencil.

TRANSCRIPTION OF A FORLANE BY COUPERIN
(Plates XIIIa and XIIIb)

RAVEL frequently gave the following advice to young composers: "If you have nothing to say, you cannot do better, until you decide to give up composing for good, than say again what has already been well said. If you have something to say, that something will never emerge more distinctly than when you are being unwittingly unfaithful to your model."[46]

In composing *Le Tombeau de Couperin* (1917), he explained that the work was a musical homage to eighteenth-century French music, rather than a tribute to Couperin himself. Nevertheless, he prepared for the task at hand by transcribing a suitable model: a forlane from Couperin's chamber works entitled *Concerts royaux*.[47] Ravel composed two bona fide pastiches for piano solo,[48] but of far greater importance was his attitude toward the art of others. He would often cite an apothegm attributed to Massenet: "In order to know one's own métier, one must learn the métier of others." Thus, to some extent, his music illustrates Valéry's curious statement that "art should be the pastiche of what doesn't exist." One of the most important characteristics of Ravel's works, and perhaps the most difficult to analyze, is how he remains faithful to a foreign culture, be it Spanish or Greek, or to a past epoch, be it the Renaissance or the eighteenth century, and still manages to impose his personal stamp on all of this music.

A LETTER FROM RAVEL TO HIS BROTHER, BOSTON, 1928
(Plates XIVa and XIVb)

IF RAVEL'S art is highly polished and sophisticated, his correspondence reveals the essential simplicity and childlike humor of the man. After the deaths of Debussy (1918) and Fauré (1924), he was internationally regarded as France's leading composer. Negotiations had been under way for several years to bring him to North America, and finally, in 1928, he performed his music from Texas to Canada and from New York to California, receiving great acclaim. After spending an exhilarating four months abroad, he returned to France. Just ahead lay the *Bolero*, whose popularity astonished even its composer, the two piano concerti, and finally, *Don Quichotte à Dulcinée*. Thus Ravel ended his career with a musical homage

[46] Émile Vuillermoz et al., *Maurice Ravel par quelques-uns de ses familiers* (Paris, Éditions du Tambourinaire, 1939), p. 145.

[47] Printed in the complete works of François Couperin, Éditions de l'Oiseau Lyre, VII, 98–105. Ravel mentioned the transcription in a letter to his friend Cipa Godebski. See Chalupt and Gerar, p. 106.

[48] *A la manière de Borodine* and *A la manière de Chabrier* (1913).

PLATE XIIIa. Transcription of a forlane by Couperin, page 1.

PLATE XIIIb. Transcription of Couperin, page 2.

to the Spain of his fantasy, and said farewell to his art with an exuberant toast to the joy of living. A similar enthusiasm and élan is found in this colorful letter to his brother.

The Copley-Plaza, Boston
13/1/28

My dear little Edward,

if I return to Europe alive, it will prove that I am long-lived! In short, until now, I've survived, and my manager assures me that I have gone through the worst. As soon as we arrived in the harbor, a swarm of journalists and cartoonists invaded the boat, with cameras and movie cameras. I had to leave them for a moment in order to see our entry into the port: it was even a bit too late, but splendid all the same. I wasn't even able to practice the piano a little during my stay in New York (4 days which seemed like 4 months). As soon as I settled down at the Langdon Hotel, a little nothing of a hotel which has only 12 stories (I was on the 8th), and delightfully comfortable (an entire apartment), the telephone didn't stop ringing. Every minute they would bring me baskets of flowers, and of the most delicious fruits in the world. Rehearsals, teams of journalists (photographs, movies, caricaturists) relieving one another every hour, letters, invitations to which my manager replies for me, receptions. In the evening, relaxation: dance halls, Negro theaters, gigantic movie houses, etc. I hardly know New York by day, cooped up in taxis in order to go to appointments of all sorts. I was even in a film, with make-up two centimeters thick. . . . I was forgetting the concert which the Boston Symphony played in New York, devoted to my works. I had to appear on stage: a standing audience of 3500; a tremendous ovation, climaxed by whistling. Sunday evening, a private concert and a gallop in evening dress for the train to Boston.

14/1/28

I continue: I have been relatively undisturbed here during the day between orchestral rehearsals (a marvelous orchestra). The day before yesterday a concert at Cambridge, yesterday at Boston: a triumph (they thought I looked English!) Koussevitzky told me that I was the greatest living French conductor. . . . When I think that I had to conduct the *Rapsodie Espagnole* at sight! I'm doing it again tonight, returning immediately to New York for tomorrow's concert, setting out again for Chicago where I will remain a few days, and from there on to Texas. Several free moments have enabled me to write to you; today, no receptions. Those at Cambridge and Boston were less exhausting than the one given by Mrs. Thomas Edison in New York: 2 or 300 persons filing before me and speaking English, more often French (it's amazing how many people speak our language here). As in New York, in the evening, relaxation: dance halls, Chinese theater, etc. Attached are several clippings. Keep them. Affectionately to all, I embrace you

Maurice

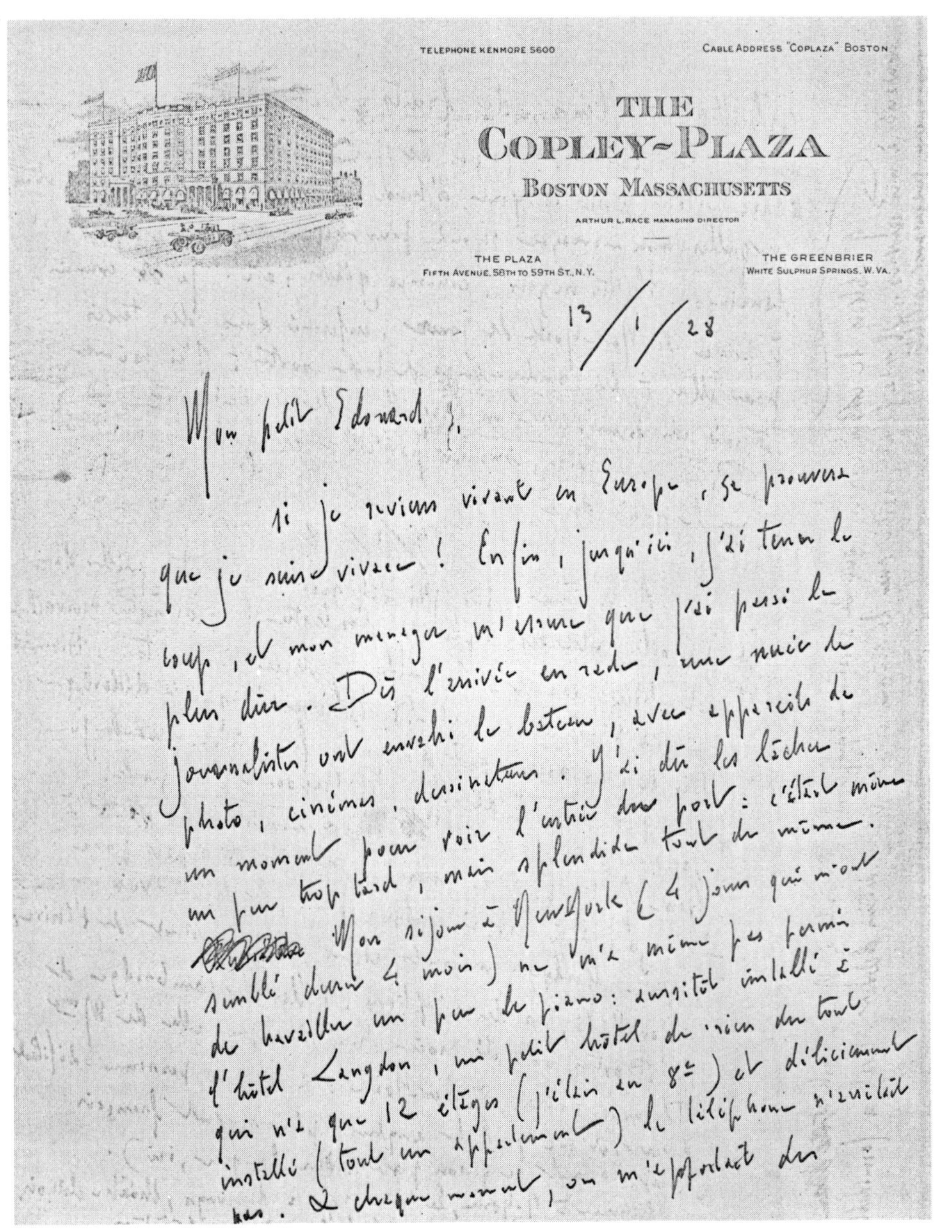

TELEPHONE KENMORE 5600

CABLE ADDRESS "COPLAZA" BOSTON

THE
COPLEY-PLAZA
BOSTON MASSACHUSETTS

ARTHUR L. RACE MANAGING DIRECTOR

THE PLAZA
FIFTH AVENUE, 58TH TO 59TH ST., N.Y.

THE GREENBRIER
WHITE SULPHUR SPRINGS, W. VA.

13/1/28

Mon petit Edouard,

Si je reviens vivant en Europe, ça prouvera que je suis vivace! Enfin, jusqu'ici, j'ai tenu le coup, et mon manager m'assure que j'ai passé le plus dur. Dès l'arrivée en rade, une nuée de journalistes ont envahi le bateau, avec appareils de photo, cinémas, dessinateurs. J'ai dû les lâcher un moment pour voir l'entrée du port: c'était même un peu trop tard, mais splendide tout de même. Mon séjour à New York (4 jours qui m'ont semblé durer 4 mois) ne m'a même pas permis de travailler un peu de piano: aussitôt installé à l'hôtel Langdon, un petit hôtel de rien du tout qui n'a que 12 étages (j'étais au 8e) et délicieusement installé (tout un appartement) le téléphone n'arrêtait pas. À chaque moment, on m'apportait des

PLATE XIVA. A letter from Ravel to his brother Edouard, page 1.

corbeilles de fleurs, de fruits les plus délicieux du monde. Répétitions, équipes de journalistes (photos, cinémas, caricaturistes) se relayent d'heure en heure, lettres, invitations, auxquelles mon manager répond pour moi; réceptions. Le soir, repos: dancings, théâtres nègres, cinémas géants, etc. Je connais à peine le New-York de jour, enfermé dans des taxis pour aller à des rendez-vous de toutes sortes. J'ai même tourné un film, avec un maquillage de 2 centimètres... Dimanche soir, concert particulier et galopade en habit pour le train de Boston.

14/1/28

Je continue: ici j'ai été relativement tranquille dans la journée, entre les répétitions d'orchestre (un orchestre merveilleux). Avant-hier, concert à Cambridge, hier à Boston: triomphe (on m'a trouvé l'air anglais!) Koussevitzky m'a déclaré que j'étais le plus grand chef d'orchestre français... Quand je pense que j'ai dû déchiffrer la Rapsodie Espagnole! Je rentre ce soir, retourne immédiatement à New-York, pour le concert de demain, repars pour Chicago, où je resterai quelques jours, et de là vers le Texas. Quelques moments libres me permettant de t'écrire, aujourd'hui, pas de réceptions. Celles de Cambridge et de Boston ont été moins éreintantes que celle de Mme Thomas Edison, à New-York: 2 ou 300 personnes défilant devant moi et me parlant anglais, plus souvent français (c'est étonnant ce qu'on parle notre langue, ici).

Comme à N.York, le soir, repos: dancings, théâtres chinois, etc. Ci-joint, quelques coupures. Garde-les. Affectueusement à tous

Tendresses Maurice

J'oubliais le concert que le Boston-Symphonie donnait à New-York, consacré à mes œuvres. Il m'a fallu paraître sur la scène: 3500 auditeurs debout. Ovations formidables, qui ont été jusqu'aux sifflets.

PLATE XIVb. A letter from Ravel, page 2.

Index